# A SINISTER BOUQUET: AWAKENING

## The Sinister Series Book 1

## A. NICKY HJORT

Lavish Publishing LLC

First Edition

The Sinister Series Book 1

All Rights Reserved

Published in the United States by Lavish Publishing, LLC, Midland, Texas

Paperback edition

ISBN: 9781944985042

Cover Design by: Wycked Ink

Cover Images: Adobe Stock

www.LavishPublishing.com

# Contents

*–For you, Dad*

*I miss you…*
*I forgive you.*

# Prologue

A MANUSCRIPT IS DISCOVERED.

The first few pages are missing, but the rest are mostly intact. The pages feel satiny and light, almost magical to the touch. Once you hold the book, you can't tolerate putting it down.

It calls you. It owns you. It beckons you read faster. It demands your absolute attention.

It calls you out from the darkness.

**Liv•ie**
**/liv-ee/**

*adjective*
   Dearly loved; Of the sun.
   *synonyms: dear, darling, favorite, loved*
   *noun*
   Nickname for Olivia; Much-loved person.
   *synonyms: sweetheart, darling, lover, sweetie, beloved*

# ONE

## Called Out

QUIET NOW, my Livie. Hush...
Can you hear me call your name?
In the center of your stillness,
In the heart of your heart,
Can you sense me whispering?
Hush now. Be quiet. Listen...
Wake up. Open your eyes. Accept the lesson.
I'm calling you out.
Finally.

...A voice from within.

"I have to get out of these scrubs—fast, before I go insane," Doctor Devyn Mitchell whispered. Only she heard her muffled words, but the whole Labor and Delivery Unit felt them. She sensed twenty questioning eyes burning holes in her back from down the halls, piercing through the walls.

*What the hell just happened?*

Her mind reeled.

*Thud!* The plastic lid of the dirty OR hamper slammed shut in judgment. Blood stained everything. *Slam, slam, slam*, the gavel fell. More blood seeped into her pores. The precious, precious blood stained her red.

3

She smelled it everywhere. It saturated her fingernails, her hair, and the mucous membranes of her nostrils. The hot and sticky heme contaminated her with the tainted scent of metal.

Blood, the giver of life, giver of love, had called her out.

Another person saved. Another mother spared. Another baby birthed. Another trapped soul she had just helped condemn to suffer the human experience of life by saving it from the jowls of death.

*Why? To what end?*

To facilitate this bizarre journey that delved deep into madness, so full of fear, illusion, and pain?

*Why?*

She couldn't quite figure out the reason she struggled so hard to rescue others while she watched her own grip on life slip precariously loose.

"Get a hold of yourself! It's not possible," she said out loud. "It's not. You didn't put that home portal order in for all those units of blood products to the lab. You were sleeping at the time. You know you were, so just stop. The only reason they called you here for this fucking disaster was because Doctor Cullen wasn't responding to the nurse's pages."

She shook her finger at the mirror, more at herself than that creep Doctor Cullen.

"You looked at the clock, remember? That damn overpriced, military, accurate-to-a-stupid-second clock."

She was practically screaming at this point, but she couldn't stop.

"As if you actually cared about coordinating time with NASA."

Her foot slipped on something sticky—blood probably.

"How could you have made sure Mrs. Johnson's rare blood type was ready for transfusion? How? She isn't even your patient, so how could you? You didn't have access to her chart. It must have been a mistake. A big, fat, life-saving mistake!" she wailed smashing her fist into the locker-room vanity.

She threw her bloody foot-covers in the garbage and shuddered, almost unable to turn back around to face her reflection. An inner magnet, far more powerful than her need to cower, spun her round against her will. Angry at this point, she demanded an answer from the confused face she saw in the mirror, the same bewildered features she no longer recognized...except for those same almost sad brown eyes.

She blinked, her irritation quickly replaced with another emotion almost too painful to consider, and her eyes moistened. She squinted, and they quickly dried. *Who am I? Why am I here? Really, who the hell am I?*

Lost in her own questions, she stared back at the stranger, the inverted image otherwise identical to her own. *Who are you? Who the hell are you?*

The reflection looked nothing like the picture of the playful girl caught dancing unaware, who smiled, clueless she was trapped in a wooden frame on a nightstand. In fact, the image couldn't have looked more different.

*Another miracle? Kiss my ass. Get a grip. This world is not made for miracles.*

She sat down on the bench and trembled. A deep and powerful sadness shook her. As the intense waves of emotion filled her, a single tear fell despite her best efforts to contain it. She wanted to sob but couldn't figure out why. Hadn't she just saved that woman and her baby's life? Angered by her display of momentary weakness, she wiped the tear from her cheek and scowled.

She stood to examine herself once more in the mirror while she washed her hands, again.

"Who are you? What do you want from me? Why me?" she asked the mutated version of the sweet girl she once was.

She scrubbed her fingers, still seeing nothing but crimson-stained flesh soaked in the woman's blood.

Flash. Her memory returned to the OR.

The last sixty minutes felt like sixty hours and sixty seconds all at the same time. It was the woman's first baby.

*It will be her last, too.*

She closed her eyes letting the memory consume her. Her hands, suffocating in gloves one size too small, felt hot underneath the fountain of red liquid oozing from the patient—all the goddamn blood. It should have been thick and burgundy, but it wasn't. It was thin and getting paler by the second.

Devyn wanted to scream.

Thankfully, her mask disguised her weakness while the doctor within stepped up and took over.

"Blood. We need blood. Whole blood. Any blood. Now! And fresh, frozen plasma. Try to get her cross-matched if you can. Fast. Get Mefoxin, two grams IV, but the blood first. Antibiotics are useless to her corpse—"

Before she finished her sentence, the OR doors crashed open. A courier from the lab had four units of rare, matched blood ready to hang.

While the OR team stared in delighted disbelief, the tech said, "With four units ahead, already prepping as per your orders via home portal entry, Doctor Mitchell. Next round up in fifteen minutes."

*"What orders from home?"* she almost asked.

The anesthesiologist stared then recovered. "How could you possibly have known? She hasn't decompensated yet."

"The blood's here but still no lousy reply from our STAT pages to Doctor Cullen," the charge nurse said. Her rage infected her tone, spreading across the floor and down the hall like a river of pus. "That man should be stripped of his

5

hospital privileges for this outrage, for not responding to an emergency page. That asshole."

Doctor Mitchell cut in. "This woman and her baby are dying."

Devyn made the emergency Cesarean section incision and said, "Whether or not she's my patient doesn't really matter anymore. Forget Cullen's pages. Scrub in, and make yourself useful at my side—here, where at least we are trying to do something, anything, the only thing left to do for her, for them."

Nurse Karen gasped at all the blood. "She's still bleeding," she said, unable to say anything more useful while she wiped and suctioned out the fluid that kept coming. It spilled over the OR drapes and onto the floor, unmistakably pink instead of red.

"It's DIC, Karen, Disseminated Intravascular Coagulation: mass consumption of her clotting factors from the placental abruption."

Silence.

"When the baby's placenta tore away prematurely."

The only sound left was the suctioning device.

"That is why the baby's heart beat stopped," Devyn said. Saying something sounded better than silence or suctioning.

She handed the limp baby to the pediatrician.

"No pulse, I'm sure. God damn this job!"

The baby monitor started beeping.

*Not good. Not good at all.*

The code team activated. Devyn looked over for a second, but the blood was still coming. She tapped the woman's leg through the drape.

"Stop bleeding, or you are going to die."

Nurse Karen rolled her eyes.

Devyn's thoughts inevitably strayed to Livie, her daughter, to how delicately the balance of life teeters back and forth always threatening the unthinkable—to how easily everything could be lost, stolen in an instant.

If Livie died, like what almost happened in the swimming pool last summer, Devyn knew she would kill herself immediately from the grief.

Then her thoughts turned to the only person she knew who had killed herself: her mom.

*Mom, how could you?*

Her mentally ill mother. The one who used to be so much fun before she essentially bungee jumped off a cliff without a rope. The one who handed all Devyn's happy birthday parties, along with the steering wheel of her mother's Toyota, over to the devil.

Devyn imagined it for the thousandth time.

As the frame of that ugly rust-covered Camry crumbled, mortality, that bitch of a killjoy, snatched Devyn's happy childhood from her mother's fragile skull as it smashed into the side of a mountain. *Smack!*

The infant warmer alarms ceased, and the resuscitation team took a breath while Devyn's mind returned to the present moment. The baby would live—probably.

Her skilled hands went back on auto pilot to save the mother.

"If I don't remove her uterus, she will never stop oozing until there is no blood left in her or the hospital's blood bank," she said to the team. "Someone step out and tell her husband the baby has a pulse now, and this is our only chance, her only chance left. It is small, very small indeed."

*At least she has one. Thanks to the mystery blood I never ordered.*

She completed the C-section and subsequent hysterectomy in less than thirty minutes. It was a new hospital record. She then spent the next thirty minutes holding pressure and begging for help from someone bigger and more powerful than she, like the miracle blood sender.

She hoped against hope they weren't too late or too slow, that the blood would take, that infection wouldn't set in, that the baby would live a life worth living, not a vegetable but a real boy full of possibility and promise.

A knock on the lounge door followed by the smug voice of Nurse Karen pulled her from her thoughts.

"The tardy Doctor Cullen is on line three. He says his pager was out of batteries—the creep. As if. He wants to know if he is still needed here."

Picking up the phone, Devyn shook her head to clear the memory of the near miss.

"Brad, how gracious of you to return my page."

Sigh.

"I suspect either you or your lawyer should meet the family in the ICU. I am going home now since I'm not on call and you are—supposedly. Expect a full root cause analysis on this from the Medical Safety and Quality of Care Committee. Also, plan on a formal inquiry to your whereabouts tonight. Know that if I find out booze or drugs are involved, you are on suspension indefinitely."

Truthfully, she felt thankful she answered her pager first that night.

If Doctor Cullen, who was famous for his ambivalence and inability to make a life or death call, had arrived first, she would be on her way in now for the aftermath anyway. The innocent but unlucky woman and her baby would already be on their way to the morgue. As Chair of Obstetrics, she would have had a full-blown sentinel event on her hands.

She was pissed, exhausted, and dismayed. Mostly, though, she felt lost and empty. Her world seemed to make no sense anymore.

When she turned to leave the lounge, a flash of light caught her attention. A

7

burning sensation attacked her neck. A stench filled the air. Nausea cramped her intestines. Then she saw it.

*"Wake up. Open your eyes."*

In the mirror, she watched the image of someone, a darker-skinned look-alike, collapse on the ground. The woman's eyes glossed over with the finality of death. The woman's skin glimmering from perspiration, smooth, shiny hair, and almond-shaped eyes commanded Devyn's attention. The stink of sweat intensified. Devyn heaved to vomit. Nothing came.

She looked back at the mirror again. There was only her own similar looking, mascara-stained reflection.

She crumbled to the floor, quivering, more from shock now than sadness.

*Am I crazy? Am I losing my mind? Did I order that blood and forget?*

A successful but overworked obstetrician-gynecologist, Doctor Devyn Mitchell had done all the right things. She had checked all the right boxes and brilliantly covered up all her imperfections. Now, no one, not even she, remembered the truth of her past. She escaped notice, slipped through the cracks, and convinced everyone of her flawlessness. Her application looked spotless. Her permanent record appeared unblemished.

Sure, her family's past was full of tragedy. So what?

She wore a size six dress and owned just the right shoes for every dress in her disaster of a closet. From the outside, she seemed to have it all together: the beautiful house, the perfect career, the skillful hands of a brilliant surgeon, the handsome partner, and a healthy daughter.

Inside, however, she was a painfully altered version of herself, injured with doubt, woundedness, and guilt. She felt lost, trapped, and ready to give up.

Well, she was almost ready to give up. There was one thing she was still certain of. One unspoiled rainbow still caught her eye and forced her to smile. One beautiful prism of color still proclaimed the flood would not wash her away again. Even as she clung for dear life in the rapids of disaster, that someone made her hang on, made her want to connect back in and be a better person, a better mother.

Her three-year-old daughter, Olivia, was definitely awake by 7:00 a.m. Sweet Nanny Rose felt the fullness of Olivia's sass by now. Even Devyn smelled the not-so-sweet side of Olivia's adorable rear end six miles across town.

By this time, Olivia, who preferred to be called Livie for short, surely marched around the living room in her Cinderella gown, demanding answers. Where was her mother, and why wasn't she dressed and ready for their morning picnic outside by the pool? What emergency possibly justified this measure of outrage? Perfectly juicy raspberries waited in the fridge. The imaginary purple tea brewed. The pretend kettle whistled while the furiously disturbed cat, Master Lucky, hissed from the safety of the couch. While Lucky licked his backside, he watched the magic of imaginary purple tea go shamefully undiscovered down the thankless drain of the kitchen sink—wasted.

With the image of an enraged Livie in her mind's eye, a tender smile crossed Devyn's face. She was done trembling. She was going home to her baby, her only joy, the same joy that could be swept away without notice.

For a brief moment, she remembered who she truly was: adoring mother, intuitive knower, messenger of love and light, and keeper of the innocent ones.

Under her current veil of illusion, though, she had almost completely forgotten her true self. The cloud around the fullness of who she actually came here to be hung so heavily and so thick that she could smell it, taste it, and feel it, but not see through it.

Little did she know that her clock ticked, too, like Mrs. Johnson, the woman she just saved. Her final bell rang. She had asked the perfect question. School was officially in session because she was finally ready to attend. The teacher had a curriculum built for her.

*Finally.*

These were the last few moments of her life before everything changed.

This thirty-five-year-old, schoolgirl-pretty doctor stood teetering on the edge of her life's culmination. Part of her was totally aware of how everything was about to change. The rest of her was simply clueless as the first bolt of lightning in her greatest storm crashed. Oh how it all changed in an instant, the final second, the last moment of uncertainty before the inevitable thunderstorm of truth overtook her, the defining moment when everything new arrived and everything old had no choice left but to fall away and call itself the past.

Her movie began. The previews were over. The popcorn smelled so delicious. The new Doctor Mitchell chose the Red Pill and swallowed. The new Devyn jumped...or was she pushed?

It was the moment she awakened to who she truly was, to who she had always been.

She couldn't go back. No one ever can.

## TWO

## Silent Lucidity
_____

*"MOMMY, WAKE UP,"* a little voice said in Devyn's head.

*"Wake Up. Open your eyes. Finally."*

The only thing she later remembered from before her nearly fatal accident was looking at the clock and thinking, *7:55 a.m. and on a Saturday, no less. Livie baby is definitely pissed.*

She never heard the great but dull smash of the final moments of the car collision. She never experienced her crown smashing against the headrest, which knocked her out of her prior reality. She was already somewhere new.

The splitting windshield shattered only for deafened ears. The metal frames collapsed only for closed and unobserving eyes. *Smack!*

Darkness.

Awake. Eyes opened. Finally.

The other driver was only seventeen. He had sent his last text message in that bizarre shorthand only teenagers understand.

His final text, *Ma I NVR*, would scream in his mother's devastated ears for a lifetime.

*"You never what, Johnny? You never what?"*

Some questions were meant to remain unanswered.

# THREE

## The Answer

TWO DAYS LATER.

From the still darkness of her coma came a flicker of movement, a flash of a small blue light in the abyss. Then nothingness returned.

Awake. Eyes opened. Finally.

Hours later, a thought, or perhaps a voice, called out. Devyn couldn't discern the difference. Not yet, anyway.

*"Mommy?"*

*"Yes, baby?"*

*"Mommy?"*

*"Yes, baby?"*

Silence returned.

After another day, the voice within her head said, "*Mommy, open your eyes. It's time for us to wake up. She's been hunted down, too. She's going to die. The first one...she was just found.*"

For an instant, Devyn smelled a fragrance that she almost recognized. She thought she remembered something, something very important, a detail she absolutely must recall.

She tried to open her hand. She tried to focus her mind. She tried to scream out for help, but her body betrayed her. Her arms, her eyelids felt so heavy.

*"Baby?"*

Nothing.

After three more days of fitful half-sleeping, a flowing tune started to play in

11

her head, very softly at first. Even though there was a pain in her head too big for words, she asked for the tune to play louder.

The melody soothed her. It called to her. It claimed her. It owned her. It reminded her of a memory from long ago.

*"At love's first sight, I knew it was always you."* The lyrics of the classical waltz began.

Was it from the tale about the seven little men? No. It was about a sleeping princess lost in an eternal dream. She was rescued, but not by the prince. She rescued herself, but how was that possible?

*"Who walked in my dreams and sang in my heart."*

She felt herself dancing along. One…two, three. One…two, three. She looked down at her fine, bare feet, such small and fragile feet that carried the weight of the entire world.

*"Who lifted me up and showed me my truth."*

She slowly looked up and saw herself surrounded by an ocean of angelic faces framed in innocence and perfection.

One flawless beauty in particular stepped forward and said, "I knew it was always you."

Without hesitation and in perfect timing, Devyn answered back, "Your eyes, forever the same, never have changed."

They sang the words together like she had always known them, known the steps, the tune, maybe even wrote it specifically for today, having known all along this moment was fated to come.

"Throughout all time in all of my lives, I knew it was always you."

As they embraced, the child seemed to melt inside her. The lovely melody continued only in the furthest corner of her scattered mind as the ache of her throbbing forehead took her back to an inkling of a world she started to remember: a world filled with illusion, hate, death, evil, and greed. A world that, frankly, she didn't want to remember.

A few minutes later, she awoke briefly and spoke part of some unknown name, "Ell…"

The same fragrance, like a rotten bouquet made of sweat and suffering, enveloped her again. It penetrated her so forcibly that it almost sickened her to vomitus. Just as quickly, she was gone again, lost in her healing dream.

Again, a few hours later, she called out, "Baby, where are you?"

She slurred, failing to effectively pronounce the words. Then once more, she slipped back into oblivion before she managed to hold out for a response.

12

The TV in Devyn's ICU room served as nothing more than a source of white noise with its boring and mindless chatter. Advertisements pushed products that supposedly offered salvation from made-up problems no one really suffered.

An urgent news report cut in.

The handsome television field reporter with slightly wavy dark blond hair and piercing grey-blue eyes pleasantly announced that a body had been discovered. The fear-provoking news fell on the wasted ears and unrecognizing eyes of the unconscious patient in ICU bed seven.

Brock Bryant, Tampa's most well-liked news reporter, smiled cheerfully but uselessly to the unengaged patient while he revealed that the now deceased homeless woman seemed to be in her mid-fifties. Police suspected foul play. Until the Tampa police revealed more information, they would return to their usual programming. Then, with his world-famous slightly crooked grin, he wished all the Channel Six News viewers, including the currently oblivious Devyn, a good night.

Devyn awoke just as the news segment finished. She thought she recognized a familiar voice, but she couldn't be sure. If only the throbbing lessened, if only the spinning slowed, if only the confusion lifted.

Another day passed before she improved, but she did.

At first, her moments of lucidity were intermittent, but they lasted noticeably longer each hour. Her strength returned with surprising intensity. In just a few short days, she transferred out of the ICU. Completely transformed by the end of the week, it seemed impossible she could have been the same woman who lay there so weak, confused, and tortured by her alternating dreams of death and visions of healing a few days before.

To the visitor's eye, she had been surrounded by the seemingly peaceful yet endless beeping of machines while the alternating crew of doctors, nurses, and nameless hospital staff attended to her body. From the inside, from the depths of within, though, she spent the last few days changing, shifting, and breaking down limitations formed over tens of thousands of years of programming. She travelled from one end of the universe that was her and back again. Once the cracks set in, though, there was never any going back, not for her, not for anyone—ever.

Awake. Eyes opened. Finally.

In between her bouts of incapacitating dizziness and insatiable periods of thirst, she rested. When she was finally alert enough, the director of Critical Care Services, Doctor Eugene Track, took the time to describe what happened. In slow and easy terms, he explained she had suffered a devastating car accident and a

13

minor closed-head injury. She was hit by a young driver distracted while texting. He died instantly. Miraculously, no other cars were involved on the busy Florida Turnpike that morning.

She had awoken after a coma of five days duration. The neurologists were still unsure why her altered mental status had lasted so long. Her endless battery of negative tests left her prolonged confusion unexplained. Her head CT and MRI, the imaging studies done to evaluate her brain, looked perfectly normal. Thus, there seemed to be no worry of any long-term damage.

"It just must have been the shock of it all," the doctor said with a look that suggested he wasn't completely convinced.

Two broken ribs, a separated sternum, some scary looking bruises, and a few stitches were the full extent of the physical damage to her body.

He hinted that she should have died immediately from the impact of the accident. Somehow, though, she hadn't…as if she had been divinely protected... She would be fine, which was a miracle—a good one.

About that, he was right.

The compassionate doctor offered up some comment about the *Big Guy* and angels on her shoulders, and then he smiled at her. With loving hands and genuine tenderness, he reached across the sterile and uncomfortable hospital bed to touch her.

"By the way," he said, "Mrs. Johnson is fine. You know, the lady you saved just before the accident. She's already home. You are an awesome surgeon. You saved her life. Knowing to have the blood ready was psychic or something. Damn, you are good. Just one big miracle after the next."

"You mean lucky. I'll take lucky over good any day. By the way, I don't believe in miracles. You know that."

"Okay, sure." He laughed. "How about both—lucky and good? Man, you are pretty much a living legend for that one. She should not have survived, and everybody with half a brain knows that—much like you, I guess."

He looked away as if he wanted to say more but couldn't or didn't know how. He shifted in his seat.

"The Johnson baby's fine, too, of course, but…"

She smiled, sure he was about to give her some really bad news.

"The best news, though, lady, is that your baby seems to be fine. Ten weeks pregnant, and you never said a word. I thought we were friends."

Silence.

He patted her on the head. "Don't worry, though. Your secret is safe with me."

"What?"

"The baby. You should have told me you were expecting, my secretive friend."

"But I... No, it's not. I mean... What? Are you kidding?" She leaned forward and put her hand over her mouth.

Doctor Track tried to hold her eyes but couldn't. "Devyn, didn't you—?"

Just then, however, Livie barged into the room with a cup of imaginary purple tea. Brock Bryant, Livie's father and Devyn's charming life partner, followed shortly behind with a fragrant bouquet of elegant flowers: an inventive mix of anemones and honeysuckle with a solitary orange poppy in the center.

"Livie knew you would be ready for some tea, and so here we are a little early, thankfully." He chuckled. "Visiting hours don't seem to apply to the VIPs like you."

Devyn tried to respond but nothing came out but a squeak. She nodded her head *no*.

"Rest. Doctor's orders. We can talk about it more later. Just rest." Doctor Track patted Devyn on the shoulder and nodded his head *yes*.

Devyn touched her abdomen and sighed.

Brock put the flowers on the bedside table. "You're hungry, baby?"

Doctor Track coughed. "Lunch. More doctor's orders. Okay?" He closed the door softly.

She cleared her throat and frowned. "You know I hate it when you call me bab—"

"Mommy. Mommy need tea," Livie said and climbed into her mother's bed. "L-E be good. Mommy see."

And finally, Devyn relaxed.

# FOUR

## Fifteen Minutes

AS DEVYN STRUGGLED, both to understand what had just happened and to choose between tuna salad and a ham sandwich for lunch, the good-natured Doctor Eugene Track rushed down the hallway to make up the extra ten minutes he spent chatting with her.

He had a trip planned to the mountains for himself and his sweet Monica, and he didn't want them to miss their flight.

*Yes, vacation. Let's go, baby.*

He squealed with delight. He hoped Monica would forgive him those ten little minutes when she found out about tonight's reservation for the dinner theatre in Aspen. He also hoped that maybe, just maybe, this would be the perfect weekend to explore the loving branded on his brains. He expected to get big-time lucky, too.

Again, as usual, he was right, now and then—both.

"Yippee," Eugene whispered while he caught the elevator.

On a hunch, he sprinted for the closing doors of the elevator to the right. The door opened warmly, suspended by the generous finger of a stranger who stopped the doors the instant before they closed.

For the five uninterrupted flights down, his thoughts wandered to Devyn Mitchell and her good luck as if good luck could explain her survival, virtually unscathed from what should have been her last trip down the busy Florida highway.

*Miracle. It was a miracle.*

He knew it. He had seen them before.

16

Like his mother always said, "If it quacks like a duck, it's probably a duck."

When he came on staff as ICU director at Holosni Regional six years ago, it was a totally different place, the kind of place you hoped your mother never ended up, the kind of ER you stayed out of, the kind of ICU you transported patients out of instead of into.

Not anymore.

Thanks to Doctor Devyn Mitchell, who grudgingly gave in and finally accepted Eugene's pleas to help with her ridiculous administrative load, everything had changed.

The two of them functioned like a match made in heaven. They had made poor outcomes and unexpected Joint Commission visits a thing of the past. The patients went from surviving in spite of their care to thriving because of it.

*"Safety first. Excellent staff. Best practice care with cutting-edge technology all wrapped up in impeccable customer satisfaction is the plan, Eugene,"* he heard Devyn say in his mind every time he thought about cutting corners to save a dollar. Her word was strong, good, and sincere.

*Doctor Devyn Mitchell is the face, the vision, the mission of this place.*

He walked past her photo in the lobby and said a quick prayer for her recovery. He added a few words of thanks for her and her ambition but mostly for her recent good luck while he stepped right out the front sliding glass door.

As far as he was concerned, this whole community owed her a debt of gratitude they would hopefully never have to comprehend. Without her, this hospital was a place he and the patients would never want to return to, and they had almost lost her for good. Thankfully, they hadn't.

*It was a good luck miracle.*

Skipping to the bus station, he acknowledged his continued good luck, too. He was making up time right and left. Monica might not even notice the ten minutes.

*What ten minutes?*

Yet even he had no idea how good his luck was getting.

What he never needed to know was that if he had taken the other elevator instead of the one he chose, he would still be stuck waiting on the third floor. Those ten minutes would now be fifteen minutes, and he would have just missed the bus, the same bus he barely caught before it drove away.

He bounced with anticipation in his second-row seat all the way home, none the wiser of his glorious advantage.

When he walked up the front stairs of his and Monica's new townhouse, he smelled the pungent distress of something burning in the oven. With all her excitement about the trip, Monica had forgotten about the poppy-seed bagels she put in the broiler.

17

Oh how she loved sun-dried tomato cream cheese on a warm, toasty bagel.

Oblivious to the danger below, Monica showered upstairs. While she sang an out of tune version of some nineties' Celine Dion song at the top of her lungs, smoke filled the kitchen. Thankfully, instead of fifteen minutes too late, Eugene arrived just in time to put out the first hint of a flame.

Sure, it was a little stinky downstairs, but no real damage occurred.

Oh what those fifteen minutes might have cost them. Instead, it was but an afterthought of a joke on the plane ride headed for Denver, some good-luck icing smack dab on top of a day made of good-luck cupcakes.

Miracles, probably.

Instead of spending the weekend in some unfriendly hotel room sorting out the fire damage details, the loving couple spent three magical days together in the breathtaking beauty of the Rocky Mountains. Together, they enjoyed a delicious long weekend just as those gorgeous Aspen leaves started dancing their famous golden jig in the almost chilly wind of a late Colorado summer.

They loved one another so much that weekend, about nine months later, Monica witnessed the awesome sight of her eight pound, two ounce daughter Elizabeth taking her first breath.

So, thank goodness the stranger held the door open for the elevator on the right, a much better story told all because of a generous finger and fifteen little minutes.

Proudly bearing discharge instructions and flowers in her left hand, Devyn wheeled straight past her picture in the lobby and right out the front door of her own hospital.

"I just love these flowers, don't you?" she asked Brock.

He whistled some unrecognizable tune and moved his feet back and forth as if waltzing to some melody in the furthest corner of his mind.

She laughed while he hummed.

"I just had to keep this bouquet. The rest I donated to the Pediatric Ward. I wonder who sent these. Was it you? What are these, anyway? The blue ones are forget-me-nots, I think."

"You say the funniest things," he said. "Just because my family happens to own a flower importing business, amongst a thousand other companies I might add, doesn't mean I have a clue what these are. So no, they are definitely not from me. Peonies maybe? We can ask my sister. She has a thing for flowers."

"Yeah, I think I'm starting to have a love affair with flowers myself," she said.

With Livie holding her right hand and Brock pushing the rickety, old wheelchair from behind with his big, strong arms, she took a deep breath of the floral bouquet surrounding her. Lungs full of life, she paused and held the air for just a second longer.

Livie shared some insight about the fairies playing in their garden, so Devyn knew she was finally on her way back to life as usual.

Devyn said thanks, almost in a prayer, even though she would have never admitted it—at least not at the time. They drove the ten minute ride on the back roads to their six thousand square foot, two-story stucco and brick abode.

Devyn was done with the Turnpike for a while.

Safe and sound, they arrived at 144 Sunnyside Way in little old trapped-in-the-past Holosni, Florida. For the first time in way too long, they openly honored their connection to one another. The daily bother, shrugged to the side, was completely forgotten, if only for a moment.

When they walked in the front door, the happy family luckily missed the latest news report that spewed its half-truth and poorly disguised disinformation. It concluded with an update on the recently discovered corpse in her mid-fifties. This nameless Hispanic woman remained unidentified. An accidental death officially ruled out, murder was apparently afoot. A request called for any information that might help the authorities in any way.

Master Lucky, the grey cat from nowhere, stopped licking his paws and danced and twirled in delight at the feet of his now-home mistress.

"About time," he announced with his tail held high in the air while he circled her feet over and over again.

Five days without her were just too much for everyone. It was about time for life to return to normal. Who knew what might have happened to breakfast, bath time, and the brushing of teeth if Mom stayed away any longer? Nanny Rose could have only worked so many miracles.

Back to the usual hustle and bustle of life as a small-town celebrity doctor in the middle of no man's land, Doctor Devyn Mitchell returned. She grinned from ear to ear. Already a thing of yesterday, broken ribs and pirate ship-sized bruises were long forgotten by lunch.

After the traditional Mac-N-Cheese and Kiki milk, Livie's name for chocolate milk, treats of childhood were shared by the Princess Livie and her parents. The clock struck nap time. This time, Devyn planned to break all the rules and snuggle her baby through magical journeys to the dragon-filled lands of their best-planned dreams.

For once, she wouldn't even bother to look over her shoulder, afraid to be caught on tape by the do-gooder doctors who screamed about co-sleeping. Right now, she couldn't care less what the pediatricians might say about her suffocating her daughter in the middle of the night.

*Ridiculous. Like I would ever sleep soundly enough to crush my child.*

She remembered all the sleepless nights, unable to rest while she watched her precious baby sleep and dream and grow. *As if.*

With the TV and its distorted stories of the crazy world turned off, newspapers discarded in the bin, and mail tossed in the corner, the house took a breath. Everything less important waited—everything.

Wrapped in her loving mother's arms, Livie giggled. She was destined to be strangled with affection and certainly doomed to barely escape this kind of love.

Brock would have to wait for now. That kind of loving was meant for later.

Mother and beloved daughter, hand in hand, went down the rug-lined hall toward the land of cuddles and kisses. Devyn yawned, oblivious to the fluttering wings standing guard over her daughter's door. She climbed past her daughter's princess table, prepared as usual with perfectly arranged settings for afternoon teatime.

She looked for Big Head Baby, Gigi the Penguin, and Sophie. The chosen dolls of the month all sat with ideal posture, patiently awaiting their staples of precious purple tea and crispy biscuits.

As she yawned again, she noticed three flowers on the table. Three gorgeous, pink Zinnias were perched perfectly, offered up as a gift from some unseen and mourning suitor.

"Huh." She yawned a third time. "Livie, I love you to the ends of the universe."

Livie answered on cue. "Back, Mommy."

With a big, open heart, Devyn took one last look around her daughter's green and purple butterfly filled room while they snuggled down for their nap. In their slumber, destined to be the best nap ever throughout all time and space, they rested safely embraced by true love, real love, the kind of love that enveloped them.

Oblivious to the love that protected the inhabitants inside 144 Sunnyside Way, a rustling out back tempted the trees. Darkness threatened. A silent, disturbing presence haunted the back edge of the swamp that soaked part of Devyn's land.

Its time had come. Its waiting had ended. It was ready and willing.

Once more.

# FIVE

## Run

FAINTLY, off in the distance of her dream, Devyn heard the ringing of a bell and smiled.

*Another angel gets her wings.*

She looked at her feet and remembered she could fly if she wanted to—badly enough, that was. With the effort known only to the movers of mountains, she gave it her best shot. Just a lift off the ground at first, and then higher and higher up she went.

Finally...wham! Up to the top of the orange and blue tree, she jumped. The fingerlike projection of its needle-shaped leaves pointed even higher, daring her to really fly. She giggled.

*Truth or dare? Dare. Definitely dare.*

Just before she could accomplish her feat of greatness, her attention turned to the mesmerizing army of red balloons that seemed to come from yesterday.

She found her focus drawn like a magnet down, down, down. Before she knew what had happened, she heard the tumultuous ground splitting beneath her while she tumbled helplessly from the heavens of the Great Listening Tree. She felt a stabbing pull inwards toward the center of the earth as the roaring of the rapidly enlarging crack spread. Quick witted, she jumped to her feet, racing with lightning speed away from her impending doom.

Her inner voice screamed: *Run or you will be swallowed up! Save yourself. No one else can help you. Not now. Not this time.*

She took a moment to peer over her right shoulder, only to find that this subtle break in her movement was enough to bring her crashing to the floor. Rocks

22

tumbling all around her weary head, she knew this must be the end. She started to give way to the swirling disaster that surrounded her and submit to her demise.

Then, just before she surrendered, she changed her mind. She shouted with every breath of life she had left, "Never! I will never!"

Renewed fight filled her lungs, and with the thump, thump, thump of a racing heart, she awoke with a gasp.

Livie, still in peaceful slumber, rested comfortably to Devyn's right side. Thankfully, she seemed totally unaware of the destruction in her mother's foreboding dream.

While Devyn dreamed her dream, the killer relived a very different one, going back in time with wicked delight to savor the last attack.

The enticing smell of fear soaked the otherwise stale air. The rancid scent of nervous body odor betrayed the damned woman's brave pretense. She fought so deliciously hard to get away, but there was no use.

The murderer stroked the place the victim had grasped so tightly, trying to escape. The bruises, deep, so deep in the skin felt satisfying. They served as definitive proof of the event that showering with soap would never wash away... for a few sweet days of remembering, at least.

The victim's struggling was wasted effort like a mouse on its stupid, eternally squeaking wheel trying to escape, trying, but unable to get anywhere.

The maniac's sin became the victim's, and she was punished for it.

Oh how it soothed when the sweet liquid of death pierced her skin.

*Penetrate. Shove. Inject. Withdraw. Ah...*

The needle felt cold and sharp yet warm and soft in the devil's hand all at the same time. It had been too long, way too long, since this kind of relief was felt. If only it lasted longer...if only.

Amusement stirred in the monster when the thoughtful image of a flower was remembered. The police were so careless they probably wouldn't even discover the secret little clues. It would remain the villain's private, personal joy.

*Oh what blossom of love next?*

Before Devyn could remember why she felt so anxious and fearful from her dream, the vision was forever lost to her unconscious mind.

How queer the idea of dreams if explored by an inquisitive philosopher. A mind could create a world within itself while it entertained its genuinely surprised

23

other side. How clever the mind that reveled in such self-deception, yet also how divided.

Or was the dream state simply a portal to another dimension, another possibly more *real* version of *reality*? Which side then was *real*, and who decided?

Who made the dreams after all? Was it the dreamer, some higher source, or the angels?

Or if you were an unlucky one, plagued with nightmares, was it the darkness? An evil entity or perhaps just some devilish part of the sinful dreamer?

Which part? The child, the fallen adult, or the playful jokester who kept pulling tricks on himself? Or was it actually a teacher offering up the next lesson of unfoldment, where blessing had been cleverly disguised as pain?

# SIX

# Heartbreak War

DEVYN ROSE SLOWLY, her joints complaining from disuse, and looked around her daughter's room. Livie slept soundly.

*Thank you.*

Devyn traced Livie's forehead and smiled. Then she shook her head to clear the cobwebs.

*How the hell am I going to tell Brock about the new baby?*

She stretched and yawned, completely forgetting her dream about flying, falling, and yesterday.

*What was that dream?*

Six months ago, Devyn and Brock decided marital prison would come before any more babies, like her opinion had mattered in the least. Brock remained adamant about this one thing. His intensity and anger about it wedged a splinter in the seat of the trust of their relationship. A seed of doubt sprouted its meddling, tiny roots into the ground of their love and dug in.

After that battle, she really thought Livie would be her one and only, her only joy, her only child.

*Oh, Livie, I love you so much.*

Despite five long years together, she still answered no every time her lover, the charming Brock Bryant, asked for her hand in marriage. Lately, though, the offers had been few and far between.

She paced the room, trying to clear her thoughts.

Actually, the flowers—mostly roses, tulips, and jonquils—from her secret admirer had stopped mysteriously showing up at her office months ago. Beauti-

25

fully wrapped surprises on the car seat seemed to be a memory from last year just like the hot, steamy nights in the bedroom.

Brock spent more and more time working in Tampa these days. Some new, big, news-breaking story broke week after week—supposedly, but maybe not.

*Maybe there is someone else?*

She doubted it, but when was the last all-night slumber party in the sheets? If she was ten weeks pregnant, it must have been about eight weeks ago. Was it? She couldn't be sure. Her memory was less than reliable lately.

Her memory flashed to life-saving blood in the OR. She looked down at her hands expecting blood stains in her cuticles. They were clean.

As far as everyone in their community was concerned, Devyn and Brock were married but simply had two different last names just like the average, modern, your name's-not-good-enough-for-me woman of today. In this case, though, there was no legal piece of paper backing it up. They filed separate taxes and technically lived separate lives outside the wood and stucco structure they called home.

Half the time, Brock lived at his family's lavish beach house in Tampa anyway, so both his closets stayed half-full—or, better put, half-empty.

She looked down at her pretend wedding band with defeat. Brock wore its identical twin to stave off the inevitable well-intentioned suitor who crept anxiously around every corner waiting for a chance to pounce on the special ones like them.

To her, the band of white gold felt like a weight dragging her down: a rock of torture, a boulder with heavy outcroppings trying to snag her, a promise of someone wanting to take something more from her—something more than she wanted to give, or had to give…again.

To Brock, it felt too light, flimsy, worthless, like a pathetic façade—irrefutable evidence something was missing. He thought it clearly symbolized her unwilling-ness to love him enough. The shining circle of precious gold constantly referred him back to the absence of that piece of expensive paper in the filing cabinet labeled *Life Documents*. It served as undeniable proof of something inadequate or unworthy about him…again.

Devyn claimed she loved him over and over to no avail. Marriage, in her mind, was not a promise of eternal love. It was a death sentence. She saw it every day,

26

sure as death and taxes. Nuptials were just a clever and expensive dose of potassium chloride meant to kill.

*How the hell am I going to tell him this? Is he going to leave me over a piece of paper?*

She twirled her expensive and heavy white gold loop around and around her left ring finger and sat back down in defeat, still surprised her nails looked so normal.

# SEVEN

## Everywhere

IN HER SMALL but adequate live-in quarters on the back half of the property, Nanny Rose took a darling swimsuit out of her meticulously organized closet and inspected it closely. She had stitched it perfectly by hand and adorned it with love. Pink and red were Livie's top two favorite colors. Meant to be a surprise reward for swimming all the way across the big, blue pool, it waited patiently to be shared with the princess.

Nanny Rose smelled the clean scent of the cloth and smiled. Livie would love it. She was sure.

She was right.

While Rose smiled, Devyn frowned. She took a detour to the kitchen for a drink of water as she prepared for the slaughter of a lifetime from Brock. She stood still for a minute and took a good, long look around. Devyn welcomed the freshly cleaned black granite countertops that formed a fortress around her. She smiled at the scent of pine-based cleaner mixed with flowers inviting her approval.

*Ah, the smell of home.*

Looking for an excuse to avoid confronting Brock, she glanced at one of the silver patterns on the countertop and followed it. Swirling and swirling, it meandered to the edge of the counter near the phone. There she noticed a drawing partially covering the magazines and newspaper overflowing onto the floor. It

28

obscured the grotesque photo of the still nameless, still murdered homeless woman.

"Was a Homeless Hunter on the loose?" She read the headline out loud and almost picked up the paper but couldn't be bothered.

Devyn took the corner of Livie's masterpiece and lifted it up into the light. Orange construction paper formed the warm background of a picture titled *Fmly*. Two large stick figures stood on either side of a smaller stick figure that had a circle at her feet.

*Is that Master Lucky, our grumpy cat?*

Devyn grinned, sucking in every fine detail.

She noticed something in the hand of one of the larger stick figures but couldn't discern exactly what it was. Was it a wand? A flower? A sword?

She felt more intensely drawn to the larger figure on the right. A few strokes of pink colored pencil decorated the triangular-shaped dress. For sure, this was supposed to represent her. Like Livie, pink was her favorite color.

*How thoughtful, my Livie.*

She offered a silent thank you for Livie's completeness while the idea of pink summoned strength within her.

*The baby he doesn't want, but I do. I want you, baby.*

If he dared to suggest the unthinkable, she already knew what her response would be: "No goddamn way. No!"

She might even drop an F-bomb, which she never did, while she slapped him hard across the face.

She thought of her favorite black-and-white movie and giggled.

"I'll slap you silly," she muttered.

*This baby deserves recognition, and I am strong enough to say it.*

She scowled, infuriated by the possibility of what he might suggest.

*Unthinkable.*

If only she convinced herself of her resolve about the situation, she could divulge her secret to him fearlessly, no matter what. She lifted up her shoulders as if donning her armor for battle—a battle she planned to win.

The back of her throat felt sore and dry, but a splash of water worked its magic. She took another big gulp from her favorite cartoon character glass and turned to leave the safety of her sterile abode.

*Could use some of that stuff people call...help.*

A slightly altered version of a laugh escaped her lips.

Before she had a chance to completely brace herself, she ran smack dab into Brock and the opportunity to challenge her fear.

29

Upstairs, gently tucked into the perfection of her bed, the Princess Livie slept. She dreamt the dreams of the innocent. Unicorns guided her down well-lit paths to rivers made of candy. Birds flew overhead, bidding her welcome to the land of joy. Juicy fruit hung from the branches of the trees, kindly offered, just low enough for the reach of her perfect little hands. Baby dolls came alive with but a glance toward them. Hands held in a circle, Livie joined in the games of chase and play. Hide-and-seek played on where no one was *It,* and no one was ever lost. Nanny Rose, taking sides, cheered while Livie won the game of tip-toe, tip-toe, their favorite made-up game of following directions blindfolded.

Master Lucky stood nearby like he was a personal escort making sure all was well. He smirked snobbishly and looked like he would rather be cleaning his paws.

Angels stood guard at every door and every window.

Love itself smiled. Love made Livie lovely. Brilliance made her brilliant. Kindness made her kind. Joy made her joyful. Perfection made her perfect. She allowed it all, as only the innocent can, never once doubting her worth. Never once did she question her purpose, which was simply beyond question. Skipping back and forth, she played and dreamed and sang…still remembering how.

Back downstairs, Devyn and Brock collided with a smack.

"Ouch. Gee, honey, you okay? Something funny?" Brock asked.

He stepped back and regained his balance.

She laughed again but said nothing.

"I heard you in the kitchen and called out your name three times. When you didn't answer, I got a little scared, but then you laughed. Are you playing some kind of weird game with me?"

She laughed again, mostly from being caught so unaware. "Maybe. Should I be? Do you want me to be?" Her questions prompted a wondering within her. She decided that yes, a game of lovemaking would be fun. *Yes, it would.*

"I can't tell a lie. I was hoping for some monkey hugs from you, lady. Livie can't get all of Mama's loving because poor little old me needs some, too."

He offered his most enticing, crooked smile and then pouted like an overgrown baby.

*Damn, your smile looks delicious.*

The pouting she could do just fine without. That familiar smile, though…it felt so comfortable to her as if it had always belonged to her—like a song she once knew but couldn't recall the words to right now.

Instantly, she fell into his muscular arms and felt the strength of him. She took in the smell of his masculinity—a little sandalwood and spice mixed perfectly. Her face scratched the scruff of a two-day-old beard, and she opened to the pain of it. She rubbed her cheek to his, loving his roughness. The slight rug burn it always left would be proof he was here so close to her.

She loved him as much as she had ever loved a man. He was her man, her rock, with or without any worthless piece of paper.

Brock found her ear first and took a sweet and tender nibble. Chills coursed down her spine like electrical impulses made of desire. Then with both arms around her shoulders, he squeezed her with a genuine oh-how-missed-you-were embrace.

She gave in, let down her guard, and opened her drawbridge. He held her outside, inside, and everywhere in between.

Ever so lightly, to share a warm tickle of pleasure, she traced her fingers across the fine line of his full and throbbing lips. Like a love scene from the old black-and-whites, minus the slap...with just a flutter of a butterfly's wing against his mouth...she pressed her lips to his. She welcomed his passion. She encouraged his intensity. She opened her lips a little wider and teasingly let just a hint of his searching tongue enter her mouth.

They both groaned in anticipation of their imminent union.

When she finally opened her eyes, she took his hand and slowly guided it to her lower abdomen where the baby was growing.

Confused at first, he started to question her meaning. She placed her finger tenderly across his lips, encouraging his silent reflection. She looked deep into his eyes and just barely tilted her head forward enough to affirm his now mounting suspicion of the meaning of her gesture.

His pupils dilated with joy, and she knew he understood her perfectly. Somehow everything would be okay. Their love would traverse this rocky terrain, this unknown path.

*Of course it would. Of course it would. I knew it would. I knew he would want it—want us.*

He swept her up into his broad, strong arms and took a long, deep breath of the scent of the woman who was his. Her flavorful bouquet filled his nostrils with joy and certainty. All doubts of her love fell away in that second. He remembered just how much he loved her in return, how much he wanted her, how much he needed her to feel complete, to feel like himself—whole, good, and righteous. He carried her slowly down the hall to their bedroom where he planned to show her.

Reminiscent of the passion of reunited star-crossed lovers, he took a long drink of the sight of her as she lay temptingly across their bed. He soaked up the moment completely before he nodded his head just like she had. Dripping with excitement, his pulse raced. He gasped as he felt her moisture gather.

It was his turn to share his secret. He nodded again.

Starting with the skin over her forehead, he gently caressed all the curves she had to offer. His fingers worked their magic down her full and flushed cheeks, over her sumptuous lips, and down to her angular and intense collarbone. He followed slowly around the rounded contour of her full breasts. Teasing, but never touching, he worked her nipples, which stood erect in attention as if screaming out they were somehow forgotten.

His firm maleness returned her glistening salute of desire, screaming to be noticed, begging to be obliged.

Her gasps pleased him. At first, he teased her by pretending he didn't care, didn't want to feel her hot, wet center.

The game was more painful for him than her, however.

A barely audible moan escaped while he licked his dripping lips.

Gently and slowly...almost too slowly...he traced down the middle of her stomach to her navel where he drew out several turns of a circle. From here, he focused on the fullness of her luscious hips, the part of her he had always secretly loved best.

A soft but louder cry escaped his throat when he finally abandoned any attempts to stave off his need to feel her from the inside any longer. He must take her now or die from the pressure building in his groin.

He took her fleshy buttocks and gently yet firmly drew her onto him as his first thrust met with hers. Deeply kissing her, he tasted the fullness of her flavor. His tongue searched down, down, down for more of her while his hips simultaneously thrust up, up, up to meet the rest of her core.

At first, she kissed him back like a nervous teenager learning the first glimpses of the pleasures of physical love but then seemed to overcome her shyness. Willingly, she opened fully to his ocean of intensity. With the ebbing and flowing movement of the tide, he shared himself with her. His body became hers, and hers his. In every way, they were one in their inferno of love as their climax swept them away on their river of ecstasy.

Not too far away, a woman feeling no joy at all hid in the shadows of her makeshift home in the woods. The last hints of tonight's fire flickered pathetically while the embers lost their battle with the wet Florida earth beneath them.

The panic in her infallible gut hinted something was terribly wrong, that danger waited to hurt her, that *they* had finally hunted her down after all she had done to evade them.

The usually comforting smell of musty leaves beneath her temporary bedding did not soothe her tonight while she tried restlessly to fall asleep. The trees rustled betraying the threatening presence of an animal watching her and her campground.

She jumped up, wide awake, to look out and investigate the source of the disturbance. Failing to find its location, her anxiety increased to full-blown panic. Uselessly, she attempted to fall back asleep, knowing two wild, yellow eyes watched hungrily in the distance.

The animal wasn't the only thing that watched, and it wasn't the only thing that waited for her, hunted her.

Her time was up.

# EIGHT

## A Fallen Swan

AS THE ROOSTER crowed to announce the first light of dawn, the frigid, metal needle delivered its deadly dose of poison into the woman's neck veins. She landed hard on the musty leaves that once felt so familiar and soothing to her while gravity overpowered her lifeless body. In complaint, her arms thrust forward exposing her marble-smooth textured fingertips.

The Homeless Hunter rubbed the abnormal smoothness of the dead woman's digits and smiled.

"As if you could have fooled me."

Opening the woman's mouth, the villain laughed.

"As if pulling your teeth could have kept me from finding you. You stupid fool. You stupid bitch. Now it's finally done, after all this time. You moron."

In a crouched position, the monster caressed the dead woman's neck, exploring the joy of the mortal puncture wound. How delicious her demise tasted. How awesome the experience of this gruesome finality. Yet how ironically peaceful she appeared wrapped in the soft, patterned quilt.

"A quilt for her, not you," the killer said angrily.

How still the victim's thoughts felt. How perfect the zinnia looked in her useless hair.

That was too easy.

The fiend tossed the flower a foot to the side of the woman's body lying so peacefully on the ground.

The killer kicked the corpse and chuckled.

"You thought she was safe. You thought you could see her...let her touch you.

34

Well, I guess we see where that got you, my swan. Where is your beauty now? Rest now, my dear. Join the other swans. I suspect they have been waiting for you...in the dust of my tracks just like you suspected. Funny how right you were. And they all called you crazy. Ha. Guess the joke's on you...and them."

When the sick-minded criminal stepped away from the body, these insane words spewed forth:

"Ah, in you I hide my treasure of gold.

In you, you barren and useless fool.

Why would they look here?

In this worthless place?

As if you ever mattered.

In plain sight, I offer my message of love.

Of passion.

Through you.

Not of you.

If you so much as smelled a bit like her,

I would eat all of you.

To prove my passion, my love, my fury.

Instead, I bury it.

I hide my happiness with your pathetic sorrow."

The devil looked up at the moon and wondered what really went on over on the dark side, why the pale globe never turned to face the light.

How numb it must have felt to be forever trapped in such a black gelid tundra. A shudder coursed through the villain's body while the idea of eternal night and ice sunk in.

*It's darkest...and coldest, though, just before the dawn.*

In a way the fiend couldn't possibly understand yet, that was absolutely right.

# NINE

## My Mommy

THE FOLLOWING MORNING, a faint hint of the calming scent of lavender tickled Devyn's nose. All of a sudden, she realized she must have fallen asleep again. Without opening her eyes, she searched for familiar surroundings. The soft side of her goose-down pillow rested gently under the left side of her face and chin.

A gritty soreness between her thighs demanded her attention, but she refused to baby it. The chaffed skin reminded her of the lovely friction of their union. She pressed into it firmly, yearning to feel the pain and pleasure of Brock's body once more.

Intensely aware of the contrast of the smooth coolness of her sheets, she gave thanks for Egyptian cotton and smiled.

"Yes," she whispered to the bed, "I love expensive linens to pamper myself with."

Soaking up the luxury of her bed and for once feeling worthy of this oh-so-lovely creature comfort, she took a big breath. Exhaling, she let the rush of fragrant air escape her lungs. For a moment, she wondered if the smell of spicy yet soothing lavender had gotten stronger, but she quickly dismissed the idea as crazy. Convinced it must have a reasonable explanation somehow, she explored the layers within the potpourri surrounding her anyway.

Her imagination called forth images of fragrant flowers draping down from the ceiling in hanging baskets. Lavender and something else, perhaps vanilla, seemed to form an outer aroma held up underneath by the musk of Mother Earth. Brock's cologne on top of his broad strength served as a base for this welcoming pyramid of scents.

A faint grin covered her face. She caressed the fine sheets with her foot, bent on reminding Brock of the loveliness of their reunion. She was surprised, however, to discover she was alone. No longer entangled with him, she relaxed into her personal solitary sanctuary within as the gentle sunlight teased her through the thin, white drapes.

The window reflected the smooth shape of her naked curves while she walked to the bathroom. She looked more like herself than she had in a long time, she realized, almost like her picture on the nightstand again. More youthful yet somehow wiser looking, her reflection pleased her. Maybe it was the hormones, but maybe it was not.

She heard a faint, childlike whisper of a voice that startled her.

*"My mommy."*

Had someone called out her name? For a second, her heart skipped and her breath caught. Fear tugged at her.

*Am I losing my mind?*

Her pulse raced.

Then she found a logical explanation and relaxed.

*It must be Livie.* "Livie? Livie, baby? Is that you, honey?"

She anxiously wrapped herself in the luxury of her bathrobe and sunk into its softness. Feeling better, she relaxed.

*I'm okay. It's Livie, of course. That's all.*

# TEN

## Daddy's Couch

WITH TENUOUS EXCITEMENT, she anticipated joining the others. She smiled with the settling awareness that she brought along with her the newest addition to the family—the baby.

*I'm okay. Of course I am. I am fine. Fine.*

*What will we name the baby? Name her? Her? Where did that come from? Am I having another girl?*

"*Yes, Mommy, you are.*"

"Livie, honey. Where are you, baby? Is that you, baby?" Devyn called again.

She hoped and prayed it was just Livie even though she didn't believe in prayer—not yet anyway.

"*No, Mommy. It's me. Ellie.*"

Devyn anxiously journeyed to the living room where Livie had arranged all her dolls in a grand circle of motherly love around her and Nanny Rose. On the floor, each baby lay face down covered with one of Livie's special blankets, napping and getting professionally patted to sleep.

Simultaneously, Nanny Rose and Livie looked up. Devyn's clicking knees had betrayed her otherwise silent, observing presence. A little giggle escaped Livie. Thrilled, she jumped up to embrace her mother.

"*Mamasita*, my little mama, what's going on here? Daycare in the living room? Were you upstairs a minute ago? I thought I heard you, baby."

"No, Mama. Just here. Mama, all better? Boo-boo all gone?" Livie asked.

"One hundred and ten percent better. All gone, in fact. Mommy all better," she

38

said with a grin that seemed to get bigger by the second. "Who's ready for breakfast? I know I am."

Livie quickly raised her hand in support. The snoozing plastic babies were all but forgotten.

When they walked into the kitchen, the front door bell rang.

The door opened of its own accord, followed immediately by the dramatic entrance of the intuitive Heather Lewiston…flowing silk scarf and all. Her long black hair, pulled tightly back in a headband, fell just beneath her buttocks, swaying gracefully side to side over her athletic legs. The clear look of honesty, much like a child's, came from behind and almost beyond her wise, pale hazel eyes. Her wrinkleless forehead gave her an ageless look. She could be twenty, or forty-five, or even sixty. No one really knew. No one really cared.

"'Bout time I was invited over for the party, don't you think?" she announced in her slightly self-inflated but endearing way.

Heather's eyes brightened and drizzled with delight.

She took Livie's hands and placed a beautifully wrapped gift in them. This was not the first time they had played this game, so Livie knew the rules.

Devyn looked at Heather as if to ask, "*Where's mine?*"

Without missing a beat, Heather said, "You already got yours, little lady. It's called another chance. Life, what? Number two? Number five? We better consult the all-knowing Master Lucky to see how many lives you have left."

All joking aside now, the two best friends embraced. Devyn remembered why she loved her wonderfully bizarre friend so much.

Nanny Rose came marching in with her famous pizza biscuits, and they all sat down to a laughter-filled meal like the accident never happened.

While they wiped their plates clean, Nanny Rose just smiled.

"Why aren't you eating?" Heather asked.

"*Doctora* says the biscuit too high for my sugar." She rolled her eyes and faked a gag.

Devyn laughed. "Yep, too much sugar will put you in a coma, Rose."

Nanny Rose gagged again and then started in with one of her jokes. "*Doctora*, why did the chicken cross the road? Do you know?"

Devyn played along. "No, Rose, I don't. Why did the chicken cross the road?"

"To get to the other side, *Doctora*, of course," Rose said and laughed.

They all joined in the roar, having expected anything but the classic punch line. This time, the joke was on them.

As the plates were cleared, Heather announced her plan to take Livie upstairs to the playroom.

39

"We have some things to do upstairs, Mama. So, if you don't mind, I will be taking the princess with me. You can have her back later...if you can find us."

She presumptuously flipped her silk scarf over her right shoulder.

Livie grabbed her present and willingly followed Heather, her step-grandmother, up the twelve winding stairs to the second floor. Heather swept her arms widely side to side in pretend flight up to the top. With a wave of her left hand, it transformed into a deadly hook. She played the bad guy, too.

Pretending she was cornered by the tick tock, tick tock of a creeping crocodile made of fear, she trembled.

Heather cried out, "Ah, Livie, I'm done for."

Slapping her hands down to her sides, she collapsed to the ground with the grace of a defeated yet somehow adorable bad guy.

Then Heather transformed into a merry mermaid displaying her imaginary sparkling green tail. She swam Livie back home to Atlantis after finally returning from some thousand-year crusade to save the Merfolk. Heather, Livie, and a band of rogue seahorses celebrated their victory with the grandest purple tea party ever seen on land or sea.

Later that night after Brock returned from work, he and Devyn played a different pirate's game. With a pleased yet mischievous grin painted on his face, Brock patted the couch next to him, urging Devyn to take a seat. She obliged and turned to face him.

Before she spoke, he put his finger to her lips.

"Let me go first, please."

She nodded.

"Just listen. Since I left your oh-so-sexy side, I have been trying to put my thoughts into words that might make some kind of sense to you. Being a man, I'm pretty lousy with all this talking stuff, but you already know that."

He chuckled getting braver by the second. For a brief moment, all tension faded from his face.

Devyn took a deep breath and noticed the smell of fresh, new leather, oozing from their comfy, brown, leather sectional. Unintentionally, she lost herself in the memory of its purchase.

She had ordered the showroom model. No other version would do because this particular couch smelled just like her dad—leather mixed with Old Spice.

The aroma stirred sadness in her she couldn't risk exploring—or risk letting go of, either.

She shook her head, refusing to go there. It hurt too badly.

40

*Daddy, where are you?*

"Dev? You okay?"

Thrust back to the moment at hand, her mind gladly returned to Brock, who fidgeted nervously in his seat, trying to find the right words.

"Lost you for a second, honey. You back?"

Again, she just nodded.

"Three deep fairy breaths? That's what you always tell Livie, right?"

After three slow and deep calming breaths, a gentle smoothness crossed his handsome face. He found his words and bravely began.

"When I look back on my life and think about what really matters, a few moments clearly stand out."

She smiled while she peered with anticipation into the best part of him.

"Without a doubt, I am proud of my accomplishments. I love my work. I love making a difference in the world. I really do. Somehow, that all seems so small compared to my best moments with you, my love, my everything, my reason to live."

Out of respect, she tried not to laugh. She tried, but failed. As a nervous giggle escaped, she admitted this wasn't easy for any man, especially Brock. She even considered dragging it out—for herself, not him, of course—but then decided that was too cruel to be fun.

"Yes, I'm listening," she said.

After another breath and a pause, he went on to say, "The day I saw you for the first time. Do you remember?"

Of course she remembered—like she could have possibly forgotten.

"No. I have no idea what you mean," she simply said with the slyness of a fox.

She flashed back to the memory six years ago.

He had come to interview her about one of her patients. Without apology, he rudely interrupted her during her always-busy office hours.

Being an ambitious investigative field reporter, busy gaining popularity for his Tampa-based news station, he was just doing his job. The business was, after all, thoughtless, relentless, and sensationalistic all in the name of getting a good and hopefully terrifying story. The loyalty of the station's viewers demanded all the bad news updates he could muster. Proper politeness wasn't his priority. In fact, it was just about last on his list. Full of charm and engaging on-camera wit, he usually got away with his assuming behavior. A ladies' man like Brock got away with almost anything—almost, but not this time.

Devyn, of course, knew most of this particular patient's unfortunate story, so

41

she was not surprised in the least by the appearance of the notoriously handsome but ill-mannered reporter.

From down the hall, she simply dismissed him by saying, "Brock Bryant and your Channel Six News Team, go away. I know you are aware of the legalities surrounding patient confidentiality. Nevertheless, here you are wasting my precious time. Find someone else's day to ruin."

She then, without so much as another glance in his direction, picked up her next chart and went in to see her scheduled patient.

Finally finished seeing her last patient of the day, she left the office only to discover a black town car waiting out front for her. Inside was a perfectly wrapped gift with a note attached that read:

Peace offering for Doctor Mitchell.

I should have asked permission before coming, but then you would have said no. I wouldn't have met you, so I am not sorry I stopped by. It was not a waste of *my* precious time.

I reserved a table at the Delectable Fork hoping to make it up to you. Not a word... I promise to be on my best behavior. Well, maybe. Looking forward to seeing you in this.

Or better yet...not in this.

My driver is at your disposal.

With anticipation,

Brock Bryant


Curiosity and that crooked smile got the best of her just like all the other times.

Poor little cat, she opened the box.

Inside the handsomely disguised Pandora's Box was an unassuming black couture dress, a pair of perfectly sized black pumps, and a single blood-red rose.

She should have known better, but didn't.

The dinner went the only way it could have gone—perfectly. They were both smitten with one another instantly. The charming duo was charmed. The impressive were impressed. The unclaimed were now the claimed.

"Devyn," he said, bringing her back to the present moment, "you okay, baby? We can finish our talk later if you need to rest. It's been a big day for you."

"No, no. Please go on. You were just getting to the really good part, I think."

"Where was I? Oh yes, I remember. After seeing you wear...and then not wear...that black dress, I thought my best memory ever was taken for sure—until Livie came along, that was."

Like always when he spoke about Livie, Brock's pupils dilated slightly, and he looked just a wee bit to the right. It was as if he saw her there, and Livie somehow washed him clean.

Devyn wondered if it was the doctor or the mother in her that noticed this.

She encouraged him by saying, "Yes, go on."

A childlike innocence overtook him.

"The first time I held her, my baby, my Livie, there was no paper I wouldn't sign. No thing I wouldn't do. No blood I wouldn't spill. I had never felt so clean, so good, so loved, and so alive. There you were, my two favorite girls, tied forever in first place...in what used to be so heavy and empty a heart."

Devyn smiled at him, touched deep in her core. She reached tenderly over to pat his arm.

"Yes, I know how much you love her. She does, too, you know."

Then a touch of sadness crossed his face. "Lately, we have just been off, you and I. You've been so goddamn busy rebuilding that joke of a hospital in this joke of a town and saving the lives of other people instead of being here with us—which just almost got you killed, by the way. Like a vicious thief, that joke of a hospital almost stole you from me for good. Damn it, Devyn."

His anger exploded. His face lit up red despite his best efforts to contain it. He stood up and started walking around, not making eye contact, gritting his teeth and pinching his upper lip.

At first, she got annoyed.

Then she decided to observe instead of react.

She had to admit that if someone even joked about taking Livie away from her, she would be livid. She chalked it up to misrepresented fear of the loss of her and tried to give him some slack. She listened intensely and tried to quell her outrage at his inappropriate display.

Pacing back and forth, he calmed himself down before he went on.

"Damn it, babe! You should want to be here with me and Livie. Honestly, it just enrages me sometimes. I get jealous, which is ridiculous, but I can't help it. I can't. I love you too much. Don't you know that? Then the talk we had six months ago really hurt us, really hurt you, and that really hurt me. So I figure I need to get over it. You are who you are. That's what makes you so awesome. I want you. I do. So I've tried uselessly to figure out how to take it all back: my words, my anger, my hurt, my disappointment."

He stopped there, struggling to finish.

Then he dug in, too far gone to turn back now.

43

"Don't let me mince words. I meant what I said when we had our fight, but I'm disappointed by the way I said it, the way I let us down. I think I almost lost you, lost me—again. I can't let that happen. It will literally kill me, kill us all."

She looked away from him now, unable to meet his gaze. The pain of that talk still stung her like the poisoned stinger of a wasp trapped deep in her heart. She wasn't sure if her heart had ever stopped burning from his hateful words even if he hadn't meant them…and he just said he had.

*He meant them!*

She had come to realize that vicious words, once they were out, could never be taken back, not really. Even if they were, they left a crack.

Much like an infection, the crevice would affect more and more of its host over time—seeping, oozing, and festering like a pus-filled hole that could never be filled back in.

Each time a similar injury happened, the host died a little more.

She died a little more. Her love got a little smaller and harder to find.

One time, her love wouldn't make it back, too fragmented, drowning in pus.

She looked up, planning to meet his gaze.

"This time," he said, "I would rather be happy than right. I guess I have to learn how to share you, but if you tell anyone I said that, I will have to kill you."

The intensity in the room lifted a little. A breeze from nowhere dissipated the heavy energy surrounding them.

Again, she noticed the slightest smell of lavender and took a big deep breath, wanting to let it in.

There was no doubt Brock injured her with his hateful words six months ago. All the arguing about her quitting her job and getting properly married had made her want to do anything but marry him.

In fact, she seriously considered leaving him.

So, she had been trying, without any success, to forget his cruelty every day since. Some fights, she concluded, were better tossed aside unaddressed than fought when surely there could be no winner—only losers.

*Damn therapists. What do they know about resolving conflicts anyway?*

With the charm of a classic perfectly crooked Brock Bryant smile, he turned once more to face her fully. His intensity begged for her to give him another chance, a real one, for him and the baby.

He took her hands and kissed them each with a slow, gentle touch of reverence, worship even.

Pushing it one step further, he said, "I could have never thought of this. This tops it all, baby. Your cleverness never fails you, does it? Really, you could have just said you would finally marry me, that we will finally be a real family. You didn't have to prove it to me by getting pregnant first."

Her heart sank when she processed what he was saying. Quickly, she pretended to hear something worrisome from upstairs so she could look away and regain her composure.

"Don't misunderstand what I'm saying. Thrilled doesn't even come close to describing how I feel right now. You know I would love to give you my name, to have you claim it as your own. I have always hoped Livie would have a brother or sister. Only child is a hard label for a kid to wear in this cruel, lonely world. A simple yes would have made my day; however, this makes my eternity. Thank you. Thank you. I love you so much, baby. I do. I knew you would see things my way one day. I knew it."

He was almost jumping out of his skin with excitement. "What a perfect gift. How did you keep it secret so long? I have so many questions. They can wait. They can wait. I know you are so tired. I see it in your gorgeous, glowing mama face. No wonder you have been sleeping so much, baby. I love you forever and always. We will have the wedding where and when you want. My sister be damned! This will be ours, baby, just ours!"

Each word he said more pressured than the last, Devyn never got another word in edgewise.

"Rest now, babe. Take as much time as you need. I will go check on Livie and your crazy best friend. Right now, I even love her and her wacky ways."

Devyn, awestruck, reeled back into the couch.

How would she tell him the truth? Her mind, racing at the speed of panic, grasped fully what just happened. He had no idea that she didn't know about the baby. He mistakenly thought she planned it all.

She had no intentions of marrying him. She never had. Never.

"Help me," she whispered so he couldn't hear.

Unfortunately, she didn't really know how to ask for help—not yet anyway.

# ELEVEN

## Separate Lives

AFTER A QUICK TRIP upstairs to tell Livie goodbye, Brock disappeared into the part of his life known only to him. He left one part of his reality to journey forth into the other.

Pleased with Devyn's commitment, his sense of self-worth flooded in. If she wanted him, he must be good. If she loved him, he must be worthy. He almost tasted her approval and licked his lips with satisfaction. The candy of her pleasure was still present on his mouth.

She would take his name and prove his value to the world. He would know the blessed bliss of acceptance.

A buzzing in his pocket startled him.

*Who the hell?*

The caller ID betrayed the source of the disruption of his brief moment of peace.

"Can't talk now, Sis. Call back later, okay?"

"No, it's not, but the short version will suffice," Victoria Bryant said.

Brock felt her disapproval through the receiver.

*You are not going to make this easy for me, are you?*

He stopped in his tracks. Emotions reeling, he tried to think of what to say next.

"Spill it, brother of mine. I don't have all day. Some of us do important work for a living."

"Just left for the beach house. Devyn's doing better than I hoped. I think I may have some really great news to share."

46

Before he could finish, the line went dead, frozen in silence by the ice in her unfeeling words.

Outside, the trees on Sunnyside Way swayed slightly from side to side in disapproval. A gentle breeze whispered its displeasure to the oblivious blades of grass while ants made homes out of the sand beneath them. A cricket wailed his song of mourning just as the sun set for the evening, calling back the light of day. An all-knowing owl silently observed from across the road but then thought better of his quietness. His ambivalence seemed inappropriate considering the circumstances.

"Hoo hoo," he called. "Hoo hoo," he cried.

He tried to warn Devyn about the car outside.

Inside it were intentions unworthy of her and the girls. With dark eyes and an even darker heart, a cunning villain lurked in the shadows.

Master Lucky, the arrogant cat, proudly stalked the halls.

*No sir, no sir, not in my house. Not on my watch. No way.*

Up and down the stairs he marched, pausing only briefly here and there to lick his backside. He hissed at a few unfortunate insects that crossed his path. He meowed to warn them which side they better take. With bared teeth, he took one last trip around the living room before settling down to sleep.

He knew what lurked. He knew what waited. He smelled its rancid scent of evil.

As the cat marched, Devyn spun. With her hands over her eyes and her foot planted firmly on the floor to slow the spinners, she thought she heard a voice.

No, not really a voice. It was more like a thought within her head, one that definitely sounded different from her thoughts.

*"Mommy,"* the voice said, *"all be okay. Promise. No break Daddy's heart now. It all okay. Promise, Mommy."*

From total shock and exhaustion, she collapsed on the couch.

*I'm going crazy. Just like Mom. Just like her...before she drove off the edge.*

She imagined the scene like always. *Smack!*

Nanny Rose and Livie, as they descended from upstairs, saw only the silhouette of Devyn resting calmly. They pleasantly joked about baby dolls, totally unaware Devyn was pretty sure she had just lost her precious independence and her mind all in one day.

With the smell of fresh, new leather filling her nostrils, she took one deep breath after another and prayed like she never prayed before, admitting only God, who she didn't even believe in, could help her now.

She stood up slowly, gathered her balance, and asked, "Can you guide me back to bed, Livie? I think all the excitement of coming home has been a little too much for me. I'm going to put on a movie and just veg out for a bit. Want to join me, sweet pea? Daddy had to catch up on some work, so it's just you, me, and Nanny Rose tonight."

"K, Mommy. Purple tea help," Livie said with the sweet helpfulness of a toddler.

"Sounds great. Let's blow kisses to Nanny Rose, baby," Devyn said while they approached the stairs.

*What if I go off the deep end? Would my family forgive me if I end up squashed on the side of a mountain, too?*

*What if I drive off the edge of a mountain just like Mom, my insane and subsequently-dead-because-of-it mom?*

*Smack!* She heard her own skull crash from the impact.

She laughed trying to clear the idea from her mind.

*Think a better-feeling thought.*

While Livie raced upstairs to put on her pretend kettle, Devyn thanked Rose for her reassuring presence, which also allowed her to delay climbing the dangerous stairs.

"Thank you for everything. I don't know what I would do without you. I'm not myself right now. I think I need more help than I realized. Will you check on me, I mean us, later? "

Rose smiled.

"Sure. *Es nada.* Glad you are home, *Doctora.* Take it easy. *Dulce sueños*, sweet dreams, *Doctora*," Rose said in her unique and reassuring way.

Devyn jokingly called it Spanglish.

She looked back at the stairs and sighed.

Doctor Devyn Mitchell took each ascending, winding stair slowly and carefully, very carefully, while simultaneously performing a shortened version of a mental examination on herself.

*I'm not going to throw myself off the side of a mountain or down these stairs. That's ridiculous, right?*

She counted forward and backward by sevens. She knew her name, the month, the year, and what puppet the citizens of the United States currently called *President*. She remembered her alphabet perfectly, forward and backward. As far as she could tell, her visual fields seemed normal, and her reflexes worked fine.

Okay, so what? She had just experienced an auditory hallucination. Big deal.

*I'm not crazy. No way. I'm fine, perfectly fine. Smells, thoughts, no big deal*

48

*really. Or were they? I must have imagined it. It was just the stress from Brock's misunderstanding. I can find a way to explain. I'm okay. I just imagined the whole thing. Silly me. Right?*

*"No, Mommy, you didn't,"* the voice said.

Perhaps the car accident shook her brain a little loose. Was that really such a shock? *Of course not.*

Was she losing her mind or just tired?

*Tired. Too tired to think anymore. Tired. Like crawling through Jell-O.*

For now, she was too spent to worry any more.

*I'm fine. Perfectly fine. Just tired.*

When she rounded the corner, Livie returned to her side, kettle in hand. Devyn hugged her. She looked over her daughter's shoulder and spied a vase on her favorite granite-topped table in the hallway. The colors of gold and orange swirled around in a never-ending pattern. Like whirling ocean currents, they reminded her of the deep beauty of the earth and her waters. She felt better, much better, much less tired, much less crazy.

Standing proudly in the table's center, a sprig of baby's breath saluted her. So peaceful and simply elegant, the many small flowers seemed to open their tiny petals built of possibility to her. She opened her mind a little and welcomed the flowers as a message of energetic support.

*"Good, Mommy,"* the voice said.

She paused to wonder why baby's breath was always behind other flowers in an arrangement. They were a beautiful message in their own right.

For a second, she expected the flowers to speak to her and say, *"Look how gorgeous we are."*

She laughed at her silliness now and relaxed further, much less tired, better by the second, much less crazy.

*"Even better, Mommy."*

Besides, she had Livie with her right now. What else could really matter? She decided to let it all go and do the unthinkable: relax and forget the silly little made-up voice in her head.

She turned on the TV, that eternally useless source of subliminal mind-warping garbage, like the rest of the world for a while. She disengaged her monkey-mind chatter and figured she probably made it all up anyway.

*A voice from my unborn baby? How silly. Pregnancy hormones? For sure.*

Her fear of madness faded into the oblivion of creature comfort, and it was gone as quickly as it had raised its terrifying head.

# TWELVE

## Brafe

UPON CLIMBING INTO BED, Devyn decided on a bit of a whim that having a strikingly handsome, financially unshakable, local celebrity like Brock falling over himself with excitement at the idea of marrying her was really not the worst problem a girl could have.

*If I have a few voices in my head, so what?*

To confirm her newfound, positive perspective, Livie danced into the bedroom wearing a red and gold wizard's cape.

"Need magic, Mommy. I got Livie's spell," she said.

They snuggled down together for the late-night movie.

"What's your fravit part, Mommy?" the benevolent wizard asked.

Devyn paused to think carefully before she answered.

"The part when the little boy tells his teacher to have courage. Then, the teacher gets very brave. He tells the little boy the truth even though he was very, very afraid the boy wouldn't like him anymore. If he hadn't told the truth, the little boy wouldn't have known what to do next. Instead, little lady, the teacher helped save the whole magical world by speaking his truth. How 'bout you, baby?"

Livie giggled.

"I like lots of parts like flying and the elsves and all the silly things that the little girl says. I know you will be brafe, too, just like the teacher. I love you, Mommy, to the ends of unifirst!"

Devyn finished Livie's sentence. "Back again, baby, and back."

By the time Nanny Rose finished what she was doing and went back upstairs to check on them, both mother and daughter were sleeping soundly. Careful not to disturb them, she turned off the television. She whispered a loving prayer over them and put something wrapped in a gold and white bow in the top nightstand drawer like Heather had asked her to.

"*Perfecto, Doctora*," she whispered.

She paused for a second, took a deep breath, and smiled. As she walked down the hall, she started to hum a tune from so long ago.

In her head, it played: "*I knew it was always you who walked in my dreams and sang in my heart.*"

Safely across the long bridge over to the outskirts of Tampa, Brock breathed a sigh of relief. Since Devyn's accident, this drive made his heart beat a little faster than usual, but the real source of his anxiety escaped him. Pulling into his parking spot at the station, he realized what an exhausting day it had been. His thoughts were focused so intensely on Devyn that he couldn't remember much of the drive at all. He thoughtlessly walked right past a few of his favorite crew members without saying a word.

His main co-reporter, Mary, indignantly called out, "Hello. Earth to Brock. Earth to Brock."

In a flash, he reoriented to his surroundings.

"Sorry, it's been a long day."

She tossed her hair and grinned.

Defeated, he said, "I think I'm actually tired. I guess there's a first for everything, even for me. Going to finish some stuff up around here and then catch some winks at the beach house."

"Sure. Whatever."

"What's up with you, Mary? A little stressed by all the new fame? Another local hero? Another local scandal?"

Her rabid attention helped him feel better all of a sudden.

"You know me, sexy superhero that I am, saving the world one story at a time. Just call me Clark-ette Kent," she said with newly discovered excitement in her voice.

He winked and gave her his famous crooked smile.

"I could join you, you know. There for a drink...at your place if you wanted me to."

"Not tonight."

She cleared her throat and looked away.

"I can't," he said.

He caught her eye and tried to bring it back in.

The idea sounded good but felt wrong–too wrong, tonight.

She sighed and plastered a fake grin on her face.

He stepped forward to share a brief hug. She moved into it, trying to prolong the embrace.

He pulled back–too quickly.

"Don't push. Not tonight," he said, not sure of the strength of his resolve.

The look of smoldering rejection burned fire-hot on her face. She shrugged her shoulders and stomped away not even trying to avoid him seeing her so furiously offended.

"Ugh. Going to have to deal with that soon," he muttered to the stack of papers on his desk.

Later though. It would have to wait.

"For now, let's do as little as we can and get the heck out of here and into a comfy bed," he said to no one in particular.

Mary slammed the office door, got in her car, and sped off.

# THIRTEEN

# The Wall

BROCK IMMEDIATELY KNEW he was dreaming.

His lucidity intrigued him, thrilled him even.

He noticed a freshly uprooted tree, which was just starting to bloom its spring flowers, entangled with a broken version of his first rusted, old truck.

*Man, how I loved that truck even if the radio sucked.*

The wind swirled with the speed of a tornado and lifted everything up in its path. Despite all the destruction around him, Brock stood in the center, amazed but shockingly unaffected. His feet walked steadily, one in front of the other, while he gasped in awe of the precious items spinning all around him.

Each step down the rocky path awakened him to another lost treasure tumbling through the air: so many irreplaceable items lost or destroyed in the twisting cloud of disaster that now embraced thunder, lightning, and hail. Spinning out of control, a child's school desk smashed into the front door of the first house he and Devyn shared. A long-forgotten, tattered, old jumping rope strangled a life-sized stuffed animal dog that once perched on the edge of his bed—Rover, his sweet Rover, who had protected him from too many monsters to count while he hid under blankets with a flashlight on the *scarier* nights.

When he rounded the corner, he approached a thick concrete wall. It, too, seemed unaffected by the terrible wind as if it were actually the storm's source. Out of undeniable curiosity, he touched the wall.

It melted like clay under his hands.

*No. Melt is the wrong word. Molded. It molded.*

"What are you?"

He heard a remote sound and turned around desperately needing to seek out the noise despite the all-encompassing roar of his cyclone. Brock's family approached from far enough away that he only glimpsed their outlines. He heard the sweet voice of Livie singing accompanied by Devyn giggling with her most tender, most endearing laugh. Unmistakably, they chuckled at something funny the littlest one just did.

Headed straight for the twister, they seemed totally unaware of the impending danger. He tried to shout, louder and louder, more panicked with each attempt to warn them than the last, but every step he took forward to try to reach them took him another step farther away. Into the mouth of a labyrinth, he descended. Each time he turned around, he was moving in the same direction–away.

Surrounded now by more and more walls made of the same horrid substance, panic overtook him. Finally comprehending the walls trapped every sound, like the grey egg-foam sides of a soundproof recording studio, he trembled. He grasped the terror that his words were useless to warn them. They were doomed, and he was impotent with his pathetic attempts of rescue.

He dropped to his knees in devastation and slammed his right arm against the floor in despair. He was unable to save them or find his way out.

"Help me. Help them!" he screamed to the unconcerned, icy-cold concrete floor.

He instantly woke up to the uncomfortable numbness of a sleeping arm. Confused for a moment, he tossed it about, accidentally striking his face with it. He giggled softly when he realized his foolishness.

The dream disappeared, already lost to the ocean of forgotten nightmares. Without another thought, he turned on his other side and re-entered the restless body of tonight's dreams.

Sixty minutes away in the small town of Holosni, Devyn dreamed beautiful visions, safe in the hugging embrace of her beloved Livie. She giggled out loud while she and Livie snickered at something funny the littlest one just did. Somewhere in the distance, she mistakenly thought she heard Brock for a moment. She quickly tossed the idea aside when she remembered it was just she and the girls.

Marveling at the intricate details of the blooming flowers surrounding her, she made a mental note of the wonder that was nature. Farther down the perfectly winding path, she observed a fresh, large hole that warned a tree had been uprooted from the moist, dark earth. The girls chuckled as they pointed fingers at the wriggling bodies of the earthworms exposed to the bright light of day. The other surrounding trees seemed perfectly fine, and she wondered what could have possibly happened to the lost one. Sad for a moment, she imagined it covered with the new blooms of spring like the others.

Distracted by a swirling dragon-shaped kite flying off in the distance, she and the girls ran through the rolling meadow to get a closer view.

"Let's go fly a kite," they squealed together with delight. They raced off for another adventure.

Comfortably hugged in the loving arms of her mother, Livie dreamed the brightly colored dreams of a happy childhood. She shrieked with joy at the pink and purple swirling sky filled with flying fairies and birds. She skipped along, now holding the hand of her new baby sister. They were going to fly a kite, and Livie could not wait.

"*This will be your first kite game,*" she said to the baby with her thoughts. "*Don't worry. I will show you just what to do, little baby. I know all about kites.*"

They whistled together and danced about in the tall emerald grass of the rolling meadow.

Warm and cozy, surrounded by the soothing amniotic fluid of her mother's womb, the baby floated about. She heard the constant pulsating of her mother's heart and knew she was loved, adored, safe, and protected. Thoughts of peace and comfort surrounded her while she tumbled about in her dream-like state. Images of one hundred and forty-four colors and sounds of blue, then purple, green, and pink filled her developing mind. Although she had no words by which to call these wonders yet, soon she would remember their names.

She felt a hand reach up to her; she opened hers to grasp it tightly.

"Love you, Mommy. Love you, Livie, " she said. "Let's go fly a kite."

Some three hours away, just across the Georgia border, an anxious college student dreamed the fitful dreams of pre-final exam nervousness. Determined to soothe herself, she imagined an emerald-green meadow filled with blooming trees and countless singing birds.

On a whim, she designed a dragon-shaped kite that sailed instantly amongst the clouds. Turning right and left, the kite jiggled the glorious dance of bliss. She relaxed into her fantasy now, and her worries of failure were a long-forgotten tragedy of the past.

From far across the distance, she spotted a woman and two children skipping directly her way. Perfect. She had an extra kite just for them. She thought she heard lightning in the distance but dismissed the silly idea of a thunderstorm on such a clear afternoon.

She sang the words of a song she knew as a little girl so long ago.

"I knew it was always you."

# FOURTEEN

## A Perfect Day

DAWN of the following morning finally arrived. Brock sipped his coffee while overlooking the beauty of the ocean. He heard the sound of the crashing waves on the shoreline and thought of Devyn, the mother of two of his children.

*How does it get any better than this?*

She loved him, and she was going to be his—forever.

He licked his lips, still searching for the taste of her sugar.

Revitalized more than in a long while, he felt ready to face the day. Barely startled by the vibration of his pager, he knew a local story had just broken. He licked his lips again.

*Wow, already breaking the news.*

Couldn't it wait for him to finish his coffee?

Pretending to complain, but really bouncing on the inside, he reached for the phone.

"Brock Bryant here. When and where?"

Pause.

"I'm on my way. There in less than twenty."

Hoping for a love story, but knowing better at the same time, he packed on an imaginary layer of armor. At this time of day, you had to be ready for the worst, but a story was a story after all.

Stealing the attention of the public was the job, and Brock was damn good at it no matter what it took. When he needed sincerity, his crooked smile was perfectly believable. When he needed to command power, his formidable square jaw line screamed out his strength. When he needed the favor of the ladies, it was over before the battle began. Handsome and then some, his mutability served him well.

Muffin in his mouth and coffee in his travel mug, Brock Bryant, Tampa's most charming investigative field reporter, headed out for the day. Happy to be back in his world where everything made sense, he remembered why he did this job.

*Sister, you can stick it.*

He gagged. He was never going back to Italy. He was done worrying about his twin brother and the posthumous wishes of his parents.

Laughing at himself a little, he jumped into his luxury convertible and sped off to catch the next story, bent on ruining everyone's breakfast.

Back in the sleepy town of Holosni, Devyn and Livie woke up to the sweet sound of singing birds.

*Awesome*, Devyn thought. *An omen of a perfect day.*

Out of nowhere, the idea of a picnic popped into her mind. She had planned on going into the office to catch up on charting but decided instead to discard the boring plan for a much more exciting trip to the park.

"Get up, baby," she said and tickled Livie. "It's time to get up, time to get up this morning."

Livie rolled over and covered her ears.

"You know that song's yuck," Livie said and rubbed her sleepy eyes. Together they laughed and started their daily morning banter.

"I have an awesome idea, baby girl. Let's go to the park for lunch today. Nanny Rose can get us some cheese and fruit ready. It'll be fun to read stories under the trees. Whattaya think?"

"Sure, Mommy. Cool."

Devyn had expected a much happier response, so with some confusion she asked, "Don't you want to go? Thought you would love that."

"I do, silly goose-goose Mommy. I just knew it, too. Heather's present was a new pinick bakset."

"Of course it was, baby," Devyn said. "Well, at least we don't have to run to the store for a basket now, so we have some extra tickle time, tickle monster. Go."

She chased Livie around the room until they both laughed so hard they cried.

During breakfast, a local news bulletin update flashed across the television: Homeless Hunter strikes again! Another victim found. More information on your local station coming up next.

Without missing a beat, Devyn quickly positioned herself between Livie and the television while she cleverly started a distracting game of *I spy*.

58

"We don't need to start our day with this stuff."

Devyn changed the channel and searched the room for something to spy. "Okay, baby girl. Space Babies or Max? I spy something red."

Livie caught on immediately.

She squealed, "Red burd. I spy red burd. Space Babies, silly Mommy goose-goose. I spy sumfing pink."

"Good one, baby. Let me see...pink."

Livie said, "You trolled Daddy off!"

"Yep. He can tell us all about it later, baby. It's Space Babies time. Ba, ba, ba, ba. Flying though space babies or TV off, little lady. You pick," she said lovingly.

Livie smirked and started eating her pancakes.

Devyn scanned the counter top and grinned.

"I spy a magic, pink princess necklace. Now I spy something white with a red top."

With cereal spilling down her adorable chin, Livie giggled. "Easy! Milk. I spy milk bottle!"

Over in Tampa, Brock and Mary played a different, more dangerous game.

"Wow, that was great teamwork. Loved it—seriously," Mary said.

She replayed the video clip of her and Brock breaking the latest news about the Homeless Hunter again.

He looked up at the screen, unable to look away.

"We look awesome up there together. Quite a pair, don't you think?" she asked.

"Yeah, actually, I thought it was good. Do you think I seemed too serious?"

She walked to his side and started rubbing his neck.

His gaze never left the screen.

"I was going for honesty with a slightly hard version of compassion for the victim. Did that come across?" Brock asked.

"I think you looked hot, and so did I, by the way," Mary said with a wink. "Hey, let's go back to the station and get to work. It's going to be a big day around here as we get all the juicy details out to our murder-hungry fans. Love a big story, but the whole murder business makes it hard for me to go for sexy, unfortunately. Will have to wear a buttoned-up shirt for the follow-up report," she said and frowned.

"Hey, I'll be back soon. Got something to do real fast, so I'll meet you at the station later. We could do dinner tonight if you want?"

In a moment of his new fame, he lost his perspective.

59

With two conflicting agendas at hand, he would have to choose. Which came first? Which came last? What mattered most? What mattered least?

Their dangerous game called forth for another player. The chess pieces assumed their starting positions.

Who would win? Who would lose?

## FIFTEEN

# A Door Opens Up

LYING on her back at the park and looking up at the trees above her, Devyn sighed while she relaxed into the musty comfort of her favorite old quilt. The light blue patterns were built with shapes she could not adequately describe. Not quite squares, triangles, or circles, the oddness of the figures soothed her. It was like the quilt demanded to be loved for what it was, unable to pretend to be anything else. She loved it, perfect in its imperfection, unaltered and genuine. Her grandmother willed it to her before she was born, gifting her with its loveliness through a message of acceptable difference.

"Did you know," Heather asked, "that this town is named after an extinct tribe of Indians, the Holosni?"

"No," Devyn said. She frowned, not pleased to be dragged from the beauty of her favorite quilt.

"Yeah, it's a crazy story. I looked it up the other day for some reason."

"You and your 'for some reasons'," Devyn said.

"It's so sad how the whole tribe died. Well, anyway, I'll spare you all the details, but the coolest part was their legend about eventually saving the future world. It has such a...I don't know...Mayan feel to it."

"From South America? I've heard of them."

"Yes, I should hope so. Like the calendar. Anyway, listen to this."

Devyn sighed.

Heather laughed and continued. "They apparently practiced a religion that recognized the sun and earth as their primary Gods. These proud, strong, and mystical Indians told the unforgettable story of a beautiful maiden with sad eyes.

Supposedly, out of great tragedy, this same maiden birthed a set of twins. One was a gift from the sun. The other was a gift from the earth."

Another sigh.

Another smirk.

Heather got louder. "In doing so, the sad maiden fulfilled her destiny as the Greatest Mother of all blessing to come. Then the story went on about bridging night and day, past and future…blah, blah, blah. It's kind of cool, like Beauty and the Beast, only better."

"Heather, you are so funny. Let me guess. It reminds you of the story of Christ—all the pain and then the resurrection."

"Exactly. Nail on the head, girl."

"I love you, you know. All the religion stuff, especially the nails part, is way above my head. Let's keep it that way, so please don't bother to explain. Keep a half-cocked eye on the princess for me if you don't mind. I feel like zoning out for a second. Sad maiden. You're nuts, by the way, but I love you anyway."

"Course, Mama. Got it all covered."

Running up and down the sloping hill, Livie shrieked with delight as she chased fairies only visible to the all-seeing eyes of a child caught up in the magic of play. With arms out to each side, she made the motion of flapping wings. She gave it her best attempt to fly, knowing somewhere deep within her it was still possible, even here on Earth, to defy gravity.

Taking juicy grapes out one by one, Heather gladly put the charming pink and brown checkered picnic basket to good use.

Wanting so badly to stick her nose in Devyn's business she said, "Thought you guys would love this. Love mine and knew you would, too, you know, since you've been through so much lately. Well, I wanted…"

Heather nervously twirled her hair.

Finally unable to contain herself any longer, she said, "You going to spill it or what? You're killing me."

"Thought you would never ask. I know you already know. That's just the way you roll, but I'm struggling with where to start. It's all so much," Devyn said.

"How about the beginning? It's always a very good place to start."

Silence.

After a few moments, Heather sweetly grabbed Devyn's hand with a supportive squeeze. "I'm listening."

"My head is spinning...with crazy things I'm thinking, and I...well, I'm pregnant. Almost three months along."

Heather just listened, knowing all too well that what Devyn needed most was her undivided attention, never once tainted with judgment.

Devyn continued. "To make matters worse, Brock thinks I want to get married. He thinks I have finally agreed to the unthinkable, but it was all just a big misunderstanding. I don't wish to break his heart, but I want what I want. It's not a wedding, I can assure you. Things are just turning around at work, but I'm still so busy—too busy—to plan a wedding I don't even want. The thought makes me want to scream, and gag, and punch somebody."

Heather nodded.

Devyn did a two-punch move in the air.

They both laughed.

"I haven't even told Livie about the baby yet. I'm too afraid. Heck, I guess I haven't even told you. It seems so insane that I had no idea until a week ago. How did I miss it? I'm an obstetrician. The Chief of my department for heaven's sake. Just out of nowhere...boom, my whole life is upside down—again."

Heather giggled in her lighthearted yet supportive way and said, "Life happens to you, too. Perfect. You are human, you know. You know they don't say the universe works in mysterious ways for nothing."

"We never planned on—"

"Yeah, yeah, I know. Who ever does? You are heading down one path, and then all of a sudden, the road takes a sharp right. You look back and wonder what happened. How did I get here?"

"That's so true."

They shook their heads in silent reflection.

Heather pointed, and Livie squealed with delight.

"She's amazing, you know."

"Yep, I do. Oh, Heather, I look back at so many things in my life and see what you mean—like when my mom died, when Livie was born..." Devyn stared off into space.

"So gorgeous, that baby." Heather smiled. "Dev, you ok?"

"Yes. I'm sorry. I'm just..." She looked back and returned the smile. "I'm just distracted, I think."

Heather giggled.

"Even when you married my dad and then when he finally died, it's always the same. Blindsided at the time, but from further down the road...always I find a blessing somewhere in it. Granted, it's harder to find sometimes...more than others, but it's always there on the other side. So here I am again, shocked and wondering what will happen next and how I will get my ass out of another tight spot.

"Well, I love you," Heather said. "That's all I need to know. You will be fine, better than fine. You are strong, and this will be the best thing ever. I know it. That's how these things work."

A sadness entered Devyn's expression when she said, "If my accident taught me anything, it's that you never know...when it's going to be over. That poor young boy who died and his devastated family. Oh, sometimes life feels so unfair."

Heather said, "Experiencing what you went through, almost dying like that, sometimes kind of changes people. It changes how you look at things, opens a door somewhere, a door you didn't know you had, a big door—deep within—that opens up to a whole new universe."

Devyn said nothing, nothing about the voices.

Laughing, Heather said, "Maybe even makes them a best-selling author on top of it, to ease the suffering."

Devyn laughed hysterically thinking about the countless near-death experience books she had seen on the best-seller list.

Heather nibbled the cheese. "Seriously, though, if you need me, some support, an ear, an editor, a book agent—anything—I'm here. In any way you might need me, I'm all yours no matter what, no matter how crazy or how bad your writing is."

For a moment, Devyn considered telling Heather about the baby's voice in her head but decided not to. She wasn't ready yet.

*Then you will think I'm really insane. Then who the hell will I talk to? Besides, it was probably just a side effect of the head trauma from my accident. It must be. I'm not like my mom. I'm not.*

They hugged each other before returning their attention to the world in front of them.

Livie came marching up to the two best friends. "Hey! Why am I alone? Who's playing with me—Daddy, Mommy, or Heather? Let's go."

"Me!" they both yelled at the same time.

Devyn suggested freeze tag, and the game began.

Darkness waited and watched in the park...playing its own wicked game. They were not alone. They were being watched.

64

The leaves crackled in complaint underneath the shoe of the uninvited observer with unthinkable intentions. Even the insects scurried away.

The murderer breathed slowly in and out trying to maintain a state of calm detachment. The girls were all too close together to be separated, so fantasizing about hurting them was all that could be done right now.

The pretty little girl danced with joy, too much joy. Didn't she know about all the vile things waiting to snatch her innocent perfection? Didn't she know what lurked in the shadows and wanted to hurt her?

A homeless woman walked past and disrupted the villain's view.

*Get out of the way. For fuck's sake, get out of my way!*

Then the unfortunate lady headed right for Devyn who was waving her over.

The sick-minded delinquent paced back and forth in anger while the girls spoke to the woman who lived secretly in the backwoods of the park, an unclaimed, unwashed version of anyone they might know in their day-to-day life who gladly accepted their generous gift of leftover picnic treats.

When the woman smiled, baring her broken and wasted teeth, a measure of honesty and strength in her expression made Devyn wonder what her mother would have been like without mental illness.

*Are you mad like my mother was? Could she have been just the same as you if she hadn't driven off that rocky cliff?*

*Smack!*

Devyn shook her head to clear the image of a smashed and bloody Toyota.

The Homeless Hunter watched the encounter with anticipation.

In one terrible moment, the next victim was chosen, her fate called forth. She matched the Homeless Hunter's profile perfectly.

Doomed to elimination, she sat in silence eating her last gifted supper, unaware of the evil intentions held for her by the demented stranger who watched, waited, schemed to annihilate her, to substitute her.

With eager anticipation, the fiend fingered the deadly syringe over and over as the woman ate. Nauseated with disgust, the monster belched. It was thrilling yet simultaneously intolerable and unforgivable for the woman to enjoy something once intended for Devyn. So for the intended victim's final judgment, the murderer offered up the homeless lady as a suitable sacrifice to the Idol of Guilt and Sin.

Her execution would wash the criminal's mind…and sins…clean.

The woman's punishment fit her supposed vileness, her unbearable evil within. She would be extinguished by the un-love, the un-good in the world, which could no longer bear witness to her light, seeing only its own shadows instead.

She had gotten in the way, contaminated Devyn's purity, and served as evidence of evil and sin. For that, the woman was condemned and must be punished with death.

Her last title, Number Three, did not honor her.

It erased her and every good purpose that she might have served had she just been forgiven instead of judged for someone else's projected sins—her murderer's, to be exact.

Loosely wrapped in an untraceable quilt of specialness, she closed her eyes for the last time this go round. Still clutching a half-withered marigold in her broken and worn-out hands, she stared at the flat, grey sky. Forever frozen in death's grip, the blossom's meaning was lost to her now oblivious mind.

Much to everyone's surprise, Brock showed up unannounced with flowers and gifts a-flowing just after dark. He looked particularly handsome that night with newness in his smile. He smelled cleaner, fresher, and shared his new-found optimism. Giggling all the way upstairs, he put Livie to bed before he left to go back to the beach house. He planned to call once he arrived safely home even though he knew they would all be sleeping—but not safely, not safely at all.

# SIXTEEN

## Fraidy Cat

FOR THE NEXT WEEK, things were pretty much normal on Sunnyside Way. Master Lucky played the ever-exciting game of chase the string. Furious he just couldn't catch the elusive worm, he eventually tired of the battle in lieu of the more important business of cleaning his backside. Rose challenged Livie in the swimming pool with all sorts of new games devised to disguise the lesson of holding her breath underwater.

Occasionally, Devyn still collapsed with fatigue wholly uncertain if it was more the accident or the baby.

Or fear of madness.

The voices came more and more, each time with less and less subtlety. Yet the effectiveness with which she dismissed them grew in direct proportion to the frequency of their attempts to communicate with her.

*What voices? I don't hear them. They aren't real.*

*"Yes, they are, Mommy. I am very real."*

Her denial would not work much longer. Soon she would have to face her own truth, her own fears, her own higher self.

Finally.

Five days later.

At her office during Livie's nap, Devyn surmised the damage of three weeks out of work.

*Job security, right?*

She scowled at the ridiculous number of charts piled on top of her desk.

Doctor Cullen's lame excuse report, she shoved to the side.

*Later, later I will be up to dealing with that creep who already hated me before I put him on suspension for drinking on call. Asshole. You reap what you sow, buddy.*

He scared her a little. She once saw him lose it in the parking lot. The encounter didn't end well for both him and the guy he boxed like a punching bag.

*Once an asshole, always an asshole.*

Distracted by a light down the hall, she decided to push the neglected catastrophe of work aside for another few minutes. A humming from the fourth examining room drew her attention.

"Oh, ultrasound machine, you want me to take a look at the baby? Well, maybe just a peek. I am busy, you know."

Trying to crane her neck around to look at the screen while scanning herself with the ultrasound machine, she witnessed some of the first movements of her developing baby.

"Beautiful," she said to the fetus. "You are gorgeous, baby. I love you already, my little one."

*"Me too, Mommy."*

She dismissed it—again.

Humming a song she struggled to recall the words to, she finished her charting quicker than she expected. As for the nasty Doctor Cullen's disciplinarian report to the Medical Board, that could wait.

She sang, "I knew it was always you who lifted me up and showed me my truth. I knew it was always you."

When she turned off her main office light and stepped away from the desk, she spied a chart orphaned from the pile of its otherwise orderly stacked brothers. On a hunch, she flipped it open and reread her orders.

Shocked to discover her careless approval of a prescription drug that interacted disastrously with another of her patient's medications, she gasped.

"Damn it. That could have hurt her, killed her even. You're too tired for this. Your eyes ache. Your brain is throbbing and useless. Time to go home. Thank God you caught that."

She closed the office garage door and climbed into her rental SUV. She felt better already, shaky, but better.

The statement, *"You're welcome, Mommy,"* washed loudly and undeniably clearly through her reeling mind.

She clicked her seatbelt into place and shook her head.

Her head snapped up. *What the...?*

*"You're welcome, Mommy."*

It was her own voice inside her head, but it clearly felt different, more child-like, more external yet from deep within at the same time. Chills and bumps assaulted her arms. The back of her neck spasmed.

*I am not alone.*

*"No, Mommy."*

Her hands trembled uncontrollably. Her stomach clenched as she gave into the insanity of total panic. Terrified and pulse racing, she gasped for air.

She knew about biofeedback. Just like she did in a crisis in the OR, she started reciting a childhood nursery rhyme to soothe herself. Once she finally calmed down, she looked from seat to seat and back to the office door. Settled now that she was alone and had simply imagined the whole thing, she covered her face and sobbed.

*I'm crazy. I'm crazy. Just like my mom.*

*"No, Mommy, not crazy,"* the voice said.

She could barely hear it for all her crying.

Nanny Rose heard the beeping of Livie's baby monitor declaring that nap time had officially ended. Livie had made it successfully to the bathroom, changed out of her PJs, and was already playing dollhouse by the time Rose trudged up the twelve winding stairs.

Perched around the room, each precious baby was assigned a very important task. Big Head Baby and Black Baby were sipping tea and gossiping about the others. Tangled Baby was down for another nap in the crib. Poor Tangled Baby. She never got to play. Sweetie Pie, with one broken blue eye frozen forever in a wink, sat perched in the high chair having snack time. Poor little Meow-Meow Kitty. He was in time-out, again, for some unknown but assuredly punishable crime. Nanny Rose giggled at Livie's proficiency and asked her if she was ready for her snack, too.

"Not yet, Nanny Rose, but Livie love some Kiki milk."

"Princess, I be back in *cinco*, five minutes."

With a look of compassion oozing from her bright blue eyes, Livie asked, "You sink Mommy always be fraidy cat with sad eyes?"

"Oh, my love, she's doing the best she can. She's strong like Livie. Don't worry, *mi niña*. Time to take poor Meow-Meow Kitty out. His time-out is all done."

"Kiki milks. Kiki milks. Popcorn, too?"

"Okay, playing food after some growing food first. Promise," Rose said and blew Livie a kiss.

"Nanny Rose, tell joke, tell joke."

"After snack. We will make up a new one together, *mi niña, mi* Livie. Promise."

"K," Livie said. "Promise? Joke about a baby mato."

"You mean a baby tomato, *mi* Livie?"

Livie nodded excitedly.

With a wink, Rose said, "Baby mato it is. Let's play tip-toe, tip-toe, tip-toe."

Livie jumped up. She loved playing this game. She looked around for something that would work as a blindfold. Perfect. A soft cloth did just the trick. Nanny Rose tenderly kissed Livie's cheek while she gently tied the cloth in place.

She said, "One, two, three. Ready you. Ready me. Tip-toe, tip-toe, tip-toe."

The game began.

Trying to sneak home unnoticed, Devyn parked out front by the fountain. Hoping Livie slept soundly, she crept quickly through the beep-beep of the front door, slipped into the half bath and examined her face. Black, wavy, mascara-lined tear tracks betrayed her otherwise have-it-together appearance. She quickly wet some toilet paper and went to work. The makeup succumbed to her efforts and only redness remained.

Looking intensely at her reflection, she mentally listed her faults one by one: barely crooked bottom teeth; eyebrows desperately in need of plucking; too many fillings to count; right ear slightly higher than the left; wrinkles around both eyes betraying her lost youth; and, worst of all by far, three stray grey hairs.

She laughed as she surmised her looks were the least of her worries.

About that, she was right.

"So let's see...mirror, mirror on the wall, who's the maddest of them all? Please tell me I'm not turning into my mother."

*What if I'm totally crazy?*

*"No, Mommy, not crazy,"* the little voice affirmed.

She took one last long look before she washed her face again with cold water.

"Mommy?" Livie whispered through the door.

"Yes, sweet pea, it's me. Washing my hands like a good girl. Coming out now. Promise. Hope nap was good. I sure missed you today, baby."

While Devyn composed herself, she heard Livie sing some made-up song about a rose.

"That's a new song, baby. Did you make it up?"

"No, goose-goose Mommy. Big Head Baby teached me. It's your song, silly,"

70

Livie said, obviously surprised her mother didn't already recognize the tune. Then she added, "I think you're bootful, Mommy."

"Oh, thanks, baby. That's just what I needed to hear. You too, Princess. I love you to the ends of the universe."

"Back, Mommy. Go play with Livie and baby now. Purple tea party help Mommy."

"Just what the doctor ordered," Devyn said.

With that, the uninvited voices were forgotten—almost.

# SEVENTEEN

## Hurt So Good

ONE WEEK LATER.

Devyn gradually started seeing patients again. First, just a few in the morning, but as her strength returned, she worked up to a full schedule. Too tender to operate, Devyn's OR schedule was cancelled. Her head hurt now and then, but she could mostly handle it with some over-the-counter pain relievers. She blamed the headaches on the pregnancy, but secretly, she wondered if they were evidence of something changing inside her brain.

*It can't be a tumor. My MRI was normal. It can't be. It can't.*

Thankfully, she had a call arrangement with another obstetrician in town, and he had no choice but to help her out. That was the contract, so there was no need to say thanks and no need to feel badly. It just was what it was. Uncomfortable with any signed legal arrangement, she was thankful, for once, that she had one.

Doctor Hamilton Drake, the doctor she had the call arrangement with, was pretty low on her list of friends, but he was several levels above the soon-to-be-dismissed Doctor Cullen. Sneaky and slightly self-inflated, but otherwise harmless, Doctor Drake was the kind of doctor no one really paid much attention to: not brilliant, not the dumbest guy from medical school, not dangerous.

Exhausted and head throbbing after a full day's work, Devyn sat at her desk and buried her head on her arm. She couldn't wait to get home to Livie.

*Just open some mail, and get the heck out of here.*

A card addressed to her using her first name sat at the bottom of the stack, so she decided to open it first. When she saw the return address was from Dallas, Texas, she tore it open as fast as she could.

*Ah, Billy, I've missed you,* she thought. *Always there when I need you. Let's see what you have to say.*

On the cover of the card was a picture of a dust-and-mud-covered cartoon character with a swirling dirt cloud above his head.

*Just like my water glass, Billy.*

In his barely legible handwriting it read:

Still the luckiest gal I know, Ladybug. Always finding your way out of any ol' mess. Call me if you need me, ever.

Laughing out loud, she recalled how funny her best buddy in medical school was. Always witty with the perfect response, Doctor Billy Thompson, her favorite doctor-turned-cop, remained a legend in his field of forensic psychiatry. Engaging, with a genuineness about him, Billy was a kick-ass author, well-respected serial killer investigator, and a shockingly elegant dancer for a humble cowboy from Texas. He had no idea how he affected the women around him with his snakeskin boots and tight jeans. He was that guy every girl had a crush on, only he never knew it, never believed it, never had a clue.

"I really miss you," she said to the cartoon boy's picture as if Billy could hear her.

The card was signed:

Always loving you, Bug. Let me know what I can do. Love, BLT

She ran her finger over his signed nickname, their personal joke about his favorite food—bacon. "Do you even know my real name?" she asked the card as if it could answer her back. "My old buddy. Miss You. Love you," she said while she returned the card to the envelope.

Last she heard, Billy and his snakeskin boots had solved some cold serial case in Michigan no one else could crack. So, he had become the guy they called in after all the other guys failed.

*Good for you, BLT. Good for you.*

73

While Devyn left the office, the murdering criminal sat silently and watched the precious video. A calmness settled in, and a soothing took hold.

*Yes, yes, the best part, yes.*

The fiend drooled, pausing the screen to enjoy it more completely, soaking it up like gravy on a warm, flaky biscuit.

Yes, some gruesome images were worth a thousand words and a thousand screams and a thousand swallows.

This was certainly no exception.

*Yum.*

The killer rubbed both hands together faster and faster, pressing the left thumb deeper and deeper into the palm of the other hand. The pain, the sensation of it, felt so good, so real, so undeniable—so empowering.

Surrounded by shadow and illusion, the villain's senses were almost completely numbed by the dark bag of repression: empty, a void full of nothing. The self-inflicted pain complemented the frozen video perfectly.

*Yes, yes, hurt me so good.*

The fiend confused the miserable sensation with delight, again, just like so many times before. After all, childhood had taught this measure of foolery well.

Yet did the criminal really have any other choice? Faced with too many forms of vileness to escape, the lunatic searched for pleasure amongst so much pain. The effort was to no avail because the content was always the same. Despite the elaborate mask of beauty it wore, it was what it was—misery. The killer, searching through the layers of torture, needed so badly to find some experience to label joy, but misery was misery no matter what false disguise it displayed.

# EIGHTEEN

## L-E

___

NOW CLOSE TO SUNNYSIDE WAY, Devyn paused to look both directions before she turned onto her street. She looped around to be safe. Had that white sedan followed behind her before?

A foreboding darkness engulfed her. A needle-like sting assaulted her neckline.

*That car is totally creepy. Am I being followed?*

Then she dismissed the idea when a stench in her car intensified.

*What is that disgusting smell? Body odor? Old, rotten trash?*

She smelled her armpits, but only the smell of baby powder scented deodorant filled her nose.

*What the hell?*

She felt like someone or something watched her. Was it that car? She kept glancing nervously in the rearview. That creepy car was still there, but was it the same white one she saw yesterday down the street? The car followed too closely.

Her breath became shallow, and her hands started shaking. She thought about calling the police. Then the white sedan turned, so she let it go.

She must have imagined it.

*What is that awful smell in here? Yuck. The car following you? Absurd, Devyn. You are losing it, girl.*

"No, Mommy, you are not," the voice said.

Her ears started ringing, and she felt a little dizzy. At least she wasn't afraid. The ridiculous trembling was over. The smell, thank God, was gone.

She opened the front door, ignored the stack of mail, and went out back to the pool where Livie just finished her swimming lesson with Ms. Connie.

75

"No more wings, Mom," Ms. Connie furiously scolded. "Didn't you learn from last summer? She could have died. I would think that a mother wouldn't forget such a close call."

"Sure, you are the expert," Devyn said, trying but failing to hide her embarrassment. Her neck burned fire-hot with the memory of that awful day. The sting still seared her from the inside—much like a few minutes ago but worse, much worse.

*I could have lost everything that day. My baby. My love.*

Devyn's hands starting shaking again.

"They make Livie think she can swim, and that is cute and all but very dangerous. Got it? So in the trash they go, Mom. Or…well, it's all on you. I warned you," Ms. Connie said.

Devyn promised no more floating devices of any kind as she tried to cool her cinnamon-coated cheeks. Relieved to escape any more scolding from Ms. Connie and the memory of the unthinkable possibility of *what could have been*, Devyn made the after-swim snack herself.

Nanny Rose and a pink-eyed, exhausted Livie joined her at the counter.

Devyn asked, "Gorgeous flowers, don't you think, Rose?"

"*Perfecto, Doctora.* Probably *Señor Brock. Nada informacion, nada.* No name, no card."

"You mean they just showed up?"

"*Sí, Doctora.* That's right.

She slid the hairband out of Livie's wet hair and combed it with her fingers a little too firmly.

Livie grunted. "Mommy, ouch."

Devyn quickly apologized.

You all right, *Doctora?* You look shook up."

"*Gracias*, Rose. I'm fine. I think I keep seeing the same white car driving around the neighborhood lately. Keep the alarm on when it's just you and Livie home alone. I have a bad feeling about that car."

"*No, Doctora.* No, no. You no thinking…"

"Forget it. I'm just being ridiculous. Distracted, that's all. Forget I said that."

"Okay, *Doctora.* You sure? "

"Forget it." She snapped the hairband in two and tossed it but missed the trash. Rose picked it up and put it in the bin.

"Oh, Rose, I keep missing the mark today."

"*No problema.* But Ms. Connie sure was mad at you." Rose chuckled.

She turned to Livie and said, "Mama was in big trouble today. Better not mess with Ms. Connie. Ha. Do you know what you call a bee trapped in the pool?" Rose suppressed a giggle.

In unison, they said, "No, Nanny Rose. What do you get?"

She laughed so hard she struggled to finish her own joke. "Ol' Ms. Connie bee mad. Get it? B-e-e, bee."

Then she roared at her own cleverness the whole way into the living room.

Devyn turned to Livie and asked about her day. She told her mother all about watching a new movie with a kid doctor and that she thought it was the coolest cartoon ever. She wanted her own doctor bag as soon as possible.

"Sure, honey. No problem. Whatever you want, we can make it happen."

Livie grinned cheek to cheek. "Mommy tell Livie now. Mommy say."

"Wow. Ok, Livie. Mommy does need to tell." Devyn took a deep breath and tried to steady herself.

"Yah, Mommy tell bee joke like Rose."

Devyn laughed, and all her fear evaporated. She, too, giggled at her own cleverness. "Ok, Livie, what do you call a bee in a mommy's tummy?"

She put her finger on her nose and thought long and hard. After a few moments, she jumped up and down. Twirling round and clapping, Livie said, "Baby. Baby."

"Livie, my love, how would you feel about a brother or a sister?"

"Okay, couse, couse, goose-goose, as long as I get to keep my toys. Can't have Big Head Baby. No stinky poo poos, k?"

"Sure, baby, no stinky poo poos. I will change all the poo poo diapers myself," Devyn said. "Would you like a brother or a sister?"

"Bruver," Livie quickly replied. Then she thought better of her answer and added, "No. I fink sissy way better. Sissy. Then we can do tea parties."

"Well, she would have to grow up a bit for big-girl tea parties," Devyn said. "I will ask for a little girl. If it's a sissy, what do you think we should call her?"

"You're so silly, Mommy. L-E, L-E, L-E is her name," Livie sang. She went upstairs to change out of her wet suit.

Alone in the kitchen, Devyn smiled to herself, thrilled her conversation went better than she could have possibly hoped.

She touched her pregnant bump and said, "Ha. Ellie if you're a girl, and let's see...if you're a boy...what should we call you?"

*"Ellie, Mommy, Ellie,"* invaded Devyn's mind. She collapsed with fear onto the floor, totally oblivious to the sudden thick smell of lavender in the room.

In the back of her mind, a tune started to play and a waltz began. *"At love's first sight, I knew it was always you. Throughout all time in all of my lives, I knew it was always you."*

# NINETEEN

## Surrender

"WHAT DO YOU WANT FROM ME?" the homeless woman asked. "You don't have to do this. I promise I'll never tell anyone. Just let me go. Please, please, please!"

"Nothing. I want nothing you can give me," the maniac said.

"Why are you doing this?"

"Hold still and take your medicine, or I will have no choice but to use my gun, and then it will have to hurt—bad, real bad. It doesn't have to. You are going to die, lady, either way. It can be painless or not. You choose."

"Help! Help! Help! Please someone help me!" she screamed.

Help would not come—not tonight.

When she heard the Homeless Hunter unlock the safety on the gun, the victim realized she had no choice left and accepted her fate.

*No pain,* was her last thought.

The needle pierced her flesh, and the monster let out an orgasmic gasp.

*Yes, yes, my love. Surrender to me. Let the liquid work its magic. Yes. Yes. Yes.*

The woman's twitching legs collapsed beneath her, and she fell to the ground. Then the criminal wrapped her in an untraceable quilt and closed the corpse's eyelids tenderly.

"Sleep now; the worst is over."

78

This eulogy followed:
"I am mad, yet they ask for my help.
I am a stranger, yet they pretend to know me.
They are like stupid fools who don't see me.
And they don't see you, either.
But if they saw what I saw,
They would finally see,
The sadness in you for sure.
Begging me to release it once more.
They would love you like I do.
And they would let me finally have you.
To sniff out the lies in you.
And lick them clean.
Let me eat you up and make you mine.
All mine forever.
But for now, I wait.
So patiently for my prize.
For you, my lovely prize."

Without looking back again, the Homeless Hunter dropped something close to the victim, climbed up the short path back to the road, got in the car, and drove away.

Devyn woke up at 4:44 a.m. with a need to share her story that wouldn't be denied. A tune played faintly in the background of her mind. She started humming along, barely able to recall the specific words. The tune, though, made her feel whole somehow, like she had written it herself for someone special too long ago to remember.

"I knew it was always you," she sang.

*I don't want to be crazy. It's not fair to Livie.*

Her thoughts flashed to the side of a mountain. *Smack!*

*Oh, Mom. I'm so sorry. What really drove you off the side?*

Devyn scoured her bathroom and found nothing suitable to write on, yet the lyrics of the song soothed her. She kept singing, and the words kept rolling off her weary tongue.

"Who walked in my dreams," she sang.

*Where would a nut job put some freaking paper?*

79

On a hunch, she went through her nightstand. In the top drawer was a perfectly wrapped package. A note from Heather read:

Just in case you need it.

Heather

Inside, a ratty, tattered old notebook begged her to write, to share her story, to get it out and set it free.

*Perfect. What mountain?*

She smelled the mustiness of the ancient pages and already felt better.

Inside was a dried flower she couldn't quite recognize.

She grabbed the attached pen, which felt light yet firm.

With it, she wrote:

Dear journal,

In case I lose my mind totally, I want to record my thoughts, and I guess...perhaps my downfall. Maybe later, someone will find this useful and forgive me my departure.

My name is Devyn Mitchell, and I am going crazy.

Livie, forgive me...as I follow my mother's fate.

Ellie and I are now several months along, and I am so scared I will not be okay by the time she gets here.

What will happen to my babies then?

I am feeling weird things and smelling scents I now realize are probably not there. Each day, the voices in my head are growing stronger.

If I tell someone, they will commit me. They will strip me of my credentials. They will take me from my children, medicate me, experiment on me with drugs I do not want to take.

I will not remember who I am. So, until I cannot take it anymore, I will keep my mouth shut.

No one knows. No one. Only this beautiful paper will be my witness to madness.

I want to be good. I want to be sane. I do!

I want to watch my babies grow up, unlike my mother.

Hopefully, I will escape from my nightmare and burn this before anyone ever reads my words. Insanity has always been my greatest fear—well, almost—second only to losing Livie.

Forgive me. Forgive me. Forgive me.

Me

. . .

With tears streaming down her face, she prayed to a God she was starting to have no choice other than to believe in. She was simply out of other reasonable options.

She prayed a silent prayer for sanity, a prayer for her babies, a prayer for her life, a prayer for her mother.

*Is this what it was like for you too, Mom?*

Rushing to the bathroom to splash her swollen face before it betrayed her completely, she spotted a feather on the floor.

*Odd. What the...?*

Too distracted by her grief and fear, she could not hear its message: *"Prayer answered. Prayer answered."*

# TWENTY

## Bottle It Up

BROCK HAD JUST STEPPED off the stage at Channel Six, Tampa's local and best-loved news station, when Victoria barged in the back, employee-only door. He heard the fallout before he saw her angular and furious face.

"Who do you think you are? You can't go in there, lady," screamed the studio room controller.

"Yeah, I just did. What the hell are you going to do about it?" Victoria hollered.

"Hey, Sis, stop it. You're getting me in big trouble. They can fire me, you know," Brock muttered behind clenched teeth.

"Wouldn't that be too good to be true. I called again, but I suspect you already know that. After three calls, Mister Too-Big-For-Your-Britches, you get a visit from me. You know that. How many times do we have to play this ridiculous game? We have some big business to talk about. I don't want any more of your silent treatment. Got it?"

"Fine. We just finished shooting the newest update about the Double H murders. The fourth lady, I mean…victim, was found this morning."

"The Double H murders? What? You mean the Homeless Hunter case?"

"Yeah, saying the Homeless Hunter gets old after a while, so we changed the name. Dubbed it the Double H murders. Sounds more mysterious. Catchier, too, don't you think? So, uh…just give me a minute, and I will meet you anywhere, far away enough from here that it's safe, where we can talk discretely."

Dressed in her obscenely overpriced, pinched at the waist, size two designer black suit and needle-sharp five-inch heels, Victoria softened intentionally. Her perfectly smooth, black hair fell just under her sharp jaw line, exaggerating it even more. She flipped it behind her ear to try to lighten her look. Aware she was anything but small in presence, she purposefully backed up a little giving Brock some space to breathe.

"That's better," she said, more to herself than him.

His jaw softened.

"How's my favorite brother, anyway? Your choice for lunch. I'm paying. Let's go somewhere with food worth the freaking calories and discrete like you suggested. We don't want any goddamn interruptions from your stupid fans. Pathetic aren't they, the way they follow you around like you're some kind of celebrity? The car's out back. Come on, Brocky-poo, my famously handsome brother. Let's go."

For the better part of an hour, Victoria filled Brock in on some sketchy family affairs. Some overseas operation looked a little shaky right now, and that meant potential big-time legal battles. Obviously, someone must take the fall, but so far, she hadn't decided which patsy would serve the company best. Any idiot knew expensive silence cost less than the alternative in the long run, so they needed a game plan, an emergency out, a fall guy. In the meantime, however, everyone needed to put their best foot forward.

As far as she saw it, the attention from Brock being the main reporter connected with the Tampa killings definitely jeopardized their vulnerable position further. The case appeared to be getting more and more national notice, which worried her about as much as another Democratic president taking office. Brock needed to seriously prepare for choosing this case or the family's support. She pleaded that he keep it low and let Mary step into the lead reporter role on this one. Just for a brief while, she promised. For Mom and Dad, she argued.

He grudgingly agreed he would do his best, but he added it really wasn't up to him. His public wanted him now more than ever. Who was he to deny them?

Victoria stuck her finger down her throat and gagged.

Brock laughed.

"I have some great news. I was just waiting for the right time to tell you. I guess that's now," he said.

"Because the rest of this isn't enough? What news? Cat got your silver-lined tongue?"

"Well, you know about Devyn and all—"

"Yes, Brock, freaking spit it out."

"It looks like we are going to have another baby."

"Are you kidding me? You jackass! I thought you agreed you were done with her. That selfish whore. I mean, really, we already talked about this. Remember, like about six months ago, if I'm not mistaken, you had your eye on some other young thing. Ding Dong. Keep your junk in the trunk, Mister Monster, because if this is about your dick..." She scowled.

Pacing back and forth, she continued. "How could you be so fucking stupid? Don't you ever learn?"

"But...I... Well, I mean, she..."

"Another illegitimate baby? Money doesn't grow on trees, not even for us. For fuck's sake."

"What does money have to do with this? I mean, she's finally agreed to marry me. It's actually her idea. We haven't sorted the details, but—"

"Stop right there, my precious brother. There will be no public wedding. Not now, not with this deal hanging over the Bryant family name. That's just asking for more publicity, and right now, we have enough, thank you."

"Well, screw you then. I love her. You can stick your family shit right up your ass. You won't take this from me. Not this. Not her. I won't let you. You, of all people, know what she really means to me. Especially after all I...after all we have done to make her mine."

He snorted, stamping his feet harder and harder into the ground like a bull.

His anger was getting the best of him, and that was not good.

"Whoa, buddy," she said.

"No! I'm sick of you and your skinny airtight ass running my life. I'm the elder brother here, so get out of my face and run. Run straight back to the diamond-lined hole you crawled out of. I'm done! If you don't watch it, I'll just claim my position in the family and tell you to bugger off for good!"

"Wait. She's done this to you. You know how she affects you. You aren't thinking straight."

She reached out far enough to barely touch him. Stepping a little closer, she said, "I'm sorry. Just slow down, honey. It will be okay. I promise. We will find a way. We always do. Relax, and let me think about it. Give me a little time to tie up some loose ends. Keep your mouth shut for a little while longer. Do your TV stuff, and let me take care of the details overseas. Then we will make it happen just like you want. I promise."

He wasn't sure if she was just talking him down or if she meant what she said. He didn't want to play the fool. He was more than done with feeling like an idiot. Then he decided he had too much at stake to totally piss off his powerful sister.

84

Smoothing things over with her was best for everybody—for now anyway. One day, the tables might turn.

About that, he was right.

He gave her a hard, long, penetrating look.

Victoria knew her brother like she knew which cops were good and which ones were bad. She sensed he needed a much bigger confirmation to trust what she was saying. She simply couldn't risk the irreparable damage of him and his wicked anger blowing up in public. Most of all, though, legally, his argument held merit.

The only reason she ruled queen of her mountain-sized throne was because of his unwillingness to embody his birthright as king of the Bryant empire. In that sense, she owed him. On the other hand, though, he owed her as well. In a fraction of a second, she dissected the innumerable layers of complicated catastrophe that bound him to her and her to him that, much more than genetics or the viscosity of his blood, demanded she fix this—immediately.

With every false ounce of warmth she could muster, she embraced him. Then she looked him squarely in the eyes to prove her honesty. Daring him to look for some hint of falseness in her intense expression, she shook her head.

"Yeah? You won't stand in our way? Promise?" Brock, gullible as ever, asked.

"Yeah. Yes, I mean yes. Of course I do. Hey, who loves you the most? Who's always been there for you?" She had him now, and she knew it.

*Sucker.*

"Remember, I really love her. I really want her. I need her and Livie. You like Livie, don't you?"

"Of course I do. Because I don't want any kids of my own doesn't mean I think they are all stinky rug rats. I'm just happier if they are not my stinky rug rats."

"Hey, Sis, like when we were little. Do you remember? Let's see. How did it go? Oh yes. Who's got my back?" Brock chanted.

She hesitantly played along. "I do, and who's got my back?" She felt stupid, like a powerless twelve-year-old kid again, but she knew better than to leave him hanging.

"I do. High five and on the side. Slide, slide, and drive by. Kick 'em, kick 'em. Bryants rule!" He finished the cheer while he did a series of claps and kicks to the beat of the words.

"Wow, I thought you forgot that little cheer we made up when we were kids." She laughed, demonstrating the same series of claps and kicks in return.

She instantly felt an overwhelming pang of affection for him that swirled around and through so many bizarre and unexplainable layers that she was lost for words.

"Never. I never forget anything," he said.

Their secret bargain flashed in her mind.

After she regained her composure, she teased him back by saying, "Oh, now I'm scared, big brother. Get in the car, have a drink, and get your ass back to work. So, the Double H, eh? I think I like that. I will have to remember it."

"How could you possibly forget? Anyways, thanks. I promise I'll answer when you call. Cross my heart. Hope to die."

"Stick a needle in your eye. Thanks. That's all I wanted," she said and actually meant it.

# TWENTY-ONE

## Secrets

BACK IN HOLOSNI, Devyn, Livie, and Nanny Rose enjoyed another yummy homemade veggie pizza. Thrilled to have a kitchen full of the smells of melted cheese, basil, and fresh oregano, Devyn forgot about everything except her stuffed and happy pregnant belly.

She briefly sensed the baby quickening now. Pizza seemed to give Ellie super energy. Even the bruises from the accident had faded gracefully away. The pain from her fractured ribs was but a hint of a memory from some lifetime ago. She was lost in the glorious living of life.

In fact, it had been almost a week since she had spoken to Brock. She had been too happy enjoying life to even notice.

The unusual and colorful flowers from nowhere shriveled and made their way to the local trash facility as one day gracefully gave way to the next.

Livie constantly played with her new doctor set, reminding the whole house of the joy of the play of children.

"Normal," Livie said, listening to Rose's heart. "Very big," she added while she ran upstairs for more purple tea.

From downstairs, Rose hollered, "*Mi niña* Livie. Knock, knock."

Livie stopped halfway up the stairs to ask, "Who's there?"

Grinning from ear to ear, Rose said, "Hoot."

"Hoot who?" Livie played along.

"*Sí, mi niña.* What does *mi* owl need?"

They both giggled and did a long-distance high five.

Rose, swept away with overflowing sadness, turned away from Devyn to hide her secret tears. She didn't want to look like a baby, but even more, she didn't want to have to explain why. It would hurt too badly to tell her story.

On occasion, the intensity of her love for Livie brought back the memory of Fernando, the baby she lost so many years ago.

Unaware of Rose's suffering, Devyn left to sneak in a shower while the purple tea party continued.

When she climbed in the shower, the baby spoke to her. "*Love pizza, Mommy. More again?*"

She almost went into a panic—almost.

*Totally crazy. I'm totally crazy. Just like my mom. Poor Livie.*

Instead, she chose to step outside herself for a moment and observe.

*Yeah, and so what?*

She held a space of allowance.

*So freaking what if I am crazy?*

Was there any value in her fear? No. Did that serve her in any useful way? No. Had it ever? No. Had it ever served anyone ever? No. No. No. She wasn't her mother. She never had been.

Didn't her baby speak to her in many ways already through the kicking, moving, flipping? Why should this intimate exchange of thoughts frighten her so? Did she need protection from the thoughts of her unborn child?

No, of course not.

Twins supposedly experienced this sort of thing all the time. Why wouldn't the connection between mother and child be as intense and effective?

So, instead of shutting it out, perhaps for once, the better response was to welcome it.

"*Baby, bring it on. I refuse to be afraid of you. Speak again.*"

"*What if...?*" She wondered with excitement for the first time instead of fear.

"*Talk to me again, my baby. Are you really there?*"

"Sure, why not? I've lost it totally now. So what's a little pizza for breakfast for a crazy lady?" Devyn said out loud to the shower door.

"*Silly, Mommy, not crazy. No. The fraidey cat hid Mommy from Ellie for long time. Ellie here, always. Mommy who goes bye-bye. Not crazy, Mommy. No way.*"

Devyn thought that sounded even more insane than pizza for breakfast, but she was done with afraid. She just didn't have the energy for collapsing on the floor anymore. It was too hard to get back up.

What would have sent her screaming a week ago seemed almost humorous.

*"I love you, baby. I love you so much. I'm not afraid, not anymore. Not of you, my baby."*

The veil thinned further for her. It was amazing how far she progressed just from one little bitty shift in perspective, how many leaps she took in one oh-so-small choice not to play with fear any longer, how many lives she saved herself by seeing things in a different way. With but a breath of an opening, a whole new world came rushing in.

# TWENTY-TWO

## A Rose for a Pearl

FROM A STATE OF GRATITUDE ABOUNDING, she gave all her secrets away.

Why?

Because she was finally ready to hear them.

Through the fear and lies of her self-made illusions, with her ears no longer deafened to our call, a sound was finally heard.

From the stillness from which everything originates, the universe called.

*Ring, ring, ring.*

Devyn Mitchell finally answered the phone: *"Hello? Is anybody there?"*

*"Of course we are. We always have been."*

Awake. Eyes opened. Finally.

Devyn looked around with fully opened eyes in her dream state and knew it was more than just an ordinary dream. She sensed her growing power to control her surroundings and felt a surge of internal excitement.

At first perplexed but soon outright encouraged, she started playing with the idea. She turned the sky a swirling color of orange. The smell of her favorite popsicles from the too-long-forgotten ice cream man invaded her nose.

*Yum, I loved orange Push-Up Pops.*

While she walked onward, she turned the ground into a beautiful, ornate carpet.

A frog jumped out of her pocket and demanded she follow him. The nearby owl hooted in approval of the sky's color. Barely visible in the woods, the smile of the sly fox confirmed his pleasure with her cleverness.

When she explored deeper, she found a rocky path to the front of a castle nestled amongst the rolling, green hills of its massive but ignored and overgrown estate.

She raised her squinting eyes to the formidable towers above and grinned.

*Long-forgotten princess, let down your hair and see who has come to rescue you.*

When she approached the putrid encircling moat, she laughed and simply floated across. With the blink of an eye, she lowered the drawbridge.

Elaborate banners applauded her gallant arrival. The image on the flag was a single blood-red rose, her symbol, as definitive and obvious as her name. In each corner, the elegant flag proudly displayed an animal: frog, fox, owl, and hawk.

She felt like they had been waiting patiently for her, declaring her royal blood for an eternity. How had she failed to notice them sooner? How could she have become so distracted?

After she took in the grandiosity of the drawing room, she glimpsed a small wooden door in the back. Her heart sank. A smothering sadness consumed her, yet she embraced it anyway and walked morosely through the doorway.

Her mind demanded more light, and the darkness in the next room quickly shifted to a welcoming glow. Now in the marvelous and splendid chamber room, the beautiful paintings and tapestries came alive, but once again, in the far back corner, she spied a small, bare, and modest wooden door. A great fury exploded within her. Her chest swelled violently with the passion of her rage.

With fists held high in anger, she ran through the opening and entered a massive kitchen. The strong smells of freshly hunted meats instantly filled her nostrils. Overtones of the metallic scent of congealed blood engulfed her memory.

This was a scent she knew, an aroma that had already called her out—blood: giver of life, giver of love.

Awake. Eyes opened. Finally.

For the first time since her arrival at her castle, people she recognized—some young, some old, some from this lifetime but mostly from others—surrounded her.

*"I remember you. I am sure of it."*

In reply, they nodded and started applauding to congratulate her accomplishment of passing so many tests, of winning many races, of uncovering many clues.

The quiz wasn't over. She wasn't done yet. Again, in the far back corner, she saw a similarly understated small doorway.

With escalating fear oozing, she approached. This time, she moved more slowly than before. Somehow she knew there was no turning back now. The door had to be opened.

When she reached the threshold, her breath became short and gasping. Her knees trembled, and tears streamed down her face despite her attempts to hold them back.

Pulse pounding in her ears, she pulled her hand out of her pocket. She fumbled with the set of ancient keys clenched in her sweaty hands.

She unlocked the door. *Boom!*

The lock fell to the floor. Then another lock appeared, and she shakily found the right key.

The others were watching her now and telling her not to open the door. They begged her to stay there where it was safe and easy.

She had gone far enough, they bellowed.

Devyn was lost to comprehend what she feared more: opening the door or keeping it closed.

A roar escaped from deep within as a hawk flew to her right shoulder and landed. It bent down and pecked the keys she was still holding.

"Open the door," the benevolent and wise hawk said. "I will help you see the goal of this journey."

She did despite a terror so consuming that she could hardly contain the sickness in the back of her throat.

Mortified, she stepped through.

The light inside the room was so bright it blinded her immediately. The panic in her throat increased, and she thought she would surely die of fear.

Just when she was about to give way and surrender to her impending demise, the penetrating heat of the light let up.

She waved her arms as if to clear the steam in a sauna, and when she did, all she saw was a reflection—her own.

Shocked, she looked herself up and down. The version in the room was older, yet also somehow younger.

"Are you me? Am I you?" Devyn said out loud.

Wearing a billowing, thin, white cotton dress, her hair braided back with golden threads into a crown of lilies and olive branches, the reflection turned and opened her arms to Devyn. The vision's words, like the lines of a magical spell, floated on the wings of glittering butterflies towards her and simultaneously echoed in Devyn's mind. "I see you, my beloved, but do you see me?"

*I see you and me, too,* Devyn thought.

The voice, so pure and soothing, mesmerized her.

Was this her own exquisite voice she heard in her head? *"You are so beautiful. I...am so perfect."*

When Devyn stepped forward to accept the gift of a large, crude pearl her flawless twin offered, the floor gave way, and she fell. Her arms flew upward for one last attempt to retrieve the pearl to no avail, but she suffered no fear while she plummeted faster and faster back to Earth.

Just before she collided with the cold, hard ground, she awoke with a start and quivered at the lingering vision of her own beauty.

Devyn rushed to write in her journal and record her dream. She was forgetting it so quickly it seemed less and less important by the second. She flipped through to the pages in the back of her delicate and tattered journal. For the first time, she noticed an inscription:

Once you remember the way into your heart-space, it's only a matter of time. And you will finally see.

In light, love, and promise,
Heather

Rushing love and support came bounding into the core of her being. She was so overwhelmed with peace that silent tears poured from her face frozen with shock.

"I'm not alone, am I? I'm not crazy, am I?" she asked while she looked at the empty space in her room with the first breath of understanding.

Awake. Eyes opened. Finally.

*"Good girl,"* filled her mind, and that was enough.

For once, she finally suspended all doubt and accepted her birthright of loving support fully and wholly without question from the place of bliss, of peace, and of purpose that few in this dense reality ever truly experience.

She had seen the light. Her light. The truth of herself. The truth of how big she really was.

Although she wasn't completely ready to hear Spirit, from a place of unconditional love for the holiness in her, a message called forth in her mind:

*"Take a precious moment now, my dearest Devyn, and put your worries aside. Do you feel the tingle on the back of your neck? Do you notice the chill in your arms, the heat caressing your feet, the ever so soft humming in the background you only hear in the presence of silence?*

*"That is love courting you.*

*"Its embrace, its gentle and tender butterfly kiss is calling you home.*

*"Put your blinded eyes aside and let them go slightly out of focus. You will see us if you want to, if you will it so.*

*"You will come to know the waving grace of Spirit's presence ever so lightly at first then stronger in time.*

*"Have no fear. It is only peace and love offered back to you. The stillness that is here, beckoning you welcome, is only good. A calmness that rests firmly in the awareness of the greatness that you are awaits you.*

*"Never does it doubt you but is as sure of your perfection as you are certain that the sun rises in the east. It has always loved you, adored you, claiming the glory that is you.*

*"It applauds your courage and might, knowing, even though you have forgotten, that you are one of the strongest amongst us.*

*"You are never alone, my brave and precious little one. You never have been. Your worth, so immeasurable, is beyond question. It simply is. Like blue is blue and truth is true, your value just is.*

*"If only you would see it.*

*"Love is here for you now. Know that it is unwavering. It is not a trick of your mind but a truth deeper than you have ever been willing to accept, up until now.*

*"Somewhere over the beauty of the rainbow's arch, way up high, the peaceful silence of knowing awaits your return.*

*"What a wonderful world made for you, you who are magnificence in physical form.*

*"My child. My twin. My Love."*

# TWENTY-THREE

## Just Say Yes

THREE AND ONE-HALF DAYS LATER.

As soon as Brock entered their house on Sunnyside Way, the banter started up. Devyn felt playful and light. She intended to spread a little of her infectious energy.

"Brock, we are so glad to have you home tonight. I've been missing the manly smells in the house," she said while making grunting caveman sounds.

"I will take that for a nice warm welcome home, I think, even if it's a weird way of putting it." Brock smirked with his sideways smiling kind of way. "Anything else you missed, like my super sexy body?" He flirted back, catching on that a game was afoot.

"Yes, actually," she said. "I think dinner has been way too healthy."

"Fine. Barbecue and French fries it is. Anything else?" He played along.

"Of course, my love. The toilet lids have been mysteriously down. What do you think could be going on? A mystery bathroom elf?"

He looked her curvaceous body up and down.

Before he could say anything particularly witty in return, she had to add one more dig. "Yes. It's such a mystery. Everything is so clean."

He smiled again. "I really missed you, too, baby. You have no idea how much. I have so much to say."

She took in his yummy smile.

"The phone just isn't good enough anymore."

She nodded in agreement.

The desire to avoid him suddenly seemed so silly. Why had she pushed him

95

away for so long? She had been so busy blocking the intensity of his affection that she had forgotten how to do anything else. Maybe her intention to protect herself did nothing more than block out all the things she really needed to bring in—all the love, all the affection, and all the warmth she craved so deeply. She had banished all that from her own world. She had no one to blame but herself.

*How ridiculous have I been? He is so handsome. That smile feels like I have known it for an eternity, as if it's part of me.*

He continued to smile, stepping toward her.

"I haven't called lately. It felt too cheap. So, as soon as I could, I stole away for the night. I will probably have to leave again in the morning, but at least we have some time right now. Tell me my girls are okay."

"Yes."

"The baby?"

"Yeah. I can feel her move."

"Her? How do you know? Are you sure?" he asked.

"Just a hunch I have." She smirked.

Devyn decided to play it safe and shut her mouth before she exposed the incredible idea that the baby communicated with her through her thoughts. That measure of vulnerability was better left for the non-judgmental paper of her journal and, maybe one day, Heather... if Devyn got brave enough to reveal Ellie's secret.

*"I better change the subject, don't you think, Ellie?"*

*"Why, Mommy? Mommy not crazy. Everyone else is."*

Brock said, "Well, you women seem to just know things, so I guess you are probably right. I don't care either way. Boy or girl, I want it. Oh how I want it. What does the Princess Livie think about the new baby? She's probably already asleep?" he asked.

"Yes, mister. It's way past bedtime for her. Don't you go waking up her adorable butt. Actually, she's thrilled about the baby. I hope you don't mind. I couldn't keep it secret from her anymore."

"Sure. You probably know best." He shrugged.

"I'm afraid the baby is going to be big this time. She seems to be growing so fast, way faster than Livie did, but maybe I've just imagined it."

"You look the perfect size to me. Did I say hot yet? Yes, definitely hot."

"Try to stay on subject, Mister Mind-in-the-Gutter Brock Bryant from Channel Six News."

Devyn put her hands on her hips and glared.

"No way, lady. My mind is all on you and those hips of yours." The need in his eyes intensified.

"Shut up already," she said. "Stay on track, buddy. I guess I should tell you.

Livie has already started calling the baby Ellie. So, Ellie it is. If it's a boy, we are in big trouble."

"Let me guess. She's planned tea parties as well. I want to peek in on her before I go to sleep. Please...just this once?" Brock asked with his handsome sideways smile.

"Okay, but you better not wake her up."

"I've missed you too, Mama."

"Yeah, me too. More than I realized. What's going on at the station? How long will it have to be like this? Once the baby gets bigger, I—"

"Don't worry. It won't be much longer, I'm sure. Something tells me this Homeless Hunter business will be over soon enough. For now, I can't really say more than the police have looked back at the initial crime scenes and finally noticed some things they overlooked the first time. They are talking about bringing the big guys in on this one. Hey, tell me everything you know about Eclamptin." Brock fumbled about in the kitchen junk drawer.

"It's a pretty hardcore medication that some people take for serious neurological problems like epilepsy. It's great if used right but can be very dangerous, too. Why?" she asked.

"Just curious? Do you ever use it?"

"Not very often if I can avoid it, but we have to keep it on hand just in case of seizures from blood pressure problems during pregnancy. If a pregnant lady has a seizure, called eclampsia, we have to respond very quickly. If not, we can lose the baby and the mom in a matter of minutes. Why? Do you have a seizure disorder I don't know about, Mister Mysterious?" she asked, trying her best to sound like a woman and not a doctor.

He appeared to sense the subtle shift in her persona from doctor back to Devyn. "Huh, no, Doctor Mitchell...soon-to-be Doctor Bryant. Ooh, that sounds tasty. Get over here and give me one of your monkey hugs. Ellie? I think I like it. Feels soft and comfy somehow, like I already know her. I hope she gets all our good parts and just skips over the bad stuff."

"What do you mean, bad stuff?"

"Well, you know. Hmm, let me think. Like I can be frisky like a tiger or dangerous like a dinosaur. Roar, roar. I'm big like an elephant. See my deadly trunk." He proudly whipped out his fully erect manhood.

She covered her eyes while her cheeks turned red hot from embarrassment.

*I can't believe he just did that.*

"You know...I'm not really sure I know you as well as I thought I did." She snickered.

"Me think lady pretty. Me swing from big jungle rope to save lady. Me love lady. Me want lady. Me need lady."

Brock grunted in his best jungle-man voice and started beating his hands on his chest.

"Lady can save herself, thank you," she said quickly.

She pretended to run away and put both hands over her mouth.

"Maybe lady need big save from Mister Big Elephant."

She chuckled, caught off guard by her spontaneous response. Then she unbuttoned her nightdress and let it fall to the floor. With her arms tucked under the back of her hairline, she did her best hip shake from some long-ago forgotten dance routine.

She danced in a slow but quickening movement, rolling her hips back and forth, urging him on.

*Yes, come take me, my jungle man.*

Brock's thump, thump, thumping on his chest got louder—teasing her dance, spurring her onward, claiming his mate.

This was the new Devyn, the kind of female animal who responded with passion. The sexuality she had repressed for so long begged to be set free. She let it all out and soared with it.

To tease him further, she stepped back to the other side of the bed.

*Bring it on.*

The chase began. Right, then left she ran. She pretended she didn't want to be caught, and then she realized she did.

*Catch me, please.*

She let him.

Fists pounding in triumph, Brock cried out with a guttural holler. Then he pounced her like a wildcat, carefully and lovingly to prove the ferocity of all the animals in his jungle.

He roared.

She growled.

He arched his back.

She arched hers.

While his grunting intensified, she hollered in unison to the rhythm of the drums of their ceremony.

Like savages, they owned the jungle of their lovemaking.

They played and owned one another's body and climaxed simultaneously.

She collapsed on the firmness of his proud and beating chest while his pleasure flowed out of her like the Nile.

98

As the white unmarked car drove by the house on Sunnyside Way again, no one noticed.

No one but the owl who cried out, "Hoo, hoo."

The blackness of night swallowed the silhouette of this house which evil watched. The calm before the storm fooled the inhabitants inside, but something haunting and hungry waited. It refused to be denied any longer.

Livie tossed and turned in her bed. The sheets were scratchy and did not smell right. Something was terribly wrong. Trying to comfort herself, she hugged Big Head Baby tightly to her chest. Fitful sleep overtook her tired eyes once more.

She immediately returned to her unsettling dream. The dolls were alive and talking, but they did not say nice things. They were pointing fingers and laughing at her. They viciously tore their beautiful clothes. They picked on Sweetie Pie and called her names Livie didn't understand.

"Not nice, babies. Not nice," Livie whispered in her sleep.

A tear fell from her eyes as she rushed to rescue poor little Sweetie Pie from the bullies.

Then they turned on her. They gathered in a pack and started walking her way. She feared they were coming to hurt her.

She was right.

# TWENTY-FOUR

## Too Close to Home

EARLY THE FOLLOWING MORNING, Brock's emergency pager went off.

The now silent scream of another lost soul demanded his attention and that famous smile of his. The Homeless Hunter had struck again, and this time, the vileness occurred in the nearby local park.

Devyn begged him to be careful. She felt a suffocating black cloud close in all around her. This attack, unlike the others, felt too close to home, almost personal—like it was aimed at her, aimed at her babies.

Would the police finally identify this fifth female and apparently homeless victim?

So far, the four prior bodies still remained nameless in the morgue. No one stepped forward to claim those dead bodies. No dental records or fingerprints matched. These unknown beauties were still a mystery to the confounded police whose few leads had so far ended up being nothing more than dead ends.

Devyn felt backed into a corner. Furiously, she cursed the situation. She tried to remind herself to focus on the positive. The only good thing she could think of was that Brock was nearby and wouldn't have far to drive. He promised he would stop by on his way to the station. He had something for Livie, something special.

Instead of worrying, Devyn decided to write:


Dear journal,

Last night with Brock was fun. I'm surprised at him, but mostly, I shocked myself. Never really let loose in the bedroom before. I think I liked it? Maybe

100

married will be fine after all. It's just an expensive piece of legal paper, right? Tell me it's just paper so I won't freak. Tell me it won't change us, break us, or ruin us. I do love him. I know I do, but do you ever really know someone well enough to take their name in place of your own?

Mom, I wish you were here. Dad, I wish you were here. I need some advice. I need some guidance. Am I doing the right thing? Will I ever stop wondering? Will I ever be at peace? Will I ever feel like myself?

Yes, yes, Mommy. I can help.

Devyn wrote the words before she realized what just happened. She shook her head and read them again. When she did, her head got a little dizzy, and the smell of lavender came flooding in.

*"Yes, Mommy, Ellie here,"* filled her thoughts.

A soothing and familiar song played in the back of her mind, the same song as before.

Just then, Livie came marching in singing an upside-down jumbled version of a made-up song about flying. Devyn immediately put her journal down. The shaky feeling in her hands subsided much more quickly than she would have expected.

She had decided not to be afraid, not anymore, damn it.

*"I won't be afraid of you. I won't, baby. I won't."*

*"No, Mommy, not anymore. You can't, or we won't survive,"* Ellie said.

Her fear of insanity was over and tossed aside like the useless trash it was. Just as Livie predicted, she was brave, same as the teacher in the movie. Yes, she was.

Livie kept singing and danced right out of the room.

Devyn thought she heard her sing, "I knew it was always you. Walk in dreams. Always you."

She was right.

# TWENTY-FIVE

## Discarded

DISCARDED and unread like so many before it, yesterday's newspaper was thoughtlessly replaced by today's unopened version and then tossed in the recycle bin. The ignored front page of today's local section screamed its headline: *Homeless Hunter Claims Fifth Victim, Others Still Unidentified.*

It was not noticed, though, not in this of all houses on Sunnyside Way.

Devyn played her messages from the night before only to discover Brock was on the Homeless Hunter scene and unlikely to be available for the next week or so. Some new leads had apparently broken, and the police thought they might have something to work with after all. Now stepping firmly into the lead role as the expert reporter on this case, he would have to be ready at a moment's notice.

She was encouraged to "just say the word" if she wanted him to schedule an appointment with a wedding planner. His sister, Victoria, intimately knew all the big names, he informed her.

*Ah, the lives of the rich and famous.*

Devyn gagged. Well, at least she wouldn't have to deal with facing Brock and the whole marriage thing for a while. That was the one blessing in his potentially prolonged absence.

102

Hopefully better late than never, Devyn showed up for her first OB appointment with another well-known OB in the surrounding community. She knew perfectly well that any woman over a certain age was considered a high-risk patient. She wanted to be in the hands of someone she knew and trusted. She had operated with Doctor Elise Phillips once in an emergency situation and knew the good doctor had excellent clinical skills. Most importantly, she actually liked her as a person. Expecting the inevitable admonishment for late prenatal care, she braced herself.

"Are you kidding me?" Doctor Elise Phillips asked as she saw the shameful look on Devyn's face. "Whoa, lady. Congrats," she said with a big smile as she closed the examining room door.

"Yeah, yeah, I know. Let me have it. I'm late. I'm non-compliant, and I pretty much suck. First visit at three months. Ugh... I know. I know," Devyn said.

"Sounds like some pretty intense self-judgment to me. All self-inflicted, by the way, just in case you were wondering—and you mean four. So, if you are going to beat yourself up, you might as well be accurate about it."

"What? There's no way I could be that far. The first scan—"

"Got the images to prove it," Doctor Phillips said. "I thought you would want to check them out yourself. Here." She handed the ultrasound report to Devyn.

"Huh? That's what it says. Well, I will add it to my list of unexplainable events these days."

Devyn sat silently looking over the photos again and again.

Doctor Phillips asked, "How are you, old friend?"

"Pretty good, I guess."

"So, let me see. In the past month, you have saved a critically ill patient with a usually fatal placental problem against all odds and then survived a should-have-been-fatal car accident unscathed. Hmmm... You found yourself engaged to the most handsome and sought-after local celebrity in town, and now you are pregnant." Doctor Phillips smiled.

Devyn nodded as she said, "I know. I know. Crazy, huh?"

"I have to ask about that crooked smile of his. Tell me it's real. I know a little something about smiles. I've met a few bad ones along the way."

Elise looked to the floor. She shook her head and sighed.

"You okay?" Devyn asked.

"Sorry. Lost me in the past for a minute."

Elise traced her finger up and down her chest and sighed again. Then she laughed. "Please tell me Brock is one of the ones worth keeping."

Devyn just nodded again.

"Anyway, I would say good is not the right word. Did I mention Livie is just about the most amazing little girl I have ever seen? Show me that picture of her again," Doctor Phillips said with genuine interest.

Devyn laughed when she realized this office was the last place she was going to get slaughtered with external criticism. As for the new due date, that was a mystery. The first calculations must have been wrong—must have been.

She skipped out the front door of the doctor's office.

"So, Ellie for sure. Loving the name more each day, more and more. Can't wait to meet you, little lady," Devyn said out loud to her developing baby.

A song played in Devyn's mind. A waltz soothed her, and she swayed along. Chills coursed down her arms. For a minute, she felt like maybe she had done this before, been right here, done this exact same thing.

That was ridiculous, so she shrugged it off and kept swaying.

A memory started to surface. Soon she would have to remember.

# TWENTY-SIX

## Lottery Tickets

WHILE DEVYN TRIED to rationalize Ellie's new due date, the memory of the fifth deadly murder played out again in the Homeless Hunter's wicked mind.

*Someone recognized you for sure, my love,* the villain cooed. *They will finally see the sadness in your eyes.*

The ecstasy of reliving the release exploded like the hot lava of a recently blown volcano. Core temperature rising with the recollection of every little crucial detail, the killer boiled. Flash! The sordid events replayed.

The clueless victim enthusiastically asked of the well-dressed stranger who approached from out of nowhere, "Do you have a dollar? I could use a dollar."

"Of course I do, dear. For you, I do. I also have something much better made just for you."

The monster in disguise fumbled through a commonplace cloth bag.

"Drink this. It will soothe your parched throat," the creep said with a sincere looking smile.

"The dollar? Then can I have the dollar?" the woman asked.

"Of course. I will give you all the dollars you will ever need," the liar said.

"Really? Hey, don't I know you? You look familiar. How do I—?"

"Don't worry about that. It doesn't matter now. Finish your drink, and I will give you that dollar. You can spend it on whatever you like."

"The lottery. I know I am about to win it. I can feel it. Today is my lucky day, and then I can get back on my feet. I just need a little help, a little boost. If you give me ten dollars, I can turn it into a thousand at the slots. Then maybe my daughter will forgive me. The horses. Oh I love the hor—"

105

The monster grinned.

The woman stumbled. "Hey you, wait a minute. What is this?

She leaned over to steady herself but couldn't stand back up straight. "I feel funny, and my tongue feels so big and heavy."

The villain's pupils dilated in anticipation.

"Hey, what are you doing? Why are you looking at me like that?" she said slurring as she tried to push the hand away from her neck.

"I'm saving you, my love. You can thank me later."

Her hand dropped, and she slid down on one knee.

"Rest now. The worst is over," the criminal said and pressed the syringe deep into the veins of the woman's neck.

She fell to the ground with a sickening thud as her skull shattered from the impact.

Nothing besides the deceived ears of the mad fiend heard her body collide with the empty promise of death. The murderer covered the victim in a soft quilt, placed something on her still chest, and walked the short pathway back to the rest of the unaware and unconcerned world.

With an ever-increasing look of peace, the villain remembered the words chosen to honor the dead woman.

"Ah, the cleverness of me," the villain called out and then said:

"Devils laugh at me. Angels mock me.

I am drunk from all your stupid jokes.

And my so-hopeful wishes of death.

Bring me the poison. Give me my poison.

I will taste it with joy like wine.

Imbibe it like the nectar of the gods.

I am claimed by it, tamed by it, shamed by it.

And seen by you, exposed for the failure that I am.

By your eyes—only.

For your eyes—only.

Forever into the sad abyss, my eternal love."

*That was just right*, the freak thought. *Just like I planned it.*

*For sure they saw the gift now. They saw the service. They would be awed by the perfection of the brilliant plan for salvation.*

This time, the freak was completely wrong.

# TWENTY-SEVEN

## I'm Listening, Baby

DEVYN MADE it back just in time for her first afternoon patient. Unfortunately, the stat referral summary sheet revealed the woman suffered from a rapidly enlarging and very painful pelvic mass. She shook her head knowing exactly what that meant.

She booked the patient for emergency surgery that afternoon. The pain was too serious to delay any longer. Then she got mentally ready. She needed her game face on for this operation.

"Jump right into work, girl. Your first case back might as well be a huge one," she told herself. "Anyone can do the easy ones, right?"

After canceling the rest of her afternoon schedule, she joined the patient in the pre-surgery holding area. At the advice of one of her greatest mentors, she always said a prayer with the family before going to scrub her hands for the case.

Breathing in and out slowly, she cleared her mind.

*Focus on your patient.*

Everything else had to wait. Even Livie and Ellie were put on the back burner for now.

Then, like always, she imagined herself on the other side of the case even before she began. She smiled as she envisioned a future version of herself in the recovery room signing the post-operative order sheet. She let the universe fill in the blanks.

When she opened the OR door, she smelled the now-familiar scent of lavender. She paused as she connected for the first time what the aroma really meant.

*"Yes, Ellie, I am listening."*

*"Don't use the camera, Mommy. Open her belly and make a big cut. It's best. I promise. You will see."*

Deciding she must be nuts for bringing her talking unborn baby into the OR, Devyn decided to go with her craziness. She put her doctor ego aside and on a hunch, took the advice. She prepped the OR team for an open surgical approach and began.

Step one, she incised the skin; step two, she opened the fatty tissue; step three, she entered the deeper layers. When she reached the next filmy inside layer called the peritoneum, she immediately encountered a very large blood-filled mass involving the intestines and the ovary. Blood furiously oozed from every surface of the disturbed mass.

*"Call for help—now, Mommy!"* Ellie cried.

"Get the general surgeon on call in here now," Devyn said. "Get blood ready for transfusion, stat. We are going to need it immediately."

As the on-call general surgeon, Doctor Biddle, entered the OR, cursing rude remarks, he started to ask what the hell all the rush was about—started, but then stopped. He got his answer loud and clear from the doorway.

"Holy shit, Devyn. If you had used the camera, she would already be dead."

"I know." She gently tapped her pregnant bump.

"Tell me. Why didn't you use the scope?"

"Just a hunch. I guess it was right on the money."

She paused to take a moment and say a silent prayer of gratitude for Ellie. She was done with not believing. Done.

Awake. Eyes opened. Finally.

With great reverence, she said thank you on behalf of the woman's family, the same loving family who never needed to know what could have been had Devyn not listened to the insane advice of her yet-to-be-born child.

Doctor Elise Phillips, unaware Devyn was up to her elbows in blood, left her office for the day feeling great. She would have offered to rush in and help, but that was no longer needed. The vascular surgeon clipped off the blood supply of the benign, but very dangerous, pelvic mass, and the battle was already over for all intents and purposes.

*How cool for Devyn and her family*, Elise thought.

She sang a tune from some long-ago-forgotten tale but could only remember a few of the words.

"I knew it was always you."

Elise Phillips was one of those souls, now anyway, who took treating others with respect and love quite seriously. She always assumed the best in people, including herself. She never spoke any evils. In fact, she tried to focus only on that which she knew to be true.

The image of a three-story house filled her mind, the one that almost killed her—twice.

*That was years ago.*

Twelve years the first time. Seven years the second, to be exact.

"Just call me Lola Littleton, the Firling," she muttered and then resumed the song. She thought about playing her favorite album for a moment, but then she remembered...she didn't need it anymore.

She loved Florida. Sunny. Warm. No snow. No mountains. No basements full of broken dolls or dead victims. No bad dreams. No maniacs trying to kill her over and over again.

She traced the scar down her chest one more time and smiled.

"Forty-three reasons to never step foot in Colorado again, my sweet Jill."

The butterfly necklace she always wore glittered in the rearview mirror, and she chuckled.

"Hello...home sweet home, my wings."

The next week of life blew by for Devyn, Livie, and Nanny Rose. Livie's swimming improved every day, and because of Ms. Connie's intensity, Livie swam safely from the steps of the pool all the way to the sidewall. Ms. Connie warned everyone again against floating toys, claiming that right now was when Livie was at her most dangerous junction as a new swimmer.

"The excitement often outpaces the child's progress," she told Rose and Devyn every chance she got.

Big Head Baby was tossed aside for a soft mermaid doll, and the topic of tails swam to the forefront of every conversation.

"Were you a mermaid before you came to planet Earth?" Devyn asked her dripping wet and puffy-with-pride daughter.

"No, silly goose-goose Mommy, but Heather was," Livie said.

"Okay, Princess Gorgeous, get that wet suit off and eat your dinner."

"I love you, Mommy. To the ins of..." Livie said.

"The universe and back," Devyn said.

At the same time, Ellie said, *"Ellie, too."*

Devyn took a deep breath and welcomed in the love around her. If only they knew how much she loved them back.

Without missing a beat, Ellie said, *"Of course we do."*

109

At work, each day pretty much led to the next. Devyn's schedule quickly filled up, and the days went by as fast as ever. When Ellie added some suggestion, Devyn hesitated at first but eventually learned to listen. She didn't always agree in the beginning, but most of the time, she obliged Ellie's requests for tests or prescriptions on behalf of a patient. More often than not, she was thankful on the other side of the well-given advice of her unborn daughter.

Over in coastal Tampa, the Double H murders of the Homeless Hunter proved to be the favorite terrifying topic of conversation. Brock and Mary's television updates took over the public's attention. Eagerly awaited by all, they fueled an ever-growing epidemic of fear. The public desperately wanted the Homeless Hunter found and punished.

No one believed the ridiculous claim that the identity of four apparently homeless victims remained undiscovered, and the fifth looked just as hopeless.

How could that be?

Were all homeless people in trouble or just the women?

The community demanded answers, or someone's head, or at least someone's badge.

So, of course, the opinion of the local police rocketed downward with the pace known only to presidents who are maliciously crucified during times of economic strife or war.

After much debate, the Special Task Force assigned to the Double H murders obliged the greater Tampa area's unrelenting public by reaching out to the national forensic experts.

The usual east coast expert for difficult cases was unavailable due to a prolonged medical absence. The next available big gun arrived willing and able to serve, wearing tight jeans, sporting snakeskin boots.

# TWENTY-EIGHT

## He Never Forgets

WHILE DOCTOR BILLY THOMPSON was being integrated into the investigation of the murder case sixty miles away, Devyn stewed, and worried, and wondered, and wrote:

Dear journal:

I'm missing Brock more and more these days. He just seems to come and go. So absent and so distracted all the time. I'm getting more and more tired each day. What will I do if he's like this when the baby gets here? We will be in trouble.

Thank heaven for Rose! What would I do without her...those crazy jokes, and that pizza, and Livie to keep me going?

Brock hasn't mentioned the wedding in a while, so I just pretend not to notice. Yesterday, he was so riled up about his crazy sister. He can't see what a manipulative witch she is. Makes my skin crawl, but I can't say a word. The thought of her as my sister-in-law is awful—her pointy nose, her skinny little ass.

Sorry. I don't mean that. Actually, I do.

On a better note, Ellie is getting so big that I can really feel the drain of her in the late afternoon now. Think I need to cut back on my schedule at work. That would help. Even Livie said something about it. She must see it in my face. She always says she feels "Mommy tired inside." How sweet is she. I'm so proud of her, my big girl. She's so beautiful. I love her so much my stomach scrunches up, and my knees go weak. And Ellie, too. I already love her so much.

Is that how much God loves us? If so, we must break his heart every time we ask if he is really there. When we don't believe, like I didn't believe, only doubted—until now.

It would break me if Livie didn't believe in my goodness.

But He knows you do. He knows your entire mind. How could He not? You just forget Him sometimes. He knows that, but...He never forgets you...ever.


It was a second or two before she realized her writing had become automated once again. The words were not her own but were instead an answer to her question. She put her journal down and said a silent prayer for all the lost souls.

"Help us find our way home," she said and meant it.

"Father, love us the way I love my Livie. Love us the way I already love my Ellie."

*"He does, Mommy. He does,"* Ellie said.


Then she signed her journal entry on an impulse:

Loving you.

Me.


She was not sure who was "you" and who was "me."

# TWENTY-NINE

## Princes

THAT NIGHT, Devyn felt a great longing for physical closeness and invited Livie to have a slumber party with her. She promised popcorn and a movie.

"In the big, white bed, Mommy? Mermaid and Sweetie Pie both need blankets, too."

Devyn readily obliged and, just for the fun of it, brought in Livie's tea-party set and table. Before bed, they watched the latest fairy movie letting it invite dreams about magical creatures and mean-spirited pirates into their sleep.

When Devyn quieted her mind, she heard the tune she now firmly associated with Ellie playing in the background. She had come to understand that this song or the smell of lavender meant Ellie was present and pleased. Every time she gave into her fears, she noticed Ellie's presence was harder and harder to perceive.

*Have to write that down.*

Somehow she knew it was critically important. She was right.

Mother and daughter snuggled in for a good night's sleep without a care in the world. Nanny Rose had the night off, so they knew it was just them at home. As usual, Devyn set the alarm from the keypad in her bedroom and crawled into her favorite fluffy, white, fancy bed.

"May we have dreams worthy of us. Amen." She prayed with Livie.

"And princes," Livie added.

"You mean princess," Devyn said with a grin.

"No, princes, silly Mommy."

"Okay, baby, and princes. Amen. Night, night."

113

Five hours later.

In the darkest dark before morning light, a cold draft entered the bedroom. Devyn shivered and trembled.

*What the hell?*

Her heart pounded. Blood rushed through her ears. Panic set in. Something was terribly wrong.

She knew it. She was right.

*"Slow your mind, Mommy, or can't hear Ellie. Breathe with me, Mommy. Slow like fairy breaths,"* Ellie said.

"Okay," Devyn said breathlessly.

Barely able to slow her spinning thoughts, Devyn shuddered again.

Livie remained peacefully asleep.

*"Livie safe. Only Mommy in danger."*

An electric zing coursed through Devyn's spine. Her face flushed with fury and fear. She wanted to scream but couldn't. Her mouth betrayed her. Her body was too paralyzed by terror. She tried to move her legs but couldn't.

*"Someone's in the house."*

*"Yes, Mommy. Roll on your side like you are asleep. Don't open your eyes. Don't open eyes. Now, Mommy, now!"*

Without hesitating, Devyn obliged. As soon as she did, calmness came over her. She felt the wings of angels were enveloping her. She was right.

A few seconds later, she heard a faint creak of the stairs. Her suspicion was confirmed; someone was coming up the stairs.

They were not alone.

Panic resurfaced. The possibilities flooded her.

Master Lucky lay curled asleep on the bed. Rose stayed at her sister's house for the night. That left Brock or a stranger.

Devyn wanted to run. Her heart exploded. Her thoughts swirled. Her gut clenched. Still, she couldn't move.

Ellie persisted in calming her down again.

Several more stairs released a slow and terrifying complaint against the weight of the obviously advancing intruder.

Her mind imploded once more, too mortified to make sense, to listen. They were going to die. She was sure of it.

Worries about Livie flooded her mind.

*"My baby, my love—please protect her, please. There's nothing I won't do. Nothing. Take me, not her—anything but that."*

Pictures flashed in her mind: broken and wounded bodies; Livie's face torn, stitched back together but no good; her innocent smile ruined, mangled, destroyed, bleeding, screaming.

Devyn heaved and was then paralyzed again.

Pressure on her chest—couldn't breathe, couldn't breathe.

Every second the intruder delayed in the hallway felt unbearably longer than the last.

Every muscle in her face and neck tightened in spasm.

How could she lay there...not defending her baby?

*What kind of mother am I? Why won't my legs work?*

The alarm. She had set the alarm. She knew she did and was right. Again.

Out of nowhere, one of Rose's well-meaning but less-than-funny jokes popped into her mind.

She flashed to a memory of it. Her breathing slowed. "*Doctora*, what did the terrible taco say to the burrito bandit? Ha. He says, 'Stick 'em up, bandit. That's nacho cheese.' Get it? Nacho, not your, not your cheese."

The distraction served to reset, to reboot her mind.

"*Hush, just hush,*" Ellie said. "*Slow your breathing or bad guy will know you are awake, Mommy. You must look asleep. Please! Slow, Mommy, slow.*"

Devyn did exactly that—slow, slower, slower still.

She heard the footsteps stop at the foot of her bed.

"*That's not your baby,*" she said to the fiend, but only in her mind. "*That's nacho baby. She's mine, damn it!*"

The heaviness of the presence on the carpet was close, too close—so close. She could feel it, hear it, taste it.

Then...smell it.

The horrible scent of a woman.

# THIRTY

## In My Heart

ACROSS TOWN, safely in her room, Heather sat cross-legged on the floor deep in meditation. The blue and purple swirls in her mind changed into green, and she knew she had successfully entered into her sacred heart-space. She entered the small wooden antechamber and relaxed.

She felt an urge to connect at a soul level with Devyn. The idea had intruded on her otherwise peaceful thoughts an innumerable number of times today, which she knew meant she was guided from a higher source.

As usual, she was right.

She entered the main opening of her outer heart chamber and rejoiced. This place brought her peace like no other. Rooms beyond rooms filled with treasures awaited her exploration. Here she encountered her guides, her higher self, and her parallel-life versions of this physical self. Any question she needed answered was game for her here.

She asked to travel to Devyn's heart, and there she arrived. The toroidal field of Devyn's heart sparked forth a light show of alternating green and purple. Heather stepped within and announced her intention. She expressed the desire to be of service to Devyn in whatever manner served the highest good. That was all. No other request mattered.

Instantly, a swirling cloud of owls surrounded her. In between flights of these winged miracles, jumping tree frogs croaked their song of transformation. While Heather took note of Devyn's totems, she sighed. If only Devyn could see the beauty of the support around her.

Heather heard giggling from the corner. Livie and a smaller little girl Heather correctly assumed to be Ellie came running in, hand in hand. They waved but then danced their way out again. Heather called them over, but they just giggled, too busy to bother.

Ellie pointed up at an ominous cloud in the sky. She spun around in circles while the first flash of lightning plummeted to the ground. Then the girls ran away together, hands intertwined, not bothered in the least by the storm.

Not Heather—she was no fool.

She suspected Devyn was in grave danger.

Again, she was right.

# THIRTY-ONE

## The Sound of Silence

DEVYN HAD SMELLED this perfume before. She tried to keep her thoughts slow so she could remember. What brand was it? Who wore it? She struggled to recall but couldn't.

The evil presence leaned even closer over Devyn. Once more, she tasted the dirty scent of the putrid perfume mixed with a penetrating odor of something else.

What?

Of sweat and stale, old body odor.

The disgusting combination evoked intense nausea in her. There was something so wrong, so bad implied in its existence that she wanted to crawl into a hole and die. Her mind reeled with so many concurrent and conflicting emotions it threatened to implode—again.

She couldn't let it, or they would all die.

Trying hard to keep her breathing soft, deep, and slow, she thought only of Livie. She knew their lives depended on the illusion of her peaceful slumber. Turned on their sides like they were, her body formed a physical shield over Livie's body. She found her only solace in that awareness.

The monster leaned so closely over them that she could feel hot, sweaty breath on her skin. Just when she thought she couldn't take it anymore, she heard the invader catch a breath in surprise.

Livie's presence had been spotted.

There was no turning back now. Her protective instincts engaged. She immediately lost all doubt regarding her ability to defend her precious offspring.

She would kill without question.

118

Stab, shoot, slice—anything for Livie.

She reminded herself of what limited but deadly defense maneuvers she knew. Hoping to catch the intruder off guard, she prepared to surprise the devil and overtake it. Seconds before she initiated her counter attack, Devyn gladly welcomed death in exchange for offering Livie a few moments to escape their attacker. Anything for Livie. Anything to protect her.

The presence stopped moving.

Devyn allowed her mind the possibility of survival for the first time. The terrible burning in her neck let up. The heavy footsteps were moving backward now. The stink let up. The air tasted better, purer, cleaner.

Terrified to open her eyes and betray her awakened state, she scrunched her eyelids so tightly they hurt.

She hung on the sound of every creaking step back down the stairs. Twelve steps exactly. She counted them each with bated breath.

*Four...five...six. Please keep going.*

*Seven...eight...nine. Go away and never come back.*

*Ten. Next time, I will be prepared for you.*

*Eleven. You better be ready for me.*

*Twelve.*

*Thank you. Thank you. Thank you, God.*

*My Livie. She's fine. She's fine.*

The front door clicked open and then very quietly shut again without another complaint. When she looked at the alarm pad, she saw the red light turn back on. The alarm had been reset. Other than Devyn, no one would have known the intruder had come at all. The invader had disengaged the alarm and reset it without a hitch. Livie's favorite teacup had been knocked on the floor, its disturbance her only proof the attacker had invaded the sanctuary of their home at all.

She started to reach for the phone, but before she dialed the nine of nine-one-one, Ellie spoke.

"*Safe now, Mommy, safe. Go back to sleep. Police won't help. Only hurt. Bad guy gone. Will be fine. Promise. I promise.*"

With that, Devyn allowed her tears to pour. Her muscles cramped again. She dry heaved and collapsed.

Her mind descended into the horrors of what could have been. She imagined a cut-up version of Livie lying next to a cut-up version of herself. They could have been tortured and... The terror took its opportunity and flooded her with full force.

Violently shaking, Devyn sought her reflection in the mirror. Other than puffy eyes, she looked just fine, so maybe, maybe she was.

That perceptive turning point gave her a whisper of mental reprieve, and she jumped on it. Starting to embrace her optimism, she announced that she wasn't cut up in the least. In fact, she was better than not cut up. She was perfectly fine. Even more importantly, so was Livie.

She reached down and patted Livie's chest. The slow, deep, rhythmic rising and falling of the baby's chest soothed her in a way she no longer knew was possible.

They were fine. They were absolutely fine. They had been confronted with the unthinkable and came out smelling like roses.

In that moment, the rest of her fears fell away from her. *Slam!* Her terror crashed to the floor. The distortion of fear shattered all around her.

Awake. Eyes opened. Finally.

She wasn't afraid of the intruder, of going crazy like her mother, of planes crashing as they landed, of swarming deadly bees, of diving in the pool.

Her deepest fears finally declared themselves ridiculous and unworthy of her. Assuredly, they always were just that—ridiculous and unworthy of her. They were some insane, almost clown-like version of a comedy turned into a horror flick by the well-meaning but ever so misguided director. Her fear had always been a worry as small as an ant that tried to face down a giant...as if it could have ever won.

She was the giant, of course, and the ant, well that was the hell of her own personal choosing—but an ant, nonetheless, that stood puffy chested up to an immortal giant.

There was humor in there somewhere, except, of course, for the ant. It just required some perspective to see it.

No one else could have told her. It was the same for every person who came before or after her. The observer decided when to see the ant for what it really was, what it always had been: a stupid, powerless ant.

So thankful now in retrospect she brought Livie into her bedroom that night, she dropped to her knees with gratitude. She knew the outcome would have been very different had she not.

She was absolutely right.

*"You did that, I know. You put her in my bed to save us. It was never my idea. It was always yours. It was yours. Thank you. Thank you. Thank you. I love her so."*

*"I know, Mommy."*

Devyn crawled back in bed and swore from that night on, unless Brock was safely beside her, Livie was sharing the nights in the big, white bed with her.

Apologies, not a single one were directed to the anti-co-sleeping do-gooders. She tried to laugh. They had lost this mom for good.

With the beep, beep, beep of her alarm in the background, Devyn woke up to the gentle shaking of Livie trying to rouse her.

"Wakey, wakey, Mommy. Hungry in my tummy."

Devyn smiled, a little shocked at the calm audacity of her return to deep sleep. The last fragment of her dream already threatened to slip away into oblivion, but she didn't care. She looked lovingly at the perfect image of her daughter who remained healthy and untouched, undamaged, unruined by the hand of the almost-forgotten enemy—almost, not quite.

She barely remembered the needle-shaped leaves of a tree from her dream that she had visited many times before, swirling colored dresses on her babies, and something about playing *Ring Around the Rosie*. Her fists remained clenched from holding a stick or wand. A man in the wood had said something about her saving herself, but then the dream was gone.

Dreams, ever elusive like that, seemed lost so quickly to her conscious brain but were never really lost—not in truth.

*Was it really a dream at all?* she wondered.

*"No, Mommy. No, it was not."*

# THIRTY-TWO

## Calling For Help

THE NEXT MORNING, Devyn thanked herself for her impeccably timed plans to go down to part-time at work. Now working only three full days at the office, she had more time to spend with Livie and prepare for the coming baby. Ellie exerted a great physical strain on her body these days.

When she started feeling guilty about cutting back on her patient appointments, she tried to remind herself she really didn't need to work at all. Brock took care of all the bills and asked her many times in the past to cut back. She always refused his requests, which had once seemed ridiculous to her. Now all of a sudden, his demands for her to take more personal time appeared to make total sense.

Lousy at accepting help her whole life, she questioned her wisdom of approaching everything like she alone had to do it all.

*What a stupid idea. Maybe I used to be crazy, and now I'm sane.*

*"Yes, Mommy. That's true."*

She could try to be a superhero and wear that burden as if it were a badge of honor—or not.

Devyn called Heather immediately after breakfast and asked for some help.

"Thought you would never call," Heather said. "I have been waiting to hear from you. I would be honored. Luckily, I'm close by. By the way, what's going on?"

"Problem with the alarm, and I don't want to scare Livie," Devyn said hurriedly. After realizing the shortness in her response, she added, "If I had it my way, she would never even know we have an alarm. No reason for her to be thinking about things like bad guys and alarms, right?"

"I couldn't agree more, but right now, you have to take precautions. In fact, I wanted to talk to you today about that very thing. In my meditation, I—"

"Exactly, my friend. Your timing is always perfect. That's one of your gifts. I will explain after you get here. Oh, and thanks for the beautiful journal. Just what I needed—just in the right place at just the right time, like always. How do you do that, always giving people gifts before they need them?"

"I don't. It does me, actually. You're welcome, of course. My pleasure," Heather said.

After Livie and Heather left for the local bounce house, Devyn called the best private security guys in the greater Orlando area. Luckily, they had an install appointment cancellation that morning and could be there within the hour.

She waited the next sixty minutes in Livie's room. She looked from doll to doll and smiled. Recognizing each one and calling them by their given name, Devyn honored the toys that shared her daughter's heart.

She returned Sweetie Pie, a gift from Livie's first birthday party, to the crib while she sang the doll the purple dinosaur song every mother knows by heart.

*Yes, we are a happy family.*

She blessed the half-cocked, broken-eyed baby with a kiss before tucking her in tenderly. Then she caressed the bald plastic head of Big Head Baby and confessed to the baby doll that she depended on her as much as Livie did. Next, she bowed to Mermaid, the newest of the chosen babies, kissed her on her cloth cheek, and placed her softly on Livie's favorite pillow, the most revered of all positions in the room.

Devyn stood to leave, but then something made her pause.

Last night's anxiety briefly returned. Her legs buckled.

She refused to be afraid, damn it.

A draft of cold air, which seemed very odd on a hot Florida afternoon, sent shivers down her spine. When she reached down to grab a warm blanket, she saw it.

In the dollhouse, on the top floor, she saw it.

The usual mother and daughter dolls both rested on the purple polka-dotted bedspread, but at the foot of the bed stood a doll she had not seen before. It was not one she ever purchased. Where did it come from?

Her mind spun. Her stomach clenched. Her heart raced.

No longer cold, she threw the blanket down and screamed. Was the intruder in Livie's room last night? Had Livie remembered what happened? Where did this

123

unblessed and unholy doll come from? If not from her, not from Heather, then from whom?

"Oh my God!"

Fists shaking, she said, "No way. Not here. Not in my house. Get the f-u-c-k out and away from my babies! You may threaten me but not my babies."

By the time the security team arrived, her shouts of fury had quieted, but her intensity remained. She needed help, and it had arrived.

# THIRTY-THREE

## Never Mind

THE KILLER WATCHED the film again tonight, like always. While it soothed, it also cut deeply at the same time. Not knowing whether to treasure it, smash it to pieces, or just throw it in the trash, the Homeless Hunter remained mesmerized. Torn apart inside and out, the villain just stared. How could love and hate occupy the same place so deeply?

After dinner, Devyn called Brock to fill him in about the doll, the security system, and her terror of the unthinkable, but mostly that they needed him home tonight of all nights.

"We need you home—now. No, tomorrow isn't an option. I will explain more when you get here. I don't want Livie to overhear what I need to tell you. They just pulled up. Get your ass home, Brock. If we matter to you, you will find a way to make it happen."

She slammed down the phone. Thankfully, she regained her composure before Livie walked in the back door still laughing with Heather.

"Heather and me did the big white slide, Mommy."

"It was awesome," Heather said.

One magical look from that baby was all it took to turn her around. Devyn laughed at her previous anger. Then she picked Livie up and started kissing her head to toe.

125

For the moment, Devyn forgot about the top-of-the-line security system install and her disappointment in Brock. She ran to hug her precious daughter again.

The image of the unholy doll flashed in her mind, and a quiver coursed through her core.

Heather appeared to notice this but didn't say a word and immediately offered to stay the night. Devyn, for once, took her up on the offer instantly. She did not want to be alone. She wanted help. She sent a "never mind" text to Brock and planned to let him have it later.

Then she confessed every detail to Heather who simply listened—never offering a suggestion in return, just her complete and uncompromising attention, which was exactly what Devyn needed.

Back at the Tampa police station, Homicide Division, Doctor Billy Thompson studied the Homeless Hunter Double H murders file. Although most of the reports bordered on acceptable, there were a few that overlooked crucial details. The first crime scene of a serial killer was never realized to be that until the second or third murder, so toxicology reports commonly screamed inexcusable inadequacy in a situation like this. By the time police were aware of the critical nature of the evidence, it was often too long gone or irreparably contaminated.

Shaking his head, Billy decided dinner might cheer him up, especially if bacon was involved.

Tampa was relatively new to serial killings, after all. Gentle redirection of the police detectives always worked better for him than brute force. This was their territory, and he was the guest. Ranting and raving would not serve him well. His clever finesse always worked better.

He planned for a group debriefing tomorrow, and that would get him back on the right page. He needed to get to know the key players and find the right allies. Disgruntled, and often horribly offended, officers tended to see an outside investigator as a threat to their reputations. They could impinge upon and, even worse, actively block an investigation in the name of saving face, their reputation, and their big fat cop egos.

He decided he wanted to talk to that Tampa TV station reporter after all and try to get the low down. He fished the reporter's business card out of the trash and dialed the number.

"Brock Bryant, Channel Six News here. Who's calling?" The famously handsome reporter answered on the first ring.

"Doctor Billy Thompson. We met earlier at the police station. You wanted to meet with me tonight...about the Homeless Hunter...I mean...the Double H murders."

"Yep."

"The two names keep tripping me up. Anyway, I'm available now after all."

"Okay, um…"

"Something just opened up for me if you still want to meet up?"

"Fine."

"Hey, didn't your team rename this crazy case?"

"Yes. I did actually, for effect, you know."

Silence.

Brock said, "Sure, I can make it. I was just on my way to visit someone, but I guess they can wait a little longer."

"Great."

"Where do you want to meet? I can be back in town in about fifteen," Brock said, grinning with the new opportunity at hand.

Brock read the "never mind" text from Devyn and didn't even give it another thought. He was hot on the trail of the next story, and no one would want to stand in his way, especially not his family. He planned to come home after dinner if it was that important, right? Devyn and Livie understood his career and probably even wanted him to go, he convinced himself.

This time, he was wrong.

# THIRTY-FOUR

## Liquid Magic

THAT NIGHT, long after Livie and Heather slept soundly in their beds in the nursery, Devyn continued to toss and turn. With the newly installed gate and camera security system in place, she felt safe enough to go for a skinny dip.

She had sent two texts to Brock since dinner and had yet to get a response. She should be pissed, she knew, but she could not muster the energy it took to get that mad. The baby drained her too much.

If Heather hadn't stayed the night, she was sure she would have felt differently. Heather embraced this soothing opening which somehow seemed to hold space for those around her. Everyone felt better, safer somehow, when she was near, and about being safer, they were right.

Startled by the size of the shadow of her pregnant roundness, Devyn reminded herself it was time for another appointment with Doctor Phillips. She was getting too big, too fast. She wondered if something was wrong but didn't want to go there, so she dropped it and dove in.

The coolness of the water splashed her softly in the face.

She had been terrified of diving into the pool her whole life. Not exactly sure why she had always felt so afraid, this time, she just dove in not worrying about hitting her head on the bottom of the pool, not fearing a loose strand of hair getting tragically caught in the pool drain.

She scoffed when she remembered those sorts of thoughts had once plagued her now fearless mind.

Once in the water, a rushing sound filled her ears. A moving pulsation like the swish-swish of a swirling drain disappeared again as soon as she surfaced. She went back under, and again, the sound appeared. Up once more, the sound-poofwent away. The image of floating on her back flashed in her mind's eye. She did, and it felt great.

Bobbing gently, the sound returned to her. In her mind, she asked what the sound could be.

Ellie said, "*That is the beautiful sound of your blood swirling around me. I am sharing it with you.*"

"*What? You can do that?*"

"*Mommy, the magic of water allows me to do almost anything. Why do you think we develop in it?*"

"*I never thought about it before.*"

"*Most people don't, but that doesn't make it any less brilliant, does it?*"

"*You sound different, somehow more mature...like you are older somehow, my baby. What is happening?*"

"*I am growing up very fast so you will be ready for what is going...so you will be ready when... Well, so you will be ready, and I will be ready to assist you.*"

"*Ready for what?*"

"*All in good time, Mommy. You can't hear what you are not ready to. No one ever can. The words might as well not even be said. They are as empty as silence if you are not ready to hear them. Soon, I promise. Too soon, I'm afraid. I'm just starting to get...*"

Then Ellie stopped.

"*Swim now. It is good for you. Good for us. I will leave you to your thoughts now. I love you. I really do.*"

"*Me too, my love. Me too.*"

"*Oh, and, Mommy, when you need help, you have to ask. Try to remember that. If you don't ask, help can't come no matter how much it wants to. That's the law; that's how it works in a free-will universe.*"

"*All right, I promise. Ask if I need help. Got it. Heather always says that, too. Night, night, baby.*"

Devyn swam like Ellie suggested. She swam away her anger at Brock. She stroked away her fear of evil intruders. She floated away her worry of ever losing Livie. She dipped herself into the peaceful state that prepared her for perfect sleep. She was going to need it. Soon, she would be lucky if she slept at all.

# THIRTY-FIVE

## Bad Plans and Bad Dreams

BROCK AND BILLY hit it off like gangbusters. Both men were famous for their personalities, so, of course, they were natural friends.

Charming and witty in a slightly self-deprecating way, Billy put you right at ease. He had the gift of gab. He was a master at idle conversation that was anything but idle.

Billy loved to tell stories about how he spent his youth tending to the family farm and still managed to keep a cow named Flossie out back on his small ranch. Flossie had adopted two orphaned potbelly pigs as her own young, which made for some pretty funny tales. Not sure if Flossie thought she was a pig, or if Millie and Minnie, the pigs, thought they were cows, Billy spun tales coated in Texas twang about the endearing trio that had you in tears by the time he was done.

That was exactly how he got people to spill their guts. Always none the wiser for their confessions, by the time they were done laughing at his slightly tall tales, he had already pegged their deepest truths by their most innocently offered responses and comments. He succeeded effortlessly at what he did. That was why he sniffed out a suspect everyone else overlooked.

Brock, on the other hand, charmed his audience with his good looks. His famous slightly crooked expression won him the loyalty and affection of his viewers, not to mention the heart of every woman who crossed his path.

Billy, after breaking the ice, cut to the chase. "Well, spill it then, Brock. What the heck is going on around here? Do you really think all these killings are about revenge against homeless people? Really? Who wants to kill street people? Are homeless people really that big a problem in Florida?"

130

"Well, I'm no cop. If you ask me, the killer is desperately trying to send a message with the murders but probably not something about homeless people."

"Like what?"

"Oh, I don't know. Maybe something about power or choice, but what the hell do I know?"

"Probably more than you think, actually."

"What's that supposed to mean?" Brock asked, slamming down his drink.

"Nothing. Just that you know this town. Give me the low down about the police. Who's my friend? Who's my enemy?" Billy asked as the waiter corked the second bottle of wine.

While Brock divulged what little he knew about the police force, Billy noticed the tan line of a wedding ring on his left hand but no ring. He chalked it up to an affair that was on the down low, which was no big surprise; seriously, just look at the guy. Even though Billy knew nothing about the Bryant family's fortune and fame, his keen observational skills honed in on Brock's six thousand dollar cuff links immediately.

Brock, possibly out of respect for Devyn, never mentioned her name. He mentioned his family of origin briefly, and that was all. He hinted that his involvement with someone was long-term enough not to turn back and then made it clear the conversation ended there.

Weren't they meeting about the case anyway?

To ease Brock's discomfort, Billy offered some personal details about his mostly empty love life. He openly professed his longing for a long-term relationship and admitted he had a way of ruining anything good that came along. He had missed his chance, he confessed, a long time ago. He had once loved a classmate, but it never amounted to anything worth mentioning. She didn't know he was alive, so that was that.

Since then, his constant traveling had brought on disaster after disaster in the ladies' department. Most chicks, he admitted, were less than thrilled to get involved with a cop or professional shrink, especially in the forensics department, and lucky him, he was both. They always expected everything to be turned against them, which probably wasn't too far from the truth. The ones who weren't afraid of him were always afraid of the creeps he helped put behind bars. Retaliation from the sick-minded weirdoes he caught was a real threat, and they knew it—or even worse, the idea thrilled them in some sick self-demoralizing way.

After the last drink was paid for, Brock texted Devyn that he was on his way home. Since she didn't respond within the next fifteen minutes, he decided it was best to just head home for his beach house. He was probably too drunk to drive.

About that, he was right.

He phoned, but there was no answer. He phoned her again but still no answer. Feeling a little dizzy, he unlocked the back door of the beach house and headed for bed. He decided flowers might do the trick, might set things straight again. He must get a present for Livie and one for the new baby, too.

This was all finally coming to a head. For sure they would get on with the plans for the wedding soon. Even Victoria hinted that things seemed better for the family business. She had supposedly solved the problem overseas. Brock knew well enough solved could mean a million different things, some legal and some not so legal, so he hadn't asked questions.

Soon, though, the wedding plans would be back in full gear. He would be happy. Devyn would be his, really his, finally and forever his prize. They would be together, and that proved his completion was eminent. Until then, he would hang on, clawing his way back to okay. Once the baby arrived, their family would be perfect. He would feel whole, and the pain, the emptiness, would finally be over.

Brock moaned and collapsed on the bed half-drunk, half-exhausted, saying, "That's all I have ever wanted. That's all I ever really cared about."

His last waking thought lingered. *How can I feel so alone in a world full of people?*

Then he passed out.

"*We know. We know, but no one is ever alone. Let us help,*" replied love in his mind.

He couldn't hear the message fully.

Not yet, anyway. He wasn't ready.

The fiend woke up before dawn. Bad dreams were bad dreams. No one, not even a murderer, slept well during nights cursed with unsettling nightmares.

The movie, the devil hoped, would do the trick. It should help ease the suffering.

People rarely grasped the torture of not having power over their choices. No one understood the convoluted mind of a raving lunatic. How could they through their clear window of normalcy?

The villain wondered who was really the insane one in this mad, mad world. Either way, it mattered not, for the result remained unaltered.

The movie played, but no relief came this time. The movie played again, but still no release offered solace. The pressure built too fast this time.

*Help me. Help,* the Homeless Hunter begged.

No help came—at least not the kind the villain had in mind.

# THIRTY-SIX

## White Horse

DEVYN STEPPED into a kitchen full of the popping sounds and delicious smell of frying bacon.

She said, "Nanny Rose, you aren't supposed to be back yet."

"No Nanny Boo-boo here. Just little old me," Brock said.

He stepped out of the pantry grinning.

"I thought—"

"Well, you thought wrong. Here I am. Rode in on my white horse before you yawned your first yawn, my lady."

"How did you get past the new security?"

"Heather, of course." Brock gagged.

Devyn chuckled.

"She's out doing yoga at sunrise. Did you know she did that crap that early?"

"Yes."

He gagged again.

She smirked and performed a simple yoga pose. "You look awful. Your eyes are so puffy. Didn't you get any sleep last night?"

"I got enough. What I really needed to get was you."

"Whatever." Devyn held the *warrior pose* and shrugged her shoulders.

"I needed to hold you—not sleep—to feel you."

Devyn rolled her eyes and dropped her arms.

"How does the old saying go? There will be enough time for sleep in the grave...or something like that. So here I am. Growing baby needs meat, and I knew—"

134

"You knew there was no way that health-conscious Rose or Heather the vegan would ever make me and the baby bacon?" She laughed then gobbled up the first piece.

"Exactly. Dig in, Mama."

"Are you okay?" she asked. "Last night, you—"

"How about we worry about you? You're the pregnant one, Ms. Warrior."

"Fine, Mister White Horse Master. I am worried about you, about us. What the hell is going on at that work of yours? You're never home, never call anymore. How's Mary, by the way? She's a disgrace, you know, flashing her breasts on the evening news like that." Devyn was a little surprised at her jealous anger.

"Mary? What? That's a weird question from the love of my life. Who cares? What's up with the million-dollar system install?" Brock asked.

Appearing thrilled that Devyn's feathers were ruffled by the thought of another woman for the first time ever, Brock chuckled.

"Just a precaution for our safety," she said.

She looked away to hide her red cheeks.

"You should have called me first. If you just hinted you felt unsafe, I would have sent the best guys."

"Stop right there, mister. I can take care of myself." Devyn tossed her plate in the sink, and it broke in two. Honestly, she wasn't sure who she was mad at—him or herself for acting like a schoolgirl a few moments ago.

"No, you stop right there," he said.

Sauntering over next to her, he put his hand on her shoulders and started massaging them.

"I'm the man around here, and in case you didn't realize it, we men are the ones who do things like order overpriced and unnecessary security systems. The women, like you, are usually way too brave and sane for this kind of stuff."

She started to relax into the tenderness of his touch, but she wasn't ready to drop it completely yet, not without a proper apology.

"You don't know what's been going on around here as you can't seem to make it home from Tampa lately, so save the superhero crap for Livie."

He stepped back from the flames in her words. They burned him hot, hotter than she planned.

She felt him stop and regain his composure.

Then he resumed rubbing and said, "You are right, exactly right. Thank you for having the balls to say it out loud. I am sorry for last night, really I am. You are joking, I know, but the words are full of truth. Sometimes it seems there's not enough of me to go around, like I get thin somewhere and my inadequacies take over."

"I'm sorry. I didn't mean it that way,"

135

"No. It's fair. You always get the short end of the stick. As of today, that is going to change. You are what keeps me going. You are the only sane thing in my crazy life. You are my calmness, my only light in a sea of darkness, my lighthouse, my way out, the only thing that makes any sense to me. Shit, Dev, you are the mother of my children, and you are about to be my wife. You should be able to depend on me. I realized that early this morning. That's why I'm here. I need you. I need more of you, so much more. I want you. I hope you still want me. Just a little while longer, and this will be over. All the pressure will settle. I know it."

His vulnerability shocked her.

"Come over here. We are fine. We are fine. All forgiven," Devyn said.

"Forgotten, right? I do hope so, baby. I need you, deep, deeply in here." He pointed to his chest. "Sometimes I swear if it weren't for you, there would be no me left inside here. I'm lost without you. You have no idea how much I love you, how much I need you, how much you fill me and give me something to live for."

"Right, buddy," she said. "I think I'm about to hear music playing in the background as you tell me that I complete you."

She tickled his belly, and the twinkle returned to her eyes.

Her attempt at humor lightened the mood immediately. This was heavy stuff for her to hear, ring or no ring.

He reached over to hold her and made a sound of, "Ah," like a crying baby finally given his bottle to suckle.

"I believe you. I do," she said. "Sometimes it seems like there are two of you—that guy, the famous, untouchable TV celebrity, and this guy, the soft and cuddly teddy bear."

She had never used those words before, but they were spot on.

"You know, we depend way too much on that lousy joke-cracking Nanny Rose," Brock said.

He started pacing.

"If I get my way, it will be me here instead of her all the time—this guy, the real me, not the untouchable me...the soft teddy bear me, to use your words. No. That's not what I mean either. I mean it will be us there, in Tampa, away from this small town, away from this sideshow joke of a city. Quit your job and move with me into the beach house. Open a practice there if you still want to work. Screw it. Quit your job all together. We don't need the money. Damn it all to hell. I'll quit my job, too. We can travel, show Livie and Ellie the world, and get away from here and all this insanity. Forget this weird little place. Forget this life. Just you, me, and the girls. No more insanity. Just us."

"It's not the money, and you know it. I love our lives. I love this weird little place. So do you, remember? You love your work. What about your sister? What would she say? Try to understand even if it seems crazy to you that I took the money for school on an exchange of a promise. I promised to serve the underserved in Holosni for five years. You know I made that promise, and you know how I feel about promises. After my Dad, I keep my promises—always. Besides, the contract is up right after Ellie will be born, so ask me again then. For now, my answer stands firm. This is my life. This is our life. This is my town, and this is our home."

Putting on his famous sideways look, he said, "Soon, woman...you will learn to obey your husband...or..."

"Or what?"

"Or he will have to beat you into submission." He smiled.

"Monkey hugs?"

He accepted. They embraced, and he tenderly touched her bump.

"She kicked. She kicked me hard. Oh, ouch. That must hurt." He laughed.

"Sometimes, when she really wants my attention," Devyn said.

Her comment made her pause for a second and try to figure out what Ellie wanted.

*"Yes, baby? Do you want something?"*

These days, Ellie usually just told her with her thoughts, but not this time.

Silence.

She checked again. Silence.

"I think she wants some more of your yummy bacon."

With that, they dug in and ate every last piece. Not a single bit remained. Once the plates were cleared, Devyn went upstairs to check on Livie. Surely she hadn't slept this late.

From the hallway, she heard Brock's phone ring, and she knew perfectly well what that meant. Their time together was up too soon like always.

From the stairwell, she overheard him say, "I'm thirty minutes away at least. Are you sure I have to be there? Are you sure it can't wait?"

"Go," she said from upstairs. "Just go. We're fine. Come back tonight. For Rose's sake..."

"Ugh, what now?" he grunted.

"What is a cow's favorite game to play?"

"What, Devyn? What's its favorite game?"

She laughed out loud while she finished her own lousy attempt at comedy. "Cowhide-and-seek. It's my new favorite joke of hers."

"Ha, ha. Enough of that Rose, though. Tell Livie I love her. I left a present in her room. Yours is in the office, and the baby's, I left in the nursery. Where is she, by the way? Rose, I mean."

"At her sister's house, of course."
"Tell her I said she will be looking for work soon."
"Yeah, yeah. Go before I chase you out the door."

# THIRTY-SEVEN

## Tick Tock

ROSE LOOKED AT THE CLOCK.

*Tick tock, tick tock, tick tock.*

She always hated this part of her weekend off the most—this odd hour just before she left when time was not on her side, when she felt the need to say something important but was lost for words.

Her sister's silence swallowed her unapologetically.

She knew it was obvious she was ready to go back to Sunnyside Way. That drove Sylvia crazy, wounded her, offended her even.

Rose felt blessed, honored actually, that she enjoyed her work so much. For her, it wasn't a paycheck. It was a purpose, a reason to keep going. It was the reason she cried less about Fernando, her baby, who would have been eighteen this year. It was the reason she forgot about her old home in Mexico and had the strength to keep going as the sun rose anew.

She loved visiting her sister, but the hours away from her home with Devyn and Livie weighed heavily down on her. She wanted to be there doing what she did: caring for them and keeping them safe and sound.

Besides, she just finished reading a new joke book and couldn't wait to try them out on Livie. One day, the game would get old, but for now, she found it a meaningful way to connect to the childhood innocence in Livie. She held a knowing within her that Livie possessed an old soul, and all the child's play wouldn't last much longer.

About that, she was right.

She flipped through the pages again. Which one would she try out first? She

139

still hadn't found one about a baby tomato like Livie requested, so an animal joke would have to do until she could make one up herself. The one about the monkeys was good, and everyone knew Livie loved her animal jokes. Maybe the lion one sounded funnier? With so many to choose from, Rose reeled with excitement.

She glanced back to the clock.

Wonderful. It was finally time. She started packing, but something made her stop. She sensed an urgency to go and speak with her sister. For once, it wouldn't be denied.

"Sylvia," she called out. She continued in her native tongue. "Sister, my sweet sister, have I ever told you how much you mean to me?"

Hands on her hips, Sylvia said, "Oh no. What did you do this time? Some kind of joke, huh? What did you break? Let me guess. You are recording this."

Rose, surprised a little by her sister's response, said, "No, I mean it. Have I ever told you how much I love you?"

Sylvia shook her head. "Never, Rose, not once in all these years."

"Well, that's bologna," Rose said. "I mean it. Total crap, but I do, sister. Always such a big, strong sister. You looking out for me all these years. For the many times I should have told you, I tell you now. Thank you. I love you. I don't know what would have happened to me without you."

Tears began to pour down Rose's face. This was no joke.

When Devyn entered her daughter's room, she was taken aback. Livie was playing with two matching dolls, both unknown to her, both the same. They were two identical versions of the androgynous doll from before, the same unholy and unlovable doll she saw at the foot of the bed in the dollhouse the other night. Her heart sank. Not sure if it was anger or terror, or maybe both at the same time, she rushed to Livie's side.

"You all right, baby?" she asked, trying to suppress her fear.

"Course, Mommy. Silly goose-goose. Morning, Mommy. See my new dolls?"

"Where did you get them?"

"Goose-goose, this Hey-N. This Bicky," Livie said, showing each one in turn.

Devyn tried very hard not to shower society's invariable stereotypes on her daughter, so she didn't comment on their lack of apparent gender. She would get a good look at them later after Livie was napping.

"Honey, where did they come from? Mommy never saw them before, so she's a little confused, baby," she said slowly, careful again not to betray the panic in her heart.

"Daddy, duh...Goose-goose Mommy. I'm hungry in my tummy now," Livie said and carefully placed the two new dolls back into their assigned positions next to each other in the doll bed.

"Let's get you some breakfast," Devyn said, thrilled to get as far away as possible from the new dolls.

She knew she would have to accidentally lose these two wicked dolls—lose them or bury them or melt them back into plastic lumps.

She had no intentions of letting them stay. As soon as Livie forgot about them, they were as good as gone. Brock wouldn't even notice. If he did, she could spin a tale to explain their absence as fast as any clever mother.

With that, they hugged. She tried to let it go but couldn't. Something was wrong, very wrong, and she knew it.

*Do I smell body odor? What is that?*

Devyn heaved. Her stomach tightened and cramped with disgust. She knew this wasn't morning sickness.

It was that same awful smell. She knew it.

She was right, again.

Brock looked at his phone before it rang. He knew perfectly well who was about to call. Victoria had phoned three times today, and it wasn't even lunchtime. The last time he ignored her like this, she showed up at the station throwing around all ninety-five pounds of her weight. He couldn't afford that today of all days. She or whomever she hired this time was probably watching him right now.

*Shit!*

He answered the phone.

"Sorry, Sis, can't talk. It's real busy around here. Can I call back later?"

"I think you already know the answer. Don't ask stupid questions, not of me. You know better. You know I'm keeping an eye on you. You know I know perfectly well what you are doing right now, so let's get this over with."

"What's so freaking urgent? What's the matter now?"

"Don't play dumb with me, brother. Don't try to pretend, not with me. You know exactly why I'm calling. The last Double H murder report was national, Hayden. I mean, Brock. Brock, shit. I…" She caught her breath and shook her head. After a few pauses, she continued. "Damn it. We can't keep this game up forever. People are watching."

"Sis, it's Tampa. People in Europe don't care about stuff like this. They chalk it up to crazy Americans needing therapy and change the channel."

"Maybe they won't see, but what if they do? Are we really willing to take that bet? The stakes are high now, brother. Big, bigger than you probably realize. We

141

are talking prison or worse here. No more slaps on the wrist. No more go away for a little while. This time, we are talking about...go away for good. There are some things even money can't fix. I'm not ready for that kind of shit. From where I'm sitting, this looks bad. I mean real bad, so I'm not going to tell you again. Get low. Get out of the spotlight. Do it for the family, or else."

"Jesus, Victoria, don't you think you are getting way too intense? I have this under control. You fixed the problem overseas, right? Why the freak-out?"

"For all I know, this line is being tapped. You think that investigator had dinner with you on accident? Yes, I know about that too, my big brother. You idiot. Dinner with him? For fuck's sake, think. Get in line, or something bad is going to happen. By something bad, I mean bad. Let's just say...you can use your imagination."

The line went dead.

"Bitch!" he said under his breath.

Then he remembered that the kind of people his sister hired read lips.

*All right. All right.*

He would do it. He was good at playing games. Victoria would think he did it for her, but he knew better. This secret belonged to him, and she couldn't take that away. Having Devyn was worth it...because he was nothing without her.

Nothing.

# THIRTY-EIGHT

## Too Much Sand

WHILE BROCK SEARCHED FOR A PLAN, Devyn searched for understanding and wrote:

Dear journal,

I want so badly to share this, to remember this, to understand what's happening to me. To us. Inside me.

Ellie's thoughts...so beautiful, are merging more and more easily with my own. I don't know if it's because she is getting so big or if it is because I am getting more sensitive to it. Either way, I like it. I feel her now more quickly than before. At first, I could only sense her with a song playing in the background of my mind or a smell of lavender. Now, I feel her in my legs—like a fullness or a pleasurable numbness or a tingling. It's hard to explain what is happening to us with words. Somehow they don't seem worthy or exact enough. Then her thoughts start to mingle with mine. They just come through, light and bubbly with ease, graceful almost—like a dance. I'm no longer afraid of anything except for losing Livie.

I know I'm not imagining it now. I'm not crazy. I feel a breath come into my being when her presence is strong. It's like I open somehow. I will even feel a pang in my heart like it has cracked a little. My thoughts slow and become more clear right as hers join and come through. It's like she opens a space somewhere within me and just moves into it. When it happens, subtle, swirling colors fill my closed eyes. I feel like I'm never alone, not anymore. I can feel her movements inside my body, and I can sense her thoughts in my mind. They are always loving and feel so pure. She quickly went from feeling like my child to feeling more like a friend, as weird as that sounds. Now, she almost feels like a mentor to me.

As my connection to Ellie grows stronger and stronger, I also find myself able to connect more closely with others in a similar yet different way. Livie carries a feeling of fullness in my hips. Almost like she is urging me forward, helping me...to just keep moving. I can feel when she is awake, and I can feel when she is sleeping. My body senses her changes in mood almost as soon as she does. Soon, I wonder if I will hear her thoughts, too.

Brock is different, though. I can't pick up on his...I don't know the right word...energy, feel, signature...like the others. I am sure it will come in time. We have been apart so much. That must be why.

Something else has started to happen. At first, I barely noticed, but it is getting more and more intense lately. My ability to smell is even better than usual. I just thought it was the pregnancy at first, but now I'm not so sure. Something about my vision has changed, yes, shifted. I see glittery sparkles in the sun-filled sky more and more often, not at night, only during the day, less on cloudy days. It's like glittery holes, I think. Like magic coming from somewhere else. The stronger I focus on it, the more I see it. It only happens when my thoughts are calm and peaceful or playful. If I'm upset or stressed, it's not there. Or maybe I don't...or can't notice it.

I feel Livie waking up from her nap. Have to go.

Loving you,

Me.


As soon as she closed her journal, Livie walked into the bedroom.

"Mommy, where's Nanny Rose? She promise, promise, promise we play swimming today. She said she got new swimsoup. Mommy wanna go swimming pool, too?"

"Sure, baby, let me call her. You're right. She said she would be home by now. Thanks for reminding me. I was having so much fun with it, just us girls, I forgot she didn't come home yet. Let me ask Heather to stay with us until we find Nanny Rose."

"K, Mommy. Let's play big fish, little fish? Livie big fish. Mommy little fish?" She ran gladly up the stairs to find her swimsoup.

Devyn dialed Rose, but there was no answer. She left a message asking her to call back as soon as possible. She had a feeling, deep in the pit of her gut, that this wasn't good. She hoped everyone was okay, that nothing had happened. She hoped Nanny Rose overslept, missed her alarm, lost her cell phone, or anything else insignificant that would explain her absence.

She already knew better—even then.

Something was wrong, really wrong. Never in three and a half years had Rose been more than three minutes late, never. No call, no answer. That was not like her, not one little bit.

*Stop it. Stop the crazy what-if crap.*

She couldn't. Her intuition gnawed.

She swam with Livie in the pool, back and forth, up and down. She swam like a nervous polar bear guarding her cubs—her Livie, her Rose, her Ellie, her body.

The water felt cool against her hot face that expressed her steaming-with-fury thoughts.

The water kept saying, "*Listen, I will tell you. Listen, I will soothe you.*" But she couldn't hear it for the worry in her mind.

The sky sparkled like a million angels dressed in shimmering suits made of diamonds, but she couldn't see it either. The fear blocked her view.

The butterfly said, "*Ride my wings. I will take you on a flight away from this insanity.*" But she didn't notice it either.

Her guilt blocked the sight of its fluttering.

The hawk cried out, "*See things from my perspective. Things look clearer up here, all the way up here.*" But she was too blinded by her own self-made illusions.

The owl could have cried out, "*Hoo, hoo. I have my eye on you.*" But he was still sleeping, now exhausted from keeping guard last night.

She couldn't get far enough outside of her ego-mind always bent on protection and attack. Swirling, the ego saw its chance and dug in. It had been waiting like a tigress intent to pounce upon its prey.

Funny thing that the foolish mind bent on thinking found the only way to defend itself was to attack. Never did it seem to comprehend it only attacked itself.

That night, Heather stayed to support Devyn and Livie and to be there for whatever was coming. She sensed the darkness. An ominous storm lurked over Sunnyside Way. She knew it, Devyn knew, and even Livie baby lacked her usual playfulness. Fearful her racing mind would betray the illusion of safety for Livie, Devyn asked Heather to sleep in the extra bed in the nursery again that night.

"Call me crazy, Heather, but I think she knows something is up. I keep telling her Nanny Rose is just at her sister's house tonight, but she knows better. I can see it in her eyes. They look grey when I tell her a lie."

"Oh, I know. You can't fool a child just like you can't fool a dog. They always

145

know better. They smell the deception, but they pretend to go along for our sake, I think."

Heather tried her best to tease like usual, but it wasn't working.

"How long do we wait before we report Rose missing?" Devyn asked, hoping for guidance Heather didn't have to offer.

"I think we give her the rest of tonight. Then we find her sister's number and go from there. I mean the 'we' part. We are in this together. I love you, I love this family, and I'm not going anywhere."

"Thank you, my sweet best friend. For once, I'm going to accept your help and just be grateful. I need you here. I need your support. I'm not going to pretend I'm strong for your sake. That's stupid, isn't it? All these years being strong for the sake of being strong. It's so idiotic. Brock, who's never around anymore, wouldn't understand, so I think it's best to wait to involve him—just until she's back. Then we can laugh about how silly all this was."

"Yes, exactly," Heather said with resolve that was anything but convincing.

"We can laugh about me mixing up the dates, her losing her cell phone, or whatever this is all about."

Master Lucky, the cat from nowhere, came up and wrapped his tail around Devyn's leg.

He was offering his support, too, she realized.

She was right.

Devyn went to bed that night distressed. Her bedtime tea hadn't helped. Her ocean sounds CD didn't soothe her one little itty bit. As a last resort, she pulled her old battered teddy bear from the top shelf of her closet.

"You're staying with me tonight, old buddy, my Bear-Bear. Long time, no see. Too long, I think. How many nights have you been by my side, Bear-Bear? Get me through tonight, old pal. Get me to the other side of this worry, old bear. Guide her home safely. Bring Nanny Rose back to us all in one piece. I would love to hear one of her silly, stupid jokes right about now."

Then she kissed the ratty, old one-eyed bear.

With that, she settled down for a restless night of dreams. To dream the dreams of the monkey-mind madness she went forth, hoping to claw her way back to sanity.

"*Claw, Devyn, claw. We will help you.*"

Devyn looked around and knew she was dreaming. The ground beneath her feet seemed to shift and slide.

"Stop it," she said, and it did.

*Better*, she thought and started walking.

She was going somewhere but didn't remember exactly where. Something or someone was pulling her forward. A great need welled up within her to get there.

Around her, the wind blew, and the rain showered. At first, she shivered, but then she decided that was silly. She asked the temperature to change, and it did. The wind was not as accommodating to her request to slow, so she decided to let it be.

She arrived at the front of a dilapidated structure. Somehow, she knew it belonged to her. It smelled like old half-rotten wooden floors doused with pine-scented cleaner. The windows were boarded up, and the front door was locked. She asked it to open, and to her surprise, it did. The plastic wrapping that was hanging from the scaffolding above the porch slid to the ground without complaint.

"Thank you," she said, and the thought of *Welcome* returned.

She followed the entryway around the corner and came upon a long, dark, and desolate hallway of doors. The smell of musty old clothes and mothballs invaded her nostrils. The wooden planks of the floor creaked their protests against her every movement. Splinters seared the underside of her bare feet, but she kept walking with purpose. She sensed she was running out of time.

The doors were all closed, but one by one, she started opening them.

First opened. Room empty. Closed.

Second opened. Room empty. Closed.

Third, fourth, fifth, all empty.

With each door, she felt a greater and greater need to find what she was looking for and find it fast. She wasn't getting there quickly enough. Her heart raced.

She reached the sixth door, now overwhelmingly terrified to open it. The room was empty except for the tattered swimsuit of a child. She slammed the door shut in horror, unable to look any longer at the devastated bathing suit.

*My only fear. No, not that. Not that! Anything but that! Don't take her. Not her. Take me. I go willingly. Not her. Never her.*

*"Hurry. Don't stop. Hurry,"* an echo urged.

Just for a moment, Devyn felt compelled to pause and look over her left shoulder. A presence demanded her attention.

As she turned her head, the images before her started to warp and melt but just at the very edges. The cracking sound of the end of a movie roll on a projector filled her ears.

147

Then she saw them.

An army. An army of...things...spirits, maybe.

She wasn't sure. She had never seen anything like them before. They looked somewhat like she imagined angels might, but they didn't have wings. There was a light, a beautiful and soothing light, behind each of them. They continued to encourage her, push her...the word came as quickly and completely as she opened to its beautiful possibility...guide her.

She looked over her other shoulder next and saw two Brocks. Both overlapping versions of him floated on a chair of sorts. Was it a leather chair? She couldn't be sure. He waved her in his direction, away from the hallway, away from the lighted beings.

He smiled his best and most engaging smile. She was tempted.

She wanted to feel his warmth, his body, and his love but decided against it. What she was looking for was too important to risk the interruption any longer. He and they would all have to wait.

She turned back down the hallway and started running but not fast enough. Then she noticed the rotten petals scattered about the floor.

Had they been there before?

She knew it was important that she remembered, but she just couldn't.

*"Remember, Devyn. Remember, or she will die, or you will die. You must remember."*

There was a different mangled and decomposing flower on the threshold of each doorway. Some she recognized as common flowers, but some were unknown to her. When she looked at each door in turn, the flower...disappeared. Poof. Gone. They evaporated into nothingness. Somehow they were an idea, just a thought, not a thing, and then forever gone. All gone. Vanished.

Except the fresh-cut red rose beneath the sixth door...drip, drip, dripping blood.

At the end of the hall was a large, dirty window.

She rushed over and tried to see out. She must look out.

It was covered with smudges or fingerprints or old smears of something she couldn't quite make out, dried blood probably.

The blood of someone precious to her?

She yearned to clean it, to clear it, to make it new again.

She looked out through the stains that wouldn't wipe clean. Blurred. Barely able to see. Sand everywhere. A great storm of billowing dirt assaulted her.

Brock screamed, but she could not see him.

Sand filled her mouth, magically passing through the glass. Her throat felt parched, dry, and an irrepressible gagging motion took over her body.

She tried to wipe the sting of the storm out of her eyes. Tempted to close them, she moaned, searching for a second of relief. She decided against shutting them.

She must stay awake.

Alert. Eyes opened.

There wasn't enough time now, not even for a moment of hesitation.

Despite the painful sting in her eyes, she opened them wide, pressing her bare eyeball against the glass.

The coolness of it surprised her. It felt good, heavy and thick, which made no sense to her. If the glass was solid, how was the sand getting through?

Then it stopped. The glass was gone. The sand disappeared. The hallway doors evaporated. The floor withdrew. The sky faded. Brock's screams silenced. Even the urge to find what she was searching for ceased.

Only three things remained: she and two gender-confused dolls both covered in blood.

Devyn choked, waking up with a parched mouth.

When she looked in the mirror, her eyes were red with irritation.

From too little sleep perhaps.

Or was it from too much sand?

# THIRTY-NINE

## Her Throne

VICTORIA ROLLED her heavy wooden pen back and forth in her hand. It felt firm, erect, and powerful, almost sensual.

She caressed it up and down, up and down, feeling its loveliness with the strength of her grip. Doodling on the paper, she lost herself in oblivion for a moment. The black circles grew larger and larger on the legal pad in front of her and merged into one another. Where did one start and the next begin? Even she, their source, no longer knew.

She stopped drawing and rubbed her tense neck. It seemed that no amount of straight-up cocktails, spa treatments, or exercise offered relief from the mounting pressure in the back of her neck. Sex, even *sex with him,* proved to be useless to her now. Fantasy through books or movies failed her as well. Her list of useless lovers ran down the hallway and out the door, but they all knew better than to think she actually cared about them. Really, she cared about nobody but herself.

Ironically, even though she never would have admitted it, the petite, ninety-five pound woman felt heavy within herself.

She rubbed more firmly, almost too firmly, digging in her nails and leaving scratches.

She thought of Brock's new baby with chagrin.

She remembered she had wanted to be a mother once, but the universe had been way too smart for that. She almost died that night in the goddamn ER under a false name, wearing a false wig to disguise her identity and subvert the potential discovery of her infidelity, her scheme, her failure.

Death would have been better than the alternative she realized and laughed.

150

The black-haired and vicious beauty, Victoria Bryant, once believed power and domination would quench her thirst, her terrible, terrible thirst. What she yearned for was lost to her, but surely power and money held the answers. The bigger, more powerful she became, the more dehydrated she got. Sometimes, she felt like a crack-head, never satisfied, never.

Insight might have told her each thing she destroyed made the emptiness within her grow ever larger, ever more inescapable, but she didn't see that. She couldn't with those power hungry eyes. All she was able to see was the need for more, more, and then still more. All she felt was the rage, the craving for more power and control.

Surely she knew better than the average peon. She acted, at least in her deceived mind from a valid superior perspective, for the good of all—at least all of those elite like her.

Daily, she determined who lived and who died, sometimes directly and sometimes more indirectly. The stroke of her beloved pen abolished thousands of jobs, bankrupted farmers, closed schools, and even endangered species. She opened banks, closed industries, and impeached the leaders of third world countries with nothing more than a stroke of her firm wooden ink stick.

As one of the backdoor keepers of the Circle of Global Nations, a savior to some and a deadly enemy to others, she reigned supreme in her kingdom. Mostly, she was a deceived puppet mistakenly convinced she was the puppet master because each level of authority in this ring of power remained fooled by the false idea that it operated within the highest circle of authority. Little did it know that a higher, more elite level managed it.

With a false sense of security, she approved the request to release her genetically altered seeds into the wild. What did she care if they would wipe out all naturally occurring competing species within the average human lifespan? That was someone else's problem for another day. The contract this small agreement demanded promised more control and more money but, most importantly, more access to like-minded contracts.

Feeling at ease now, she took a breath and leaned into the fullness of the luxury of her office chair. It felt so good to make such seemingly difficult decisions and clear her desk.

*Next*, she thought. *What next?*

The smell of fine Italian handmade leather filled her nasal membranes. She flashed back in her mind to when she purchased it. This chair served as the excuse she used to visit her other brother in Italy.

She flew in without notice on her private jet on what seemed like just the whim of a rich brat. No one, including her closest advisors, knew that excuse was just that—an excuse.

Made by hand and designed specifically for her tiny yet intensely overwhelming and angular body, this chair had become a symbol for Victoria that everyone else was simply oblivious to. It served as her throne, her battle chamber from where she influenced the shockingly unaware and unobserving world. Here she sat in luxury and kept an eye on the family empire.

She controlled, at least she thought she did, much of the modern, disturbingly uninformed world. Here she extracted, bit by bit, many rights that the common man still foolishly thought he possessed. Here she dominated the economic machine that helped the unaware trade their lives for money—the same money which was once actually gold, then paper printed by a bank answerable to no one other than the rich and powerful, but now was just an electronic sequence on a computer screen. It was easily manipulated, made, destroyed, abused.

People were too busy working to pay the mortgage to ask the kinds of questions that exposed the reality of the types of scams the modern world functioned from. Ironically, these pawns were the same fuel that fed the machine bent on their destruction.

Masters like Victoria Bryant were kings at the game of create a problem, divert blame to someone else, and then rush in and save the world from the problems they themselves created at the oh-so-small price of yet another small liberty or freedom. These champions of the Circle of Global Nations were the devil incarnated deceptively masquerading around as self-appointed saviors—foolish, so foolish in the audacity of their process were those like Victoria who depended on the very thing they sought to destroy.

It was as if a daft parasite had forgotten it depended on its food source and decided to kill the very source of its livelihood.

Ten years ago, she gave up the courtroom to run the family business after the tragic and untimely death of her parents. She had no intention of relinquishing her domain. If she had wanted to do that, some popsicle-faced kid would be calling her "Mom."

Victoria was stronger than the others. She made decisions that the boys simply weren't unbiased and determined enough to make. She told herself she saw the big picture, how each piece connected to the others. She almost always found the most effective way to personally benefit in situations that, to most, seemed to have no possible benefit at all.

So, when a fly got in the way of her picture-perfect position, she squashed it without hesitation in one sweeping grand motion of her wooden pen.

Brock's newly found popularity with the public was looking more and more like a fly that needed squashing. Her pen was always ready and willing.

"Shoo, fly. Don't bother me," she said to the imaginary fly hovering over her desk.

With a hint of a smile, she slammed her fist down obliterating the pretend, pretentious horsefly. "Better. That made me feel better."

For a moment, she reflected on her too-handsome-for-their-own-good twin brothers. She felt genuine concern for them if she tunneled deep enough.

Brock and Hayden, the twins, couldn't have been born built more differently. One was charming, debonair, and the center of everyone's affection. The other, plagued with a nervous twitch and a confused mind that was best described as different or broken, often isolated himself in fantasy.

One was popular, yet preferred to keep to himself, while the other one always found himself standing in the center of a crowd—some good crowds, some not so good—trying to figure out with whom he really belonged. After years of this adaptive behavior, he perfected the art of wearing just about any costume.

"Brothers, stupid idiot brothers!" she said to her desk. "Pain in my lily-white ass brothers. Why didn't you give us sisters, Mom?"

*A peace offering, built just for Hayden and Brock,* she thought. *That will hold him over and quiet his furious little pistol for a bit.*

"Leslie," Victoria called out to one of her personal assistants.

"Yes."

"Book out the Spa for ten o'clock tomorrow. Schedule lunch to follow. Something light but yummy. Not too expensive. Quaint is better than fancy. Call Brock and that useless girlfriend of his."

"Sure. Right away."

"In fact, no, better, send her some flowers this afternoon from the family with a note attached. Something sweet, like welcome or whatever. I think yellow roses would be perfect. Get some, oh I don't know, names or lists of wedding planners. Good but not the best. Make it happen by noon today. I need plenty of time to prepare for the little meeting. Send me a text with the details."

"On it. Right away."

"Now."

"Yes, ma'am."

"Snap to it so I don't have to fire you for screwing up like usual."

Victoria strutted out of the office. Fake smile, ear to ear, she purposefully stamped the impression on others that she was the happiest woman on Earth.

No one ever questioned her peace of mind.

She had never given them any reason to.

# FORTY

## Taken

THE KIDNAPPER PACED UP and down the hallway unsure of the next best move.

*Think. Think. Think. Use that brilliant noggin of yours. Think. How are we going to get out of this one? What have you done, you fool? Your impulses got the best of you, you silly clown. I think we all remember what happened the last time that happened. It didn't go well, not for you, but it was worse for her. Shit. Think. There's always a way out if you think quickly enough.*

From farther down the hallway, a scream shattered the peace of the otherwise quiet afternoon air.

"Help! *¡Ayúdame!* Help me!" the woman yelled again and again.

The Homeless Hunter stopped pacing to listen.

"Let me go. Me no tell. Me no tell. Me run. Me go away and never come back!" she said. "No *policía*. No police."

Sometimes in English, sometimes in Spanish, she wailed. Sometimes she cried out in a mixed-up version Devyn would have called…Spanglish.

In between her terrified screams, Nanny Rose wept.

She couldn't remember how long she had been here. She didn't even know where here was. Her head throbbed the dull aching of a drug-induced sleep, worsened by no food and her refusal to drink water. Soon she would have to give in. The dehydration was going to kill her. Her brittle diabetes required close control. Without insulin, her time was marked. She knew the clock ticked. If she didn't get

154

help or medication soon, she would get very sick. That would be the end of everything.

Her thoughts quickly turned to Livie. They were supposed to be swimming today in their new, special suits. Livie promised to bravely jump off the diving board today for the first time. If she did it, Rose had a present waiting for her.

"*O, mi niña, mi* baby girl, *es* good, *es* good swimsuit, *mi niña, mi* Livie."

Rose was full of self-pity. She missed Livie so badly that she secretly wished for a swift death.

She imagined Livie jumping into the pool without her, and a tear fell from her eyes. She was so dry she didn't think another tear was possible, but it was. It fell.

*Thud*. It splattered on the floor.

Unbelievably, her thoughts had totally turned from what could happen to her. She was out of what ifs and done caring about what could happen to herself. There was no more room for fearing the cut-up, the poison, the beating, or the battering. The only thing she feared was not seeing that baby again.

In this moment, she acknowledged the intensity of her love for Livie. That was her baby and her reason to keep going.

All of Rose's family was gone now except for her sister, Sylvia. In this place of torture, she came to the awareness that was not actually true. She had friends. She had a family. Devyn and Livie were her family, and if she couldn't hang on for herself, she would hang on for them. They depended on her, and in this dark and desolate place, she admitted she depended on them, too.

She closed her eyes and imagined embracing them. She pretended they were all on the other side of this together and a family again.

She looked at the water in the glass on the floor and grasped it. In a flash, she drank it.

Then she demanded with every ounce of strength she had left, "More *aqua! Más aqua, más* water. Need *más aqua. Por favor*. Please."

She knew the rules. Once the fiend opened the door, she had to close her eyes tightly. If she looked out, she would die. That was the kidnapper's promise. That was the rule. She knew it was true.

Not even trying to peek, she listened as her captor refilled the water glass. She took it urgently in her hand and downed it again and again until her parched throat sizzled with relief.

"*Gracias. Gracias*," she said and then collapsed into a deep sleep.

The monster left Rose where she landed. There was no reason to risk fingerprints, scratches, bruises, or the like. The killer had done a pretty damn good job at covering tracks up till this point and had no intention of messing up that streak of luck now.

The police missed things and overlooked critical details.

The flowers, for God's sake, had never even been mentioned in the press. Obviously, the authorities failed to notice the most important detail of them all, including the beautiful message they contained. To think the useless police really blamed the motive of the killings on the hatred of the homeless. Idiots! When would they ever learn how to decode a killer's intention and message?

The criminal's attention shifted now to a more ominous fact.

Doctor Billy Thompson was no fool. His reputation preceded him, and noticing fine details left him with a record of no unsolved cases to date. His clever and almost sickened mind tricked the suspect by getting inside and figuring out the clues from within the devil's mind. Perhaps if he weren't so good, Doctor Thompson could have been so bad. He reeled in the guilty party by considering the usually unconsidered and unnoticed details.

*Doctor Thompson will figure it out if given half a decent chance. Stay smart and stay alive—don't and you won't,* the Homeless Hunter thought.

Just as the mad-minded criminal left the small space of Rose's chamber, something brushed up against the killer's shoulder.

The fool turned to face the victim, heart pounding with confusion, but she was still unconscious on the floor.

*What the hell?* The killer shifted weight from one foot to the next, unable to stand still while the various possibilities filled the fool's mind. *No, not possible. What are you?* Goosebumps assaulted the monster's skin, and the criminal ran out the door to get away from the answer to the question.

An angel leaned over Rose's chest and whispered in her ear, *"Good girl, my sweet niña. Dream of your safety now. Dream of your rescue. That is the only way you can serve yourself, the only way you can serve her. Stay strong, don't give in, and don't go to fear. There's nothing there. There never has been. Find our light, your light, her light, and scratch and claw your way back to it."*

# FORTY-ONE

## Missing

DOCTOR BILLY THOMPSON read the Double H murder case file over and over again.

What critical, unrecognized detail was in there? More importantly, what wasn't? If he answered that question, he knew the assailant invariably would fall into his lap like usual.

*Think, Billy, think. If you were the killer, who would you be? The poison, the blankets...all mean a female assailant or someone desperately disguising gender. Sexual abuse, maybe? Hatred of their mother? What is the motive? What connects this killer to these victims?*

Was the murderer so consumed by self-hate that he or she tried desperately to be someone they were not? Why?

Four unidentified victims still baffled him. How was that possible in this day and age? He demanded a logical answer from himself—even better yet, an illogical one, one he was overlooking.

Staring at the photos of the first four victims, he pushed harder.

"Are you locals?"

They must widen the outreach effort to other groups, other nations. No fingerprints on file for the women virtually ruled out prior criminal history, military service, or most high-paying professional careers these days.

Most bizarre of all, the second victim had no fingerprints.

What did that mean? Did she do that? Maybe burn them off with acid in a lab? Or did the killer do it and if so, why?

He answered his own question—most likely to avoid identification.

That meant that someone, somewhere, knew this particular victim. Either she didn't want to be named or the killer didn't want her recognized.

He knew this piece of information must be critically important; otherwise, he wouldn't keep coming back to it.

He was right.

"Who are you?" He begged for an answer from the silent faces of the victims, but no answer came.

These women were lost or possibly hiding in a world almost impossible to hide in. Homeless, probably, but it must mean more than that. Were they afraid and unable to come out during the daytime hours? Off the grid but uncovered? Trying to escape but found?

Each of the disheveled victims wore old, tattered, and untraceable clothes without unique brands or jewelry. If they lived on the streets for long enough and had journeyed far enough from home, that would explain no family, no people to claim or recognize them.

How could the Homeless Hunter possibly plan for that?

What or who brought them here...of all places? What was the connection he was overlooking? How were they related?

So far, he couldn't discern the elusive link. If he figured out who knew these four women, who could identify them, he was certain he would know the murderer's identity. He was sure of it. The missing link... What was it?

He laughed at himself when he suddenly remembered the idea of six degrees of separation. If he could sniff out the degrees of separation here, either he would find the Homeless Hunter or Kevin Bacon.

That made him giggle and his tummy growl.

"Appetite, you win again. Time for lunch, good ol' belly o' mine. Besides, I do my best thinking with a full and happy stomach. Bacon will do, smack dab on top of a juicy burger. Fully loaded, thank ya'll very much."

He smiled as he rubbed his always-hungry tummy and took his sexy blue jeans and shiny boots to lunch.

"Devyn, did you get the invitation? Did Leslie get in touch with you?" Brock virtually shouted over the phone.

"Yes, and I can't believe that little—"

Before she could finish using the proper term for a female dog un-affectionately, he cut her off.

"I know. I can't believe how awesome it is either. Isn't it great? She's finally accepted the wedding. We can start making plans with the family's blessing."

Devyn wanted to say just what she thought about Victoria and her little plan, but Ellie kicked her good and hard. She gasped instead.

Rude was the word she was searching for—rude, assuming, rotten, self-inflated bitch.

She wanted to tear into Victoria again, but at the last second, after another good kick from Ellie, she decided to keep it to herself.

Instead, she simply said, "Yes, but I'm not sure I can rearrange my schedule with one day's notice."

"Sure you can, baby. You're the boss, right? Why not? What would your patients do if you had an emergency delivery? You cancel at the very last second for that reason all the time. It's just one afternoon, baby. Please."

"Well, I'm not sure. I don't really think... Can't we do it on Friday instead? I'm already off then. Surely she can wait one freaking day," she said, gritting her teeth.

"Baby, you know how she is. I'm terrified she—"

"Stop calling me baby, please. I hate it."

Devyn smacked the phone on the countertop. "She will what? Not want to be part of our wedding planning? Not give her blessing? Really? Are you serious? 'Cause I couldn't care less what that overpaid, psycho, bony-assed sister of yours thinks of me and our wedding."

She slammed the phone again still shocked she just used the words "our wedding."

"You don't mean that, and if you do, I don't want to hear it. It does matter to me, baby."

"Stop that!"

"Sorry. She's my sister, and I know she can be intense, but she loves me. I hope one day she will love you, too, and you will love her. She already loves Livie. She said so just the other day. Give her a chance, baby."

She groaned.

"For me, please."

She gasped, toying with the idea of tossing her phone in the trash.

He continued in such a way that she could hear his crooked smile over the phone.

"It would mean the world to me, baby."

"I said—"

"Yes, but..."

He sang some bordering-on-scary signature Brock version of an Italian opera. That did the trick and nudged her back to humor. She lightened a little.

"All right. All right. I will think about it," she said.

"Yes!"

"Let me see what I have scheduled, and then I will get back to you. Don't expect an answer before the end of the day, Mister Pain-in-my-ass, opera or no. By the way, don't quit your day job. Cute but tone deaf doesn't pay well unless you are British."

Her other line clicked in, and she took the call.

Her office manager informed her that some moron had apparently damaged the main gas line for the office's street block while doing some landscaping work across the street. The dangerous fumes had been cleared, but the repair work could take a while. The city utility crews immediately shut down the gas line, so no one had been harmed. The office, though, would have to be closed via a city enforced mandate for at least three days until the gas line could be safely repaired. All her patients this week were already rebooked, so she was off for the rest of the week.

*What are the odds of that? Coincidence?* She thought not.

By now, she knew better. She didn't believe it at first, but then she did. She had just been rescheduled, too.

She clicked back over and gave Brock the impeccably timed news. After the line went dead, she wondered what was so important about this stupid meeting that would justify a broken gas line and three cancelled days of work at every office in her plaza.

*"Just wait, Mommy. You will see."*

Later that night.

Just before Devyn went to bed, a great sense of well-being overtook her. Her heart felt warm and fuzzy.

*"Mommy, close your eyes, please."*

Devyn obliged Ellie her request and breathed into the space of where their thoughts mingled. She sat comfortably on the leather couch that smelled so much like her father and smiled.

*"I'm here. I'm present."*

*"Present, yes. That's the perfect place, thank you. You are getting better and better at connecting. You reach me quicker each time now. Can you feel that?"*

*"Yes. Like a rocking back and forth. Yet I know I am still. What is happening?"*

*"I am soothing and supporting you from the inside. You are feeling my vibration, my energy, my soul's signature."*

*"The swirling purple colors. What is that?"*

*"That is the most sacred of connections. That is love connecting its mind with your mind. You are tapping into the one mind."*

*"Are you telling me—?"*

*"Yes, that is exactly what I am telling you. The divine is in your mind,"* Ellie said.

*"Thank you. That feels so beautiful. Why me? Why am I so special? Why now?"*

*"Because you are finally ready. Love and support are available to all who are willing to receive them. You are unique, but you are not special, at least not in the way you mean by special. The desire for specialness is what maintains all the mad separateness in this world. So no one is special, yet all are unique at the same time. Can you see?"*

*"Not really, but okay. Keep going, please."*

*"Everyone, even the least amongst us, possesses gifts too numerous to count, too special to comprehend. Unless we awaken to them, we cannot know or possibly share them. We must first ask and then open to receive, receive ourselves, or we will not see the love and innate gifts that are waiting for us all. It is our birthright. Same for everyone. No one is special, yet everyone is. Love is always patiently waiting for us to wake up, always loving, always holding and soothing, nudging us back...back to ourselves, back to home, back to all that is."*

*"How can I possibly be worthy of such greatness?"*

*"Stop,"* Ellie said. *"That thought no longer serves you. Your worth is beyond question. Soon you will learn who you really are and that to question your worth is like asking a number what color it is. Stop asking questions that no longer make sense. The question, inherently flawed, has no valid answer; therefore, considering it is useless. Asking why now, that is a valid question,"* Ellie said with loving reprimand.

*"Can I try to answer it myself?"*

*"Of course. That helps you understand the answer."*

*"I can feel, no, sense...sense is the better description, something coming, something big. Right?"*

*"Exactly, Mommy. You are moving from perception to knowing. Right now, you are partially awake, traveling in the borderlands between what is perception and what is truth. In truth, there is only knowing, but that is not so with perception. Perception's laws are opposite to truth. In fact, most things in this world are opposite to truth."*

*"I don't understand, Ellie, but I want to. Help me understand better. Tell me more, baby."*

*"I want to explain more clearly. I really do. Nevertheless, there are still some things I cannot tell you yet, things you are still not ready to hear. Some things you must discover on your own or my purpose will be lost. You are right though, Mommy. Something big is coming."*

*"Should I be afraid?"*

*"No, there is nothing to fear. You will do perfectly fine as the shadows and illusions fall away from you. Forgiveness is always the key to happiness. You must remember that. You must remember. Do you hear me? It is the key to everything you want. Make no mistake; it will not be what you would call easy. It will seem like you will have very difficult choices to make. Try to understand though, Mommy. You have already chosen. Now you are just trying to understand why, so you act it out. You are learning, or remembering if you will, very fast this time. I am very pleased."*

*"Is that why I get the dizziness and the dull headaches more often, because I am learning? It feels like my brain is changing somehow. I thought it was you, and I guess it was, but in a different way than I understood."*

*"Exactly. Very good. Drink more water, which will help. Eat chocolate, too, if you feel out of balance. Rest now. You need it. Mommy, just in case some things happen that seem to make no sense, know they do from somewhere even if you can't see it right then. Sometimes, the highest good doesn't feel good until you can see the whole picture. Know I love you in a way that words cannot, in this world at least, do justice. I'm always here. Even when you cannot see, hear, or feel me, I am here, in the best and even the hardest…especially in the hardest… moments."*

For the first time, Devyn noticed a deep sadness in Ellie's words. It was as if a tear had welled up in her throat, but that was crazy. Why would Ellie have felt sad?

Although Devyn felt like she had spoken with Ellie, a word had not been required. Some connections were beyond words, and some conversations were too holy to require them.

Sleep fell hard on her while the night's dreams enveloped her. As part of her brain slept, the other parts worked overtime to help get her ready for what was coming, what waited, what wanted to hurt her…and her babies.

# FORTY-TWO

## Aliens Are Coming

FIRST THING NEXT MORNING, Devyn phoned Sylvia, Rose's sister. Sylvia claimed Rose left her house for the bus station just like always, and there had been no problems she was aware of. Everything seemed to be in order, but why was Devyn asking? Had something gone wrong? Was there a problem?

Devyn didn't want to unnecessarily alarm Sylvia, so she lied.

"No, no. Everything is fine."

The Holosni police station was minimally staffed during the best and laziest of days, and today was no exception. The town sheriff was out on vacation, and the few police officers employed there were all dispatched on calls. Apparently, a local stray cat appeared to be stuck in a tree at Ms. Frazier's house. Mr. Littleton had gotten confused again and was running down Main Street naked and screaming the aliens were coming.

Devyn laughed while the visual image of a naked, demented, wrinkly, old but invariably sweet Mr. Littleton filled her mind. She asked Lucinda, the kind switch-board operator, handy woman, and police secretary all-in-one, what she suggested Devyn do next about reporting a missing person.

Lucinda giggled before asking, "You mean other than Mr. Littleton?"

The question made both of them explode with uncontrollable laughter.

"Yes, unfortunately, Rose hasn't returned home after leaving her sister's house a day and a half ago," Devyn said.

"She's probably just—"

"Yeah, I thought of all the probably this and probably that. None of them really make sense. So, I thought I better report her missing just to be safe."

"Oh, Doctor Mitchell, what if, you know, with all those murders in the area? Maybe the Homeless Hunter thought she was homeless and—"

"Stop it right there, Lucinda. That's impossible. Rose couldn't be further from looking homeless. If anybody ever did her harm it would be for cracking one of her ridiculous jokes," she said, as much to reassure herself as Lucinda.

She really hoped what she was saying was true. The local hospitals didn't have any admitted patients listed under the name Rose or Jane Doe, so she was really out of leads.

"Listen, I know it's a real pain in the butt, Doctor Mitchell, but if I were you with all this crazy Homeless Hunter stuff, I would drive to the coast and go talk to the police out there."

"There?"

"In Tampa."

"Oh."

"Let's face it; we are not equipped to handle a real investigation here anyway. The last big crime in this town, other than Mr. Littleton's streaking, of course, was a third grader who shoplifted some shoes at the local Kmart. That was big news if you know what I mean."

"I remember."

"So just go on down there to see the real police. Visit the TV station and that handsome husband of yours at the same time. I just watched his last segment. Boy can he smile, Doc."

"Thanks, but actually he's not my husband—not yet anyway."

"What?"

"Never mind. I will do what you suggested. That's a great idea. You are a real police station, so don't sell yourself so short. You do a lot of good in this little town—for example, getting the wild, nude, maniacs off Main Street. Thank you for doing what you do."

"By the way, I was supposed to see you tomorrow as a patient, but they cancelled me until next week. You okay? Is this why?"

"Oh, no. It's because of that gas line leak."

"That makes sense," she said.

"Thanks...for making me laugh. I needed that," Devyn said.

"No prob, Doc. Good luck. She'll be fine. I'm sure. Just lost or forgot. Something like that."

The phone clicked off, and Devyn sat there for a minute. She convinced herself

Lucinda was right. She then prayed a silent prayer for the next step. She prayed for Rose's safety, and again, she prayed for help.

If she considered the worst, she had to admit that without the insulin locked safely in the medicine cabinet at home, Rose would be pretty sick by now. In a few days, she would be dead.

The Homeless Hunter sat down, frustrated and confused. One part of the fiend's wicked mind argued for an immediate execution of Nanny Rose. The other part debated as strongly for her dismissal. She couldn't possibly be important enough to risk killing, but could she be unimportant enough to risk releasing? The kidnapper played out several potential scenarios, none of which were satisfactory.

*What did Daddy always say when he was pissed?*

The maniac answered out loud. "Goddamn mother fucking son of a bitch. Yes, exactly. Thank you, Father, for teaching me one thing worth repeating."

The Homeless Hunter laughed at the joke, feeling much better.

"We all know where sayings like that got you, Daddy, don't we? I hope you are watching me now, marveling at the mess you and Mommy made. A failure in every sense of the word just like you said. Yes, that's me, the fuckface who never amounted to anything, not worth my last name, not worth the space I take up. Can't even kill a useless Mexican bitch right. Can I, Pops?"

No reply came. No answer shared its glorious perspective.

So the fool sat in the same place, swirling the same inadequate ideas over and over again in a confused and conflicted mind: broken, split, injured, ruined.

Sometimes making no decision was the easiest decision, the Homeless Hunter finally concluded. The criminal would just wait and see, hoping that perhaps the right plan surfaced on its own accord.

With that final assessment made, the mad-minded fool unzipped the costume of fearful inadequacy and tossed it on the floor. Looking down at the imaginary brushed-aside layer of being, the monster decided not to care anymore; laughed sinisterly with wicked overtones of hate, joy, evil, and childishness; and simply walked away.

# FORTY-THREE

## All the Wundiful Think

ON BENDED KNEE, Livie recited her prayers. She had seen it done this way on last year's made-for-TV Christmas special, so it must work better if you really wanted something big-time—and Livie really wanted something big-time.

She wanted Nanny back. She knew better than to think Rose was still at Sylvia's house. Rose miss Livie's new swimsuit and first jump off the diving board party? No stinking way. That was simply not possible. Something must be really wrong.

Heather was talking on the phone with one of her clients, so she decided now was as good a time as any to start.

"Dear heaven above, help Livie," she said. "Help Mommy, and help Lucky, my cat, too. If you have Nanny Rose, we want her back, please. We need her. We miss pizza, and Heather can't do my socks. Ouchy, okay? Hurt my foots. So hurry, Nanny Rose. Thank you for all the wundiful thinks. Amen."

She smiled, pleased with her cleverness.

Then she remembered something Heather always did.

She placed two fingers in the air, winked, and said, "So it is," with the heartfelt grace and tenderness known only to the open and beautiful hearts of undamaged children.

Billy entered the police station feeling more nervous and unsettled than usual...as evidenced by the breakfast burrito stain on his brand-new shirt. Somehow, today,

166

his luck was off. The coffee was too hot and burned his tongue. Then he used sugar substitute accidentally instead of the real stuff. To top it off, the hotel informed him that they lost his one good suit—thus, the new and freshly ruined golf shirt tucked into his jeans minus a jacket.

Worst of all, while sitting at another red light, he realized he forgot to charge his cell phone. Its power was at twenty percent.

Out of nowhere, he envisioned Tootsie, his long-lost imaginary childhood best friend, running down the sidewalk shaking his finger with a full-faced grin.

"*No, Billy. No. I don't think so.*"

"Okay, Tootsie." He laughed. "I know you were always a figment of my imagination, but I'm going to listen to you anyway. Back up, turn around, Billy, and start over. I'm missing something. I'm going in the wrong direction. I'm asking the wrong questions. Is that what you are trying to tell me? What would my colleagues say about me if they knew I consulted my imaginary old best friend?"

*Billy, you've lost your friggin' mind.*

"By the way, Tootsie, old Mister No-show, where did you go all those years ago?" he asked.

The idea that he was being rerouted, not reprimanded, popped into his mind.

"Reroute me, old pal, old buddy. I'm listening, and my radar is beeping," he whispered.

Silence.

"Nothing to say, eh?"

Billy sat down with a thud into his makeshift chair in his makeshift office. Overall, despite a few critical errors with evidence, the Tampa police had been mostly friendly and supportive, but they were busy. Tampa was a big place, and the Double H murders were just one of many "priorities" around here. After all, no one really cared that much about the dead street people, who were a nuisance to the police anyway, so why should they work overtime to find their killer?

Billy, thankfully, couldn't have disagreed more with that philosophy.

He served as the forensic and lead investigative consultant alongside a team of two other relatively well-respected but less motivated investigators. One worked pretty hard; the other worked harder at not working than working.

He knew this case was on his shoulders, his back, his conscience. If he didn't solve it, no one else would. Years from now, it would be nothing more than another unsolved cold case tragically locked and forgotten in a cabinet in downtown Tampa.

The *People Magazine* article from seven years ago that made him so famous popped into his mind.

*Doctor Billy Thompson, Master of the Cold Case.*

"The author loved my boots, Tootsie," he said, briefly recalling the affair that it brought on. "Maybe it was the jeans."

In all honesty, so far, his team had gotten pretty well nowhere with the ID of four of the victims. As for the fifth, she was finally recognized yesterday as local, but her murder never fit in. It was as if it was an impulsive move by the killer.

*A red herring, perhaps?*

They were still no better off than before. Maybe the back room was where the Double H murder file was headed no matter what. The thought of coming back to the case in a few years made him sick to his stomach.

Other than being obviously homeless, the victims still seemed to have no connection, but he knew better. Somehow, somewhere, there was a common link. Finding that was the answer to solving this case, and no one could convince him otherwise.

The missing fingerprints from the second victim's hands maybe?

He knew it. He did.

He was right.

# FORTY-FOUR

## Crack the Shutters

NANNY ROSE WOKE UP BREATHLESS. Her heart raced. Her pulse pounded so loudly in her ears all other sounds drowned away. She noticed the sweet, sick taste of sugar on her breath. With her glucose level so high, she didn't have much time left. Without her insulin, her hours were numbered. She risked slipping into a coma at any minute. She opened her eyes widely but saw only darkness. She couldn't tell if the room was in total blackness.

*Oh no. What if...?*

Panic took hold.

She reached up to find no cloth blinder over her eyes. A scream of terror escaped her mouth. She was blind from the sugar level.

Sobbing, Nanny Rose realized she was most certainly going to die.

*I'm going to die. No. No! I don't want to die!*

Then the image of Livie rushed into her mind. She wept harder.

"*Mi niña, mi* Livie!" she wailed. "*Por favor, mi niña, mi* Livie." She gave into the full body tremors of total and complete misery.

Brock felt lousy today. His mind jumped from one worry to another. What if Victoria was in full-bitch mode at the meeting? What if she changed her mind about helping them? What if she acted more like a lawyer than his sister? Too many what ifs forced his mind to spin out of control. He didn't want to admit it, but he knew he needed Victoria's help with the legal details. Marrying a Bryant, especially him under his unique circumstances, meant a paperwork monstrosity capable of scaring any normal lawyer. That, of course, assumed a normal lawyer existed.

Again and again, he rehearsed his speech. He refused to sign a prenuptial agreement. His desire to stand up on Devyn's behalf enraged him. He felt angry and defensive but afraid and guilty all at the same time.

Yet he was also a realist and knew the treacherous nature of his situation. He expected to agree to any other kind of arrangements Victoria might suggest. Damn it, he would do right by Livie and Devyn if given half a chance.

If something happened to him, Livie must be protected at every cost. Devyn was a clever and able woman, and his money meant nothing to her. If it did, she would have quit working and moved into the Tampa beach house with him years ago. If that weren't proof of her financial intention, well, nothing ever would be.

"Surely Victoria will see that," he shouted, pacing back and forth.

He sensed his blood pressure rising. He had better get himself under control fast. That was harder and harder to do these days.

Victoria's uncanny ability to sense fear terrified him the most. If she smelled so much as an ounce of weakness in him, she would engage her attack mode and go for the kill.

He had seen her do it in court a thousand times before. Other lawyers often underestimated her. She looked tiny, after all, and how could someone so small assault with such force? Opposing attorneys only made that mistake once.

He must convince Victoria, without her realizing what he was doing, of course, that she wanted to help him. She must think that somehow she needed him more than he needed her. Then, she must think helping him was the best thing for the family—not from a point of weakness, but from strength. He planned to beat her at her own game. He was the game-face king, after all. He just had to go in knowing which game and which face to stay on top.

He was so close to having Devyn...in every sense of the word...that he couldn't afford any mistakes, not now. If tomorrow's meeting went well, then his dream realized might be enough to satisfy him. It might be enough to last the rest of his life and even might be enough to make the terrible pain stop.

He loved Devyn so deeply it ached in his bones. It pulled at his sternum. He smelled her in the air. He tasted her in his food.

"Please," he said, "let me have this, just this one thing. Please. I'll never ask for another thing again."

He meant it in the only way he still remembered how.

170

Doctor Elise Phillips read the schedule again. Devyn Mitchell's appointment passed one hour ago. Either Devyn was going to be over an hour late or she had forgotten her follow-up ultrasound appointment. She probably had a delivery to attend.

Doctor Philips knew better, though. She always had. She had a sense, an intuition about her.

She reached up and touched her butterfly necklace for comfort.

Something big was up. She hoped for Devyn's sake it was something good.

Unfortunately, it was not.

Another smile crossed Devyn's face as she adjusted her rearview mirror while driving to Tampa. The image of the butt-naked Mr. Littleton crossed her mind again.

She couldn't resist laughing at the idea of his arms flailing while he hollered about aliens. Out of respect, she knew she shouldn't laugh, but some things were just plain funny, politically correct or not.

She sighed when she looked about the new car. It seemed like she would never get used to the new SUV. The accident felt like it happened a lifetime ago to someone else.

*Whose car is this? Not mine, surely.*

She was different these days, and somehow the day-to-day crap didn't seem very important any more.

*What accident? I don't even remember almost dying.*

The mail waited. If the dishes piled up a little, well, who really cared?

She shrugged her shoulders as if to say, "*Not me.*"

For the next forty minutes, she let her mind go where it wanted to. It wandered from her accident to downtown Holosni and back to Livie's swimming lessons.

Ellie brought her back.

"*Mommy, focus your thoughts, please. We are almost there, yes?*"

Devyn nodded.

"*You need to gather yourself so you will remember the details. Also, I want to open you up a little.*"

"*Thank you, Ellie. I don't see why not. Will it hurt?*"

"*What would Livie say? Goose-goose, of course not. Good. We are here. Just close your eyes for a minute.*"

"*Sure. Eyes closed.*"

"*Take a deep breath with a wide-open mouth until your jaw clicks. That opens your throat, which is a chimney of sorts for the heart. That will help you speak your truth. Good. You are doing great. Next, pretend you have a set of keys that unlock your heart. As it opens, grab another key in your imagination and keep doing that over and over again, very slowly, until I say to stop."*

*"This seems a little silly, but if you say it will help Rose, then I will do it. It actually feels settling. Is that my imagination?"*

*"No. Your description is valid. Sink into the chair and open. Allow it to happen."*

Devyn sighed as a feeling of warmth overtook her. Her legs felt tingly, and her feet felt hot. She took a slow, deep breath and sighed again.

Ellie continued. *"Very good. You are doing very good. We are ready now. Just remember, everything is perfect. You are doing exactly what you are supposed to be doing. Your timing is no coincidence. In truth, there is actually no such thing as chance or coincidence. That idea is a great big myth. Last big breath, Mommy. Your heart is open enough to help Rose and us all, for that matter. Here we go."*

Devyn walked up to the front door of Tampa's central police station. She had never been here before, but she knew she was in the right place. When she opened the heavy glass door, a feeling of purpose took over her. She was going to get her Rose back, damn it.

The image of Tootsie popped into Doctor Billy Thompson's mind once more.

*Funny, dude,* he thought. *Why did you pick today of all days to remind me of my childhood fantasies?*

In a flash, he felt lost…just like a six-year-old, trapped and twirling his snakeskin boots in his oversized chair. He went back to the day he came home from first grade, and his imaginary best friend was gone, never to reappear again—until today that was.

Devastated, just like all those years ago, he wondered who he would hunt with in the backyard after Tootsie was gone. Who would play pirates and die gracefully at the imaginary tip of his pretend sword now? Who would promise him everything would be okay, that his parents would stop fighting one day?

He was convinced Tootsie had been the single most important reason he survived his parents' ugly divorce. No one, except Billy's mom, even knew about Tootsie. The day he told her, she laughed at him. She told him Tootsie wasn't real, a figment of his childish imagination.

That comment effectively destroyed Billy because her dismissive tone took him straight from innocent fantasy to adulthood pessimism in one painful swoop. He was ruined instantly. If only she had acknowledged the sweet boy inside, maybe he would have been able to really relate to people around him instead of manipulating them into the people he wanted them to become and then hating them for it. He wondered briefly if something so simple as his mother's reaction could have such lasting effects. After all, he always hid his true self from others because he was still hiding his inner child from his mother. Maybe? Probably.

*Get over it, Billy. Stop shrinking yourself.* He sighed.

Growing up after old Tootsie left turned out to be a blessing in the end. If he was being honest, he wasn't really sure he ever got over the abandonment from Tootsie or recovered from the deep sense of loss over his prematurely ended affair with make-believe. *Mom, I miss you. I wish I could tell you how much.*

He swallowed hard and touched his stomach. Then he took a deep breath and slowly let it out. *"Tootsie, why the heck are you here? Now of all times? You got my attention. I'm playing along. How's Mom, by the way?"*

The imaginary Tootsie danced a jig. He waved and flew in a big circle around the office. He did his best pirate salute and then stepped to the side. As quickly as he had appeared, he was gone again.

Just to the left of Tootsie's absent image, through the window of his office, Billy saw something even more incredible.

He blinked his eyes twice to be sure his hallucinating had really ceased.

She was still standing there.

# FORTY-FIVE

## Tip-Toe

ROSE SAT BLINDED by her sugar, or was it the situation?

Who knew, but did it really matter? She was lost in a world of terrible darkness, enveloped by a fear she could smell and taste all around her. Again, the idea of Livie filled her mind, which, thankfully, distracted her from her useless and horrific thoughts. Without the further distraction of sight, she sunk into the image of Livie.

Livie smiled at her as if to say, *"See me. I am here."*

Back in the far corner of Rose's awareness, she heard a thump, thump, thump, like the start of some tune she didn't quite recognize. The rhythm soothed her, and she welcomed it. A childish grin took over Livie's face that suggested she wanted to play a game.

*"Tip-toe, tip-toe, tip-toe,"* Livie called, even though no words were spoken.

Rose heard much more than just those simple words.

She understood the full implications of them instantly.

This was not a new game. They had played it before. Rose giggled while the idea sank in.

*"Yes, yes, I will play with you."*

She knew the rules. After all, she had invented the game when she was a little girl.

Rose nodded her head to confirm she was in.

The game began.

174

Victoria stood naked staring at her image in the bathroom mirror.

*How ironic that I was born captive to such a small body.*

She definitely didn't feel small and, to be honest, hardly recognized her image each time she looked in the mirror.

She played tomorrow's meeting with Brock and Devyn over in her mind. She would be ready. It was important for them to think she wanted to help with the wedding. She did want to help, of course—just not them. She wouldn't have to pretend much longer. The end of this stupid nonsense was close at hand. She had been here before and recognized the importance of appearances that eventually would reveal themselves to be illusions.

This time, she was wrong.

A notion of a plan started to form in the killer's mind. A way out started to crawl to the surface of the monster's thoughts. Sometimes sacrifices must be made for the greater good, for the higher will.

Whose will was higher? That was the only real question left. A divided mind always forced a battle onto itself. One side must lose for the other side to win. Insanity? Yes, it was, but only from the perspective of the sane. To the demented mind of a madman, insanity was the only perfectly sensible choice.

Someone must lose for the other person to win, yet something so sensible couldn't have been further from the truth.

Paralyzed in his creaky, old, sunken too-much-in-the-middle chair, Doctor Billy Thompson reviewed his options. He couldn't figure out why he felt so overtaken. If his eyes deceived him not, that was his old best friend walking directly his way. Running out the back door failed to catch his attention as a reasonable option and was, therefore, immediately dismissed. He decided he would sit it out for another few seconds. Twenty seconds of courage was all he ever really needed to over-come any fear, and surely he had twenty seconds to offer her.

*Her.*

She hadn't seen him yet, so for a moment longer, he still had the proverbial upper hand.

*Whatever.*

He choked. Why would he need an upper hand?

Devyn Mitchell wasn't scary, mean, or evil. In fact, she was anything but. She was simply everything else.

175

Perhaps guilt explained the almost panic-like sensation in the back of his throat.

*Sure, why not?*

He was feeling pretty crappy about not telling her he was working so close to her hometown, but even then, he knew better.

In his photographic memory, he flipped to some page in an old neurochemistry book that had always perplexed him. In the physical body, as the nerve cells fired, the neuro-chemical reaction to fear appeared to be exactly the same as the neuro-chemical reaction to excitement. The difference, then, was only the perceived value of the provoking encounter or thought in the mind of the affected individual.

Excited. Maybe he was just excited. That sounded much more fun than afraid. Quickly, he assessed his pulse. It beat at well over a hundred.

*Also a sign of excitement.*

She grabbed the doorknob, and his stomach flipped. He was about to come face to face with his fear or, better yet, his excitement of seeing her for the first time in over six years.

"*You understand, Nanny? Tip-toe, tip-toe, tip-toe?*" The vision of Livie probed in Nanny Rose's mind.

"*Si, mi niña. Mi* remember, *mi* Livie," Rose said out loud.

On the verge of a full-system collapse, it no longer mattered to her if she was hallucinating or not. Delusions were pretty insignificant in the face of imminent death.

"*Good, Nanny goose-goose. Now close eyes. Ready, play. One, two, three. Ready you. Ready me. Tip-toe, tip-toe, tip-toe.*"

Nanny knew the rules. Tip-toe meant step forward. Green light meant turn right. Yellow light meant turn left. Red light meant stop.

She was ready to play, and without a doubt, she knew this was her last chance. All questions regarding Livie's intention fell away from her with a thud as they struck the concrete floor.

A sliver of hope entered Rose's mind for the first time.

Maybe she didn't have to die. Maybe, just maybe, she would see Livie's face again in the real world.

"*Mi niña, mi* Livie," Rose cried.

Oh how she meant it.

Oh how she was right.

Heather watched with amazement at Livie's intensity. Never had she seen the child play this way with her dolls. She was marching them up and down the stairs of her dollhouse, in and out, up and down, over and over again.

Heather offered a snack, but Livie refused. She was too busy to eat, she explained. There was no time for a snack. Heather left the sandwich on the doll table just in case. Ham and cheese with orange slices and lemonade was Livie's favorite lunch, but today, even a favorite would wait.

"Are you kidding me?"

Devyn squealed when she looked through the police investigator's office window.

"If that isn't BLT, I don't know a cow patty from a clump of dirt," she said with a twang mimicking her best version of a Texas drawl.

With a big fat grin from ear to ear, she turned the doorknob as quickly as her hand would move it.

Billy jumped up instantly and rushed to greet her. Arms out and open wide, his gesture welcomed her completely. The breakfast burrito stain and neurology books were long forgotten as they connected with the full-bodied hug of old pals reunited. All worries about who didn't call or should have this or that were lost in the absolute joy of their embrace.

She filled her nose with the scent of him and smiled. She had forgotten how good true friendship smelled.

No wonder she thought of him often. How could she not?

He felt like her favorite pair of comfy old socks. He tasted like Grandma's apple pie. He sounded like the crashing waves of the ocean tide calling her home.

*Oh, Billy, I missed you.*

She looked at him and smiled. Words failed her. Her hands shook. She rubbed them to make them stop.

He giggled and touched her cheek lightly.

She blinked, unable to otherwise respond.

*What happened to us? How did I lose you?*

She felt frozen, unable to move.

He moved for her, reached over, and embraced her again.

Finally, her words returned.

"Billy."

He laughed again and mimicked her. "Bug."

Then he sighed and smiled with his glittery eyes.

She touched his cheek.

"Well, in a million years..." Devyn said.

"No. Two million."

She laughed and hugged him once more.

Billy pulled back to get a good look at her.

"I never would have guessed you would come marching into my office today, Ladybug. I guess that's what Tootsie was all in a flurry about."

"What?"

Billy squinted his eyes and looked her up and down once more.

"Who's Tootsie?" Devyn asked, her cheeks turning slightly red.

"Never mind. I'll explain some other day. It doesn't matter right now. How the heck are you? Wow, you look like you swallowed a balloon. I had no idea you were pregnant again. The accident...the hospital...the coma. Oh my God, Bug, it is so good to see you. You look—"

"Yeah, yeah, I know. Let me guess—so womanly. Scary, eh?"

"Something like that."

"I even wear dresses these days. Can you believe it? Having little ones changes you. All for the better, I think."

"Yep. I'd agree."

"Don't tell anyone, Billy, but I think I like it. I spent my life trying to be like the boys so I could figure out all I really wanted to be was one of the girls. Life's funny like that."

"Bingo."

"Not you. Same jeans, same boots, same sweet face. You look exactly the same, just like I remember."

"I remember, too."

"Why are you here? Why didn't you tell me? I would have come to visit you sooner. I'm back and forth all the time. Well, I used to be at least. Anyway, for heaven's sake, we are old best buddies. I would have loved to know you were here, but why?" she asked.

She stopped herself, answering her own question.

"Oh my God. You are the outside guy they brought in."

"Yep, bingo again."

"I should have known. It's because of the Double H murders, which means you are exactly who I need to answer my questions."

"What questions, Ladybug?"

"About my Rose, sweet, sweet Rose. You are the guy who can tell me that it can't be related, that it just can't be, that Rose is fine, that she will be coming home," she said, each word more desperate than the last.

She collapsed into his arms and shuddered.

It felt so good, too good.

She couldn't resist and pulled him tighter welcoming the strong arms of the boy who always adored her just the way she was.

Only she never knew it, never saw it, never noticed.

He was the only one who always saw the truth of her and wanted her anyway, not in spite of but especially because of it, broken just right in all the best ways and perfect, too, in all the wrong ways.

She buried her head into him like she might explode from the situation, forgetting it was years since she saw him last, feeling like it was only yesterday that he held her like this.

Thankfully, like usual, he knew how to hold all the million layers of Devyn Mitchell together...rolled into one big mess of wonderfully fragile disaster.

Once her blubbering stopped, he raised her chin and stroked her cheek again.

"Okay, Ladybug? It's okay now, honey. I'm going to help you."

"I know."

"You were always my rock, so 'bout time I get the chance to settle my debt. Tell me what this is all about, and don't leave out a single detail. I want to know every little thing."

From behind Devyn's head, Tootsie appeared again. He winked and blew her a kiss. A sparkle of light, seen only by the amazed and confused Billy, traveled through the air and landed right on the top of her head. It stayed just a second longer before he and it both disappeared again.

Devyn looked up for a second trying to find the source of the air that seemed to blow her hair but couldn't. The smell of oranges invaded her nostrils and instantly was gone again.

Exhausted in the deepest part of her soul, she collapsed in the chair across from Billy and sighed. Then she started from the very beginning.

179

# FORTY-SIX

## A Child's Dream

HEATHER CHECKED ON LIVIE AGAIN. The sandwich was gone, and every orange slice was sucked dry to the core. Livie, fast asleep, still clutched the empty lemonade cup in one hand and her doll in the other. A proud grin pasted on her face, Livie clearly dreamed the hopeful dreams of the young.

Heather sighed with relief. She was no fool. She was well enough aware of the subtle realms that she took nothing for granted. A smiling, sleeping, content child meant more than most people realized. Children were not as blindly innocent as most people thought. They knew more, sensed more, and did more than most adults.

Heather scooped up Livie and put her in the bed. Then she gently pulled the covers up to Livie's collarbone and finished with a gentle kiss on the baby's forehead.

"Oh, my beloved Livie, may your dreams sing a song fit for the ears of a queen, for you are a queen, and I see you for what you are."

Brock and Mary discussed their day in the break room at the television station lounge, but Brock, distracted by tomorrow's meeting with his sister, kept losing his place in the conversation. To no avail, she tried to keep him engaged with taunting smiles and sultry gestures.

He wanted her physically. She knew that. The rumors around the station

180

weren't for nothing. Anyone could see, and almost smell, their passionate connection from across the room. They had insane chemistry; of that, she had no doubt.

If it wasn't for that stupid doctor lady of his, she would have nailed his ribbon to her wall. For goodness' sake, Victoria, that bizarre snooty sister of his, loved her. Although she felt weird taking advice from someone she hardly knew, every tip Victoria gave her seemed to work. It was creepy his sister would know how to work him so well, but what the hell. She would take any upper hand she was offered.

Mary flirted. "Brock, you look nice today. Love a man in pink, by the way. It's so sexy, you know, if he's man enough to pull it off, that is. We all know you can pull it off. Kind of yummy, don't you think?"

"Oh, yeah, well thanks, I think. What did you say? You like pink? Sorry, Mary, my brain is a little scattered today," Brock said.

"Tell me all the dirty details if you like. I'm all yours. I mean, I'm all ears."

"Na, just home stuff. Trying to sort out some plans. My mind is in a few thousand places at once."

"I have just the remedy."

"Like what?"

"A nice glass of wine and some slow music. We should go to the Cigar Bar after work. You can lay all your troubles in, I mean, on me," she said, twirling her hair with her finger.

She rocked her hips slightly. "Then, whatever, I'll be happy to drive so you don't have to worry about how much you drink. Oh, now that's scary—me playing the responsible designated driver. What are you doing to me, making me pretend to be such a good girl? I assure you I am not."

"Really, I should go back home to Devyn and Livie tonight. They are expecting me. At least, I think they are. Devyn never called today."

"Seems to me like you do all the work in your relationship. What's wrong with her? I think she must be nuts. If I were your woman, I would be calling you every ten minutes. I would be driving out here to meet you tonight. I think she's got you wrapped around that itty-bitty pinky of hers. I think, no, I know you deserve better. Come with me tonight. She can have you back tomorrow...if you still want her."

Mary laughed and disappeared into the bathroom.

A few minutes later, she stepped back out in half a dress with tattered edges.

"Come on, sexy. You're coming with me. I'm not taking no for an answer this time."

His reserve was too low to argue, so he followed her right out of the station into the big wide world of bother.

# FORTY-SEVEN

## A Blind Eye

ROSE ASSESSED THE SITUATION SLOWLY. Her mind ached to wander in the oblivion of death, but her heart wanted to fight.

Her pulse pounded rapidly, too rapidly, in her ears. Her legs felt much too weak to hold her weight. Fine. She would crawl if she had to. This was her only chance. She could sense that as certain as the sun rises in the east.

Most assuredly, she was right.

Her head pounded, her wrists were bruised from struggling against her bindings, and her body was on the verge of absolute collapse, but she would try, damn it. One last time, she would try. How could she not? Livie was counting on her. Ellie, well Ellie hadn't even met her yet. She may be old and alone, but she was not done for—not yet, not this Nanny Rose.

The picture of Livie flooded her mind's eye again. Swirling around Livie's outline, a brightness, almost like the color of perfect sunshine, warmed Rose from the inside as the child smiled the sweet smile of love. Then a terribly loud, almost unbearable buzzing sound assaulted her ears. It warned her to get ready. The game was on. Her timer had started.

Livie crossed her arms in front of herself at the wrists and then quickly and forcefully pulled them apart. Rose understood. She sat up and steadied herself.

*This is going to hurt,* she thought.

Livie nodded. "*Yes. Yes, it will.*"

Livie held up her fingers because the high-pitched buzzing made any sounds otherwise useless. She held up one finger, then another until she got to three. She nodded.

Rose understood. On the count of three, she was supposed to yank her wrists hard against their bindings and pray she survived the pain.

So it began. One, two, three, and she pulled. The fabric at the edge of the backside of the binding tore only slightly, but she recoiled in horrible pain. Blood dripped from her damaged skin.

The clock ticked louder. She didn't have much time before she passed out again.

*"Go again,"* Livie said with an angry face and another demonstration of her hands.

"So pain, *mi niña*, so bad," Rose said, doubting her own reserve now.

With the maddest face known to a three-year-old ever, Livie's image said, *"Get over it."*

"Okay, baby. Only for *mi* Livie," Rose said as the tears of pain poured down her face.

With the strength of children who lift cars off their fathers, Rose gave it her all. She tore the bindings just enough, and they fell to the floor.

Livie's fury turned to joy, and she opened her arms in delight for a moment. Then quickly, so quickly, she raised her fingers again.

*"Move fast, Nanny,"* she said, and Rose understood.

Rose, blinded by her diabetes, looked down at where her feet would be if she could see them and knew what came next. Livie nodded again.

She picked up one leg as if to explain that Rose needed to just get one out. One leg was enough. Rose understood.

The fingers went up: one, two, three, yank.

Some skin was left on the binding, but most of her leg was freed. Now, Nanny Rose understood the gift of her blindness. If she could see, the horror of this self-inflicted mutilation would have stopped her. Her terror would have frozen her right there and left her to bleed to death.

The pain sliced so intensely Rose knew she would have to turn it off or die, so she did. She imagined the dial of a radio in her brain and turned the volume down with her hand.

*Much better*, she thought. *Keep going.*

She knew there was no turning back now.

She was right again.

The hot metallic scent of blood disappeared. In its place, the smell of pizza teased Rose's nostrils. She laughed. She understood. Livie was distracting her from the present and willing her to the future.

"*Si, mi niña. Si, mi* Livie." Rose laughed at Livie's joke. Turnabout was fair play. Oh, the irony.

The idea of making pizza for her family again filled her with a sense of purpose. She was coming home one way or another, or she would die trying. She would not simply lie down and die, not today. She was ready to give everything she had left, and she was going to make her Livie proud. She would make pizza every night for the next twenty years if that was what her beautiful baby wanted. She was coming home, damn it. She was coming home.

And she was right.

The only question was how.

Billy listened intently while his Ladybug spilled her story. She started with the car accident and then moved on to her wild dreams and memories from the coma. She started to tell him about her visions of death, but something stopped her. Then she revealed how she could remember with shocking clarity every single detail of that time period except the actual accident itself. Her only memories of it were patched-together versions of someone else's description. Very carefully, she broached the unexplainable pregnancy and hinted that her connection to Ellie was stronger than other people would consider normal.

Billy was a shrink, after all, and would surely have an opinion about her new miraculous experiences. He would say something about brain trauma, she was sure, but these days, her mind worked differently.

Awake. Eyes opened. Finally.

She was not the same person. The world possessed a new mystical quality for her. In that moment, she realized she now believed in a whole new world, a world where miracles happened and the unexplained things were just that—unexplained and wonderful and full of possibilities for her.

Undeniably, truth simply became true. The easiest thing ever learned had somehow become the most difficult to accept—but not for her, not anymore. The same illusions of the insane, that were hardest to see with a sleeping mind, fell away from her.

How had this world come to be a place like this? What happened to cause this? Why would a loving God allow it to remain that way? He hadn't, she remembered—not for her, not anymore, and not ever again.

Awake. Eyes opened. Finally.

She wiped the crust of sleep from her eyes and beheld the beauty of a hint of her true reality. She yawned the yawn of the refreshed dreamer now waking from her own mad nightmare.

If only she had the guts to tell Billy everything. Would he still care for her, or would he call her crazy and dismiss her experiences as silly? Would she also lose his trust after finding him again?

184

Her mind reeled with what ifs, but she couldn't stop. She had to tell him more, had to share it all...except the parts about Ellie, that was.

She told Billy about the intruder, about the alarm, about the stairs.

Her confession reminded her that she hadn't even told Brock about it yet. He never showed up, so she never told him. How could they have not had that conversation of all conversations?

What did that mean?

How could she marry a man she didn't even talk to, didn't find support in, didn't find safety in, or security, or trust? A man who didn't even know her way of looking at life now? A man who knew nothing about Ellie, and the visions, and the smells, and the...

She stopped herself there. Her painful disconnection from Brock was too much to face.

She forced her thoughts back to Billy and their conversation. She sounded like a madwoman, and she knew it. She kept talking in circles, not getting where she wanted fast enough. Yet still he listened, like always. He offered no reply, but instead, his silent reflection was witness to her ravings.

When she finally stopped talking, somewhat unsure of what she had and what she hadn't said, she took a deep breath and laughed nervously.

He said, "Honey, I hear you."

She took a deep breath and sighed.

"Life has been really big for you. So much trauma."

She shook her head.

He squinted his left eye like only he knew how and smiled. "I think this place isn't good enough for this. Let's grab some dinner and catch up—the easy stuff, you know. I'll tell you the latest stories about my crazy cow-pigs and my new favorite boots."

"Perfect. That sounds perfect."

"You can tell me all about Olivia, right?"

"Yes, Olivia's her name," Devyn said. "We call her Livie at her own request, though, and that sounds lovely."

"Good."

"Oh, BLT, I have so much to say. Around here, I don't have anybody like you. I mean, I have Heather, but there are some things we can't talk about."

"Heather?"

"My best friend. She is also my dad's much younger widow. I guess she's my step-mom, which is weird, even though she tries really hard to be my best friend. It's just not the same as it always was with you."

"That does sound a little weird."

"Six years without you is too long. I have too much to say."

She threatened to spew again. Her lip quivered.

He reached up and touched her cheek again. The lip stopped.

He gave her his eye squint again. Then he reached over and hugged her slow and soft yet tight and intensely at the same time. She smelled oranges again and relaxed, comforted by the strength and security in him. She slowed her racing thoughts and opened to his support.

She suddenly remembered the real reason she came here in the first place.

"The real reason I'm here, Billy, is Rose, my Rose, our Rose, my nanny named Rose. She disappeared two days ago. She's gone, and I have to know that her disappearance can't be related to the intruder or the Double H murders. Tell me it's just a coincidence and that she will be all right."

He pressed a button on his phone and said, "Listen, I need a missing persons report. I need to take a copy of my case files home for the night."

"Thanks," was the best response she could muster.

"I'm coming home with you. We'll stop to pick up Olivia, I mean Livie, and get some dinner. Then we can get to work. After Livie's asleep, we can get all this sorted. I want you safe with me tonight until I can figure out what all this means. I have a gut feeling about this, Bug, and I don't like it, not one bit. Even if they are not related, you had a home invasion, and now someone from that same home is missing. You might be in serious danger. Livie, too. Do you understand?"

He grabbed his gun and quickly strapped it to his belt. Then he reached down for his travel bag and slung it over his shoulder. With his right hand, he grabbed hers. He looked her in the eyes and nodded as if to say she was safe now.

For the moment, he was right.

As they left the office, Tootsie the Great appeared for one last flight about the room. He winked and waved at Billy as the two old best friends walked down the hall. Tootsie had done well, and that was a good thing, a very, very good thing.

Heather checked on Livie once more. The beautiful child slept soundly. She tried to wake her to no avail, so she blew her a kiss and closed the door softly. She prayed that Livie's deep sleep would serve whatever purpose was required and then went back downstairs.

With the baby monitor on, she could effectively be there without being there. She would come running at the first sound of trouble. Just in case, she came back with another glass of water to place on Livie's table. Then she left again, sure she had done the right thing by letting the baby sleep. Hopefully, Devyn would agree. Livie needed her sleep. The princess must have her sleep.

As usual with Heather, her intuition was right.

In the back booth at the bar in Tampa, Mary teased and flirted like the expert femme fatale she was. Drink after drink, she fed Brock the love potion of uninhibited liquid confusion. One drink led to the next.

She told him how important he was, how adored he was, how irresistible she found the power in him, stroking his ego until it swelled so firmly he lost his better self to it.

She even offered to pretend she was someone else if he wanted, anyone else, even Devyn, like that was the final argument he needed to want her in return. Then she swore herself to secrecy.

Pretending to cry, she confessed her terrible loneliness and longing need to feel the touch of a man, a real man like him.

Her real fangs came out ever so indirectly at first and then more forcibly. She reminded him of how much Devyn didn't seem to need or want him, not like she did, not even close.

Victoria had, of course, suggested she use this last little helpful detail if ever in need of turning his attention. Brock's cheeks burned red with fury. His brow furrowed from the sting of her words, her words that affirmed his greatest fear and weakness.

Somewhere deep down in his wounded core, he had always feared he was unworthy of Devyn. If the mother of his children didn't want him, it would be the final proof of his uselessness.

Oh how perfectly the devious plan worked. The camel's back broke, and he fell. He fell right into the evil trap set to capture his injured ego that fractured into a billion glass fragments on the icy-cold marble dance floor.

Completely and totally without apology, Brock and Mary left the company of unconcerned strangers. Straight to his cave of idols, she took him. In her lair, she did what women do when they want a ribbon of guilt to pin to their wall of shame. He made a handsome ribbon, shining proudly on a wall stained the hideous colors of illusion and fear. The paint, dark and dirty, covered the wood that made another unlivable house built on a foundation of sin.

# FORTY-EIGHT

## Fried Okra

WITHOUT LOOKING BACK, Devyn climbed into Billy's rental car. For some reason, it seemed to be the safest choice. She strapped her seatbelt low and tight under her pregnant bump. Her thoughts strayed to Ellie for a moment.

Ellie immediately responded with, "*All is well. Do not fret. We both know I am just fine. How could I not be? We are exactly in the right place doing exactly the right things. You also know this to be true, yes?*"

"*Yes.*" Devyn did know that was true and nodded her head in agreement.

"You okay, kiddo?" Billy asked after noticing her gesture.

"I'm fine. Better than fine, actually."

She reached across to grab his hand, took in the beautiful smell of oranges, and then gave herself over to whatever was about to happen. It was big. She knew it.

She was right.

Out of nowhere, a craving for fried okra overtook her. She had to have it and now, right now. Finally, she understood the wild and urgent cravings of a pregnant woman. This was her first such experience. Ellie's demand was big, and it would not be denied.

"Billy, I need fried okra, and I need it now," she said.

"What?"

"Can we stop at a Down-Home-Kookin restaurant? There is one on the left-hand side, a half mile beyond the Tampa Bay Bridge."

"Sounds good."

"I will call Heather and tell her and Livie we will bring their dinner home. I

188

can't make it all the way back. Ellie demands I eat okra now. Sorry, pregnant-lady madness, I guess."

She laughed at the absurdity of her request.

"Sure, Ladybug. Anything the baby wants, the baby gets. If she's anything like her mother, she's already running the show," Billy said with a grin.

Ellie kicked hard in agreement. Yes, she would get exactly what she wanted. Billy was right. He was going to help her do just that.

On the slippery floor, Rose assumed a crawling position. Her legs wobbled horribly and would not support her weight. The hot wetness continued to drip down her leg. She was bleeding badly. There was not much time left. With eyes closed, she searched only for the glowing outline of Livie in her mind.

Livie smiled, encouraging her in the best way she could, with absolute love. Her fingers went up.

*"One, two, three."*

Nanny Rose knew the words that came next: "Ready you, ready me. "

Livie mimicked a tip-toe motion. Rose knew to crawl forward. Each slow movement forward hurt in a way Rose could hardly bear, so she kept turning the volume down on her pain. She refused to listen to the pain. Only Livie's unwavering image held her attention.

It was ironic, wasn't it? Today, Rose's last chance for salvation was held so perfectly safe in the hands of the image of the child whom she had always protected. Livie, once the child, had become the protective mother.

How many times had Nanny Rose saved Livie from danger? Now, every fall caught, every bite of food extracted from the choking infant's throat repaid the favor a million times. Every knife, pair of scissors, electrical outlet, or other household danger came full circle and tenderly patted Rose on the shoulder.

Tip-toe, tip-toe, forward she went. When a green hue exuded from Livie's outline, Rose veered to the right. With yellow, she moved to the left. Livie's image guided Rose out of her prison chamber and down a long, dark hall to a chance for another life.

Of course, Rose retained no memory of this. She would never be able to explain how she got out a locked door and away from the monster that held her captive. She would never know how many dangers she avoided, how many near misses she circumvented.

Those details were just that—details, matters of no importance, illusions of nothing at all. Out was all that mattered; out was all that could matter.

They finally reached a juncture where Rose had no choice but to stand. Her ultimate redemption required shattering and then climbing through a large glass door that blocked her safe exit.

She had come so far. Surely, this could not stop her now.

Livie guided Rose to stand and then demonstrated smashing the door with a chair. Nanny Rose leaned up against the chair in front of her, but she could hardly hold her own weight. How could she possibly pick up and throw the chair?

The child's furious face appeared again. She flailed her arms. She screamed a wicked temper tantrum. The sound no mother could bear screeched like fingernails down the chalkboard of Rose's soul.

To stop the gut-wrenching torture, Rose gathered herself together once more. With great effort, she stood and slammed the chair against the glass door. It remained unaffected. Rose crumbled in defeat and pain to the floor. Her head swam with dizziness. Her hands shook. Her eyes struggled to stay open, battling to remain conscious in so much pain. She had come so far. Had she met her final match? Was this the end?

"*No más, mi niña. No más!*" Rose wailed.

She mouthed the words, demanding no more, and Livie understood—but Livie did not listen. She refused to be denied. This would not be the end of this story, not if she still had a say, not like this, not when they were so close.

"Get up," she said.

Then Livie started jumping up and down with outrage.

While Livie flailed, Victoria twirled round and round in her oversized leather chair. She pulled out the picture of Devyn and Brock she kept hidden in the top drawer. With a pair of scissors, she carefully and tenderly cut out his image. Then with a kiss, she returned it to its assigned place in the right compartment of the suede-lined drawer.

Scowling, she sized up the rest of the photo. An idea crossed her mind. She took out a paper clip and untwisted it, and then she gouged out Devyn's eyes. First the right and then the left, she mutilated them. Vicious laughter erupted while she inspected the fruits of her labor. The holes were small, but they brought her great satisfaction. She held up the picture to the ceiling to further inspect her work.

190

A cloud passed overhead, and a penetrating ray of sunlight entered the skylight above the desk. At that same moment, the light flashed brilliantly through the holes that had replaced Devyn's almost-sad brown eyes.

Victoria screamed.

She threw the photo on the ground and ran the hell out of her office.

Heart pounding, she reached the safety of her car intact. She reminded herself of her power. She reminded herself there were no gods except people like her. Then she relaxed into her self-made illusion of safety.

She felt better and decided she had imagined the whole thing.

Most assuredly, she was wrong.

The phone rang. Heather rushed to catch it before it woke Livie.

"Yes. Devyn, is it you?"

"Of course. Tell me everyone's all right, Heather. I have found the help we need, or should I say it found me? How's my Livie?"

"Fine, of course, but she went down for her nap late and then stayed asleep longer than usual. I'm letting her sleep now."

"All right."

"If she wakes up in the middle of the night, I will gladly get up with her, that's if you still want me to stay again tonight. I didn't have the heart to disturb her rest. It seemed like she really needed it. I hope that's fine?" Heather asked, hopeful she hadn't overstepped her boundaries.

"Are you kidding me?" Devyn asked. "I trust you completely."

Heather took a deep breath.

"If you think she needs sleep, then she does. I won't lie, though. I am a little bummed she won't get to meet Billy tonight. I'm here with Billy Thompson, my old best buddy from medical school. He's the forensics expert on the Double H murder case, and he's going to help me make sure Nanny Rose gets home safely," Devyn said.

"I've heard you talk about him before. The guy with the pigs, or was it cows?" Heather asked.

"Exactly. I have to have some okra, so we are stopping at the Down-Home-Kookin restaurant on the other side of the bridge. We are pulling up right now."

"What? Okra? That's hilarious. Tell Ellie I think she has a great sense of humor. You hate okra. Let me remember your exact words: green, slimy, vegetable abomination from hell. Yes, I remember." Heather laughed.

"Okay, missy, button it. Yes, that sounds like something I would say about okra, but I need some right now. Somehow, I will get this unborn baby back one day for making me eat my own words." She laughed. "Can I bring you anything back?"

"Yes, I love their biscuits, and I'd like one of those old-fashioned candy bars. That would be nice, too. Thanks. Take your time. I'm loving helping you and loving knowing that if Livie calls out, I will get to rush to answer her."

"Thank you, Heather."

"You're welcome."

"That really helps. You are right to let her sleep. I don't know why, but somehow I have a hunch that it's important. Billy and I can take our time eating mountain after mountain of disgusting, yet shockingly enticing, slimy-green okra. Anything for my Ellie, anything, just like my Livie. For you, biscuits and candy it is. I won't tell your crazy vegan friends, I promise."

Ellie immediately popped into Devyn's awareness. She smelled lavender and then expected the familiar yet still somewhat surprising thoughts that would follow.

*"So, Mommy, I guess a vegetarian diet is off the options list for us?"*

Devyn smiled knowing full well Ellie heard her thoughts loud and clear. She took a deep breath and sank into herself.

How unbelievable that she sat here now, next to her old best friend, and listened to the voice of her unborn child. How much life changed and how quickly she adjusted.

*"Human beings are pretty amazing at adapting."*

Ellie said, *"Yes, exactly and perfectly. That is why they are so adored."*

As always, she was right.

# FORTY-NINE

## How to Save a Life

THEY PULLED into the parking lot, thrilled to see the closest spot open.

"Ha," Devyn said, "Ellie must have called ahead for the best parking spot. Let me guess. We will get right in, sit at the best table, and have the most wonderful server."

"Okay, alien. What did you do with my best friend, Ladybug? Known previously to the rest of us humans as Doctor Devyn Mitchell: eternal pessimist and sarcastic tomboy. Who is this happy, positive, dress-wearing impostor?"

"Funny, Mister Stay-in-Tampa-for-how-long-without-calling-me."

Silence.

She immediately corrected her attack. "I don't mean that, not even for a breath of a moment."

"You're right, Ladybug. I should have called." He shook his head side to side and frowned.

She reached over and touched his arm.

He relaxed, but only slightly. "I didn't want to bring you into this mess. Honestly, that's the only reason."

She rubbed his arm softly and her shoulders softened to match his.

"I wish you knew how many times I had to slap my own hand while it tried to pick up the phone to call you." He laughed, slapped his own hand and said, "Stop it."

She grinned. "My Billy. It so good–"

He shook his head again and swallowed. "I know…it's good to see you like it always, always has been. Think it probably always will be."

193

Devyn slapped his hand next. "Don't stop it, you mean."

He sighed and relaxed even more.

Reaching down and patting her bump she said, "Come on, Ellie. Lead us right into okra heaven."

They walked up to the hostess who already had two menus in her hand.

The hostess smiled like an old friend and said, "Doctor Mitchell, I would know you anywhere. You probably don't remember me, but I remember you. Debbie Talten," she said with a deep Georgia accent. "You delivered my baby two years ago. I was very different then. I did some stuff I am not proud of, but I will never forget what you said to me."

Devyn didn't interrupt. She just nodded and listened.

The hostess continued. "You said that sometimes the first step to getting found is getting completely lost. You told me you had faith I'd do the right thing by my baby. Well, I did. I got out of a bad situation, got myself sober, and got a real job. I've wanted to call and thank you a thousand times. I find out next week if I get my baby back. They took him to foster care 'cause of the drugs. I've been clean ever since, all mostly 'cause of you and NA. Thank you."

"You're welcome, my dear."

"So here we go. I'm gonna get you the best table and the best server in the whole stinking place. Dinner's on me. I won't take no for an answer. I pretty much owe you my life. That simple. Got it? I don't want a word in return. Not a one." She walked them to the back corner of the restaurant.

Devyn gently took Debbie's hand and said, "Good job, Mama. You get that baby and make him proud of you."

They embraced, and Debbie went back to the business of deciding who sat where.

"Nice to know we can still make a difference, ain't it?" Billy said with a full southern drawl.

Devyn noticed how the southern in Debbie urged forth the southern in Billy. It was almost like he hid that side of himself until someone gave him permission to share it and connect with that part of who he was.

She recalled her best memories of him and decided unequivocally that the southern small-town version of Billy was her favorite. It felt like the truest, most authentic version of him.

About that, she was definitely right.

As they snuggled into their seats, she asked him to tell her the latest news about Millie and Minnie, his two orphaned pigs.

After they ordered their dinner and an extra serving of okra and biscuits to go, he filled her in on the latest news. Not surprisingly, Flossie, the mother cow, was as stubborn as usual. She could hear just fine but would still pretend she was deaf, even with him, who knew better.

Lately, the local university sent some students over to study the unusual family. Interestingly enough, the idea of cross-parenting seemed like an avenue worthy of research, and several hard-working agricultural students spent countless hours gathering data on the triad for their thesis papers about the subject. Billy laughed out loud at the idea of saving all the future pigs, which settled him right back into the place of exactly who he was.

The smell of oranges filled Devyn's awareness again, and she finally made the connection. The smell of orange with a hint of mint was the perfect scent of Billy's truest, most authentic self.

"Do you like orange juice?" she asked.

He squinted and laughed at her odd question. "No, weird preggers version of my old pal. Actually, I don't, but I do love the way oranges smell. I've never told you this, but my mother always smelled like oranges. She grew up near an orange grove, so the smell made her feel like home: orange soap, orange candles, orange incense, oranges everywhere."

He stared off in the distance and grinned. *Mom, where are you?*

*"Right here, my son. I'm always right here, Billy."*

Devyn sighed softly and took another full breath as the smell of oranges intensified and then disappeared.

"Lovely."

"So, when I smell them, I think of Mom. She was a neat lady, straight talking, and she made the best chicken pot pie our side of the Mason-Dixon Line. Y'all woulda loved each other."

"I bet. I love chicken pot pie."

"Talking about Mom always brings out the cowboy in me. Anyway, back to your Rose. Tell me exactly what happened," Billy said with his clinical voice, all Texan notably absent from his words.

# FIFTY

## Screwed Up

BROCK'S HEAD POUNDED. His brain hurt. His neurons misfired. He refused to awaken. He didn't want to know what he had done.

For a few minutes longer, he restlessly slept to prolong the inevitable storm bound to follow his failure. His river of disappointment swelled and threatened to break a dam within him. A flood was eminent, he knew.

This time, he was right.

Devyn told Billy everything. She explained that Rose went to visit her sister, Sylvia, on Friday for her weekend off this month as usual. Rose's sister took her back to the bus station on Sunday morning, also as usual. Sylvia didn't actually see her get on the bus, and that's the most she knew for sure. Billy asked Devyn if she had called the obvious places like hospitals.

He wrote down everything she said and then left to make some calls.

While he was away, Devyn recalled Rose's diabetes. By now, without her insulin, she was critically ill. Devyn acknowledged for the first time that even if they found her now, it might not matter.

Billy returned and sat down. He took off his gun and set it in his lap.

"Good. That's a start. I have an officer on his way to the bus station and to visit all the local hospitals. I don't want to panic you too much, but I am very worried."

Silence.

"Not just for Rose's sake."

Devyn frowned.

"You and Livie are in very real danger. We could be dealing with a serious criminal here, maybe even the Homeless Hunter."

"No."

"Yes."

Devyn looked over her shoulder and clenched her teeth.

"Until we know more, there will be a plainclothes officer watching your house. Headquarters sent out a black-and-white already. He's almost there as we speak. You need to call and warn Heather. Let's get home and make sure your Livie is safe."

They left a large tip for their server and waved at Debbie as they walked to the door. They almost forgot Heather's candy but remembered at the last second. When Billy ran to pay, Devyn looked around the country store to distract herself from what he just said.

She walked over to the quilts and stared. For some reason, every time she saw them, she froze in her tracks. Like some kind of ornate shroud, they flooded her with ideas of death.

After they left, she shared with Billy her visions of dying wrapped in one of those quilts.

"Not gonna shrink that one. Okra and quilt-patterned shrouds. You are one funny lady these days."

He helped her into the passenger seat and watched her buckle in before he returned to his seat. He started the car, but before he backed out of the parking lot, he looked her square in the eyes.

"When I get his permission, we will get a cop trailing your fiancé as well."

She clenched her teeth again.

"I will let you choose. You can call him first, or I will. Let me be perfectly clear here. He will be informed of every detail. Do you understand what I am saying?"

She nodded her head in agreement but didn't say a word.

The various scenarios filled her imagination. Every option ended the same—with Brock furious and their tenuous relationship in even deeper trouble.

Billy continued with his interrogation while he drove the thirty minutes back to Devyn's house.

"Tell me more about your new security system and who has the codes or passwords. Your fiancé, where exactly does he live? What has he said about all this?"

Her cheeks flashed hot. She knew where this conversation was headed.

"He lives mostly on the outskirts of Tampa. Basically, he lives at the TV station where he works."

"Okay."

197

"He usually stays at his family's beach house near Clearwater when he's not working. When he's not there, he is with us in Holosni. He doesn't know about Rose. He doesn't know."

She stared out the window, hoping it would slow the dizziness that plagued her while the gravity of her foolish actions took hold. For a second, she thought her teeth might shatter from the pressure in her jaw.

"What? Are you kidding me?"

"Nope."

"How could you isolate yourself...and Livie, totally unprotected, exposed and vulnerable to this kind of danger? What were you thinking? You should have told him. That's not fair to him or Rose or Livie."

"I know you're right."

She rubbed her cheeks, hoping to save her teeth.

Her shoulders slumped further while she beat herself harder and harder with a wet noodle from a large bowl of guilt.

Not telling Sylvia had been selfish, done to avoid feeling lousy. Not telling Brock was stupid, plain stupid, and dangerous.

She imagined the cuts along the side of her tongue from the fragments of teeth exploding in her mouth.

What had she been thinking?

She didn't have a good reason for withholding the truth from Brock. Her motivations eluded her.

It was almost like she wanted to keep this problem for herself. Maybe she was determined to fix it all alone like that would win her some prize of value. But why? For what prize? Martyrdom? What? That was ridiculous.

Was she weak if she asked for his help, or was her fear of intimacy spreading like a virus, infecting him with her deception?

Or maybe something even worse than that.

Did she withhold the information to subconsciously sabotage the relationship by setting him up to fail her and Livie? Asking her mate for help was normal. She knew that in her conscious brain, but the relationship wires in her lower brain were horrifically crossed.

She wanted to be a good partner. She wanted to share her ups and downs with someone completely—at least she thought she did.

Or did she?

Maybe this proved what a failure at love and trust she was. Maybe she didn't deserve a loving partner.

Then it hit her. It smacked her hard in the face. Her lips stung from its slap. *I am not afraid of relationships or marriage. I am afraid of my own failure at them.*

She had declared herself unworthy of love and true companionship. She served as defendant, attorney, judge, and jury all rolled into one big mess. She had always convinced herself her fear of commitment was about the man, but in truth, it had always been about herself.

*Slam!* The gavel fell. The sentence cried out. She had been so busy projecting her worthlessness onto others that she blinded herself from her own self-made distortion.

Immediately, her throat tightened. She tried to catch her breath, but it escaped her.

How was she going to marry Brock with her self-judgment hanging over their heads? What lousy and inadequate explanation would she attempt to use for this move? A catch in her throat warned that tears threatened to flow. Guilt hovered overhead like a black rain cloud.

*Man, I suck at guilt.*

She tried desperately to pull herself together.

"We will drop that for now. Moving on—about that anyway. I tried to get the Holosni Police Department to send the intruder incident report you filed to my smartphone, but they can't seem to locate it. I must have the dates all mixed up. When exactly was that night again so I understand the timeframe a little better?" he asked.

She closed her eyes and begged to be anywhere else. In her mind, she placed her head over the dull bottom board of a guillotine. She tensed her muscles, ready for the sharp upper blade to fall.

*Brace yourself, girl.*

"That happened, what, Friday? The same night Rose left for her sister's? I need to get my hands on the report so we can see what leads they have, see what the fingerprints looked like and—"

In a final moment of self-torture, she got the courage to face him and stopped his questions with just one look. She shook her head right to left in shame and then looked down at the floor mat.

Tears threatened to flow from her burning eyes. She denied them. She wasn't worthy of them.

She felt guilty, rotten, useless, worthless.

Looking back at Billy with that sweetness in his big brown eyes still searching to find the goodness in her only made it worse, much worse.

Why should he make her feel bad?

What did he have to do with this?

Brock, sure. Rose, of course. Maybe even Livie. But him? Why did she feel like she had failed Billy?

199

She flashed back to the day she left him all those years ago. She adored him too much to love him even back then. Didn't he understand? Couldn't he see why she left him? It wasn't because he wasn't good enough for her—just the opposite.

She had given him some lousy excuse…about closets and space, some stupid reason they joked about for years after. Really it was because she wasn't good enough, not for those tight jeans and big sweet brown eyes of his always seeing the best in her…even back then. She never deserved him, never could have deserved him.

Her brain, unable to handle her own cruel punishment any longer, scoured the surroundings for a distraction. She thought about floor mats in cars and wondered who invented them. She thought about car doors and seat belts. She thought about surrounding herself in a beautiful quilt and welcoming death. She thought about eating candy until she exploded. She thought about the white tablecloths at the restaurant they just left and wondered why they would have such nice ones in such a mid-priced restaurant.

Then she flashed to a memory of helping her mother set the table for dinner—the last time.

Her memories of her mother were rare and mostly from around the time of her death, just a piece here and there: a flash, a color, a dress, a smile, a song, a game of Ring Around the Rosie.

She recalled her mom talking to herself more and more just before the end, but not much more than that, almost like she was talking to somebody inside her—someone like Ellie.

*Oh my God,* she thought. *What if I'm really just crazy?*

*"Ellie, Ellie, are you even real?"*

Then she flashed to the day her mom forgot to dress her properly for school. It wasn't long after that day. That was near the very end. Her mom died about a week later when Devyn was only five.

Died was one way of putting it. The other more accurate way of putting it was killed herself—drove herself right over a cliff, to be exact.

Everyone assumed Devyn believed the preposterous story of a slippery road during a rainstorm that supposedly caused the fatal accident, but she knew better. She had seen the freaking letter, read every goddamn word. Never had she told a soul she knew the truth. Never had she confronted her father with his lies. Never. And she wasn't going to start today.

Damn shrinks. She cursed Billy, knowing even then she was displacing her anger to survive the pain of her mother's memory—and her guilt, the terrible guilt.

*What does this crap have to do with Mom anyway? Why does Billy make me feel so guilty? Why is he bringing all this out?*

She tried to hide the answer but couldn't.

No one ever really could hide things from themselves completely. One might cut off one's awareness, deny it, and look the other way, but it was still really there, wasn't it?

Deep down, she still feared she was going crazy.

*Maybe all this is just crazy me. No magical baby thoughts, just crazy, stupid Devyn—like Mom.*

These idiotic things she had done proved she was crazy, didn't they?

*"I'm just like you, Mom. Nuts. Mad. Insane."*

She sighed, trying so hard not to cry.

*Billy, if I had only known then what I know now. I would have chosen differently. I would have. I swear it.*

*Thud*! Heather heard the crash from Livie's room.

She ran upstairs to check. The blanket and all the dolls were scattered about the floor. It looked like Livie had flailed her arms in the bed and sent them flying in anger.

*Of course, that is ridiculous*, she thought.

This time, she was wrong.

Billy waved his hand in front of Devyn's face, and she hesitantly returned to the present. She should have called the police. She knew that now. At the time, it all seemed so disconnected from her. It all appeared so totally, unbelievably, and ridiculously stupid in this moment.

She never really thought she was in danger. She started to blame it on Ellie and then stopped herself.

Who was she kidding? That was bullshit, and she knew it. Now she had placed Livie and Ellie in real danger in the name of what? Pride, strength, stupidity? Who the hell was she kidding?

When she finally got the courage to look Billy in the face again, she saw a mountain of disappointment, fear, concern, anger, and shock all rolled into one expression of bewilderment. He breathed slowly in and out. He was calming himself down. Any three-year-old could tell that.

"Devyn."

In the twelve long and crazy years he had known her, that was one of the only times he had ever called her by her real first name. Sometimes she wondered if he even remembered it. He did, and he had saved it for effect on a day like none other. Today was that day.

They pulled up to her neighborhood in total silence: screaming, shrieking, horrid, deafening silence, every word unspoken heard louder than the last. Every single damning, destructive reprimand made of silence burned like the fire of hell in her ears and in her brain, but most painfully of all, in her heart.

*"Mommy, Mommy, Mommy."*

Ellie flashed thoughts and surrounded her mother in the smell of lavender, but Devyn was too busy beating herself with that damn wet noodle. Finally, she kicked and kicked hard. Over and over she kicked until Devyn shifted to the side.

Billy noticed the movement and asked if she was all right. That made Devyn pause, and she put her hand on her belly.

*"Ellie, you okay, little one?"*

*"Yes, better now. Mommy, please listen. Tell him you need to rest for a minute."*

"Billy," Devyn said, "can you pull over for a second? There's a convenience store on the corner. Can you run in and get me water? I'm very thirsty. Please."

Billy agreed and went into the st0re, totally unaware of Devyn's true intention. While he was away, she closed her eyes and sank into the center of herself. She slowed her breathing until the swirling colors filled her mind's eye and Ellie's voice came forth.

*"Very good, Mommy. Thank you. We need to talk. I wasn't ready to share this so soon, but now I know I must, which means you must be ready."*

"Baby, I'm all ears. Tell me what you would have me know," she said out loud.

*"You must drop the guilt, Mommy. Guilt is but a disguised version of fear. When you are afraid, you cannot hear me. I am still here, but you are lost, our connection interrupted until you return to the peace of yourself."*

*"I don't understand. Shouldn't I feel guilty when I have done something wrong? When I failed others by my ignorance or wrong doing?"*

*"I understand your insane way of thinking tells you this is so, but you are perfect in truth, and there is no such thing as wrong or right. If there is no such thing as wrong or right, how can you, whose function is not to judge, judge yourself as wrong? You cannot judge, and you cannot be wrong. In thinking you can, you have attacked yourself. Your attack is a desperate attempt to punish yourself so that God, whom you really fear, will not punish you instead. See, Mommy, you are trying to usurp God by beating yourself up. Of all the things you can do, the self-afflictions of guilt, self-attack, and self-punishment are the most insane and most blasphemous. It proves you have sinned, deserving punishment by death. God doesn't want to punish you, so why would you want to punish yourself? In doing so, you commit true blasphemy. There is no value in it but only attack, attack upon*

*you, me, and love itself. So please stop. When you act with such insanity and investment in fear, you paralyze us all."*

"I have done wrong. I have foolishly endangered Livie, myself, and probably killed poor Nanny Rose."

*"Forgive yourself. Remember, that is the key to happiness—forgiveness of self. You are your most harsh critic. From this side of things, there was never anything to forgive. When you forgive, you offer an opportunity to correct an error that was made. Errors can be corrected, but sins can only be punished with death to wipe them clean."*

Quivering with shame, she looked into the rearview mirror. She took a breath and tried to accept what Ellie said. She didn't and couldn't yet understand, but she would try. She knew deep within her that she needed Ellie right now more than ever.

She was absolutely right.

If release of her own guilt supported her connection to Ellie, she would do it—if not for herself, for her children because there stood no mountain tall enough that she wouldn't climb for her babies. That included her self-absorbed, man-made peak of doubt and guilt.

After the guilt passed from her mind, she relaxed and felt better. The cramp in her left shoulder lessened. Her jaw softened. Her breathing slowed. Her heart rate returned to normal.

*"Much better, Mommy. You can hear me again. You need me. Livie needs me. Rose needs me, too. I love you, Mommy. No matter what, please remember. Like the sun loves the earth...I love you forever in every time, space, and dimension, to the ends of the universe and back, through all known and unknown, forever and always. Always."*

She, too, was absolutely right.

# FIFTY-ONE

## Déjà Vu

BROCK AWOKE with an urgent need to void. He laughed a little at the idea of wetting himself and rushed to the bathroom. His foot slipped while he ran down the hallway, reminding him to slow down.

Head pounding, he thought he better get some water. Surely he had one glass of wine too many. He looked for his watch, but it was not on his left wrist as usual.

All of a sudden, his prior dream swirled back around him. He closed his eyes, sat down on the toilet, and let the dream swallow him. He could not resist. It demanded his attention.

He had dreamed this dream before. In front of him stood a wall of grey material that melted under his hand when he touched it—no, not melted, molded.

Panic filled his heart. Again, he was trapped deep in the center of the monstrous labyrinthine structure. Surrounded on every side by wall after wall of this white-grey nastiness, he tried furiously to change his viewpoint but couldn't. He flailed uselessly, unable to escape.

The smell of putrid acid burned his nasal membranes. The fullness of the imagery enveloped him. These walls exuded some toxic substance that poisoned the very air he breathed. Even though partially awake, he could not escape the fear that his lungs were melting, not molding.

Then the whirling sound of destructive winds reminded him what had woken him up in the first place. It wasn't the noise of the storm in his dream that stole him from peaceful slumber but its shocking absence.

After emptying himself, he walked slowly back to the bedroom.

The dream, already mostly forgotten now, slipped quietly away. The only evidence that remained of it was a disgusting taste in the back of his throat.

How had he gotten home from the bar? He remembered going, but leaving? That he couldn't remember. Then he saw Mary's shoe in the corner, and every terrible detail came back.

Back in Holosni, Heather checked on Livie one more time. When she looked into the butterfly and princess room, she smiled. This was a chamber suited for a juvenile queen.

She recalled the day Devyn picked the olive-green color for the walls. Heather laughed. Was she kidding? Green? They all attacked her.

Devyn stood her ground. Green walls, a green and purple rug, and hand-sewn curtains that matched a bedspread covered in adorable butterflies were the decor. Each wall bore a different message, a different theme. There was the fairy wall, the dragonfly wall, and the princess wall. Interspersed were priceless photos of Livie at every memorable stage of her development.

Unbearably inadequate, the couch just wasn't good enough anymore.

Heather climbed into bed with Livie. Oblivious to the world around her, the child never moved. She kissed Livie on the cheek and wished her sweet dreams. As she drifted off to sleep herself, Heather said a prayer.

"Heavenly spirit, guides, and angels, protect us while we sleep. Direct our dreams to wonderful places that you would have us see. If Livie needs me, in any realm or dimension, I am hers. I give her all my love and joy. We are thankful for your guidance."

Heather wasn't sure if it was her imagination or not, but she heard the softest most subtle breath of, "Welcome."

A faint breeze crossed her forehead. Livie squeezed her hand lightly.

While the fog of sleep surrounded her, Heather welcomed the reprieve of the world inside her mind. The sound of ocean waves played faintly in the background. A dolphin friend came up to greet her and welcomed her into the world of waters below. She replied with gratitude that tonight's dreams were not for playing with the Merfolk. Instead, they were for service. She would come again tomorrow, and they would play then.

For now, she walked along the golden streets of light in the city of the Golden Orb toward the place she was most needed. Candy fell from the trees. Puppies played in the grass. Unicorns bowed their heads amongst rainbow colored clouds in the dream of a child.

This was where she was needed, where she could serve the most.

She walked confidently forth into the subtle realm of childhood vision where what is easily dismissed with blinded daylight eyes makes all the difference.

Subtly now, the sound of the ocean disappeared. In its place, she heard the melodies of a princess singing in some long-forgotten tale.

"I knew it was always you who walked in my dreams and sang in my heart, who lifted me up and showed me my truth."

The waltz played louder, and she danced along, unable to resist. She knew every step, every turn, every rise and fall of the beautiful melody.

It was Livie's song. She was sure of it.

Heather knew she had arrived at her destination as planned, as guided, as needed.

As usual, she was right.

Billy reached the car and stopped. Something about this corner store was familiar. Déjà vu hit him hard. His head swam for a moment before he recentered himself. They got in the car, and he drove off.

Had he seen just this view before? As he searched his mind, the memory escaped him. Something told him it was important.

He, too, was right.

He passed the plastic bottle of water to Devyn.

"Perfect," she said. "Much better now. Thank you. We live just around the block from here."

His stomach tightened.

*Notice, Billy, notice!*

Something about the memory of this place clicked deep down in his brain. Before long, it would surface.

He smiled at her with forgiveness in his eyes.

She nodded in acknowledgement. The weight of the horrific silence lifted. As they turned the corner, he told her about some more unbelievable details of his pig-cow family life.

Once he pulled into the driveway at 144 Sunnyside Way, Billy stiffened his back and transitioned into full investigator mode. He got out of the car and examined the view of her house from the street. He noticed all obvious potential weaknesses of her new security system. He planned out potential attack points so that they might be avoided in advance.

Ever so subtly, he waved to a car down the street at the officer stationed to protect her home. Billy returned to the car and hopped back inside the driver's seat.

"Looks good. Let's get in the garage. Once inside, I will search the house.

After that, I will go back out and again secure the perimeter. We can continue our work at that point," he said.

She nodded. "Okay, tough guy. You look good in those jeans, by the way, cowboy." *You always did.*

"Yea. Thanks. Get a snack ready. It's gonna be a mighty long night round here, and I don't want no hungry pregnant ladies sending me and my jeans to that joke of a store at two o'clock for ice cream and pickles." He smiled.

That final joke offered complete release of all the tension in the air between them. They both laughed, the forgiving and the forgiven, at the same time. Devyn grinned.

# FIFTY-TWO

## Home

ROSE ROLLED on her back in total dismay. She could no longer gather the strength to struggle. She ignored the pain in her back and the stickiness of the congealed blood on her leg and accepted the buzzing in her ears as the eternal status quo. She was going to die—that simple, that true.

Her heart was broken. Her faith was fatally wounded. Her body was destroyed.

She gathered what little energy she had left to rotate her wrists back and forth making the sign.

*No more. No more. All done.*

Livie dropped her flailing arms and cried like the baby she was.

She had nothing left to give either. The glass door was too thick. She couldn't break it for Rose. She could only guide and encourage her. The final step had to come from Rose herself.

A soft, glowing light shone from not too far away and kept getting stronger. A subtle off-white sparkling filled the air. Livie recognized its meaning immediately.

They were coming to claim Rose.

The entourage from the other side of the Rainbow Bridge had arrived to help her make her transition. As usual, a great celebration called forth in her honor to recognize her bravery for having the courage to come to this place, to this planet in a human body…the most difficult of all spiritual journeys.

It wouldn't be long now.

The trumpets blew from far off in the distance, and the drums boomed. The ground shook from love's dance.

They only had a few minutes left together now. Livie understood.

They had failed, but not really. Death was also a great gift—horrible from this side of the Bridge but gorgeous from the other.

Livie felt the pressure of a hand over her right shoulder.

She knew she was being asked to step aside and gracefully accept Rose's fate. The deal was signed, the final contract called forth.

Thankfully, this time she was wrong.

The gentle hand on her shoulder did not belong to the Angel of Death but to Heather.

She whispered in Livie's ear, "It is Rose's call now. She must decide. You cannot decide for her. I think it's time we ask her."

Livie nodded.

With her permission given, together they reached down to Nanny Rose. Words were not necessary, not in a moment like this. The spirit image of Livie's highest self leaned over one side of Rose's head while the spirit image of Heather's was on the other. They pointed to the light which brilliantly penetrated Rose's blinded eyes. The buzzing sound ceased.

For a brief moment, Rose heard the music of her eternal song.

Then they turned back and pointed at the glass door. Heather motioned to a filing cabinet nearby. The message was obvious enough. Either Rose could choose to submit to physical death and cross over to join the gathering on her behalf, or she could choose to stay and fight.

Here...her only option was to climb the cabinet and with the force of her weight, shatter the glass door blocking her escape. She would survive—barely. She would have a long, difficult, and painful recovery, but she would get out alive.

The choice was hers to make. No one else could decide for her, not even love itself. Rose had only a few moments left to choose to go home.

Rose nodded her head. She understood.

Tears spilled forth as she considered her options, each one both wonderful and terrible at the same time. She took a deep breath and prayed in her mind. She asked for the strength to choose the best, for the highest good of all.

"*Prayer answered*," she heard loud and clear in her mind.

A thousand images filled her mind simultaneously. With rapid but complete clarity, her vision revealed what would be the result of each possible choice. She would decide for herself. Without judgment and only from the place of total love, the entire unseen realm embraced her. Adored beyond measure, her decision would be honored.

What would she choose?

The kidnapper gasped with horror and looked up at the clock, realizing how long Rose had been left alone. The murderer rushed into the closet, changed clothes, and ran out the front door.

*How could you have been so stupid? What if you are too late? You have to see it, or it doesn't help. If she's already dead, it's been a waste, a total, absolute waste, a risk too big to be justified—all for nothing, you imbecile.*

With self-betraying thoughts of panic mixed perfectly into a frozen concoction of delusion and deceit, the freak raced back to the warehouse.

Each red light was an experiment in torture. "For fuck's sake!" the fiend screamed, more at the reflection in the mirror than at the other drivers.

As the distance between the normal side and the delirious side of the monster's mind grew, the Homeless Hunter's fear multiplied in measure. Currently, the criminal could still play both sides, easily switching from the version of Jekyll into the version of Hyde. How long could the liar play this game and still decide which version came out? The drive to kill mounted more and more by the hour, perhaps by the minute.

Taking Rose had been an impulse, a foolish move not thought completely through. It was time for this game of chess to end. She was going to die—if for nothing else, to quench the horrible thirst of the maniac's mind.

"Calling all pawns. March, march, march," the murderer announced to the air.

Or was it to the reflection in the mirror or to the other person imprisoned within, clawing and screaming to get out.

"I don't have much time left, do I? Until the rest of me is gone," the Homeless Hunter asked, more as a statement than a question.

The cruel scoundrel, this time, was right.

Perhaps it is worth considering whether or not the insane are really content being mad. Perhaps the crazy are just as offended by their madness as the rest of the world. Isn't a criterion for insanity not knowing you are crazy, not having a choice to be something else? Something better? Something more normal?

Maybe, or maybe not.

Maybe some victims are just too wounded to turn around from the path of their own invented demise. Maybe they are so damaged they cannot see any possible solution except their own inevitable destruction and the loss of everyone and everything they will take down with them. All destroyed for the hope of what? A reboot, another chance, another better, more productive go round?

Perhaps, perhaps not.

# FIFTY-THREE

## Zumba on Tuesdays

IN AGONY, Rose rolled over once more. She buried her blinded eyes in her arm and shuddered. How did one make a choice like this?

She imagined the joy of petting her dog, Chico, again. She envisioned holding her mother's hand and kissing Fernando, the baby she lost at nine months of life to SIDS. She could even hear his sweet voice calling her name, cooing and reaching out for her love. Finally, she could rest with the broken promises of a difficult life perfectly repaired—or not.

In contrast, she could fight and take care of her babies here.

She could hold Livie again and watch her jump off the diving board in her new handmade pink and red swimsoup. She could watch *La Doctora* eat her pizza, eyes wild with joy as if she had never tasted it before. She could see her sister again and take that Zumba class on Tuesdays with her.

Every time she passed the sign, she had hesitated. She thought she would call tomorrow, but that tomorrow never came. How shockingly unexpected came the day when you realized there were not going to be anymore tomorrows.

She imagined herself wearing handsome, black-strapped Zumba shoes on her feet that twirled her faster and faster across the concrete dance hall floor, shaking her middle-aged ass like a hot Mexican cutie.

In the image, Sylvia laughed, thrilled to see her baby sister so unbelievably happy.

That was enough. Rose chose.

She would climb that stupid filing cabinet, and she would crash that wimpy glass door.

What goddamn door?

It was nothing to her compared to her will.

No useless wall of glass would keep her from watching Livie go on her first date or dance her first dance across the junior high stadium floor. Just like no kidnapper would keep Rose from shimmying her way across the Zumba stage to tease her wonderful sister. Certainly no pathetic bindings would keep her hands from reaching in the oven and pulling out the perfect pizza for *La Doctora*.

She climbed on all fours and rocked slightly back and forth. She gathered momentum for one last maneuver of grandeur. It would take everything she had left in this beaten and broken body, of this she was sure.

She was absolutely right.

She asked for the strength to do it honorably. She begged that in the aftermath, she might forget the pain of what she was about to do and recall only the beautiful choice she had been given.

She blew a kiss of mother's love to Fernando. She said she would see him soon, so soon. For now, he would have to wait. Hopefully, he would forgive her this one last thing. She knew he would.

She was right, again.

# FIFTY-FOUR

## Flowers and Wildcats

DEVYN AND BILLY stepped in the front door and disengaged the alarm. The code worked as expected, and the countdown ceased.

Or did it?

The big clock from the gates of hell still ticked. She knew it. She felt the weight of the world on her shoulders. The heaviness of the situation settled with a hard and painful cramp in the back of her neck and a click in her jaw.

Panic threatened, but she did not bite back. There was no time and no value left in fear. She had finally learned that lesson.

Guilt—useless. Fear—useless. Worry—useless.

All those horrible emotions were different names for the exact same thing, the same thing which served only to cut her off from the very connection that helped her most, that she craved the most.

Fear.

She laughed out loud when she fully realized how absurd fear had always been, for her and everyone alive.

*Fear has never been real.*

It was only guilt projected into the future, which doesn't exist—not yet, anyway. How could fear be real? It was nothing, always had been a joke, an illusion, a trick of the mind against itself.

*Why do we go there, to this useless place called fear? Why have we ever gone there?*

She started to think about how different her life could have been if she had learned this critical lesson sooner. Then she stopped. There was no value in that, either. She was here, and all the what ifs were just another version of fear disguised as something easier to look at.

What if she had wasted her life? So what. What if she could have been more, done more? So what. All questions of that nature revealed their true selves as nothing more than fear pretending to be reflection.

She had wasted her last second on guilt and fear, which finally displayed their ugly backsides for what they always were—an illusion bent on maintaining separation of the self from all that is true.

Devyn's mind came back to the present, and she took a breath.

"You okay?" Billy asked. "You went to la-la-land again. What's going on in that brilliant brain of yours?"

"Nothing and everything all at once, but more importantly right now, where is Heather?"

They looked in all the usual places without success. She noticed the tiger print throw on the floor, so carelessly tossed to the side, and knew the answer to her own question.

Hands on her hips, she winked.

"Ten bucks, superstar investigator, they are safe and sound in Livie's bed."

"I will take that bet because if you are right, we all win."

Up the stairs with bated breath, they traveled to Livie's room. Sure enough, just as Devyn suspected, they were there cuddled tightly in a spooning hug.

Devyn tried without success to rouse Heather. Something whispered in her thoughts to leave Heather be.

Thankfully, she listened, because it was right.

After blowing kisses, they went back downstairs. She found milk, bread, peanut butter, and jelly while Billy journeyed back outside to reaffirm their safety. Snack devoured and thirst quenched, she snuggled in on the couch with the tiger print throw.

Although she had no idea why, this blanket always reminded her of her father. She pulled the comfy covers up tightly under her neck and closed her eyes.

Almost instantly, the swirling of colors of love filled her mind's eye. The smell of her father, new leather entwined with Old Spice, penetrated her nostrils. She imagined herself as a young girl crawling into his arms.

Flash!

She looked at her seven-year-old feet in her dream. Her childhood-lovely, silver, glittery shoes snuggly embraced her perfect little toes.

She heard children laughing cruelly at her in the background and knew instantly what day it was. As the street signs rushed past her, she remembered all the details of that awful day.

This was the day little Bobby Simpson broke her second-grader heart. She had wanted so badly for him to be her valentine, but she was just a quiet and shy smarty-pants, and he was way too popular with the other girls for that. While she ran furiously away from school, she clenched his devastating reply in her right hand. The note she had been so brave to give him in the first place burned like fire in her palm.

He had checked the "no" box.

Her heart shattered in a thousand pieces. She ran straight home from school, mortified by her classmates' cruel jokes.

With her mother gone, who would help her now?

At first, she thought she would run away from home or maybe even worse. Her life wasn't worth living anymore.

Magically, her dad came in at the right time and said just the right words. While he rocked her crying eyes to sleep that afternoon, he covered her tenderly with a tiger print blanket. She accepted the comfort of his fatherly love and sank completely into the strength of his protective chest.

When Billy came back in the front door from his perimeter check, he smiled. Devyn slept on the couch with the most peaceful face he had ever seen. There was an innocence there so beautiful to look upon he could hardly break his stare. Something in her expression made him think of family, camping trips, and the perfect love of a parent for a child. He smelled roasting marshmallows faintly wafting up from a memory in his own mind.

At first, he planned to wake her and then thought better of it. Something made him think she must need whatever inspiring dream she was dreaming.

Of course, he was right, too.

Billy toured around the house and eventually ventured into the kitchen. He smiled at the pictures of Livie everywhere. There were child-like drawings interspersed with photos covering the front and both sides of the refrigerator. A magnet of remembrance from some old, but not forgotten, vacation held each treasure perfectly secure in its assigned position.

He saw several photos of Livie laughing with an older Mexican woman he

216

accurately assumed was Nanny Rose. Her genuine smile reached out of the photos and touched him.

He pretended to go back in time and join them for each of their adventures. In his mind, they quickly visited New Orleans for Jazz Fest, the Bahamas for deep sea fishing, Italy for world-class wine tasting, California for a Gay and Lesbian Rights Parade, and a remote Indian village accessible only to the natural descendants of the Chippewa line.

Then he envisioned all the places he would love to take them in return. They could visit west Texas during a chili cook off, visit the mountains in Wyoming just before the snow fell, travel to...

He scolded himself for getting so far off track. He better get his brain back on task. He had a job to do. He couldn't let his feelings muddle his actions. Devyn, Livie, Ellie, and Rose were all counting on him.

He made an executive decision to take over the dining room table. This room, close enough to hear Devyn if she stirred and far enough away not to bother her with his flipping of pages and pictures, afforded him an excellent viewpoint of the images on the security camera screen stationed in her office across the hall.

He settled into his work as always. His brain entered perpetrator mode so he could connect into the thoughts of the assailant.

He had no definitive proof yet, but deep in his almost always spot-on gut, he knew Rose was in the hands of the Homeless Hunter. The next logical jump changed everything. If Rose was involved, then it was possible none of the murders were really about hatred of the homeless. It was always about something else, but what? Who?

In his mind's eye, he could see Rose bound and tortured.

For what? Why? Information maybe. Or was she a target or a substitute for someone else? If so, for whom?

There was no other benign yet reasonable explanation for her absence. It surely meant death or capture. By now, though, her body would have been discovered if she was dead. More ominously, Rose's disappearance just after the intruder invaded this house suggested the possibility that somehow this home was connected to all the murders.

Just under the surface of his awareness, Billy became more and more concerned that his Ladybug was somehow dangerously involved in all of it.

*What happened to your good luck, Bug?*

Was Rose just a symptom, an unfortunate casualty of circumstance?

Billy decided he needed more information about Devyn and her seemingly always-absent fiancé's life.

Maybe this was all about him. Who was he? What did he do?

Unless Rose had run away, which made no sense to him at all, this scenario of imminent danger for the entire household was really all that was left. The more he pressed the issue in his own mind, the clearer the picture became. They were in trouble, big trouble.

Again, he was spot on.

Billy turned on the TV in the kitchen for the soothing effect of its white noise. It kept his front brain distracted so that his deeper, connecting brain could work.

The volume of the TV increased out of nowhere forcing Billy to overhear a breaking news story. A large wildcat had been seen on the outskirts of Holosni near the Turnpike, not too far from the warehouse district. Several first-hand accounts of the cat reported that the deadly feline had been seen stalking in and around this area for about three days.

With the newsbreak over, he returned to his work, and the TV's volume returned to normal. He never gave the wildcat another thought.

Lucky rubbed his leg, but he pushed the cat away, not wanting to waste time petting animals. He had work to do.

He spread out the photos of the Homeless Hunter's victims. He looked at each one very slowly. Sometimes, if he turned evidence sideways from a new viewpoint, he would see something he previously missed. It was rare, but even he overlooked the smallest, most significant detail on occasion.

He took out his notes regarding each murder. To date, none of the first four victims had been successfully identified. Still puzzled by this incredible detail, he kept looking closer and closer at their pictures. Frozen in death, each woman was carefully wrapped in a quilt.

The quilts reminded him of something Devyn said in the restaurant. What was it? What had she said?

His right hand started to go a little numb, forcing him to adjust his wrist slightly while holding the photos. That was when he saw it.

Just at the edge of each photo, a few feet from the victim, he noticed a flower that didn't quite fit in.

With his undergraduate minor degree in botany, Billy had knowledge of plants that few others possessed. In fact, he had encouraged the development of a course in the Victorian Language of Flowers at the University of Texas during his graduate work. The class never took off, and after a few years, the university dropped the curriculum in favor of some new and more exciting course about the biochemical properties of plant behavior.

Billy looked intently at each photo. The first victim's shoulder touched a withered...what? Lily.

*Oh my God.* The intimated message was, "A message waited here."

The second victim lay near a pink zinnia. The intimated message was, "Absence or sorrow."

Then a marigold–"Bittersweet confusion."

Then a columbine near a blackberry–"Desertion and envy."

Then a pink carnation–"I will never forget you."

Obsession–the flowers were all about sinister and painful obsession. Who was this message of sick love intended for? Rose? Devyn's fiancé?

Then, just as his jaw dropped in disbelief that he hadn't noticed this critical detail sooner, his brain clicked into hyperdrive. One of the photos contained the exact image he saw at the local convenience store in the picture of the witness who finally identified the fifth victim. It was taken from the back part of the same parking lot. The trees were the same, exactly the same.

That meant the fifth victim had most likely been in this very neighborhood at some time. The significance of this dawned on him instantly. Without a doubt, Devyn was in grave danger, and Livie, and Rose—all of them.

"Help me connect the dots," he said. "If I ever asked you for anything, please, I'm begging…help me keep my Ladybug safe. Help me. Help me do this right."

He felt tired, so tired from the worry of all it, deep down in his bones. He wanted to keep working, but he knew a brain that worked properly was critical right now. He searched the house until he found what looked like the guest room. Billy left a note next to Devyn. He was in no condition for driving back right now. Even if he could, he never would have. He felt his place was here at her side to keep her safe.

He was absolutely right.

# FIFTY-FIVE

## She Talks to Angels

FUMING AT THE CLOCK, the Homeless Hunter clenched the steering wheel painfully tight. The drive to the warehouse felt like an eternity. Time was distorted as if somehow each second lasted an hour.

A pressure in the pit of the killer's stomach grew stronger by the second, or was it by the hour? Not sure whether to scream or throw up, the maniac chose rage. If the villain's yearning remained unquenched, the good Doctor Mitchell would have to die. No longer able to push the urge deep within, the scoundrel faced the smolderingly obvious fact. Soon, the substitutes would no longer work. Devyn was doomed. There simply was no other way for the fiend to survive.

As the sleeping guests on Sunnyside Way dreamt, the cameras rolled. They surveyed up and down, right then left.

A shadow near the back fence moved but turned out to be nothing more menacing than a wild coyote pup lost from the safety of his mother's side.

From the heavens above, the house glowed purple. The protecting love of many angels gathered on every side. Every window, every door guarded by the presence of divine love remained undisturbed for now.

Not for much longer. Evil intended to threaten these souls. A hint of guilt and hate contaminated the sweaty air.

The subtle realms prepared. Love herself readied. She would not be denied her plan.

Rose glared at the darkness and willed to see through it just enough to find the filing cabinet's edge. The darkness, previously penetrated only by the lighted image of Livie, opened a little more.

Nanny Rose sensed the presence of another figure more fully. Its identity did not matter to her. It was loving, and that was enough information for her. The throbbing in her leg ceased completely. The pain was replaced by the numbness of infection and death. It was finished. Of that, Rose held no pretenses.

The new presence tapped lightly on the center of Rose's forehead and then drew out the shape of a figure eight turned sideways. Over and over, the presence made this shape. Slowly and ever so subtly, the outline of the cabinet appeared.

Rose crawled very slowly but assuredly forward. Something definitive declared she would be given all the time it would take for her to perform this last noble feat. Time stood still for her.

When she reached the corner of the structure, she smiled. It was almost over now. She had come so far. This was but a tiny bit more.

What little thing like this could hold back the love of a nanny from her Livie? What insignificant task could dare suggest it might make her fail? The absurdity of the idea of failure shone like a light of certainty so sure, so complete that she gasped, unable to believe she could have ever doubted herself. Her faith blossomed with love's kiss of absolute confidence.

Rose, without a doubt or another care in her mind, simply crawled one hand and foot over the next up to the top of the cabinet. Her weight disappeared underneath her faith that boosted her body up, up, up to the top. She wobbled not. She faltered not. The irreparable injury within her left leg seemed utterly unaffected by this oh-so-easy maneuver of love for her Livie.

At the top of the cabinet, Rose took one last deep breath and rocked her weight back and forth, side to side, and then back and forth again.

She danced the Zumba dance of victory—today, this Zumba Tuesday, not tomorrow—for herself, for Livie, for Devyn, for Sylvia.

She had done her part well. "*Good girl,*" she heard in her mind.

The rest, well, that was up to someone, or something, else. There was nothing left for her to do now. As soon as the cabinet shifted, she slipped peacefully into oblivion. Her glucose hit the critical level, and a coma set in instantly.

The glass shattered all around her, but she felt no measure of pain. The blasting sound of the crash of the cabinet hitting the pavement outside the warehouse exploded but fell on only deafened ears. She was not here. She was playing fetch with Chico and holding Fernando somewhere almost unreachable from here—almost.

221

Rose looked out at the expanse of green rolling hills in front of her. Balloons and butterflies filled the air. Pink and green, the colors of the heart, surrounded her.

She knew she had just done something important, but she couldn't be bothered to remember exactly what. She had, even if ever so briefly, entered the perfection of her heaven. She would remain here until her body was ready to take her back again. For now, she was suffering-free and worry-free.

Fernando suggested it would be fun to roll down the great green hill together out into the expansive meadow below. She agreed and immediately obliged him his request. Rose rushed to the edge of the hill, lay on her side, and without a trace of fear, soared in a rolling triumph down the hill.

"Very good, Mama," Fernando said. "Let's go play. I've missed you so much."

She gladly took his hand in hers and walked forth into the light of all that is.

After the cabinet hit the ground, Rose's empty shell of a body catapulted forward. A large smacking crunched when her ribs shattered under the impact. She landed just at the edge of the hill that the warehouse overlooked. For a second, her body's movement seemed to stop, but then it began again. She rolled right down the hill all the way to the edge of Fifty-second Street about ten miles from the Turnpike.

Several hours later, another urgent newsbreak would cut in to share the good news.

The Florida Fish and Game Department set out early that morning to save a life, and that's exactly what they did.

The wildcat they hunted was spotted off Twenty-fifth Street lurking at the woods' edge just as dawn cracked the day Rose was found. A hitchhiker had reported the cat after quickly reaching safety himself at a nearby gas station.

Twenty-fifth Street was located just off the Florida Turnpike, but Fifty-second Street was deeper in the warehouse district some ten miles away.

They must have mixed up the numbers.

Or did they?

Not two hours after Rose's mostly dead body crashed at the end of the hill, a shout rang out. The officers had arrived.

"Guys! Guys, get over here. I think I see something," the leader of the wildcat search party shouted. "Help! It's a victim. The cat must have attacked her. Look at her leg. It's almost completely severed. She must have tried to crawl to safety after she was attacked. Get an ambulance. Fast! She might be doomed already. Her pulse is spotty at best. Watch yourself, guys; there's a big cat nearby."

In a way that was very different from what he comprehended, he was totally right.

Master Lucky paced back and forth in front of Livie's room. Right, then left, then right again, he marched. He held his chest high like a soldier on a critical mission. His tail pointed straight to the heavens. There was an air of service about him. He had waited a long time for this juncture, and he was ready. Barely allowing himself the luxury of purring, Master Lucky felt the weight of the burden of the task at hand lessening. They were almost done, so he was almost done.

As the mission neared its end, he started fantasizing about breakfast.

*Just make it through this last little hour, and I will feast. She will make me something special today*, he thought.

Somehow, his mistress would know he deserved a treat. She would see it in his stalk. She would feel it in his vibration.

Then he would nap, for days if needed, to recharge.

He was spent, his energy traded for a gift of unimaginable worth. He had offered his life if necessary. This might just be his last morning if they took too long to help her, if they took too long to get back. It was a bet he was willing to take. Yes, it had been a good trade, a good wager. He was proud even if no one...well, almost no one, ever knew the difference. He had served his mistress well. He knew he would not go unrewarded.

About that, he was right.

When the unidentified victim arrived at ED dock number three, the trauma team prepared the OR. Based on the assessment of the paramedic team, the woman's leg would need immediate amputation, or she would surely die; that's of course if she even made it to surgery following transport to Tampa.

As the siren sounded, the ED staff rushed in. A large bore IV was placed in her right arm. The doctor inserted an interosseous catheter in her good leg directly into the marrow of the bone. This technique, perfected in the battlefield by the army, allowed for the direct infusion of massive amounts of fluid into the circulation. Large quantities of blood would be pumped in next. Insulin dripped in as fast as her veins would allow it.

Despite all the fluid resuscitation, the Hispanic Jane Doe's pressure continued to drop. Her heart rhythm destabilized. She went from an irregular rhythm to a bradycardia—slower, slower, and slower still. Her pulse continued to decline while her pressure dropped to fifty over Palp.

They were losing the readings and losing her.

The cardiac monitor alarmed because the ventricular pauses increased. Now her rate was thirty, too low to maintain oxygen flow to the heart or the brain.

Cardiac arrest was imminent.

She decompensated into ventricular fibrillation next, a rhythm that could not sustain her life.

Overhead, there was a call of, "Code Blue in ED bed three!"

"Code teams engage. Begin CPR now!" Doctor Track said.

All the appropriate staff rushed in.

The AED paddles charged as CPR ensued.

In perfect cycles of compression to breaths, the miracle workers of the ED did their thing.

There was no hesitation. There was no fear. Only grace.

The whole team waltzed to the fluent movement of the dance of life: birth, death, and eventual rebirth. Another trip on the cycle of the eternal merry-go-round completed itself and brought beautifully forth the opportunity for another go, another chance, another turn.

Rose held Fernando's hand while they watched from above, or better put, from within. A thin and lightly shimmering string of something beautiful and gold seemed to trail from her empty shell of a body to the perfectly healed version of a youthful Rose watching with slight amusement.

She was too busy to watch for long. She already knew what would happen. In truth, it had already happened.

The charge delivered its power. Rose had started to look away but turned around again.

"I'm clear. You're clear. We're all clear," the barefooted doctor declared, and the second more powerful surge coursed through the body that served Rose's spirit.

Her body jerked forward and then again more forcefully the second time around.

"We have a pulse. Stop. Observe. We have a pulse," the doctor announced with pleasure, still trying to hide his lack of shoes.

The Epinephrine raced through her veins and her pulse quickened. Beep...beep...beep...beep...beep..beep..beep,beep,beep,beep. Rose's heart rate reached twenty, then thirty-seven, then forty-eight.

Her pressure climbed back to the range where it could be measured again.

The team took a breath. Rose and Fernando smiled.

The gurney quickly rolled past them. One by one, the heroes felt her body's gratitude as they waved her goodbye and wished her luck. Somehow, each of them knew deep down she would survive. They sensed no lingering odor of death on her.

They were absolutely right.

When the elevator doors closed, so her destiny closed with them. The surgeon would do a perfect job. The leg would be severed at just the right place.

She would live.

For over two weeks, Jane Doe would go unidentified as a supposed wildcat-attack victim in the SICU of Tampa General Hospital. The cat would be found and returned to the Miami Zoo.

Soon, her coma would pass, and she would remember her own name. She would leave the other side and her beloved Fernando once more, so briefly from the perspective of eternity. This life, so short, was nothing more than a blink of her eye, a fleeting memory of a moment in the passing of forever.

Not now, however, not this second, this oh-so-insignificant flutter of a dragonfly's wing.

For now, he was hers, and she was his.

# FIFTY-SIX

## Point of No Return

DEVYN AWOKE CONFUSED.

*Where am I? What time is it? What day is it?*

She caught her breath then quickly scanned the room.

*Oh, duh.*

She remembered where she was and laughed a little. She must have fallen asleep on the couch when Billy checked outside again.

Oh no. She had abandoned him while he was helping her. Her heart sank.

*How selfish could I be?*

She started to go down the winding path of guilt, straight to hell and madness, but stopped herself quickly this time.

*"Good, Mommy,"* Ellie said.

He would forgive her, again, like always. She would forgive herself her own error. Her error would be corrected unlike a sin worthy of the separation it reinforced. Guilt was not worth it anymore. It had simply lost its attraction to her now that it was exposed for the uselessness it truly was.

*"Very good thinking, Mommy."*

For a moment longer, she still smelled the lingering scent of her father—musky and comforting, warm and soft, but strong all at the same time. The memory of her reunion with him faded as quickly and completely as she had jumped into it. Part of her deeper mind remembered, but her conscious mind forgot. The effect, however, had not been lost. The message of love remained even if the experience faded from her conscious awareness.

226

She looked back down at the tiger print throw. For some reason, this blanket always reminded her of her father, but she couldn't recall why.

Ellie flipped over with excitement. She felt strong today, which was a good thing.

She sent her mother the images of the foods she wanted to experience. She desired chocolate and cheese and some pickles after all.

Devyn looked in the cabinet and remembered Livie had some old chocolate-puff cereal way in the back.

*Yuck*, Devyn thought, but she had to try them nonetheless.

She reached in the fridge for milk and noticed Livie's string cheese.

*That will do. Oh, and a pickle. Yum. Last one in the jar. Lucky me.*

Ellie giggled within. *"You mean us."*

*"You did this to us, didn't you?"*

Ellie answered back with a firm, strong kick.

"Thought so," Devyn announced out loud.

Over the baby monitor, Devyn heard two distinct snores and knew both Livie and Heather slumbered peacefully.

Master Lucky entered the kitchen with a grace about him that made her take pause. His regality overtook her, prompting her to reach for his favorite treat. On a hunch, she set out two of his favorite snacks, which she had never done before.

*"Told you so,"* he announced with his head held high.

He ate his treats, cleaned his paws, and did his business in the litter tray. Pleased as punch, he went back upstairs for a long nap in his favorite spot in the far back corner of his mistress's closet right next to her best pair of red shoes.

Devyn laughed at the absurdity of her weird and wonderful breakfast. She felt so satisfied she could cry, but when she washed her hands in the kitchen sink, a noise made her look over her right shoulder.

Through the doorway of the dining room, Billy's notes on the table caught her attention. She went forth to investigate.

227

She didn't mean to pry. Her intention was to catch up on Rose's case. She felt horrible for falling asleep on him last night. If she read his notes, maybe she could just jump in where he left off. Maybe he wouldn't have to waste more time catching her up. Maybe he could sleep a little longer if she explored on her own.

What awaited her discovery there, so far beyond the wildest reaches of her mind, there was no way to prepare her for it. Ellie didn't even try.

When Devyn picked up the folder she thought contained the notes on Rose's disappearance, the Double H murder photos spilled all over the table.

Ellie braced herself for the inevitable flood.

There was no going back now. Devyn was going to see. She was going to find out what the murders were all about.

The end was near, and nothing and no one in the world, seen or unseen, could change that now.

Victoria paced back and forth nervously. Her closet contained hundreds of perfect ensembles each designed for its own unique purpose. She owned courtroom outfits, tough-lady suits, nice-lady dresses, but nothing seemed just right for today. She knew Brock would translate her choice of clothes, her intention obvious to the finely tuned eye. His eyes were always finely tuned. They had to be for him to survive in his world. He would notice.

Maybe, for once, she would wear what she wanted to. Who cared, after all? Who was Devyn anyway? Victoria convinced herself she was giving this clueless opponent of hers way too much thought and, therefore, way too much power. Only Brock's allegiance mattered.

Or did it?

Now that she thought about it, she didn't care about his feelings that much either. Her goal shone clear and bright to her—to get herself free and clear from all this deadly crap.

She twisted her ankle back and forth pretending to put out Devyn, the old dirty cigarette butt in her ashtray.

Victoria congratulated herself in advance.

This wedding meeting need be nothing but a pretense. How could she be anything other than perfectly calm from this perspective of sureness? There would be no marriage gala, of that Victoria remained absolutely certain. It was just a matter of time before the whole issue went away and was swept under the rug of the Bryant family living room floor. In the grand scheme of things, this little distraction was a freaking joke. Brock just had to get over it. Simple, that simple, she told herself. She had always convinced him before. Why should this time be any different?

She decided that black and plain would work just fine. She finally chose some no name shoes from the back of the closet. She didn't want to get a good pair dirty—not for this useless whore.

She should have dealt with the bitch already. She knew that for sure now. She let her chance slip by once, but not again.

Clueless little peons didn't scare her. They never had. Who did this fucking lady think she was anyway? How did Devyn Mitchell think she could compete with an avatar of the game of life and death like Victoria Bryant?

Thoughts of a broken and barren Devyn flooded her mind.

She smiled looking her gorgeous figure up and down once more. "He's mine, you stupid bitch. You clueless, stupid bitch. I've had enough of you and your influence over my brother. I hope you hear me loud and clear. This bullshit is done and so are you and your precious Livie."

She was heard, but not by whom she would have expected. She was answered, too, in a language far too beautiful and innocent for her to understand. Love itself heard her call and answered back.

The image of Mary's shoe in the hallway burned a brand of worthlessness and sin on Brock's brain. Every time he closed his eyes, he saw the outline of that damn shoe, staring, screaming at him, and demanding he be punished.

*How could I have been so reckless, such an imbecile?*

He swirled the addictive drain of guilt and jumped down the long-rusted pipe of misery straight to the hell of the broken, sinning, and damned Son of God. The scenarios of deceit played over and over in his now obsessed mind.

Devyn meant everything to him. Why had he done such a useless and moronic thing? How many offers of sexual favor had he dismissed over the years for her? How would he tell her? How would she find the grace to forgive him such a base and disgusting indiscretion after their engagement?

Before...that was one thing, but now after she finally agreed to marry him, what if she wouldn't, couldn't forgive him? What would that mean? Would he lose her, Livie, and Ellie forever?

The guilt swirled faster and faster by the second. Panic and terror set in. Fear consumed him.

He had done so much to keep her, so much to own her, so much to control her.

229

All the nights of self-denial, all his attempts to be a better man—wasted. The anticipation of a new and clean life with her demolished and washed away into the abyss.

Or was it?

Did he really have to tell her? Really?

What if he just denied it ever happened? Couldn't he claim Mary was crazy and that she made the whole thing up? Everyone had seen Mary flirting unapologetically with him at work before, and he had never so much as hinted that he felt the same in return.

So what if he had screwed around a few times before? Nobody else knew that. In fact, every half-attractive woman on planet Earth wanted to bang him. So why would Devyn suspect this allegation was any truer than the rest?

Or maybe, better yet, it was Devyn's fault.

If she had made more space for him in her life, if she had married him sooner, if she had just moved to the beach house like he wanted, none of this would have ever happened.

Who knows? Maybe she had done the same thing to him...which explained everything. All this time, he thought she was afraid of commitment when really she had a lover. That's why she didn't want to move in with him. That's why she forgot to call him so many nights. It wasn't cold feet. It was freaking crowd control.

All those lies of how she wanted to see her loan-repayment commitment through exposed their deceit to him. All those nights she claimed she was at the hospital, she was probably sticking it to some other doctor, kissing, loving, screwing some pair of sunglasses in scrubs.

Was Ellie even his baby? The treachery stabbed him.

Devyn was just like all the others.

It had always been about his money, never him. How could he have thought it would have worked out? He had been such a fool...again.

His madness descended further and further into the insanity of the guilty, terrified fool. He gave out deceit and dishonesty, and it returned full circle right back to him. What one gave, one always received. That was the universal law.

The past misery of darkness sank in, took hold of him, and the shadow of his own making blotted out the true image of her. She was nothing but a shadow figure to him now. His past replaced hers, forced out the present, and condemned his future. He had chosen fear instead of love...again.

The separation between them grew so great and so deep in that moment of his ego-protecting lie that a shudder was felt throughout the universe. Smash, crack, crunch—everything good between them gone, destroyed, and erased by the wish of a madman bent on making his guilt hers and thinking that somehow his would be washed away. So foolish and fatal an error he made.

When would he learn that when he attacked, he always attacked himself first?

# FIFTY-SEVEN

## A Purple Chair

DEVYN LOOKED at the lifeless faces again. How was this possible? The photos tumbled to the floor as the significance set in. She stumbled backward in disbelief. She knocked the newly reupholstered faintly purple paisley chair on its side but didn't even notice.

She used to love that now-forgotten and swept-aside purple chair. The print reminded her of her mother's favorite dress, which she still saw so clearly. The image of that one-size-too-large brown dress with the purple paisley trim that perfectly matched her mother's favorite hat went unrecalled today. No memory of walking into church with her purple-paisley-trimmed mother blessed her this morning.

Her mind focused anywhere but on that seemingly old and useless chair. What chair? The only thing here was a series of photos that screamed out the unavoidable truth.

She knew every single one of these murdered women. She recognized every frozen face. These weren't unidentified strangers. These were real people, real women, and women she knew. Not just victim number one, two, three, four, or five; these were mothers, daughters, sisters, best friends, and patients. She couldn't believe her eyes. How did she miss this for so long?

Sadness, so thick and sticky it smelled like rotten cotton candy, threatened to suffocate her. The loss of life, the loss of promise and possibility, enveloped her.

She was the hub of a wheel where every spoke led straight to death, yet the wheel turned on, claiming more, killing more, as it flipped and twisted its evil.

She found herself trapped aboard the roller coaster of terror, tumbling down the rickety-rickety cliff of hell. Her arms flew upward, not in joy but horror while she turned the sharp corner of panic. Yet there was no exit sign here. There was no bar to lift to get out of this carnival car. The ride had to be finished, followed through every terrifying twist, every horrible scream, every maniacal turn, every blood bath until the brakes shrieked to a sudden stop, until it was finally over—until either she or the Homeless Hunter was dead.

She and her beloved babies were in imminent danger for sure. There could no longer be any doubt.

Either she was the Homeless Hunter and had killed each one of these women herself or she was the only person in the greater-central Florida region who could identify each and every one of them, the one and only person. What could that possibly mean?

This synchronicity, this coincidence could not possibly have been a mistake. These women had been killed for her, instead of her, or in order to send her a message.

She immediately acknowledged what Rose's disappearance meant. Certain she was murdered, too, Devyn collapsed on the dining room table.

"It's all my fault!"

She slammed her fist in rage on that useless purple chair, that joke of a piece of furniture, like her—nothing but the bringer of pain and damnation.

If she had just spoken up sooner, maybe this wouldn't have happened. Each one of these women had died somehow because of her. She held no illusions from herself. There was no use in pretending it wasn't true.

*Rose, sweet Nanny Rose, dead because of me.*

Her heart turned to ash and littered the floor.

Who knew what suffering the villain inflicted on sweet, innocent Rose? How would she admit to the others that this was all her fault?

Devyn felt the weight of the world hanging on her shoulders. Heavy, so heavy with the burden, she slammed her fist again on the chair.

"Morning, Princess Sleepyhead," Heather said in a crackling voice over the baby monitor.

*Livie!*

Images flooded her mind: mangled, tattered, torn, slashed.

This drove the knife of fear straight into the center of Devyn's gut. She reeked of terror and gagged on her own stench.

Who was she to pretend she could conquer fear?

Livie was awake. Her precious, darling Livie was awake, alive, and in mortal danger.

*"Get her out now, Mommy!"* Ellie said.

That was enough.

Quickly, Devyn explained the situation to Heather. She handed over her pager for future contact. They must not take any chances so no cell phones or radios.

Heather and Livie quickly gathered together enough supplies for a few days on a road trip. Thankfully, Heather's travel RV trailer was garaged right around the corner from here. They could hook up to the SUV and disappear into the unknown and unreachable world of the Florida RV campground.

Heather told Livie they were on vacation and that Devyn would join them soon. For now, Livie played along. She pretended she didn't know the truth.

Of course, she already did.

Heather and Livie pulled out of the driveway just as the fullness of the sun opened upon the beauty of the day.

Outside, the undisturbed birds sang their merry tunes. The otherwise distracted dew drops dripped down the fresh green blades of grass into the greatness of Mother Earth. The excited butterflies gathered around the fountain out front, fluttering back and forth, up and down, and then around once more, each one so taken with flight it had forgotten its terrifying struggle out of the long-gone cocoon. That was yesterday. Who could be bothered to remember? What cocoon?

The moss-coated trees swayed lightly in the fresh morning breeze as if nothing new happened here. The police officer in his unmarked car nibbled his donut and sipped his coffee, oblivious to the change afoot.

What could be more ordinary than today when Heather waved goodbye to Sunnyside Way? What could possibly be the matter when Livie giggled as her doll danced a childish jig on her lap?

Today could have been any old day in any old week in any old year, but it was not. Today was the day that changed everything for Devyn, Livie, Ellie, and everyone else, too. There was no going back now. The sun had risen. The clock ticked, and love had patiently waited for her turn. Oh how long she had waited. There would be no more delays, distractions, or diversions. The curtain drew, and the music started to play—a waltz, to be exact.

*"Mommy, this is very important,"* Ellie said. *"You cannot tell anyone about where sissy Livie is going. No one, not even...well, not even the people you think you know. Soon you will see more clearly. Tell no one. No one. Do you understand what I am saying? Do you understand what will happen if you do not listen to me? Please don't make me say any more than that. If you love our Livie as much as I*

*know you do, this will forever be our secret, a secret sworn in love, sealed in intention, and survived in truth because of its sacredness."*

Devyn nodded her head in agreement. She would not fail. No matter what happened to her, she would not tell. Never ever.

*"Very good. I feel your intention. I feel your resolve. Pretend you have not seen the pictures. For now, you must keep that part secret as well. Soon, you can tell Billy but not now. Do you understand? Hear me clearly and fail us not. Everything, and I mean everything, depends on it."*

# FIFTY-EIGHT

## Who's Driving the Bus?

BROCK LOOKED LONGINGLY at his phone. The urge to call and confess his indiscretion shocked him. His soul yearned for cleanliness, for forgiveness.

He thought of a thousand ways he could tell her.

What words? What words would he say? Flowers, that was a start—flowers and maybe, maybe no words were necessary.

After all, he wasn't sure he really needed to tell her every nasty, little, useless detail. Shouldn't he spare her this unnecessary pain?

If he loved her, which of course he thought he did, shouldn't he place her needs first? What was this little need of his for truth compared to her greater need for protection? The protection was of course from him and this all but forgotten, meaningless thing he had done, but the protection served her nonetheless. Weren't women, especially pregnant women, weak, tender, sensitive, and easily injured? After all, they were the inferior sex. Injuring her was simply a risk he dared not to take out of thoughtfulness for her.

His ego took over. In his brokenness, it saw an opportunity to strike, a chance to usurp the driver of the bus called Brock and claim superior knowledge. It declared information formidable enough that it must demand control of the so-easily misguided steering wheel of Brock's that was obviously veering in the wrong direction.

Forgiveness. What a joke. Who needed forgiveness? Surely it could more wisely steer him back to a place of guaranteed safety, back to a superior position.

If his total self just moved one step aside...for but a minute... surely the ego

236

could salvage this catastrophe. It could set things right again without any more unnecessary injury.

He had been here before. Had he forgotten so easily?

The neurons kicked in and carried him right back to that moment so many years ago when he was a boy of about fifteen—the day his stupid twin brother walked in on him and their mother, the day she rejected him so completely, so unabashedly in the name of properness.

Was a son's love for his mother not proper? Was her love for him so base that others couldn't see its value? Why was his serenity sacrificed for the greater good? Who exactly defined greater? When she had loved him, it had been good, had it not? It was good, at least until someone else placed their demands of appropriate behavior on them.

She forsook him in exchange for amnesty of her sin from the machine of society entrenched in their good, old, and precious family name. Hushed, hushed forever by the shroud of secrecy, she never touched him again in a loving way.

What about him? Poor little defenseless and shattered him? Wouldn't he be hurt again in exactly the same way if he exposed his soft underbelly to Devyn, seeking solace she didn't have the ability to offer him? Not unlike his mother, denied and then denied again.

Different woman, yes, but the insult was surely the same. His vulnerability must not be risked once more, his ego argued brilliantly. The potential for injury was too high. Would not the grand canyon of pain within him come splitting forth once more and expose the barrenness of his internal and weakened shadow of manhood?

The need for survival declared itself paramount. His need for integrity was but a back door to what—weakness? He wasn't weak. Why should he pretend he was? He was a man, after all, not a useless woman. The power belonged to him.

Yes. The plan formed more cleverly now.

The ego grabbed that wheel, sat down with self-inflated importance, and buckled the seatbelt.

Should he show up with flowers as an apology of sorts without divulging details of his affair? If he cleverly designed his words just right, he could extract an agreement from Devyn that would not violate her free will. Maybe he could convince himself that she didn't need more details. He would have, in one fell swoop, washed away all his guilt and most likely hers as well.

He calculated all this exchange so perfectly that another potential injury, like the trauma his mother inflicted on him so many years ago, would be impossible. A silent agreement they could all live with worked best. If only the terms were undisclosed. Thus, each party was most nobly served if his dishonesty masquerading around as virtuosity went undiscussed. His power remained intact. He was sure of it. At least his little, barking mutt of a dog that guarded the depths of his self-identity and self-protection was.

The filter of egoic control colored things perfectly from its yapping and manipulative perspective. After all, wasn't this really her fault to begin with?

Like an inexperienced child, he observed his own reflection on the screen of his smartphone. He made the same mistake so many toddlers do when they process their own image looking back at themselves, albeit inverse, for the first time. He told himself that the image was him.

Which version of him was it? It was impossible to tell by just looking at the picture. The image, the form, was all the same, but the content was totally unique and different depending on which him it was.

While his egoic structure was distracted with the brilliance of the plan of its own deceptive making, the genuine version of Brock's self wondered who he was. Was he Brock or his identical twin brother, Hayden? Was he that damaged fifteen-year-old, or was he the image trapped on the other side of the phone screen? Most terrifyingly of all, was he none of the above? Was he nothing more than a pretense, a computer program in some imagined Matrix, a version of some soulless creation made by some outside and unseen higher sentient being? Was he an ant in an anthill that marched forever to someone else's song, someone else's life? Was he a holy deity playing a board game on planet Earth who pretended to be a mere mortal whose masquerade had become so entrenched with illusion that he himself lost the awareness that he had invented the sport to begin with?

Brock's ego corrected his thoughts quickly and reassured him with total conviction, albeit total deceit, that it was he, and he was it. There simply was nothing more left to ponder. The monkey-mind chatter, so effective at stopping any further honest self-reflection, resumed. His opportunity for growth and subsequent salvation evaporated into the dismal abyss. The distortion played its perfect tune of distraction, and he was instantly and irrevocably lost like so many others before him, and after him as well.

This had been his last chance to turn it around. There would be no others on this go.

The chess piece took its rightful place in a now settled match, and the remaining plays were obvious.

*Checkmate.*

Love had accurately predicted what the final result would be.

She, as always, was right.

*Checkmate.*

Yet his ego just smiled. It had succeeded in taking over, controlling, and quelling the will of its now useless puppet master. The conniving pet declared itself boss and celebrated its own victory. What it, the delusional and insane fool within Brock's mind, had not realized, as was usually the case, was that it had assured its own demise simultaneously. The pet couldn't survive without the master who served it food and made its bed. Dreams of dominion blurred the ego's ability to realize its own complete and utter self-induced destruction.

*Game over.*

So foolish by design, so useless in truth, when would it ever learn? The nose chopped off to spite its face. The vicious cycle, like a record player made of eternal failure, turned round once more.

The wound from one lost soul chose spreading the virus of injury instead of self-contained quarantine, understanding, and healing. If only he had explored the extents of his wound, absorbed the fullness of the beauty of his pain, and turned to face the joy of the lesson at hand instead. Oh how gloriously the reddened-from-blood tide would have turned out differently.

No matter how contrived and layered the illusion, woundedness always remained impersonal. From mother to child, it did its evil deed because it had been done to the doer and to that doer before him. It was always but the need to spread the disease. With the infected thinking, he might be able to rid himself of the calamity if he just passed it on to the next victim.

Yet the flawed approach never achieved its intended effect. It only made it worse. The only traversable course through the septic shock of psychological pain required the individual to go within, take the lesson head on, and surmount the illusionary challenge offered up again on this go round. That was the only way to turn off the game's song of perpetual torture.

This soul turned from the opportunity in disgrace and yet again doomed itself for another turn on the painful wheel of growth through disaster. The lesson, which has always been the same, was much better learned through love, not pain.

It didn't have to be this way.

# FIFTY-NINE

## Backward

DEVYN EMBRACED the liquid gold that leaked from her faucet of a face while the last view of Heather and Livie's escape vehicle disappeared around the corner. She bothered not to wipe those salty drops dry. Somehow the warm wetness of them felt good, sacred, pure, and full of grace. They were visible, undeniable proof of her love for her beautiful daughter. Somehow that made them all the more precious.

Livie would be all right even if Devyn wasn't. It was all that really mattered to her. She was willing to gamble with her own life, but not Livie's.

She rubbed her pregnant bump while she tried to sniff back the moisture gathering in her nose.

*"I am glad we are in this together,"* Ellie said.

*"You hear my thoughts very clearly now, I see."* Devyn stifled the last remnant of the sniffles.

*"Yes, I always have. The only one who didn't hear clearly was you, but that is over now. You have fully committed your will to hearing me, and so you shall. That is how powerful and big an intention is."*

*"Yes, I am beginning to understand, at least a little bit, I think."* Devyn breathed into the space her sadness had previously occupied.

She already felt so much better. A knowing enveloped her. Livie was safe and sound. Tear time was over.

*"Mommy, it is time to wake up Billy. He likes his coffee black but just a little on the weak side, according to Tootsie."*

*"Tootsie, huh? My silly baby, I will get the coffee ready for Billy, my BLT. Did I ever tell you I always called him that?"*

*"No, but I already knew."*

"Of course you did," Devyn said softly as she gathered the coffee maker from the top shelf. *"I hope he will forgive me for falling asleep last night. I really didn't plan to."*

*"Yes, that is a given. He has and always will forgive you. One day, you will understand why. He knew your rest last night was of paramount importance. He is more connected and observant than he knows. He supposes he is a brilliant investigator, but really he is just well connected. Just like you think you have always been such a great surgeon. You are well connected, too. Your intention, like his, has always been good. Your hands become a vehicle for your gift much like his detective work is a vehicle for his. Through you, not of you. Do you see?"*

She stood silent in a moment of reflection, trying to grasp Ellie's meaning.

*"As your confidence in your gift, whatever that happens to be in this life, builds, the skills of it that you possess move more easily through you. The skills are not actually better, but your ability to share them with others is, so the net effect is the same. Does that seem clearer?"*

*"No, not really, but I'm trying to make sense of it in my way."* Devyn plugged the Keurig in the wall and turned it on.

*"Your way, the human way of thinking, Mommy, is basically backward in this and so many other circumstances. I'll give you another example. You say: when I see it, I will believe it. But that is backward. The better way to put it, the most accurate way to describe it is to say: when I believe it, I will see it. In this case, Mommy, you believe you are a very skilled surgeon, so you see it. Your level of skill is irrelevant, but because you think your skill level is high, it is. You believe it is true, and so it manifests as true. The gift is able to come through you more perfectly than another surgeon because of your belief that it will, and so it does. Enough talk for now. Go on. I will leave you to your own thoughts for a minute. Billy is almost awake now, and you will need to be ready for him."*

As she scooped the coffee into the filter, Devyn wondered. She wondered how this would all turn out. She wondered who the Homeless Hunter was and why she was involved. She wondered most of all if she would see her beautiful Livie again.

For Devyn's sake, Ellie offered one more juicy nugget of wisdom. *"If you but understood who and what you are and what she is to you, then you would know that is a silly worry. For now, let me just say if that is your will, so it shall be done."*

*"That feels good, Ellie. Thank you. It feels light and true."* She poured the water in.

*"That's because it is, Mommy. Truth always feels lighter than a lie. Always."*

241

*"Good to know for sure, my wise little baby, but I think I already knew that somewhere deep inside."*

The invigorating waft of warm roasting coffee beans filled Billy's nostrils, tempting him to wake. Espresso, with just a hint of mocha, tickled his brain. He could still feel the warmth of the bed begging him to stay snuggled up in sleepy comfort.

A flash of last night's dream distracted him. It had been about Devyn and rescuing her and somehow about him being in the way, too. It was about how the only way to keep her was to let her go. His paradoxical dream seemed so odd in the light of day despite having made so much sense a few minutes earlier.

From across the room, a faint sparkle of light teased his eyes. The outline of something caught his attention and then lost it again. He wasn't ready to see it yet—almost, but not quite. His will wasn't strong enough. He wasn't motivated enough to see. Soon, though, that would change.

Wake up. Open your eyes. Finally.

Devyn entered the guest room just as he walked over to investigate the light in the corner.

"Just as you like it," she said as she passed him his coffee.

"How in the hell do you remember how I like my coffee?" he asked, turning around and trying to locate his pants.

"It's a mystery."

"You remember my favorite movie about Shakespeare, too?" He reached for something, anything, to cover his morning joy and laughed nervously.

Devyn, unashamed by his nakedness said, "Another mystery."

He took a sip and sank into the perfection of the moment at hand. "Thank you," was all he had the strength to say, warm anticipation filling his heart.

"You were right, right about everything. I know that now. I have finally faced the situation and have come to the same conclusion that you did almost immediately. This is no ordinary coincidence. Rose was taken captive and is most likely already dead because of me. I am in danger, and I need your help desperately. I can't and don't want to do this alone."

"Wow, Ladybug. I don't know what to say. That's a big start, especially for you. How about good morning first? How about I'm not going anywhere except where you are until we have some answers. I won't let anything happen to you or your girls. I am yours. It sounds kind of stupid to say, but I feel like adding...eternally. Yes, I am eternally yours. That's precisely what I mean. I think I always have been."

Of course, he didn't understand why, but he was right.

"That feels light, and so it must be true. I believe you, completely, in the center of my heart."

They embraced with a love so deep and honest that time stood still. They had seen the truth in one another, pushed all veils of separateness aside, and jumped into the completeness of one another's support.

Heather stopped at the storage facility to hook up her luxury twenty-eight-foot travel trailer. It was a simple four-step process that even the least experienced camper could do with grace. She made it look easy. She was a pro.

From the back of her top-of-the-line SUV, she lifted the box of non-perishable food goods previously intended for a donation to support an uprooted family at the local women's shelter. When she had packed the box, it had never occurred to her she was packing it for Livie.

Last week, the urge to prepare it had consumed her. No expense spared, she collected all the things a small family might need for a weekend on the run. She even included some first-aid supplies and cash tucked under the coffee tin, which removed the need for her to visit the bank.

Literally without a trace, they disappeared into the underworld of the RV traveler. No unwise observer would do as much as blink at the pair. Heather wisely disengaged the satellite and navigation systems. She powered down the cell phone. Without the pager, they would be totally cut off from Devyn. Heather kissed it now, replaced its batteries, and stuck it safely in her pocket.

"Ready, baby?" she asked Livie.

"Couse, couse, my goose-goose!" Livie said.

"Roger that, little Livie," Heather pretended to announce into an imaginary CB radio.

Livie immediately caught on and cleverly said, "Biker, biker, ten-four, got a princess on the loose. Fly, fly, like big bird, Heather. Love you, Mommy, to ins of unifirst."

Heather grinned at her engaging step-granddaughter and laughed. She responded like they always did "Back. She loves you back, my baby."

She was right, of course.

## SIXTY

## Seek, But Do Not Find

THE HOMELESS HUNTER finally arrived at the warehouse district after stopping for flowers for the intended victim first. Oddly, the need for the signature parting gift that verged on obsession earlier was now a fleeting thought. The blood-red roses were tossed aside, forgotten and wasted. The killer laughed sinisterly at the mad idea that time had stood still to prevent a timely arrival.

*So what? The clock doesn't have special powers aimed at subverting me from killing Rose.*

Or did it?

The victim was probably dead already from her diabetes, but there was still a chance to witness the last few breaths of her struggle.

Really, the villain offered a glorious gift to the victim, a release—ah, the ultimate release.

The criminal was sure that somewhere deep inside, deep under the cobwebbed layers no one ever talked about, the victims were grateful. Relieved of their need to pretend to want the suffering of life any longer, they could finally succumb gratefully to the joy of oblivion. That's what the fool thought.

The fool was wrong.

The devil's car heard the crunch of glass under its tires when it pulled into its parking place, but the scoundrel didn't notice. The black soles of the monster's shoes acknowledged the truth of the situation as they slid slightly on the slippery

244

surface of glass slivers underfoot, but the murderer didn't see. The missing pane of the door shouted with the complaint of more falling knives while it opened and shut, but still the kidnapper didn't observe. The filing cabinet, turned on its side, shrieked with frustration as the oblivious villain walked blindly past.

"She has escaped," they all boldly announced, each in their own way.

The distracted idiot didn't see anything but the mad world of shadows and death.

The lower, more diabolical undercurrent of the Homeless Hunter's mind witnessed a perfect opportunity unfolding. This situation called for a true savior, a savior like this fiend.

If the conscious portion of the kidnapper's mind explored the significance of Rose's escape, decompensation would be unavoidable. It meant total failure, total impotence, and total worthlessness. The shock of this simply wasn't survivable.

If the maniac accepted this meant nothing, then nothing was completely risked. After all, Devyn was the real problem, wasn't she? This must be her fault, too.

In a fraction of a moment, everything shifted into place.

The fiend's subconscious mind distracted the higher mind from this failure and sent it wildly searching for something else. The distortion demanded another ever-confused master-turned-puppet look everywhere for an answer, absolutely everywhere, except in the one place it might be found. Seek, but do not find, was always the ego's mantra—stay shackled, confused, and trapped in a world of madness with no way out.

"Submit. Surrender. Hand over your power. Lose your will. Deny yourself. Follow me. I will save you."

The goal changed from killing in place of her to killing her. This little pitiful escape of Rose's was proof that Devyn deserved the punishment of death for her guilt. Surely any idiot saw that.

"We are no idiot," the depths of this egoic darkness assured.

The real criminal should finally pay. It had been a long time coming, obviously. No more patsies, no more fools, no more stand-ins would suffice. She must die, or it—this seeping blackness in the most fearful corner of the fiend's mind—must die instead. They could not both exist, and who was the murderer going to listen to? The evil void correctly suggested that the master could only choose one: this crazy, guilty bitch, or it, the dark savior, who could always be counted on. Surely the right choice had been obvious for so long.

The game entered its climax. The final play positioned. The last chess piece, a pawn pretending to be a knight, threatened the queen.

Checkmate.

Victoria was ready for the meeting. She looked flawless. She spritzed on her favorite cologne, ate a bird's helping of breakfast, and downed two espressos. Her driver's car waited out front, humming patiently in the circular drive. She gathered the appropriate pretend effects: several calendars, books, planners, possible venues, bands for hire, photos of wedding tent options, cake samples—all aimed at suggesting her desire was to help with the planning of the wedding.

*The wedding*, she thought. *What a joke*. Like there was ever going to be a stupid fucking wedding. Like Devyn Mitchell came even close to being worthy of her brother—of their name, of the family's fortune.

As far as Victoria was concerned, Devyn was a dirty fly, and flies were made for squashing.

*Weren't they, Daddy?*

From her pocket, Victoria pulled out her locket. It contained an old photo of her and Brock, intending to remind her of their bargain, when she knew where he stood.

*How can he think he loves that whore?*

This was the first time anyone really got in the way. Every other lover had been nothing more than that—a lover. She started to dive into her pain, injury, and jealousy.

Instead, however, she stopped short and chose rage.

That felt better. Yes, fury. That felt much better than misery.

Revenge sounded nice, too.

She sniffed the red roses on her vanity and grinned. She had a message to deliver.

# SIXTY-ONE

## Uninvited

VICTORIA PICKED up her cell and dialed.

Marxston, known to the rest of the word as Mr. X, answered on the first ring.

"You aren't supposed to call me on this number. Do you think we are the only ones who trace phone calls? What do you want now? I'm busy following your orders in case you forgot, Boss Lady."

"I'm calling to tell you I've decided what your reward will be after you've completed your next assignment," Victoria said with a smoothness that suggested something sultry was in the works.

"Yeah, boss. What's that?"

"Me and a night on the yacht—just us. No brothers or spouses invited. No watching—only doing."

"Oh you think so, huh? If I still want you, you mean."

"I have some new shoes and new toys specially made for you," she said to egg on his excitement.

"You have my attention. When and where?"

"After the meeting today, after I have fooled them all. At the usual place. Will text the details after I'm done with that bitch."

Click. The phone line went dead.

Victoria puffed her chest out even further. Little did she understand the finality of the deal she just made.

Play with fire, little lady, and someone always gets burned.

247

Devyn asked Billy for his trust, which he, of course, offered blindly. She explained Livie was gone and that he was not to ask where or why. If he did, she could no longer have faith in his trust. When the right time came, she would confess all the details.

He seemed perplexed but agreed nonetheless.

Next, it was his turn to share. Billy relayed the startling revelations that he came to last night, which proved, if anything, they were both on the right page. He briefly added that the assailant seemed to leave something at each murder scene but didn't go into further detail. He explained that the little store on the corner was where some of the witness photos were shot. That meant, most likely, the Homeless Hunter had been in this neighborhood recently. Each fact further supported the idea that Devyn appeared to be centrally involved in the case of the Double H murders. She was in mortal danger until the criminal was captured or killed.

He went on to say he was still puzzled about the motive. He couldn't quite figure out why the criminal jumped from poisoning homeless women to kidnapping a nanny. Something was amiss. It didn't jive. Of course, sometimes there were multiple explanations for a series of events, but that was the exception and definitely not the rule.

Just like in medicine, serial murderers usually followed the principal of Ockham's razor. The one diagnosis, or motive, that explained all the symptoms, or in this case, murders, was the best bet. There was obviously some crucial piece of information that no one, at least no one on their team, possessed that linked or bridged the events. Why would a murderer who sought out homeless women want to kidnap a nanny?

Why would the criminal have taken Rose when he or she did? Why had the intruder left the other night without taking or harming anything? Why not just try to kill Devyn? Things just didn't add up.

She turned around to face the other wall. If he took one look at her, he would know she was holding out on him. She kept telling herself over and over Ellie must have had a good reason to demand her secrecy about knowing all the victims personally. The link was, the bridge was...her.

These women weren't homeless. Everyone had assumed that crucial piece of information, but it wasn't true. Decoy perhaps? Distraction? Who knew why the killer chose that façade. Devyn knew these women, and she was starting to admit they had most likely been selected for that very reason.

Perhaps the fiend wanted her to be the only one who could identify them. The more she thought about that, the more terrified she became because only one logical conclusion remained. Either she knew the Homeless Hunter intimately and at some point had confided in the killer about these women, had a complete split personality, or had been watched closely for a very long period of time.

Her only solace stemmed from Livie's escape—unless, of course, Heather was the Homeless Hunter.

The thought lasted a millisecond. Ellie would have warned her, surely.

The fear in the pit of her gut threatened to take over, but she simply wouldn't allow it. If it did, she would be useless. She was going to have some faith, too. If she ever had faith in anyone, it was in Heather and Ellie.

She rubbed her belly for assurance. Ellie swiftly and firmly kicked in response.

Devyn took a big breath and turned back around with her game face applied. "Crap, we have to hurry, or I will be late for my meeting with Brock and his snooty sister."

"Did you say Brock, as in Brock...Brock...Bryant?" Billy's jaw dropped to his chest.

"Yes. My fiancé, Brock, is coming. I suspect you've watched him on TV—"

"Damn, Bug. He's the lead reporter on the case. Of course I know him. I've been working with him. Why didn't you say you were a couple?"

"Well, I didn't really see how it mattered until right now. Oh my God. Are you thinking what I'm thinking?" She stumbled backward slightly but caught herself before she fell.

"You are about to marry the lead reporter on a case that somehow involves your household. The odds must be..."

Silence.

She stretched her arms out like she was on a balance beam.

Billy cleared his throat and grabbed her shoulder for support.

Devyn shook her head. "Astronomically low."

"Shall I continue?" He gently put her arms back down for her.

Nod.

"The guy who is hired to solve the same case is your old best friend from medical school. One of the victims was from your local neighborhood. We have every reason to believe the assailant has been in this very house and probably took Nanny Rose, too. Yeah, I would say Brock's identity was freaking critically important." He stamped his boot on the floor.

"Holy crap," was all she could say.

Her brain chewed over the fact she was the only one who could identify all the victims. She withheld that information.

"Well, it's settled then. I'm going to this meeting, and I plan to have that talk with Brock afterwards. He's in grave danger, too, and he deserves to know," he said.

249

A weight heavier than the world sunk to the bottom of his always-hungry gut when he imagined Brock and Devyn intimately embracing. He was happy for her and Brock, really, so why did he feel so awful about it?

*Must be the thing about the ring.* He tried to convince himself, remembering the tan line he had noticed at dinner the other night.

Even then, he knew better.

They grabbed their coffee and headed out the door, down the winding path of brick-red pavers, past Master Lucky, and straight to the car that was destined to take them right into the heart of darkness.

The unmarked police car waited. Down the street and around the corner, the honorable, but easily distracted, officer waited inside. He was busy reading his e-mail and didn't notice he was not the only one watching this house on Sunnyside Way.

The villain drove past, discretely and slowly, unobserved and unnoticed. Devyn, however, whose hand gripped Billy's tightly, was anything but unnoticed.

A mounting and undeniable rage surged within the murderer. That bitch was supposed to be alone and vulnerable, not protected and safe in the company of Doctor Billy Thompson.

Yes, the Homeless Hunter knew exactly who Billy Thompson was. If they were together, that meant someone had connected at least some of the dots. That also meant they might suspect the identity of the now-observing guilty party. Most terrible of all, it meant hurting her would have to wait. The lust for inflicting pain on her, the source of the maniac's rampant suffering, must be denied a little longer.

The blood-red roses wilted uselessly on the back seat, awaiting the opportunity to share their distorted message of love. They expressed an affection so wrapped up in conditions, exclusions, and deceptions that hate described their intention better. So confused the ideas of love and hate were in the villain's mind, there seemed to be no difference.

The freak calmly applied another layer of protection so effective at temporarily hiding the pain within. Another layer of makeup in place, another film of deceit tacked on, the mad fool postponed the glorious release of murder for now. There was a meeting to go to. The clock...said so.

# SIXTY-TWO

## Spa Treatments

THE SPA on the Green at Holosni's only small but well-maintained golf course awaited its guests with undeserved anticipation. Innocently enough, the lounge had no idea who or what intention planned to walk in through the back door.

The details, perfectly arranged to Victoria Bryant's demands, suggested friendship and partnership. The colors were soft and easy to look at. The sounds of ocean waves played soothingly in the background. A hint of incense blessed the air. The place settings were perfectly straight. The wedding catalogs and booklets were strewn about immaculately appearing to have been causally placed without thought, but they had not been. To the innocent and unsuspecting eye, the event was a light, enjoyable gathering of friends aimed at helping one another. To the trained eye of the skeptic, however, that was anything but the case.

Ellie spoke to Devyn when they pulled into the parking lot. *"Mommy, listen for a minute. Some things are about to happen that I cannot possibly prepare you for. Try to remember, though, that everything happens for a reason. I love you very much. One day, this will all make sense."*

*"Honey, I don't think we have to worry. We are safe here. Victoria is your soon-to-be aunt, and Daddy will be here, too. We are going to make the plans for our wedding, which will make you legal. That's a very good thing, so let's get this over with. Chin up, baby. Everything's okay."* Devyn felt calm.

Billy had gotten used to the moments when Devyn seemed to go inside herself. He didn't ask questions and gave her as much space as she needed.

*"No, Mommy, it's not. It's not. Soon you will see, and then you will finally see. Know I am here, and no matter what it seems like, I am okay."*

*"Of course you are fine. How could you not be? This is the one happy moment we have today. I'm actually a little excited, baby."* Devyn was shocked that the idea of marriage had transformed from horror to blessing in her mind.

*"No, you are not. Actually, you are afraid. Fear and excitement feel exactly the same. Only your heart can tell the difference—not your body and not your brain."*

*"That's silly, my baby. I think I know when I am afraid. You are fine. I am fine. Everyone's fine."*

*"Yes, that is true in ordinary truth but not from this perspective."*

*"Anything else, baby?"*

*"Just one more thing. Although this may make no sense yet, try to remember you can trust Billy. He is your...family."*

*"My family? What? That's the wildest thing I ever heard you say. I attended his mother's funeral. We are not related—"*

*"Your soul family, your mirror in Spirit, Mommy. Later you will see...when you see."*

Devyn recalibrated her energy to current time and space. Of course, she didn't know those were the terms to describe what she was doing, but she did it flawlessly nonetheless.

Victoria splashed on a fresh spray of cologne as she rushed out of the limo and in through the back door of the lounge. If Devyn arrived first, the concierge had instructions to delay her until Victoria took her own self-appointed seat at the head of the table. While her team prepared, the charade began.

"Ah, Doctor Mitchell, so nice to see you again. It has been way too long," George, the head attendant, said.

"Thank you, sir," Devyn said.

"We have some new maternity services I should inform you about. I see they would now be helpful for you as well as your clients," he said in some difficult-to-pinpoint accent.

"Okay," Devyn said. "But I am here for a meeting, not for a personal appointment."

"Of course you are. Here is our list of maternity massage services. We are thinking about adding acupuncture options, but the community here is a little, how should I say, hesitant to explore such alternative therapies"

"Thank you, George," she said with mounting frustration. "If you could be so kind as to mail the details to my office, that would be perfect."

"Of course. Let me just check on things before I take you back. Feel free to check out our new cosmetic line while I'm away."

She immediately turned around, looked in the mirror, and noticed she had forgotten her makeup. How did she forget makeup today of all days? Quickly, she took George's advice. She rushed to the cosmetics counter and tried some samples. They were not her favorite colors, but they would do. Her only complaint was the intensity of their aroma.

When George returned, he flagged her over. "Excellent choices, Doctor Mitchell."

A gala of sorts awaited her. Victoria sat at the head of the perfectly set table, flanked on either side by some stuffy wedding planner representatives. Brock remained notably absent.

"Where's Brock?" Devyn asked.

"Oh, don't you worry about that. He's on his way. He's just running a little late. We can do most of this without him, can't we?"

Victoria peered over the rim of her glasses to the right of Devyn, looking through not at her.

"Maybe, maybe not."

"By the way, hello to you, too, Devyn. It's been a while. How are you doing? You look so fa...I mean big. Crazy how a baby changes your body, don't you think?"

"Well, it's the natural way, I suppose. The price of motherhood. Actually, I kind of like the way I look."

Without a trace of feeling in her icy voice, Victoria said, "Let's get started. I don't have all day. I am very busy. I have some unmovable plans on the yacht later. Why don't you begin looking at the books and asking questions while I take a phone call?"

"Sure," Devyn said.

Just as Victoria stood to walk away, Devyn caught a whiff of the scent she had come here to smell. At first, she thought it was the odd, new cosmetics.

It was not.

She smelled hate, jealousy, envy, greed, and superficial snobbery. Most important of all, she inhaled a scent she could have never forgotten, never in a million lifetimes. It was the same scent from before...

She tried to deny it, but there was no use, no mistake.

Her nose was infallible.

She had just smelled the terrible scent of a woman.

*Oh my God!*

Victoria must have been the one who was in her home that night. She must have been the monster standing over her bed—and she must be the Homeless Hunter.

*God help me!*

Victoria must have slaughtered those women and kidnapped Nanny Rose.

Devyn reeled back in her chair, almost falling backward.

Should she run? Should she scream? Should she pretend she didn't know?

She gagged, her words frozen in her mouth. Vomit burned the back of her throat.

Instantly, she was reminded of a dream. Sand filled her mouth. Sand stung her eyes. And something so bad, so wrong entered her awareness that she flailed desperately to suppress it.

*Shove, shove, shove!*

She rammed the awareness of truth down deep and hard.

The first surging pain of repression hit Devyn, and her abdomen grew as rigid as a washing board. The second came while Victoria laughed on the phone, oblivious. Then another struck Devyn...not a minute later. The waves of painful contractions pulled her right out of the chair and onto her knees.

Her teardrops streamed over her silent lips. Were they tears of pain, tears of disgust, tears of sadness, or tears of fear? Not even she knew.

She stood up quickly after the next surge let up, grabbed her purse, and rushed to the door.

"We haven't even started," one of the planners shouted.

She gasped and held her abdomen. "Tell Brock I'm sorry. Tell him I love him, and tell him I'm sorry, so sorry. I don't want to run out on him, I really don't. I can't explain, I... Right now, I have to go. Tell her whatever you want to."

In the lobby, she grabbed Billy's hand and pulled him away from celebrity hairstyles, massage menus, and mud bath options. She yanked him right out of his seat and through the doors to the parking lot.

"What the hell?" he asked.

"Just get into the car and drive me to the hospital. Ellie's in trouble. I'm having premature labor. The surges are very strong, too strong."

"What? Oh no!"

"We're only five months along with no chance for her survival. She will die. I know the odds. My baby is going to fucking die!"

"Oh my God."

Devyn shuddered and collapsed in his arms.

He half carried her to the car.

"My Livie and all those women, all those poor helpless women. How will they ever forgive me? How could I have been so deceived?"

"You're making no sense."
"I'm so stupid! Why didn't I see it sooner?"
She sobbed and clicked her seatbelt in place.

Billy, more than confused, obeyed her every instruction. There was nothing he wouldn't do for his Ladybug. It didn't matter. He was hers. It felt like he always had been.

About that, he was right.

# SIXTY-THREE

## A Priceless Doll

ON EVERY TIRE, beside every window, and in every seat of Heather's travel trailer, they rode. The Lighted Ones held true to their intention. Love herself made sure they stayed. Some babies required protection no matter the cost.

Child of the glorious sun, unaware of her importance, glittered brilliantly. Light of the light, she played with dolls, oblivious to the fact she was the most valuable doll of them all.

*"Not today, not now, not ever!"* they declared to the evil that hunted her.

*"Not this baby. Not this glorious Livie. Not her,"* they said with reverence to the darkness that followed.

For they knew she was supposed to take the rocky steps of the very last journey back home. Weary eyed and tired, the Lighted Ones rallied still. They could not fail her. Everything depended on it.

Brock pulled in at the same time Billy and Devyn sped out of the Spa parking lot. They drove right past him without even noticing.

He witnessed the fury stamped on her mascara-stained face.

That was enough. Her expression confirmed all Brock's rotten suspicions in one fell swoop.

She didn't want to marry him. She was running away with that stupid Doctor Billy Thompson, who was probably her ex-lover from medical school.

Now that he thought about it, hadn't they gone to the same school in Texas? Of

256

course she knew him. The only real question was how many times she had blown that jerk behind his back...when she was supposedly on call or at a medical conference.

*You lying bitch!*

He clenched the wheel with a force of hate known only to the shadows of the darkness. He could see nothing now except her guilt and sin. He no longer saw Devyn's truth. It was shattered beyond repair.

His ego had full control of his divided mind now. The bus named Brock drove off the cliff of distortion without any hope of regaining true perspective. The final course was sealed forever—at least for this lifetime, anyway.

He immediately knew he no longer had a choice left. His ego made sure of it. He had to do what he had to do. It was that simple, that true to him.

The only sight left for him now was complete blindness.

Perspective inevitably followed desire. Wanting so badly to extinguish his guilt with hers, he accomplished his goal perfectly. The means ideally suited the purpose, and a false reality set in.

He had won his dear and painful prize of being right instead of happy. What a sad, lonely, and horrible carnival souvenir he claimed in exchange for that validation. Like so many fools before him, he proved you may not get what you want, but you always get what you believe.

Victoria Bryant returned from her phone call just after Devyn slammed the door. She had witnessed the whole drama. Assuming Devyn ran away instead of staying put and fighting for Brock, she grinned with satisfaction.

She shook her head up and down and chuckled.

She thought her strength had called out Devyn's weakness. From her foolish perspective, she had attacked and then convinced herself she came out the winner. Apparently, she, too, would rather be right than happy.

Foolish Victoria. She didn't see that the strong don't have to battle, because the battle never really determines the winner—the real winner, at least. She didn't comprehend there was no point to war, no reason behind defense at all.

So Victoria fought the sad useless war of the weak, insane, and lonely. This was all, of course, self-imposed by maintaining and reinforcing separation from Source.

Again, she attacked only and always herself—her one true enemy.

Unfortunately, she, too, decided not to learn the lesson this go round—always the same lesson, again and again, ignored. The gift of free will was wasted on fools once more.

"What the ever-living fuck was that?" Brock screamed when he entered the back door.

He stamped his feet and sucked air in between his clenched teeth.

Victoria rolled her eyes and laughed.

He pointed at her, shaking his head rapidly back and forth.

She rolled her eyes again.

His right eye twitched.

"What d...d...did you do to her? What the hell happened?"

His madness and hate spread like a ripple of misery from him to Devyn, then on to his sister before returning back to him again.

"What I did brother? Oh ye of little faith in your sister who loves you so."

He shook his finger at her and kicked the wall.

"What about what she did to me? That bitch of yours was wasting our precious time."

He gasped.

"When will you learn that I am the only one who ever loved you? Our mother abandoned you, that girl from high school spat on you, and now this bitch, too."

He kicked the wall again.

"Always the same, you moron. But then here I am, this idiot always waiting with open arms to hold and rescue you from yourself again."

"Why can't it just be different? Why is it always the same? Different woman but always the same problem." Groaning, he hung his head so low his lower jaw touched his chest.

Victoria wisely escorted her staff out the back door. She knew where the conversation was headed.

When she returned, she said, "See, my sweet and unappreciated brother, you can only count on me. I'm the only one worthy of your affection."

He sat down and covered his face.

"Has this not always been true? How many times do we have to go through this? You don't want to go back to Europe, do you?"

He shook his head. "No."

"Certainly you don't want to go to jail over all this shit, this worthless little piece of ass, this whore, this tramp."

He tapped his right eye to stop the twitching.

"Let's forget about her. We could just take care of things my way. I'll take care of it personally if you prefer."

"No, Victoria! What about the baby?"

"Are you serious? It's probably not even yours. You saw her with that investigator, didn't you?"

He moaned.

"Why don't you go home and watch our movie? That will help. It always helps me. I'm sure it will make you feel better."

"Probably."

"I have something else to take care of first, but then I will meet you. We can have the whole night together, just you and me. I'll make it all better. You'll see," she said and stroked his arm tenderly, too tenderly.

She stood and guided him to the car while rubbing his neck.

"Driver, make sure he gets home."

They parted ways, each insane in their own right, each consumed by the monster of their egos, each convinced their perception of reality was valid.

Oh how misery loved company. In their sickness, they found the perfect match between them, and so their woundedness multiplied.

The rippling wound spread perfectly from their mother to them. Who knew who spread it to their mother before that and, of course, to her perpetrator before that, and so on...

Perhaps, if it would help, the injury could be traced back to the original insult, back to the first separation—to that wicked snake.

# SIXTY-FOUR

## Ironic

THE HOMELESS HUNTER tossed the wilted blood-red rose on top of the dead body that previously housed the traveling spirit of Ms. Cecilia Hayes.

Unfortunately for her, she had looked too much like Devyn for her own good. From the side, they looked the same. The longish brown hair, the slightly pointy nose, the square-framed glasses, the big, almost sad brown eyes, and her round cirrhotic belly had served her not.

She lived a life wasted on addiction and had welcomed her death. About that, this time, the killer's theory proved correct. With gratitude, she imbibed her last drop of poison after so many glasses of poison before it.

Never once did she even gag. Never once did she ask why. Never once did she argue.

She took her final dose of poison with grace and even almost a smile. Tenderly, she wrapped herself in the quilt and lay down for the last time this go round.

She wasn't homeless, and her body would be immediately recognized. The long-time town drunk knew too many people for it to be otherwise.

When she came in this time, she planned to be a musician, but woundedness distracted her. A bad marriage that never honored her had been her undoing. No longer in pain, however, the sweet Cecilia rested peacefully in the gutter... wrapped in a quilt adorned with a wilted blood-red rose.

The Homeless Hunter snapped off the gloves and tucked them in a back pocket. No release came. No soothing sensation oozed forth. It had been too easy, and it wasn't Devyn. This similarly featured woman hadn't substituted for her, not even the slightest bit. The terrible rage remained unquenched. The lust for death called out still.

Only Devyn would do now.

For a moment, the murderer wondered what ever happened to Rose and why she hadn't been found. She must have died, but who really cared? It meant nothing, the monster's ego affirmed.

Then with a trifle more than a whim, the maniac simply walked away from the sixth, and if Rose counted, seventh victim.

The idea of the catch phrase "Homeless Hunter" teased the villain now.

*What a joke. If they only knew the truth. The victims have never been the homeless ones. I am the homeless one.*

No wonder the Double H murders sounded better to the killer...who laughed when the irony sunk in. The victims, all the wasted and useless versions of Devyn Mitchell, had died in vain—because the Homeless Hunter was still homeless.

A love and hate so conflicting and so intense for this woman surged through the veins of the scoundrel. Every beat of the maniac's heart served only to allow one more instant of obsession to persist. Her presence haunted the fiend in every moment. The insatiable need to be as close to her and yet as far away as possible consumed this fiend. The madness of the killer's consciousness swirled and swirled—always and forever—around the center of a vortex that was Devyn Mitchell.

Now it was time for her to die.

En route to Holosni Regional Hospital, Billy notified the appropriate authorities. Two top-notch police officers were dispatched to meet them.

Other than expressing extreme concern over their safety on the ride over, Devyn divulged nothing. When they finally pulled into the secret doctor's entrance on the far side of the hospital, she confessed her dishonesty, yet Billy asked no questions. Her intention left no room for doubt.

He placed his right arm behind her back while they climbed the flight of stairs up to the second floor. When they approached the nurses station, a hush settled over the unit. No words were spoken. The pain stamped on Devyn's face answered every question.

The charge nurse flagged them into the closest open room.

"Admit her under a false name and gather all the staff in the lounge for a debriefing," Billy said while he secured his gun.

The nurse nodded.

"After you have done that, page the Chief of Security and get him up here. No one, I mean no one is to know she is here. That is critical for everyone's safety," Billy said.

The nurse nodded once more and applied the appropriate monitors.

"Are you in labor, Doctor Mitchell?" she asked.

"Call me Devyn, Joanne. Yes, I think so. Go ahead and get some Terbutaline drawn up. Put an IV in and get ready to start magnesium. I think I'm going to need the hard-core drugs to stop my contractions."

"Got it."

"My private doc is Elise Phillips, who doesn't have privileges here. I guess you're my doc for now."

The gears of the L&D machine engaged. Several nurses came in and did all the right things in all the right order. The monitor showed Ellie's heart rate was fine, but she wasn't moving. The contractions still surged every two minutes with severe force, so Joanne checked Devyn's cervix. It was one centimeter open but dangerously thin suggesting Devyn's labor appeared to be the real deal.

There was only a sliver of hope left. If the medications slowed down the labor, Ellie might have a chance—her only chance left.

While the L&D team did their thing, Billy did his.

He secured the perimeter and spoke to each attendant on the unit. A false hospital ID substituted for Devyn's, so no one from the outside would have access to her admission information. All things considered, she was in a pretty safe place.

For now, they would wait and hope: wait for the drugs to kick in and hope they worked.

"What do you mean you lost her signal?" the Homeless Hunter asked the security experts. "What do you mean you have no idea where she is? Tell me you are joking, for fuck's sake!"

"All we can tell you is that her car is parked at her house."

"Idiots."

"Thermal and vibrational scanning tells us the only living object in the house is a small dog or cat. Her cell phone signal stopped when she was at the meeting."

"Fools."

"When you were supposed to be in charge of her, you said you had that part under control. How were we supposed to know there was a problem?"

"Find her. Find her fast, or it's your ass." The killer spat and wiped away the remaining moisture. "I need to know where they are, now. I think you know perfectly well what will happen if you fail me! Use whatever means necessary. Get on the police scanner."

"Immediately."

"It will help you find that asshole Billy Thompson."

# SIXTY-FIVE

## No More Lies

"VONDALEE SWAN WAS HER NAME," Devyn muttered to Billy as the initial sedating effect of the medication took hold.

The drugs, acting like truth serum, brought forth every dirty, little detail.

"What are you talking about?" Billy asked.

"The second victim. I saw the pictures on the dining room table. The second victim was named Vondalee Swan."

"What?"

"She wasn't homeless. She was a patient of mine about a year ago. I have wondered what happened to her so many times. I guess I know now." She shuddered.

"Are you trying to tell me you know the identity of a woman no one has been able to identify?"

"Yes. That's exactly what I'm saying."

"If you know her"—his eyes bulged—"that means you are the link. All the messages of obsession were left for you."

"What messages?"

"The flowers were left for you," he said as her news sunk in.

"I don't understand—"

"She had no fingerprints. It was like she had never been alive. How could you know her? I saw the reports. I double-checked the investigation. It must be the drugs talking."

He paced around the room.

"She burned them off. She burned off her own fingertips with acid so that the

264

bad guys couldn't identify her. She was a paranoid schizophrenic—at least, that's what I thought the time I saw her."

"That's crazy."

"She even pulled out some of her own teeth so they couldn't follow her with this new implant device she swore up and down they had started implanting in so-called dangerous people."

"What are you talking about?"

"She told me her family was killed off one-by-one by the same bad guys. She told me she was being hunted down."

Silence.

"So she lived in the woods with a band of nudist gypsies she called the Prism People. She said they had some kind of machine that deflected the scanners."

"This is nonsense."

"I delivered the baby of one of her unit-mates, so they apparently trusted me. She felt safe seeing me because my office was small and we didn't take pictures or have an electronic chart system. She thought I was safe, and I'm the one who got her killed."

"What are you saying?"

She swallowed hard trying to stay strong enough to finish despite the slur in her words. "She disappeared and never came back for her follow up."

Billy's jaw dropped.

If this was true, then maybe this case was bigger than anyone could have guessed. They were possibly dealing with an enemy with major tracking capabilities and a long-standing history of evil doing.

Who could believe the ravings of a crazy lady like Vondalee Swan about implants and scanners? If Swan was even her real identity...

"What else can you tell me? Anything, anything else?"

"That's not all," she said.

He stood still and stared.

"Heather, Livie, and I gave Kimberly, the third victim, our leftovers after a picnic in the park. She was so kind, so sad, yet so grateful. Now she's dead, too, because of me. Just like Rose, they are all dead because of me." She sobbed.

"Why didn't you tell me sooner? You didn't have to carry this terrible burden all by yourself, so why now? Why are you telling me now?"

"Because I know who the killer is."

"Oh my God. Who?"

"Now you need to know to help me and my babies," she said while thoughts of Ellie and Livie flooded her mind.

"Who?"

"I would have told you sooner, but Ellie told me not to. My poor, poor Ellie.

265

She's so quiet now. Now I'm going to lose her, too. Why does everyone I touch die?"

Billy looked dumbfounded.

"The first victim. She used to work for us for maybe a week or so. I don't remember her last name, but her first name was Maria. With eyes shaped just like mine, she looked like a thicker Hispanic version of me."

Devyn's memory flashed back to the day in the OR just before her accident. The reflection in the mirror was Maria's. Ellie was trying to show her even back then.

The blood...the life-saving blood order must have come from Ellie, who already knew. She must have already known all this would happen and was trying to save her mother's patients even back then.

Devyn struggled to return to the present. The drugs were getting heavy.

Billy shook her back, and she started again, slurring worse by the word.

"She...I mean Maria, made Brock so angry. That's all I really remember about her. He kept telling me to fire her. After he walked in on her going through my jewelry box one afternoon, we had to. She denied stealing anything. Said Brock was lying, but what else could I do?"

"Go on." Billy sat down beside her. He touched her cheek softly, just like yesterday.

She tried to smile but couldn't. "The fourth, I can't remember her name, but I know her face."

He stroked her again. Lightly. Softly. Tenderly.

"From somewhere...from something long ago. She's much older, more broken in the photos. I know her. I am sure of it."

"Oh, Bug. I'm lost for words."

He shook his head and stared at the floor, unable to look at her face.

"There's more," she said, but the words kept getting stuck in her throat.

He kissed her on the forehead.

"The fifth victim, she's a local homeless lady I used to see at that corner store all the time. I never once asked her name because she drove me crazy asking for lottery money."

"Bug," he whispered.

"I would give her food and then get as far away from her as fast as I could. You already know who she is."

"Yes," he said softly.

"The first four unidentified women, though, they are not nameless. They are all real people with real names, real lives. Vondalee, Kimberly, and Maria, those were their names, at least the ones I know."

He rubbed her hands.

"They all died because they knew me."

He held her, and she heaved.

"I'm so sorry, so sorry. Now my Livie, she's away, and my Ellie, she's in trouble. I'm here, so scared and so helpless." She sobbed again.

"You are anything but helpless. Do you hear me?"

He looked her square in the eyes.

She closed hers.

"Livie is fine. I know it. Ellie will be, too. I'm going to put this person behind bars. Tell me who did this. Please, for your safety, tell me who."

She opened her eyes the tiniest bit.

"I told you about the intruder, but I never told you I smelled her perfume that night. The scent—it smelled like sweat and flowers."

"Flowers?"

"Yes."

He held her shoulders, trying to keep her upright.

"So terrible, so disgusting, I will never forget that horrid smell. When we were at the meeting, I smelled it again."

"What?"

"Not the sweat, just the flowers."

"What do you mean?"

"It's Victoria. It's her perfume I smelled hovering over me and Livie that night."

"What? How is that possible? You must be mistaken. Why would she? It makes no sense."

"I know. At first I thought the same thing, but then it all clicked into place. She hates me. That's not news."

"It is to me."

"The reason she didn't kill me the other night was because Livie was in the bed with me. Livie saved me, saved us. Livie protected me, not the other way around. Victoria must have reset the alarm so it would look like no one had been there. She thought I was asleep, so she has no idea that I know. She must have gotten the code from Brock. It's so creepy, so sick and twisted."

She suppressed a gag.

"I still don't understand why," Billy said while he paced back and forth in front of her.

Devyn lay back down on the bed, unable to hold her weight. "It just doesn't make sense unless, unless… Oh no."

"Unless she was trying to set you up. She was trying to set you up to take the fall. Your patient, a lady you gave food to, and someone who stole from you once, and then the local homeless lady. They were all killed by a drug you have access to," he said in rapid conclusion.

"What do you mean, I have access to?" she asked, totally confused by his last statement.

Her eyes closed. They would probably not open back up...too heavy.

"The drug, the poison that has killed all these women, was a very high dose of Eclamptin, which, as you know, is an anti-seizure medicine. You probably have it in your office in case of an eclamptic seizure for when a pregnant lady's blood pressure goes so high she has convulsions."

Silence.

"The circumstantial evidence would have shaken even the fairest skeptic," he said.

He stopped pacing and sat down once more.

Devyn's eyes didn't open even after he kissed her forehead again.

She slowly muttered, "As the only one able to identify them, I would have looked guiltier than hell if I came forward with any of their identities."

"You didn't. You never did."

She shook her head, almost imperceptibly.

"Why not? I have to know why not."

"Don't watch TV. Never saw their pictures until today. What are the odds?"

"Slim to none. Slim to none. Bluer than a blue moon," he said with a Texas twang infecting his tone.

"This all means I can't say a word to Brock."

"Not until Victoria's behind bars. You're both in very real danger."

With her last bit of energy, she opened her eyes.

"His crazy, manipulative sister is probably still with him. I look like the crazy one who ran out of the meeting. I can't imagine how he must feel right now. I can't call him, or she will know where I am. What am I going to do? How will I tell him this? He will never believe me."

Her exhausted eyes fluctuated between open and closed.

"Let's get her ass behind bars. I think I've got plenty of evidence for a warrant. Then we'll tell him, together. For now, this is our secret. We really have no other choice."

"Have to rest now. I'm so weak."

"Bug," he whispered.

"I have to sleep. Don't forget, this is the Bryant family. They have a hand in every pocket on the Atlantic coast. I have to rest. I'm so tired," she said and closed her eyes for the last time.

He caressed her cheek.

She said one more thing, unable to stop herself.

"I never once asked why you wanted to do forensics. Why do you want to do this kind of terrible work?"

She fell asleep before he answered.

He squinted, trying to find the best answer.

"I guess it was so I could meet you in medical school. Somehow I loved you before I even met you."

A deep sleep overtook her, and Billy stepped away.

Tootsie winked and swirled his arms around Devyn as if to say he had her safely covered. Billy rolled his eyes at his hallucination. For a moment, he pondered if he was the crazy one but decided better of it. He had too much work to do to be thinking about things like that.

Besides, Devyn was right. The Bryant empire was no mere calf to wrestle. It was a big, fat, stinky, mad, and powerful bull.

Thank God he had his best boots on today.

# SIXTY-SIX

## A Spider's Web

UNDERNEATH HER BLACK DRESS, snug against her tiny body, clung Victoria's corset of domination. The Bryant matriarch stepped stealthily aboard the yacht like a secret agent for some clandestine government crime unit.

She had played this game before. Sure, Mr. X had suggested it might be fun in the beginning, but she had perfected the play.

The red wig itched slightly at the nape of her neck, trying to tease her with distraction. It hinted at the glorious suffering yet to come.

In the right pocket of her overcoat, she fingered the pistol of joy. She imagined how fun it would be to actually pull the trigger instead of giving orders to do it. The idea thrilled her so completely that her mouth watered.

What a shame the dirty work usually had to be handed over to some poor stupid goon destined to be disposed of later by the next doomed goon always willing to take the last idiot's place. Tonight, though, the fun was hers. Afterwards, she'd kill him while he slept to tie up all the loose ends.

She took a breath to slow down her racing heart. Was it fear, or was it excitement? Who knew? What was the difference anyway? Nothing, in truth. How deliciously he waited for her not too far away.

The rules of the game gave her ten minutes of safety before launching any counter attack. Whoever subdued the other one got to give the orders, any orders. That was the enticing prize to be won.

270

Mr. X rubbed his hands together, more for excitement than warmth. His heart pounded in his chest. The heat of his dark-red blood surged to fill every organ, especially his groin.

Quick-witted and physically intense, Mr. X was no fool. He knew playing this dangerous game with the boss lady led him down a path to nowhere. The fun of it, for now, persuaded him to deny the obvious and look the other way.

Ms. Victoria Bryant, born and bred as one of the elite few who determined who lived and died in times like these, served up a tasty prize...herself. Her submitting to his every whim excited him to the point of insanity.

Of course, he usually let her win, but not this time. It was time for her to learn a lesson. He fingered his neck in glorious anticipation.

For the last six months, he had done her bidding. He took photos. He stayed up all night watching that bimbo Devyn Mitchell, the most boring lady on the planet. The good doctor never did anything wrong. What could Victoria want with her anyway?

There was nothing juicy to report on the bitch because there was no dirt to find. In fact, the most interesting thing about the useless doctor was that her mother had died of a supposed accident—an obvious suicide to him.

Then, of course, there's the bizarre detail that her best friend, some mystical healer named Heather, had married her father later in life. The guy died mysteriously not too much later and gave all his money to his spiritually minded widow. Crazily enough, the good doctor seemed to still be best friends with this chick.

So, all in all, there were no significant underhanded details to report. He was sick of following her. Why the boss lady was so against this bird marrying her creepy older brother was beyond him. Finally, after months of serving, it was his turn to be served. He intended to cash in.

Victoria's ten minus ran out.

She came around the corner quietly, but not quietly enough. He reached his hand around her neck and covered her mouth to stifle the screams. Within seconds, her hands were tied, and he put her over his shoulder. With ease, he tossed her on the bed.

She acted genuinely shocked to have been caught so easily. She struggled to get free, but it was no use.

He couldn't believe how hard she fought back. Didn't she want to be tied up? Wasn't that the game? He considered letting her go but decided against it. The excitement was just too good.

He motioned for her to be quiet. She obeyed. He slowly and tenderly cuffed her legs. He also cuffed her left hand but thought it might be fun to leave her right hand free so she could obey him better.

He didn't know about the gun. Why would he?

271

He loosened the gag over her mouth and waited for her to beg. She remained silent. He ripped off her red wig and squashed it with his heavy boots. That was the game. He played it perfectly.

"Let me go. These bindings hurt," she said calmly.

"Hmm, let me think about it. No."

She was not amused. "For fuck's sake! Release me now, X!"

"I love it when you say that. It's hot. And no, baby. I know you like it. It's just getting good," he said as he clicked her bindings tighter.

Getting really upset, she started shouting more forcibly. "I said let me go! This is no longer any fun."

Her voice quivered faintly, but he missed it.

She was getting scared now. She knew what Mr. X was capable of. He wasn't her top goon for nothing.

Absolutely no one knew where she was. Her complete and total vulnerability overtook her like a flood. She was defenseless, tied up in bondage she had foolishly arranged for herself. She was completely at the mercy of a hired assassin.

She shuddered, ironically snared in the same position she spent her life putting others in. She, once the spider, had become the fly entangled in a web of her own miserable design. She was about to get quelled, or worse—eaten.

Mr. X laughed.

The game had gotten really intense.

"What an amazing actress, my sweet spider."

He clearly underestimated her role-playing abilities.

"I can see I'm really frightening you, you helpless little thing. Do what I say, or else," he said.

She started bargaining. "Please let me go. Whatever you want: a new car, a new house, whatever. I don't want to play anymore. Dammit, X. I'm serious. Release me."

He heard what he wanted and not what she really said. He took her words to mean turn up the heat, and so he did.

Terrified, she remembered the gun. She stuck her right hand in her pocket and starting fumbling for it.

Mistakenly, he thought she was reaching down to pleasure herself. He was terribly wrong.

She pulled out the gun and aimed it at him, but still he thought it was part of the game. He struggled with her just for the fun of it.

He slapped her hard. Then he bit her shoulder.

She moaned in pain, but he heard only pleasure.

He kept going. Over and over, he smacked her.

Expecting her to climax any minute, he grinned.

That was all she could take. She reached up to show him the gun so he would back off.

At the same time, he pulled a knife out of his back pocket to tease her.

She wasn't in a teasing mood anymore.

She aimed.

He blocked.

She screamed.

He laughed.

She screamed again.

He pulled her hair.

The gun fired.

He laughed again at the fun.

She gagged from pain.

He staggered back.

She closed her eyes.

Blood spurted everywhere.

Just as the echo of the gunshot reverberated off the water, which lapped so peacefully in the Tampa Bay, her heart stopped. Fatally wounded, no EMT, no surgeon, no healer could help her now. She was already gone.

She finished this go round sitting exactly where she had seated so many others—in bondage, begging for her life.

Maybe next time she would do better.

Mr. X, still deep in denial, laughed again at her brilliant idea to bring a gun loaded with blanks. The fake blood was perfect...convincing...wicked...lovely.

The fake blood kept oozing on the floor, however. It looked real, too real. He smelled its familiar sticky metallic scent.

He reeled back in disbelief. The game was over, and it hadn't ended well. Accidentally, no doubt, but the result was still the same. He just killed the most powerful woman on the Atlantic coast while playing a sex game he couldn't possibly explain. He knew where he stood. There was no way out of this for him.

He took her out of the chains, laid her on the bed for a moment, and threw the evidence overboard. Then he lifted the gun to his head and pulled the trigger once more.

Ticket traded in, he fumbled his way back, too, back to the start just like Victoria, back to the womb of Mother, hoping next time he chose better. Wasted life, wasted chances for sure, but back-up plans for as long as forever waited to save them. Eventually, they would learn. Eventually, they would see. Until then, though, back they went into the nursery of souls dammed to play in the Great Arena of Life until they won their game of chess.

*Checkmate.*

The bishop fell. The knight fell. The playing board slammed shut…again.

Brock arrived at the Bryant family yacht just as the second gunshot rang out. He came looking for Victoria, but this tragedy was all he found. He stumbled upon this bizarre game of misery and witnessed nothing more than a broken, bloodied, old chessboard with no players left to play.

*Game over.*

An interesting idea sprouted in his right mind, in the only good part of it left. He could play this for his benefit and for her benefit and for the girls as well.

He found the one juicy golden nugget hidden deep in a huge pile of dog shit and sniffed it.

*Sniff, sniff, sniff.*

Delicious morsel of shit held firmly in his mind, he climbed right back out of the boat, returned with some things from his car, and finally went out into the big, wide world to find her—to find them all…for the very last time.

# SIXTY-SEVEN

## Purple Tea

ONE DAY LATER.

Livie woke up from her nap very determined. "Go home soon and see Mommy? I know Ellie needs Livie's help." She stomped her foot.

"I don't know yet, baby," Heather said while putting away the dishes in the small camper kitchen.

For about a year now, Heather had recognized the truth in Livie's abnormally large, clear, light blue eyes. She held no illusions about the power behind them. Livie was special. She was an Intuitive. Possibly even a Crystal Child, Starseed, or Blue Ray. There was no point in wasting anyone's time by lying to those all-seeing eyes. The child would see right through it.

"I fink so," Livie said, more as an answer than as a question.

Heather sighed lovingly.

"Let's have some purple tea. Always better. Then Livie can see more," she said.

Heather obliged and helped Livie prepare the special blend of imaginary purple tea brewed just right at the perfect temperature in the ideal cup. Then something clicked. Heather observed Livie with new clarity.

Awake. Eyes opened. Finally.

For the first time ever, someone other than Livie realized exactly what purple tea meant. Heather gladly took her assigned cup with pinkie held high in the air. A warmth filled her throat while the magic commenced. A calmness settled over her. She opened to the connection with love that the purple tea brought forth.

"Yum, yum, in my tum tum." Livie rubbed her belly.

"Let's have some fruit and mini cakes," Heather said.

275

"Sure. Open door, pease. See Mother Ocean now, pease? Mother Ocean make Livie stronger."

"I don't know, sweetheart."

Livie frowned.

"Remember we are playing hide-and-seek, just in case."

Livie was not impressed.

"No. Heather open door."

Heather was hesitant but wanted to oblige Livie as well. "Okay," she finally said.

Livie smiled.

"Only if we wear our spy glasses and our big sun hats. We must be very quiet until we know it's safe."

Livie put her finger over her lips.

"Like a mouse. Quiet like a mouse. Livie no tell bad guys watching."

Heather cautiously opened both the front and screen doors. After scanning the empty surroundings to her satisfaction, she gently welcomed in the salty breeze that flowed off the ocean into their new makeshift home.

A knowing filled her. One way or another, they were going home. Livie was right. The purple tea helped her feel into a new level of awareness.

"Sandcastles, yeah." Livie giggled.

"You bet, sweet darling."

They gathered the appropriate supplies. After Heather slipped on her swimsuit, they marched together down the two steps of their travel trailer onto the white, sandy beach of the Beachfront Resort and RV Park they now called home. There were no other campers for as far as they could see, so Heather let down her guard a little...even though Livie had said something about bad guys.

She knew they were still in danger, at least until the pager went off. Until then, they would do what they had to, whatever that meant.

The heat of the sand burned Heather's feet intensely enough to remind her how lucky she was to be here alive and breathing, with Livie safe and sound. Here she stood, in perfect health, entrusted with the great honor of keeping the oh-so-special Princess Livie safe. Somehow she knew that in this moment, her purpose was fulfilled.

As usual, she was right.

Heather put her toes in the ocean and let them sink into the soft yet grainy surface of the wet sand.

"Thank you," was all she could muster to say as the awesomeness of the moment overtook her.

No other words sounded worthy.

Pacing back and forth, Brock considered his options. He played the part of pretty boy well, but he was no fool. Mad, obviously, but his faculties otherwise never failed him. If Devyn had left with that asshole Billy Thompson, Livie had to be somewhere and with someone else. He surmised the probabilities quickly. Then he made a phone call and demanded she be found.

Brock knew Devyn well enough to know that no little meeting would drive her butt out of town. A fancy beach house couldn't get her to leave this freaky little place. She was here; of that he had no doubt. Her cell phone matched no appropriate signals on his scanners. She had obviously turned it off.

Devyn never did that unless she was at the hospital delivering a baby or doing surgery…or screwing some diploma in scrubs.

Missing for twenty-four hours? No way.

*I know you better than that. Where the hell are you?*

He tossed the odds around in his mind like a gambler in Vegas. Winner, winner, chicken dinner… He picked the hospital.

While he drove to Holosni Regional Hospital, the potential scenarios played out in his mind. None, except one, seemed acceptable.

He thought about his dead sister, killed in a fatal web of her own making. Not a single tear fell for the fallen arachnid. She made her bed. Time she laid in it.

Then a crucial detail rattled him.

With Victoria dead, he was the only one who knew the truth of what had happened, not just lately but from the very beginning. She was the only one—well, almost the only one—who knew his true identity. She was also the only one who knew what he had done, what they had done together.

The scene from their precious video washed through his mind, and a sinister laugh escaped.

The only other living person who really knew who Brock was couldn't have cared less having wiped his hands of the matter years ago—ten years ago, to be exact. Brock's twin brother proved he was smarter than they originally thought by giving up the family name, money, and fame for a fresh start as an honest olive grove farmer in Italy. He was the same brother who had accurately predicted how this would all turn out, who turned his cheek, changed his name, burned his clothes, and never looked back—never turned to salt like Brock and Victoria had.

The terror of turning to salt infused him with a fresh dose of paranoia.

He stared over his right shoulder and checked the back seat. He was certain he was being watched.

He reached for his wallet to pull out his favorite photo. While he stared at his girls, who didn't even love him, his anxiety multiplied. Then he looked for the picture that commemorated the day all this obsession began.

He found her, Devyn Mitchell, staring back at him in that black dress he gave her so long ago.

*How many people has that little black dress killed?*

Brock Bryant—whose given name was Hayden Bryant—glanced at the back seat once more. The blood-red roses waited their turn patiently.

After wasting one of them on that tramp, that drunk, that not-even-close-to-acceptable version of her, there were only eleven blossoms left. That would have to do, or maybe just one for each of his intended victims conveyed the message of his love more perfectly.

One by one, he picked up the other eight roses and ate them.

He drove to find her, to find them, to kill them all.

# SIXTY-EIGHT

## Lightning Crashes

THE FISH PECKED at the eyes of the female corpse as it sank to the bottom of the Tampa Bay. The strappings of her leather corset easily unwrapped with the ebb and flow of the water's motion. A locket slipped from the now pulseless neck that once held her elitist little head up so high. Nothing more than fish food now, her body returned to the Mother of us all.

Grace accepted her gladly with open arms, another chance given, another life offered up.

With a gasp, Victoria's soul entered a new physical body. Somewhere in the distance, lightning crashed.

The first breath of air filled the newly functioning lungs while the infant cried her first cry. She screamed with fury and shook with icy fear.

Was it the coldness of the delivery room that startled her? Was it the light of the delivery bed that blinded her blurry new eyes?

Was it the horrible memory of cruel life before?

Perhaps she would do better this time. Perhaps...

Visions of the release that would finally complete him washed over Hayden Bryant like a fountain. Devyn and Ellie together—what could have been more perfect than that? Then Livie, his final gift of silence offered to her, for her. Yes. That felt like the perfect plan for murder.

Like a baptism, the wicked dream swept away all his doubt. The veil parted in his mind, and he saw the light of day, the light of annihilation. Death screamed welcome and demanded it be realized for the gift it was to him and the others. The light of the darkness of oblivion shone so brightly it threatened to blind him in blackness. The mad chatter in the back of his mind ceased while a calm cruel certainty overtook him.

He reached up to stop the twitching of his right eye.

He had found his plan and dug his heels in.

Carefully, to escape notice, he edged his car to the side of the road. He took out a piece of paper and started writing. He must explain why he had done it the way he did so she would understand, so they all would understand.

He desperately needed her to appreciate his gift, his final gift, with her final breath, so she would finally see. She would finally know just how much he had loved her.

He cursed his poor handwriting while he wrote the last words she would ever read. They must be perfect. They must be worthy of her. They had to be the vortex of his obsession, the climax of his lust for death. She was, after all, the epicenter of his insane universe. His everything. His always.

He looked back again at the three blood-red roses and smiled. It was time for his final performance, his final work of art, his final move on the game board.

Yes. It was time for his final murders.

He checked his watch one last time before he signed his true and given name: Hayden Bryant. Not Brock. Brock was alive and well in Italy...picking stupid fucking olives.

He folded the precious paper and placed it in his back pocket.

He possessed no envelope, no fancy box, and no expensive jewel with which to garnish it. That didn't matter, not really. After all, he was the gift, not the meaningless fibers from some long-forgotten and wasted tree-turned parchment. The ink remained useless compared to his intention, the form of the words themselves but a farce compared to the content that birthed them. The expression of worth was not this silly, cheap piece of paper but the death it claimed. The beauty need not be declared with perfect penmanship but by the end of suffering the unattractive letters announced.

Thus, he went to see her for the last time—at least this go round.

His timing, impeccable as always, landed him at the hospital at change of shift, the most vulnerable time in any hospital. Confusion reigned supreme. Patient care was typically shrouded with disinformation when one shift took over and, only sometimes, corrected the unintentional mistakes of the weary outgoing crew.

They wouldn't notice his arrival. If they did, he would play it perfectly. That, after all, was his greatest talent—one costume, smoothly strapped on, easily replaced another.

His eye twitched once more. He tapped it and laughed when it stopped.

The excitement intensified. He was finally ready.

*6:57 p.m. Perfect*, he thought.

It looked like time was finally on his side.

This time, he was right.

The thought of seeing her in another life briefly entered his maniacal mind. Would he recognize her with those same sad eyes again? Would she remember him with that same endearing smile? Would she recall what he had done to her? Would she love him or hate him for it?

At exactly 7:02 p.m., he pulled into the most discrete parking place in the back corner of the employees' parking lot. The cameras recorded his arrival—not. It was too far from the main doors. Here in this passcode-protected lot, they were supposed to be safe.

They were not.

# SIXTY-NINE

## Holding Out for a Hero

A PRESENCE, a great gathering rallied on the other side of the veil. This night mattered. The outcome determined everything. The stillness knew. The silence heard.

Of course, if this chance passed by, there would be another. They knew that. This had all happened before, and perhaps it would all happen again. This time, though, it happened in Holosni, Florida. This time, it happened to the residents of 144 Sunnyside Way. It happened to Devyn, Ellie, and Livie. It happened to the royal child of the sun. It happened to the still unborn royal child of the earth.

The wills of too many heroes to count called forth for another layer of reality's unfoldment to move forward. It was simply time for the onion of life to peel away and toss aside another of its outgrown coatings. The snake's skin begged to shed, begged to birth anew, finally anew. A throbbing, a field of intention, pressed onward. It would not be denied, not this time.

The subtle realms sat not in the stands but on the sideline. They refereed the game.

As the whistle blew, the cheers called out: *"Darkness, beware."*

Devyn glanced at the clock, barely able to open her eyes from fatigue.

*7:02 p.m.*

She slumped carelessly back into the hospital bed, defeated. The medication's effects were so strong. Her arms and her eyelids felt so heavy.

282

*Stay alert. Wake up!*

She just couldn't do it.

The sting of sharp, hot pins assaulted her neck. She had felt that before, right before Livie fell in the pool last summer.

*"Danger,"* it warned. *"Trouble,"* it announced.

Last time, the searing pain in her neck saved Livie. It caught Devyn's attention just as her beautiful baby sank to the bottom of the pool. She ran out in time to save Livie and brought her back with CPR before brain damage set in.

The burning was a warning.

*"Get up!"*

She was different now.

Awake. Eyes opened. Finally.

With her new eyes, she understood what happened last year. She hadn't saved Livie. They had, and they must be here now or her neck wouldn't burn like that. She and Ellie were in mortal danger.

*"Run away now."* The needles pierced.

Or was the burn for Livie? Was someone coming for Livie? For them all?

The medication was too strong. Her thoughts wiggled, trapped in the Jell-O of her slowed-down neurons.

*The drugs, the damn drugs*, she cursed while she slipped off to oblivion.

The clock ticked so loudly it woke her again. *"Get up!"* the little hand screamed.

*"Move, now. He's coming for you!"* the big hand shrieked.

A tapping at the window demanded she rouse.

Outside, a hawk flew by to get a better view. He wanted to see how this all would end. The frogs leaped in the fountain, croaking forth her name. They called. They all claimed her, but still she fell back asleep.

A memory returned to her in her half-slumbering state. A dream from some time ago resurfaced. She walked down a long hallway in an old, dilapidated house, her house, a house that intended to consume her—ruin her, devastate her, murder her.

There were more doors now: seven, eight, nine, and ten. They all simultaneously appeared. Beneath each of the last three doors rested a wilted blood-red rose.

The scent of oranges flooded Billy's nostrils. Stillness entered his mind. He felt safe like a toddler peering out from behind his mother's skirt. He felt satisfied like a recently nursed infant ready for a nap. While he marched up and down the corridors scanning for the Homeless Hunter, he felt as if he was coming home.

They had been here for almost twenty-four hours, but he faltered not. He rested not. He marched on.

It was like he was returning to his family after a long, long journey.

Of course, he was right.

An idea popped in. Something he had to check on just in case.

Tootsie did a thumbs-up fly by announcing his approval. Billy would be where he was supposed to be as the Lighted Ones entered the playing field.

Hayden Bryant, the madman, entered the stairwell when the nurses gathered for shift change report. He counted the steps to the second floor—twelve stairs to reach her, just like last time, just like in the house.

He punched in the code Devyn once shared with him so he could pick up Livie during an emergency delivery.

*One, two, three, four. What a stupid code*, he thought while his fingers worked the keypad.

The light turned green. The metal door unlocked to admit the evil coming to greet her and creaked in complaint.

*"Don't do it, not again,"* it cried. *"There's another way."*

The gum that caught the underside of his shoe tried to hold him back but couldn't. The air weighed down on him while it tried to push him backward, back from the way he came.

He thought he had imagined it.

He had not.

# SEVENTY

## Hunted Down

HEATHER OVERHEARD the lyrics Livie sang in the bath: "Bad guys, bad guys, bad guys coming."

"Baby, you all right?" Heather asked.

"Play game. Like Daddy. Play kill Heather. Play kill Livie. Play kill Mommy. Play kill Ellie, too." She forcefully submerged the dolls and held them by their necks at the bottom of the tub. "See me now?" she hollered, ripping off their heads and throwing just the bodies across the tiny bathroom.

Heather sat gasping, mortified with shock as the heads bobbed up and down in the dingy water.

*Thump, thump, thump.*

A loud fist pounded the travel trailer door.

From the half-sized bath, Livie caught her breath. Heather observed terror course through Livie's fearless eyes and braced herself.

Had she failed her purpose?

*Knock, knock.*

Heather looked around the trailer. The back window was open. She could crawl out and climb around the back. If she got in the far side of the SUV, she could drive off. Maybe the man wouldn't see her trying to get away. They would make it out alive—maybe.

Her trailer would be ruined, but she didn't care. At least it was a chance—their only chance.

The pounding on the door came again.

285

"Ma'am, I need an answer."

Livie shuddered and cowered in the tub.

Then Heather heard footsteps coming to the back, to the window, to their one possible way out—to the one way in other than the door.

She ran to the back and slammed the window shut.

Livie screamed.

Heather ran to the kitchen, searching for a weapon.

"Ma'am," the stranger said firmly. "Ma'am, you and the little one in there? I'm not here to hurt you. I'm not. I swear it. Open the door."

Not sure if she should reply or play it quiet, Heather froze.

Livie nodded with certainty and put her finger tight to her lips.

"Hush," she whispered. "Quiet like a mouse."

Quickly but silently, they dressed. Heather grabbed a knife and put it in her pajama pocket. She motioned for Livie to climb under the table. Underneath it, she wouldn't be seen as quickly. At least she would have a chance for escape while the killer took out Heather.

Pepper spray in her right hand and knife in her pocket, Heather approached the door when the knock came again.

"Yes, fine. Thank you," she said. "What do you want? Who are you?"

"My name's Brian. Brian Stillwell. This is my park, lady. Well, I thought I better tell you just in case."

"Tell me what, sir?" Heather asked, still quivering.

"That your husband called to make sure you were still here. Told me not to worry if you guys took off soon after he arrived. He said it was all a big surprise and not to tell you."

Heather reeled. "How long ago did he call?" she asked as the significance set in.

They were still in danger—not from this man but from her supposed husband who was coming to kill them.

"Just now, ma'am. Just hung up. Because you checked single on your paperwork, I thought I'd better check it out. I've seen some crazy stuff in my life, ma'am. I want you and your baby to be safe."

"Thank you," Heather said as she opened the door to greet the man who just saved their lives.

He smiled, half his face frozen from an old injury.

"Please tell him that we must have left. Tell him we went south. Tell him whatever it takes to make him leave. Thank you. Thank you so much."

"Ma'am, if I was you, I would lie about my license plates next time. That's how the computers track our guests."

286

"I..." It dawned on her that license plate numbers never crossed her mind.

She watched their savior slowly walk back to the main office of the Beachfront RV Resort and Park. He limped with the deformity of a body broken one too many times by life.

Instead of sorrow behind his eyes, she saw the grace of an angel. Instead of a damaged and weak body, she saw the strength of a thousand deities. All he offered was his holiness to them, and they received it with honor.

She blew him a kiss of blessing when he closed the office door.

While she pulled away from the RV Park, a thought entered her mind. They would hide in the single last place anyone would ever think to find them—home. Livie had been right. They were going home soon.

*Crazy but brilliant,* Heather thought.

As always, she was right.

Hayden Bryant the villain walked discretely down the labor floor hallway and chuckled. Her secret entrance would now be his. How ironic.

Finally. Finally, peace would be his reward. He felt the serenity that awaited him. It called him out from his darkness.

He flashed back to the first time he experienced the intoxicating drink of death. He could still see her perfectly, eternally frozen in his mind. Forever trapped in the perfect body of a teenager, she lay on the floor. The warm stickiness of her blood spilled so gloriously all around her beautiful body.

She had given her flower to him for the first time that night so many years ago. Her priceless innocence lost, she became useless to him. No longer a symbol of his purity, she instantly transformed into proof of his guilt and sin.

*"She must be extinguished,"* his ego demanded, *"so that we won't have to see or smell her foulness, her vulgarity, her vileness."*

The family managed to negotiate a trade that kept him out of prison. Money, lots of money, and banishment to a boy's school in Europe had not rehabilitated him properly. It did, however, teach him how to apply the costumes that served him so well after his escape.

His eye twitched again.

The idea to switch identities with his twin brother came from the diabolical mind of his sinister sister who, after the death of their parents, felt so lonely in her wickedness. The bargain made included physical favors in exchange for her eternal support and silence. The locket was her reminder of the deal. The video, the delicious video, was his other reward.

*Where is it now?*

Saliva gathered in his oral glands. The stinky sweat of evil covered him, and he smiled. Fully erect with anticipation, he sneaked his way to her. For the last time this go round, he went to play his game again, to play the game even he didn't understand.

# SEVENTY-ONE

## At Love's First Sight

LIVIE PASSED Heather one last cup of purple tea when they took the exit for Holosni off the main road. Carefully and slowly, they drove guided on the wings of too many angels to count.

They pulled into the drive as an owl across the street hooted to greet them welcome. The trees swayed, dancing with pleasure at their return. The fox grinned, once more pleased by their cleverness.

A snake, too distracted by the movement of a mouse doomed to be his dinner, slithered through the grass. The reptile, so evil in his ways, was busy prowling, so love could accomplish whatever she was up to tonight without any more of his attention. After all, wasn't he a vermin, a creature not to be trusted like the monster that had been watching the house earlier? What the hell did the snake care about the people who had just come back home?

Gulp. The mouse, that hadn't been so clever, was gone.

Livie slowly climbed the twelve winding stairs and crawled into the big, white bed with Heather. Every imaginary drop of her purple tea kicked in. This was one party she planned not to miss. Heather understood Livie's intention. She saw it clearly in

289

those eyes and promised she would protect Livie's slumber with every breath she had left to offer.

She sang a song from long ago while Livie drifted off to sleep. The beautiful lyrics rolled off her tongue:


"At love's first sight,
  I knew it was always you
  Who walked in my dreams
  And sang in my heart,
  Who lifted me up
  And showed me my truth.
  I knew it was always you.
  Your eyes, forever the same,
  Never have changed.
  Throughout all time
  In all of my lives,
  I knew it was always you."


Heather felt the melody all around her, encompassing her spirit. It penetrated the walls and blessed the floor. The air smelled cleaner somehow, worthy of the princess she held so lovingly in her arms. She sensed the presence of grace itself soothing and holding space for them.

Of course, as usual, she was right.

# SEVENTY-TWO

## Forgiveness

TEARS POURED from Devyn's physical body while she tried to crawl back to awareness. She could see herself from above, strapped to the monitors and paralyzed by the strength of the medication. She checked the monitor for Ellie's heartbeat, still strong and reassuring. The contractions were rare, only every fifteen minutes or so.

That wasn't why she grieved.

From her higher perspective, she remembered it all, every life, every chance taken from her and her babies too early.

He was coming to murder her–again.

She smelled the sick stink of him in the hallway. She remembered every time she smelled him like this before: the same nauseating scent of evil sweat on his breath, the same horrific aroma that was mixed with Victoria's perfume the night the intruder came, the same fumes she smelled in the locker room just before her accident, and all the times in all the lives before—the same horrible smell.

Why did her hell have to repeat itself again and again? It could have, it should have changed by now.

"Please, Father, please, Mother," her highest self said, "let them survive this time. I don't care about my body. It's nothing, just an illusion. I know that now. It was never me. It is an idol, a trick of the mind, an effect of our separation of the illusion. But my Ellie, my Livie, spare them this horror, this pain, this curse!"

Then she remembered something important. "No! Stop. Stop. Cancel, cancel, cancel. What I meant to say was that I am as you created me—perfect, whole, and

291

complete. I understand now. There is a world beyond this world. I want to see that world, not this one, not the one I made, not this one anymore. Please!"

Awake. Eyes opened. Finally. The lesson learned.

"I take total and complete responsibility for all this, this horror I made that I imagined in a horrid dream you never wanted for me. I claim my birthright. I claim your power and wisdom moving through me. I claim myself. With the gift of your grace, I accept my salvation. I accept my atonement. I am that I am. I am as you see me. I am determined to see this differently. I am determined to see things another way. I am determined to. I will forgive him for this, for everything, for always..."

Just as the heavens cracked wide from within her, he opened the door and slipped to her bedside. He sniffed her scent and chuckled. He traced his finger up and down her pregnant roundness. He licked her hair and swallowed a loose strand. His erection was so big now that he had to adjust his pants to lessen the suffering of it.

While she watched him and her physical body with initial horror from above, her expression turned from terror to shocked compassion. Lightness entered her being. Stillness filled her spirit.

He reached into his pocket and grasped the sacred syringe filled with liquid death. He caressed it with his tongue while the sick, sweet smell of his breath infused the room. Carefully, so tenderly now, he kissed her cheek for one last time. Then he took his priceless letter and placed it in her hand.

The blood-red roses, one by one, he placed on her bedside table with reverence.

She turned away, unable to watch her own death again—the death always offered up by the hands of the same man with a slightly crooked smile.

How many times had he murdered her, the woman with the almost sad brown eyes? The count was too high now to recall.

Why must she keep reliving this same nightmare time and time again? Why hadn't she learned the lesson properly?

She knew they were headed back to the Great Arena for another go round in the circus called life. She was doomed. Perhaps she would do better next time. Perhaps she would see her babies grow up on the next loop. Perhaps she would remember his smile and make a different choice next time—perhaps.

Then something struck her, something so obvious she couldn't believe she missed it before.

Awake. Eyes opened. Finally. Lesson mastered.

How many lives had she missed this crucial detail? Ellie had told her. Ellie had warned her. As she looked down at her physical self with total love and acceptance for the first time in eons, she bellowed.

"Most importantly, I forgive myself. I forgive it all!"

The maniac paused for a moment when he felt the shift of vibration in the room. A peacefulness he had not experienced in over a thousand years enveloped him. He closed his eyes again to savor this, to remember this moment.

Then he lifted the syringe to her delicious neck. He lightly and tenderly located her pulse while he prepared to pierce her skin with the glorious needle. Something made him stop.

Flashing lights—so bright they burned his eyes—danced in his mind despite his closed eyelids. The visions rapidly replayed every scene from their sordid past.

*Flash, flash, flash!*

The horror scenes played out. He lowered the syringe to take in the insanity, trying not to fall over in shock.

Then he remembered.

Every time, every countless horrible crime, came spewing forth into his awareness.

How many times had he murdered this same woman with the now-explained sadness in her eyes? The babies? The babies? How many times had he slaughtered his own children?

Rivers of salt streamed down his face while his sins washed over him. The metallic scent of their blood drowned him from the inside. He gargled in misery.

Then, just as his mind threatened to explode into eternal madness with the weight of his guilt, a vision of his three girls appeared to him.

Devyn, Livie, and Ellie all nodded.

Holding hands, the triad stepped forward.

He dropped the mortal syringe when the beauty of their perfection struck him.

In melodic unison they spoke to him with their thoughts.

"*We forgive you. We forgive it all, Daddy,*" they whispered. "*It is an illusion. We take its power back. We see the perfection in you even if you cannot.*"

Their spirits lovingly embraced one another, ready yet again to temporarily return to Source, to the all loving Presence, to Mother, to Father, to the Divine, to the glittery perfection of absolute love before the next go round.

A song started to play: a waltz, to be exact.

They each recited the words, their words, their song of remembrance:


"At love's first sight,
    I knew it was always you

293

Who walked in my dreams
And sang in my heart,
Who lifted me up
And showed me my truth.
I knew it was always you.
Your eyes, forever the same,
Never have changed.
Throughout all time
In all of my lives,"

They sang the last line in flawless harmony, expecting the torture of separateness to begin again.

"I knew it was always you."

Then they held one another, completely, even if for only a fraction of a second before the cursed loop began again. Hopefully, it would be enough, enough to soothe their souls for another lifetime: for another chance, for another way, on another street, in another town, another, hopefully, better day.

Perhaps, just perhaps, next time it would end differently.

Heather jumped as a gut-wrenching cry escaped Livie's beloved mouth. Pain, torture, and overwhelming sadness were its undeniable source.

The loss it described sounded like a great canyon had divided heaven itself.

Heather knew Devyn was dead.

Not even tears were worthy. She shook, imagining the horrific suffering for Livie still yet to come.

The baby awoke, turned to Heather, and said, "Mommy at hopital. Go Livie, go now!"

Livie grabbed two of her dolls and her purple teacup and, with only her pajamas on, ran out the front door screaming.

Hayden opened his eyes and jumped away from the hospital bed. Devyn lay there, still, strapped to the machines that monitored her contractions.

He heard the pulse of her heart beep, beep, beeping on the cardiac monitor.

The visions faded, but their effect had not.

The beauty of their song played eternally in his ears.

He turned to face himself in the mirror and, for the first time in eons, saw the truth in his own eyes reflecting back at him.

He saw the hope in them. He saw an answer. He saw an option for another way, for another chance, for another life.

He took the last three roses and ate them one by one as quickly as he could. They were always meant for him—not her, not for them, not this time.

He picked up the deadly syringe and put it back in his pocket. It, too, was meant for him—not her, not them, not this time, not this day, not this life.

He leaned over to offer the woman with the sad brown eyes one last kiss, one last embrace, and one last thank you. Having been shown the possibility of grace in himself through her forgiveness, he quivered. The beauty of pure unconditional love opened his eyes, too.

Awake. Eyes opened. Finally. Lesson learned.

He could do this for her, for Livie, for Ellie, for himself.

He slipped back out of the hospital for the last time this go round.

There was another way. He saw that now. Next time, he'd do better. Finally.

Obviously, this time he was right.

Livie skipped through the doors of the Labor and Delivery Unit, demanding to know her mother's whereabouts. The charge nurse, recognizing a younger version of Devyn's intense nature—so obvious in the child—smiled and pointed to bed four.

She marched straight to the head of her mother's bed and stomped her foot. "Wakey, wakey, Mommy. Hey-N all gone. And Bicky, too. All okay. Ellie, Livie, Mommy okay," she said with the joy known only to undamaged children.

She flipped her hands back and forth to make the sign for *all done* and tossed the two gender-confused dolls in the biohazard bin, damning them to the incinerator.

Finally strong enough to open her eyes, Devyn took in the look of her adorable Livie and cried tears of joy known only to mothers who get the chance to hold their babies again. Only partially able to remember why she felt so much relief, she was shocked Livie was here at all.

Heather nodded and gave her the look of, *Later, I will explain later.*

That was good enough for Devyn, who noticed her contractions were all gone. She slipped the paper in her hand under her pillow and smiled. She would read it later. It couldn't possibly be important right now.

295

She called in the nurse and demanded the medication be stopped. Not five minutes later, she heard the beautiful thoughts of Ellie returning to her mind.

In unison now, the girls declared, "*We love you, Mommy, to the ends of the universe and back.*"

Devyn realized she just heard Livie's thoughts for the very first time. A giggle sounded somewhere in the back of Devyn's mind, which she suspected came from Livie.

She was right.

A minute later, Billy came rushing into the room, running as fast as he could behind Tootsie, who made it clear Billy's presence was required. Delight crossed Billy's face when he witnessed the love still palpable in the room. He looked deeply into Devyn's eyes and noticed something missing from them.

A great sadness, perhaps?

Somehow, no words were necessary. A stillness came over the room that acknowledged the significance of this moment for them and everyone everywhere. A new era of hope and possibility called out.

A new day had come when the past need no longer drive the present. When fear, recognized for the illusion it has always been, need no longer be the way—when forgiveness could change everything.

The sky opened, and peace settled in. The danger, for now, was gone. That was obvious to them all. They were going home—safe, sound, and together.

The subtle realms took a breath and smiled. Love herself grinned. The cards had played out perfectly. The Age of Aquarius, the Age of Hope, had finally arrived.

A song started to play...


"At love's first sight,
I knew it was always you
Who walked in my dreams
And sang in my heart,
Who lifted me up
And showed me my truth.
I knew it was always you.
Your eyes, forever the same,
Never have changed.
Throughout all time
In all of my lives,
I knew it was always you."

A new chorus was added:
"And you knew me, too,
Of course.
The way you did first
At love's first sight."

# SEVENTY-THREE

## Baby Matos

THE POLICE BROKE down Victoria Bryant's front door only to discover she wasn't there. Soon after, they found her car in the parking lot at the marina that docked the Bryant family's now blood-stained yacht.

Three days later, the authorities dredged two half-eaten, decimated bodies out of the Tampa Bay. Dental records matched perfectly for both the fallen son and daughter of the Bryant empire. Bullet wounds in the body of Tampa's deceased favorite Channel Six News reporter matched Victoria's never-to-be-recovered hand gun. Some preliminary forensic reports suggested the presence of Eclamptin in the tissues of the male corpse. He had, apparently, been murdered by his own sister in the struggle that killed them both.

After the yacht and her office were searched, multiple pieces of critical evidence suggested she was the Homeless Hunter and had planned the entire run of the six Double H murders—seven, if they counted Rose.

Devyn soon discovered that the last will and testament of her fiancé, Brock Bryant, made her heir to the Bryant Family empire. That was, of course, until Livie was of legal age and could take over the reins. The financial fortune of this ironic arrangement made her the wealthiest and most powerful woman on the Atlantic coast overnight. Her commitment to the hospital was released due to the extenuating circumstances.

Devyn's doctoring days were over, at least temporarily, while she recovered from the strain of the whole ordeal.

If it weren't for the letter, she, too, would have been convinced. The evidence documenting Victoria's guilt seemed to explain everything. The only thing the

298

police couldn't quite figure out was why she would have kidnapped Nanny Rose and why Rose remained missing. That part of the case didn't seem to fit.

Livie kept reassuring them not to worry because Nanny Rose was just busy making up new jokes.

Billy Thompson had two more questions he couldn't seem to answer to his satisfaction. Why did Victoria use the quilts? How did her body fall overboard?

Devyn kept her mouth shut for Livie's sake. Where was the value in destroying her daughter's father's name? Branding her the child of a crazy killer? No one, except she, knew about the letter, which was her little secret. Besides, if anyone could turn the Bryant empire around and make it a blessing, they could.

About that one thing, she was right.

Two more weeks passed before Rose was discovered. She eventually woke up from her coma in Tampa calling out for her Livie, her *niña*, her mato. It would be two more weeks before she was strong enough to return home to the pizza party held in her honor.

While the others prepared the table, Devyn sat down in her favorite purple chair. She thanked her mother and prayed that one day she would finally understand what really happened to her. Was her mother really ever crazy or perhaps just awake in a world of darkness and illusion?

She couldn't be sure anymore. Then she took her journal, ripped out a few pages, and tossed them in the roaring fire. It felt good. It felt right.

Billy stood in the doorway and watched. He almost interrupted Devyn, but then he stopped himself. He would let her keep her little secret just like he had. Besides, he understood that some things were better left undiscovered—like secret journals and even secret videos.

After the first toast tinkled, Rose handed Livie the swimsuit.

Perfect. It was perfect. Perfect except for a small stain just over Livie's heart, that was. Years later they would argue if it looked more like a sun or a tomato. Both, they decided. It looked like both.

They were right.

When they served the pink and red cake that night, Rose offered up her newest joke.

"*Mi* Livie, what did the baby tomato say to her Nanny tomato with only one leg?"

Livie played along, of course. "What, Nanny Rose? What did she say?"

She replied, half choked with tears, "Oh, *niña*, she said, 'Ketchup, Nanny Rose. Ketchup.' "

They all laughed and cried, and cried and laughed again. As the world turned round them, the greatest mother, the royal child of the sun, and the not-yet-born royal child of Earth rejoiced. All of them were desperately loved by BLT the investigative shrink, Heather the mystic, and the one-legged tomato, Nanny Rose.

In a world where the first battle of love vs. fear was won, they rested. Tonight, their dreams would be filled with blue and orange needle-shaped trees, green and pink balloons, dragon-shaped kites, the smell of oranges, and funny, new jokes.

For a while, perhaps. Perhaps...

Tonight, though, they felt safe, at least for the moment.

For a moment, they were right.

Somewhere not too far away, a father looked lovingly into the grey-blue eyes of his newborn and smiled. There was something beautiful in his son's eyes—a knowing, a clearness, a brightness he had never seen before. Perhaps it was a message even—about forgiveness and second chances, for a better way, in a better world.

The baby smiled back at him even though he was too young to know how, supposedly. It was a perfect smile: charming, engaging, adorable, just a little crooked. Somehow that made the father love it even more, made it even more perfect for the lovely little face.

# SEVENTY-FOUR

## Postscript:

BLESS YOU, my Livie. May the heavens whisper in your ears, too. May they sing you a song worthy of your magnificence. May you remember your brilliance so that you might remind all the others:

At love's first sight,
    I knew it was always you
    Who walked in my dreams
    And sang in my heart,
    Who lifted me up
    And showed me my truth.
    I knew it was always you.
    Your eyes, forever the same,
    Never have changed.
    Throughout all time
    In all of my lives,
    I knew it was always you.
    And you knew me, too,
    Of course.
    The way you did first
    At love's first sight.
    Remember, my Livie, you are loved...

To the ends of the universe
And back!

# Epilogue

THREE YEARS after the original manuscript was found, a prologue was discovered. Its appearance made the intention of the first book clear. It is included here for completion's sake:

If you are reading this, you have obviously found my original manuscript. Each of my volumes serves to tell a story within the greater story yet stands complete and meaningful in and of itself. Each also, of course, leads naturally and unforgivingly to the next, much like you imagine the beauty of a single planet is breathtaking to behold. Yet when it is viewed within the context of the entire solar system, it becomes so much more. In its completeness, it creates an even more meaningful work of art from the works of majestic beauty that were each a work of art in their own right.

If this is the only text initially found, then I suspect you will find the way to the others as your internal teacher so dictates.

It is the story that ended, or should I say, began all stories. I know. I can feel you whispering under your breath. You have heard this story before. Yes, that is true. Of course you have. After all, you helped call it into being.

I better add that this manuscript is not intended for the faint of spirit. Thus, at any point along the way, I give you my full permission to close the book and simply put it away until you are ready to read the rest of it.

One day, if not today, you will be. That is because you will seek the truth now. That will be your new way...when you are ready.

Awake. Eyes opened. Finally.

Sit here, my Livie. Marvel at what happened and begin to understand why you will use the term Livie for your most beloved ones.

Our story unfolds just at the crack of the glorious light of dawn in a small hospital in the little town of Holosni, Florida in the early twenty-first century. Just like the old legend said it would.

Back when we didn't know very much about life, we knew about hate, fear, and struggle. We knew about density, cancer, pain, and scarcity. We knew nothing of love, and we knew nothing of ourselves. We didn't understand the power of our hearts and the incredible value of forgiveness. Of course, there were a few of us who did...to some extent, but not enough, not enough until...

Well, there I go, already getting ahead of myself and my story, our story—your story.

Listen, my Livie. Listen with open ears and open eyes and, better yet, an open heart. Uncover the story of your awakening, for the first time, at love's first sight.

Awake. Eyes opened. Finally. Lesson offered. Again.

Oh we have missed you so.

Four months later...the next manuscript arrives.

Books in the Sinister Series
A Sinister Bouquet: Awakening
A Sinister Vision: Know This Much Is True

# About the Author

A. Nicky Hjort is originally from the greater Dallas-Fort Worth area of Texas. She writes stories that cross multiple genre lines, from paranormal romance to Sci-Fi thrillers and back again. And in some subtle way, all of her manuscripts are connected, with their purpose to explore all facets of love and what it has to teach us. Her journey into writing began with her clinical background as a medical doctor when she wrote her first fictional short story about medicine. She hasn't stopped writing since.

Facebook author page: https://www.facebook.com/Author.A.N.Hjort
Twitter: @A_NickyHjort
Website: www.anickyhjortbooks.com
Blog: www.ANickyHjortBooks.com
Instagram: https://www.instagram.com/nickyhjort

# Other Works by A. Nicky Hjort

https://www.amazon.com/A.-Nicky-Hjort/e/B01M30LVVM/

**A Sinister Vision: Know This Much is True – Book 2:** Elise Phillips, a doctor in training, has successfully repressed her kidnapping five years prior. The only problem is...she has six and one-half days to remember every terrible detail, or a total stranger will die. But to make matters even worse, in order to save this nameless woman, Elise will have to face something that scares her even more than death–intimacy. Another paranormal romantic thriller, A Sinister Vision: Know This Much is True, the second of the Sinister Series, will take you even further over the edge of what you know to be possible and guide you right back out through the only way left...impossible. Wake up. Open your eyes. Accept your assignment.... The problem is not to find the answer–but to face it. Know this much is true. (MA18+ for graphic sexual and violent content)

**Where Tyndra Turns to Ardnyt – The Norn Novellas:** In the center of a magical world there grows a beautiful and terrible chasm of climbing plants. On one side of the Ivy Wall we find the hell-of-Tyndra, on the other, the heaven-of-Ardnyt. But legend has it that in the middle...lives a preternatural beast that imprisons and tortures the children from both sides. When the war against time begins, Azza will have to cross over the Ivy Wall, something that has never been done before by a living being. But if she does make it through, she just might discover who she really is and how she became trapped in this alternate reality. A fairytale at heart, this is the first chapter in the epic saga of the youngest and most fickle of the four

Norn Sisters. The same feisty immortal creature who must escape her inherent inner darkness to learn the meaning of love. A veritable palindrome from start to finish, the narrative of Where Tyndra Turns to Ardnyt journeys through duality to discover what shocking truths emerge when up becomes down, life becomes death, suffering becomes release, and the most unexpected endings become the most surprising beginnings. Welcome to a place where forwards and backwards are exactly the same direction. Here Where Tyndra Turns to Ardnyt.

**The City: The Jane Harvest:** Winning battles means Ink honors, prestige, and life itself. ... Yet nobody understands what losing truly means. On another planet two hundred years in the future, twenty-one-year-old Isla Jane struggles helplessly to figure out who she is and what her world really means. Marked with a forbidden tattoo of the rising sun, she is a natural champion of humanity and a gifted warrior in Heats– lavish battles fought in the conjoined minds of the participants for the morbid amusement of the masses. Despite Isla's desire to fade into the background, she emerges as an obvious leader of her people when the senseless assassination of a youth forces her to face the truth. Her volatile world, disguised by its elaborate battles and constant mayhem, is a prison without bars and a coffin, the lid already half-closed, that they must escape. But when she vows to find a way to bring her people back home, Isla will have to deconstruct consciousness and the very nature of the space time continuum to unravel good from evil, truth from lies, and survival from true love. Welcome to the City–where it takes lives to save lives...

# Also from the Lavish Family

**Behind Blue Eyes Series**
Sara J. Bernhardt
http://mybook.to/BehindBlueEyesSeries

A father's desire to save his child presents him with an unthinkable choice that leaves him darker than human, forced to roam through time alone as he searches for the place he belongs.

**Adam Gold – Book 1:** Fleeing the French invasion of Geneva Switzerland in the 1700s, Adam Gold books passage to America with his family. On the ship, Adam's daughter falls fatally ill. A mysterious man comes to Adam with a way to save his child by turning Adam into something darker than human.

**The Medallion – Book 2**: Adam Gold, an immortal with sweet eyes of blue, rushes through the centuries on a quest for reason and a thirst for revenge. To cope with his pain and regret, he sleeps away the years and awakes in a new era with a powerful, ancient vampire who sets her sights on him.

**Golden Shackles – Book 3:** When the ancient queen, Sekhmet snatches up Adam, he is faced with a terrifying decision. To help aid her in her vile plans or dare to stand against her.

*Plus 3 more segments!*

Also from the Lavish Family

**Rosinanti Series**
Kevin J. Kessler
https://books2read.com/RosinantiSet

The Rosinanti Dragons are no more. Since their extinction nearly one thousand years ago these primal powerhouses have fallen into the obscurity of history's forgotten lore. In that time, humans have come to dominate the world of Terra, peacefully ignorant to one horrifying truth: ancient evil stirs around them, waiting to reclaim its lost world.

For Valentean Burai, animus warrior of the kingdom of Kackritta, the details surrounding humanity's victory over the Rosinanti are more than just a history lesson. The long-buried mysteries of this archaic conflict may hold the answers that he has so desperately sought regarding his own past.

As the awful truth of the Rosinanti's supposed demise comes to light, Valentean must stand together with Seraphina, a magically gifted princess, to embark upon a mission to maintain order and light throughout Terra. Only together can these two lifelong friends face down the resurgence of the Rosinanti legacy and combat the greatest threat their world has ever known

www.ingramcontent.com/pod-product-compliance
Lightning Source LLC
Chambersburg PA
CBHW070650180626
46817CB00006B/2304